BLAME
fòt (Haitian)
Schuld (German)

Also by Simon Mayo

Itch
Itch Rocks
Itchcraft

BLAME

SIMON MAYO

CORGI BOOKS

Dedicated to prison reformers everywhere,
campaigning for those who are *not to blame*

CORGI BOOKS
UK | USA | Canada | Ireland | Australia
India | New Zealand | South Africa

Corgi Books is part of the Penguin Random House group of companies
whose addresses can be found at global.penguinrandomhouse.com.

www.penguin.co.uk
www.puffin.co.uk
www.ladybird.co.uk

First published 2016

002

Set in 11pt ITC Bembo Standard by Jouve (UK), Milton Keynes

Printed in Great Britain by Clays Ltd, St Ives plc

A CIP catalogue record for this book is available from the British Library

ISBN: 978–0–552–56907–1

All correspondence to:
Corgi Books
Penguin Random House Children's
80 Strand, London WC2R 0RL

The secret of a great fortune made without apparent cause is a crime that has never been found out, because it was properly executed.

Honoré de Balzac, *Revue de Paris*

No one has locked up families before. I can't think what took us so long.

Assessor Grey, HMP London

SPEAKING IN SPIKE: SOME PRISON SLANG

Ant	Abigail Norton Turner
Basic	Removal of privileges
Bax	Go away
'Bin	Cell – short for cabin, the cells of the Spike
Bingo	A riot
Bug group	Resistance group (from German *Bug* meaning prow, strut)
Castle	Holloway Prison
Collar	A strutter parent on day release, allowed to work with their wages paid to the state so as to repay their debt to society sooner
Cons	Convicts; what strutters call all non-strutter prisoners
Dixam pas	Leave us alone
Doing a six	Serving a six-year sentence
Ghetto penthouse	Top-floor cell
Happy Hour	The hour before *Correction*
Heritage crime	A previously undetected crime committed by your parents or grandparents for which you are held responsible
Hunchies	Non-strutters
IR/Indoor Relief	Prison-organized work
Jammer	Home-made knife
Jug up	Meals
Ladies/ Ladies of the Castle	Prisoners in Holloway
Molopaa	Dickhead
Na	Hey! How are you?
Naa	Hey! Good, and you?
Pat down	Body search
Pol-drone	Police drone
POs	Prison officers/guards
Rub down	Cell search
Screws	Prison officers
SHU/bloc/box	Single Housing Unit – solitary confinement
Solo	A strutter in prison without any family
Spike	The family wing of Her Majesty's Prison London
Spikeout	On release or escape from HMP London. Anything that is 'outside'
Strap/handle	The tag worn by strutters
Strutter	Someone found guilty of heritage crime. The term comes from the altered posture and gait of those wearing the plastic and steel tag, placed in the small of the back
Village	Pentonville
Villagers	Prisoners in Pentonville

The girl with the pudding-bowl haircut crawled out of her bedroom, edging her way to the banisters. She lay flat on the carpet and peered down into the hall. She watched as a white man in a smart coat half steered, half carried a black woman through the open front door. She heard the opening and closing of car doors and, behind her, the shuffling of her brother's small feet.

'Get down,' she said, and he lay next to her, copying her exact pose, pushing his face against the white wooden slats. He too had a straight fringe, the rest of his hair cut to the same length. They looked at the packed suitcases, some bursting with clothes which had spilled out onto the tiled floor.

'Are they going away again?' he whispered.

'Looks like it,' she muttered.

'Where are they going?'

He felt her shrug.

They both tensed as they heard their father walking back from the car. He strode into the hall and scooped up the piles of loose clothing, shoving them into one of the suitcases. He disappeared through the door again, and the girl realized he would return just once more to pick up the two remaining cases. Then they would be gone.

Hardly breathing, they heard his every step. They heard him curse their mother, heard the thud of the cases as he threw them in the boot, heard him humming an old hymn tune as he walked back to the house.

'He's happy,' whispered the boy.

'He's drunk,' whispered the girl.

He stood in the doorway and looked around, a man unmistakably taking his leave. He caught sight of his children staring at him from the landing, and froze.

The girl and the boy froze too, breath held, hearts pounding.

She wasn't sure how long this moment lasted, but when he eventually stepped inside, her chest was bursting.

The man picked up the cases, looked once more at his daughter and then at his son.

'You'll be fine,' he said, then turned and walked out of the house.

1

She knew she was late and she knew she was in trouble.

She'd feasted on double cheeseburger and fries: beef, pickle, Monterey Jack cheese, bread, ketchup, fried onions.

She'd also enjoyed the café's wifi; trawling and posting on all the banned sites she could find.

And the final treat – she'd even managed a few minutes hidden in her old garden, staring at her old house. Her fake ID, debit card and phone were safely buried back there too.

Everything had been timed, every moment of freedom accounted for, but these boys had messed it all up. Whatever the reason for their delay, Ant now needed to hurry. She was beginning to worry that she'd missed them altogether when, finally, she heard them coming.

There were just two of them, both rangy, loud and full of swagger. She didn't need her vantage point behind the stinking industrial-sized bins – you could have heard their bragging streets away. She felt the steel handle of the bin lid in her hand and crouched lower.

The two Year Ten boys strolled down the cut-through to the park. Ant's whispered count was to four, the numbers spoken instinctively in her Haitian Creole.

En, de, twa, kat.

She stepped out into the alley. In six silent paces she was behind them, in step, grinning. This was her favourite part, *the anticipation*. This is what she did, and it felt good every time. Her agitation and six-o'clock deadline forgotten, she pulled her hood over her shaved head and leaned in close.

'And what have you done today?' she hissed.

The boys whipped round and a wall of steel hit them. The crunching sound of metal on bone rang through the alley and they dropped like stones, hitting the tarmac hard. One was out cold; the other rolled around clutching his bleeding nose. Eyes wide, he tried to scuttle backwards, to put some distance between him and his attacker.

And then she was on him. Sitting on his chest, she placed a hand on his broken nose and pressed. If her other hand hadn't been over his mouth, he would have howled. He tried to punch and kick her off, but she pressed harder and he stopped.

She leaned forward till her mouth was next to his ear. 'I said, *what have you done today?*' She watched as he tried to work out what he was supposed to say. His eyes flitted over her, and she saw him recoil. Ant smiled; it wasn't her goose tattoos that had made him react.

'I know . . . a girl! And a halfie too! Under all that blood, I actually think you're blushing.' Keeping one hand on his nose, she edged up his chest. She knew she was taking too long and forced herself to speed up. 'Last time: *what have you done today?*'

The boy finally found words. 'Dunno what you mean!' he shouted. They came fast now. 'Been at school, haven't I? You want my timetable or something? ICT, maths, English, all that stuff. You're like that advert . . .'

Hurry up, Ant.

She pressed down again and he squealed. 'You have French today?' He nodded. 'Were you a good boy, Sean? Did you *behave*?'

The boy combined horror that this crazy girl knew his name with a frantic nod.

'So you didn't call your teacher "strutter filth" like you did yesterday? And you didn't threaten his family like you did yesterday? And you didn't cut his clothes like yesterday?'

Really hurry up, Ant.

With her free hand, she felt in all his pockets. She found the knife and held it dangling from her fingers.

'You take it!' he gasped. 'It's not mine anyway.' The knife disappeared into her hoodie and she leaned forward again till her face was right above his. She could smell cigarettes and chocolate.

'Thanks. I'll find a safer home for it.' She pressed down on his nose and felt him arch beneath her. She was whispering now. 'And if you *ever* threaten Mr Norton again, I'm coming straight back to find you and your pathetic friend.' She nodded at the other boy, who was still out cold. 'Clear?'

Sean nodded furiously. She lifted her bloodied hand and wiped it on his T-shirt.

'*So, what have you done today?*'

'Nothing. Done nothing.'

'Good boy.'

Now run, Ant.

She ran.

She threw the knife into a bin as she passed and heard the boy shout, 'You'll go to prison for that!' And even though she knew she *really* shouldn't, she turned round and sprinted back. She knelt down again.

'That's the whole point, Sean. *I'm already there.*'

2

As she ran out of the alley, Ant cursed herself. The job was done, but she had always known how long she could be out for; known when she had to be back. And she had blown it. Anyone who saw Abi Norton Turner run for the Underground station knew that she wasn't merely in a hurry – everyone in London was in a hurry; she was in danger. There was a mania to the way she tore along the street. Her eyes were fixed on the traffic lights, calculating light changes and gaps in the crowds. She yelled at anyone who was, or might be, in the way. Most froze when they saw her coming, a few edged aside. One oblivious headphone-wearing tourist was sent sprawling as he stepped into her path, her free hand hitting his shoulder hard. There were no apologies, no glances back. Ant barely heard the curses that were hurled her way.

A memory of her kid brother alone in his cell, bruised and miserable, came to her.

Not separation. Not this time.

When the pavements were too full, she took to the road. Using the gutter, she accelerated past the beggars and shoppers, some of whom watched her with alarm, instinctively glancing back down the street looking for a pursuer. Hers was the speed of someone running for her life.

She saw the red and white Underground sign. Two minutes to the platform, thirteen minutes' journey time in total, on two trains, ninety seconds to the prison . . . It wasn't possible.

A crowd of students wandered across the station entrance, then hesitated, apparently lost.

'Out of the way!' yelled Ant, sprinting across the road, her voice all that was needed to create a path to the steps. She took them three, four at a time, smacked her pass on the barrier and ran for the escalator. 'Coming down!' she shouted, and most of the commuters shuffled right to let her come by.

She jumped, squeezed and pushed her way down to a man with a buggy who blocked her way. He glowered at her, daring her to challenge him. She hesitated. Then, to the man's astonishment, she climbed onto the moving handrail and tightrope-walked past him, then leaped for the ground.

A train was in – she could hear it. There'd be another in two minutes, but that would be two minutes too late. She rounded the corner – its doors were still open, but the beeping sound meant she had seconds before they slid shut. She cursed as she swerved past more slow-moving tourists but their vast trundling luggage briefly hemmed her in. In the split second it took her to side-step the cases, the train's doors closed. She cursed again and tried to prise the doors open. On the other side of the glass, a teenager in a Ramones T-shirt dug his fingers into the rubber edges and pulled. The doors opened a few millimetres and Ant plunged her hand into the gap. She had some traction now, and between them, she and the Ramones fan edged the doors apart, forcing the driver to open them again.

Ant crashed into the Tube carriage. She ignored the stares from her fellow travellers – some irritated, others perturbed by this sweat-soaked crazy girl who had just joined them – and nodded her thanks to the Ramones guy.

She took great lungfuls of air, her chest heaving; then bent down, hands on knees. '*Please stand clear of the doors,*' said the automated message, and Ant just had time to grab a rail before the train lurched away from the platform.

'You in trouble?' said the Ramones boy.

Ant, her eyes closed, nodded. She was grateful, but didn't want a conversation.

'You a strutter?' he persisted.

Startled, she opened her eyes. A few passengers edged away from her, disgust etched on their faces. She flashed him a warning. The boy retreated and stared out of the window, but Ant was annoyed she'd been spotted.

Am I really that obvious? Even without the strap?

She had assumed that, free of her debilitating tag – currently in her brother's bag – she would move just like anyone else. Then she felt the sweat pouring from her and answered her own question. It had nothing to do with how she was moving. If you were as desperate as this, two stops from the biggest new prison in Britain, then yes, you probably did look like a strutter.

The train was slowing, the platform sliding into view. Through the glass, Ant saw the crowds waiting to board her train and readied herself for the scrum.

Running was impossible. As she jumped out of the carriage, she met a wall of travellers who weren't about to get out of the way of a diminutive girl in a hoodie and trainers. She shoved, pushed and swore, but was moving at barely walking pace. With each hopeless half-shuffle she felt her brother fall from her grasp, her foster parents disappear. No Mattie, no Gina, no Dan. She had learned to pick her battles. Ant had thought that this revenge mission was small-scale. Achievable. Fair. She had been right too, but if she wasn't back for inspection, then everything changed.

Desperation seeped into her mind. *Do something drastic, do something crazy.*

Ant screamed – a wailing banshee howl that made the whole platform stop and look. Those who could see her backed off as far as possible, and she screamed again. As this shriek was delivered to a near-silent station, the effect was dramatic.

A path cleared for her and she ran, taking the steps in enormous leaps. Where new crowds threatened her progress, she screamed again. Steps, escalator, sprint, Ant flew towards the Piccadilly Line. In the enclosed walkways that linked the Underground system, her yells and threats bounced off the tiled walls.

The platform was busy with the usual number of construction workers – all with their tell-tale prison security passes still visible – but she could still choose her spot. If she stood by *that* poster, she would be right outside the lifts at the next station.

She knew the poster well. It showed a troubled-looking man in an armchair being questioned by his two young children. The caption read: *Daddy, what did our family do before the Depression?* It then dissolved into a smiling suited man holding up a pledge card. Underneath a bold *Your past is your future!* were the five 'Freedom Questions'.

Ant knew them by heart:

What have you done today?
Have you talked to your parents?
What have you inherited?
What are you passing on to your children?
Is your family now, or has it ever been, a criminal family?

If the ad hadn't been on the wrong side of the tracks, she'd have thrown something at it.

As the sound of the approaching train filled the platform, she suddenly realized she wasn't the only strutter in trouble. Never having done this trip so close to inspection, it had never occurred to her that she might have company. Ahead of her was a small group standing apart from the crowd. Or rather, the crowd stood apart from them.

There were five in total: exhausted, sweaty, fearful. Three men, two women. She knew they were strutters from the way they moved – the way hands constantly shifted to the small of the back. She was used to this inside, but out here Ant saw again how the restricted, robotic nature of their actions set them apart. The strap had originally been intended as both a punishment and a tag, but it changed the wearer's posture and gait, and had given the new prisoners their nickname. When Ant had had the plastic and steel belt fixed in place around her lower back, she swore she'd never be comfortable again. To ease the pressure on her spine, she had been forced to stand straighter, to walk taller. To strut.

Some adapted; others couldn't. Stealing the stapler-like key that removed a strap had been the best five minutes' work of her life. She just needed to put the strap on again before the assessor arrived. If she had the strap-key with her now, would she offer it to the others? Maybe. Would they take it? Probably not; they all had families to return to, beatings to prevent. If any of them failed to show, they knew the punishment.

They were straining towards the train, one of them actually waving it in, trying to make it come faster. Every instinct told Ant to stay separate, stay hidden in the crowd. If she recognized them, they would recognize her, but she had learned not to trust anyone. They were all strutters, all on the same side, but apart from her brother and maybe her foster parents, she had faith in no one.

All the same, she knew that she was out of time and out of options. She needed to be standing where they were standing, and if that meant five more people knew that she had been Spikeout, then so be it. As the train slowed, she joined the strutters. They turned in surprise, but the arrival of the train meant nothing was said. As it stopped, they approached the doors together. The doors slid open, and they stepped aboard together. There were seats free but they all stood. Ant noticed everyone look up as they got on, then hurriedly get back to their screens.

She glanced at her companions. They were known in Spike as *collars* – the member of the family group designated for outside work. It was sold as a privilege, but it was a financial necessity – too many key workers were being lost inside the prison network. This way the family were punished and the state took the salary. Any abuse, any lateness would be punished. The whole family could expect to be separated. A petite woman with a huge backpack looked close to collapse. In a previous life Ant would have offered to help, even carried her pack for her. But such generosity belonged to the past. Next to her, a lad barely older than her banged his head against the metal handrail.

We might all be strutters, thought Ant, *but you're supposed to be out and I'm not. And you get to go in the front entrance.*

The tannoy broke the silence again.

'The next stop is Caledonian Road. Alight here for the HMP London, formerly Holloway and Pentonville Prisons.'

Ant swallowed hard. So this was it. The final sprint. Like runners waiting for the gun, they crowded round the doors, leaning against each other for support as the train slowed.

'Out of the way!' called the headbanger, waving his arms frantically.

She glanced at his watch before she got off the train.

Ninety seconds.

The barrier was open.

The two women turned left to Holloway, the men turned right for Pentonville. Spike was dead ahead, but Ant sprinted for the side road and glanced skywards. At least the guard drones were somewhere else – presumably at the main entrances, counting in the stragglers. She was sure any footage could be 'lost' if necessary, but it would be one less problem.

The thirty-second siren wailed from somewhere inside the walls and dread flooded through her. She had always known that six o'clock was the cut-off, the time the assessor would visit her cell. She had to be there . . .

Security tunnel one rose in front of her, looping from the prison a thousand metres down the hill to a cavernous metal building with grooved, windowless walls. It sat like a grounded container ship looking down over a sea of dilapidated housing.

Home sweet home.

The two old prisons had effectively become a single

huge prison, joined by massive walkways, vast fences and new-build construction. Ant weaved her way around the cranes and diggers. The guards' station, all glass and concrete, was straight in front of her, surrounded by three-metre-high fencing. She saw a guard look up, frown, then smirk. From under her top she pulled a swipe card with ID attached; the photo showed a short-haired man in his twenties and the name B. MACMILLAN. She lunged for the electronic keypad, stabbing the card through the slot and picking out digits as fast as her shaking hands would allow. The gate sprang open and she tore down the rubble-strewn path that ran alongside the tunnel.

'Cutting it fine again, Ant!' called the guard, laughing. She just had time to give him the finger before crashing into a security door.

3

Day 788
My favourite things RIGHT NOW:
Drawing pictures with Gina.
Found a butterfly on 4. Flew off.
Also hot again and I'm invisible. Went 1hr 38m without anyone seeing me.
Ant seems mad again.
Things I want: games, wifi, friends.

It was only a minute after six when Ant reached the 'family annexe' of the new, sprawling HMP London. It had soon been nicknamed 'Spike', the name often given to Victorian workhouses. A prison within a prison, the midpoint between the requisitioned Holloway and Pentonville was now Britain's first family prison. The vast hollow shell now housed eight levels of accommodation, stacked on top of each other like decks of a ship. On the top level, a locked and gated bridge linked it to the prison offices. Elaborate scaffolding and metallic walkways, sometimes called the spirals, framed and connected the eight floors, each holding ten portakabins – the family cells of the annexe. They had originally been considered temporary holding areas, but two years on there was no sign of any upgrade.

Forty-three families and twenty *solos* served their time here, with sentences varying from five years to thirty. Electronic boards outside each cell showed the names of the inmates, the heritage crime they had been found guilty of and their punishment. If you tapped the screen, it displayed your case history, details of the offences your parents or grandparents committed and how they had escaped punishment. If you tapped again, it ran a film called *Paying the Price*, which explained how the last global Depression had devastated whole countries. How an 'undeserving few' had survived – but had now been caught and were no longer part of the 'national community'.

No one tapped.

Drenched with sweat, Ant barely noticed the greenhouse-like heat she had returned to. Continuous summer sunshine heated the prison like an oven, the extensive use of fans and de-humidifiers on every floor ineffective against the radiating metal walls.

It was 6.01. One miserable minute out, one Sean-the-bullying-schoolboy minute out.

Please, Grey, go somewhere else first. And please take your time, she thought.

Ant stopped in a stairwell, breathlessly listening to the sound of the Assessor and his team giving a family a lecture. They'd reached the cell at the far end of the first floor. The two youngest children spilled out onto the deck in tears. They caught sight of Ant and she swiftly put her finger to her lips; they got the message. They were only ten and eight but had learned that Ant was usually on their side, gave the assessor a hard time and could get them stuff. She waved them back into their cell and they understood. A distraction was needed.

As the high-pitched whine that the little girl had made her speciality filled the annexe, Ant dashed up the steps. She was exhausted but still fast. At sixteen, she was short for her age, but wiry and strong and well used to darting around the levels unnoticed. The screws knew, but the screws got paid. Ant ran the length of the deck, bent double. She reached the steps to the second and third floors, adrenalin and fear powering her weary muscles.

Cell 33. The fifteen-metre-long cabin ran lengthways along the third deck, its door open for assessment as the rules dictated. Through one window she could see her brother Mattie, and Dan, her foster father, sitting quite still, apparently not talking. She caught a glimpse of Gina peering round the door; her foster mother, attention caught, nodded briefly – relief flashing across her face – and spoke into the cell. Mattie and Dan jumped up – Ant knew what was happening now. She looked briefly at the other cells, counted to four, and ran.

'They're thirty seconds behind me,' she exhaled in a whisper as she leaped through the door. Gina was poised with the strap held in both hands, her face taut with concentration. Ant's little brother looked happy and cross at the same time; Dan, she knew, would be furious, so she didn't look at him at all. She had already turned her back to Gina, pulling her hoodie and soaked T-shirt up above her waist. She watched the doorway as she felt the three-part strap snap into place. Gina wasn't as fast as Mattie at re-strapping, but now wasn't the time to mention that.

Ringing, clanging footsteps on the stairs.

'They're coming! Lock it in!' hissed Ant. She felt Gina push and twist; then the end clamps tightened into her flesh.

'You're done!' whispered Gina. 'Lose the hoodie.' It had served its purpose of disguise, but now, in the sweltering conditions of the prison, it looked ridiculous – a red flag to the authorities – and Ant threw it on her bunk. 'Table, next to Mattie,' said Gina, pulling Ant's T-shirt back over her strap. 'You've been working on German verbs, *geben* and *essen*. Go!' and she pushed Ant towards the open textbooks, just as Assessor Grey, short and stiff, with wire-framed glasses, appeared at the top of the stairs. He glanced quickly at the ten cells, narrowed his eyes and chose the family in cell 31 to visit first.

Ant, Mattie, Gina and Dan all breathed a sigh of relief.

'OK, we have a few minutes,' said Gina. 'But once

he's come and asked his stupid questions, let's get him out as soon as we can. We don't argue, we are not difficult, we don't swear.'

'Why do I get the feeling that was aimed at me?' muttered Ant, writing as many German sentences as she could think of in her book.

Dan leaned over from the other side of the table. 'Capital M for *Mittag*. And we'll talk about what happened today once Grey and his lot have gone.'

Ant carried on writing and said nothing.

Mattie hooked his arm through Ant's and she ruffled his thick curly hair without looking up. 'We were worried,' he said. 'Where were you?'

'It's like you're my fifth parent,' she said. 'And you're eleven years old.'

'But I didn't know!' he whispered hoarsely. 'If you hadn't come back . . .' His voice caught and he buried his face in Ant's neck. She put her pen down and hugged him.

'*Mwen sonje'w*,' he whispered, resorting to the Creole slang their mother had taught them. Originally they had used it to keep secrets from their father; in prison they used it to keep secrets from everyone.

'*Mwen mem too*,' she whispered back. 'I missed you too. But I came back and I was doing good stuff.' She glanced at Dan. 'Honest.'

Mattie let her go. 'Your "good stuff" is usually bad,' he said, but he was smiling. Ant grinned back. 'Thought so,' he muttered.

There was a tense silence in the cell as they waited for the assessor and his team to finish in 31. Dan polished and repolished his glasses, Gina played endlessly with a strand of brown hair until Ant inhaled sharply.

'Look busy, Death-breath on his way.'

4

In a few steps Assessor Grey was outside the cell, his staff of two deputies and two guards hovering just behind. He was wearing his usual 'casual wear' of black polo-neck and black pressed trousers, though Ant knew from her unauthorized visits to his office that he also had a traditional black gown. The deputies were stern-faced as they looked at their tablets, the guards bull-like and twitchy.

Gina stepped forward to greet their visitors. 'Mr Grey. Gentlemen.' She nodded at the entourage. 'All is well here – please come in.'

Grey strode to the door, pausing as he always did to read the electronic board. His rich Edinburgh vowels filled the cell. '*Dan Norton, working teacher, ten years, fraud, extortion. Gina Norton, eight years, fraud and embezzlement. Abigail and Matthew Norton Turner, serving, until they are eighteen, at Her Majesty's Pleasure. Children of (disappeared) Kyle and Shola Turner, GBH, fraud, armed robbery.*' He shook his head sorrowfully. 'Quite a family. Quite a crime list. In fact you're really our celebrity family – if anyone needs convincing about heritage crime, all they need to do is check the crime list for cell thirty-three, eh, Gina?'

'And none committed by us, as you well know,' said Gina wearily. 'Do we have to do this every time?'

'Yes,' snapped Grey. 'Absolutely. If it helps you remember why you are all here . . .' He smiled thinly. 'If it helps you remember the debt you owe society. You and your kind poisoned this country. We've just taken back what you took from us, that is all. You have a son on the outside?' Gina winced and nodded. A deputy held a screen in front of Grey. 'Yes, of course. Max Norton. You should be grateful he reached adulthood before your sentencing.' He leaned towards Gina. 'I do hope he's being careful,' he said softly.

She said nothing but stepped aside. The assessor came in and leaned over the table to look at Mattie's work.

As he spoke, Ant mimed his words with well-rehearsed timing. 'And what have you done today?' he said, his voice light, unconcerned. Mattie said nothing – didn't even look up – just spun his exercise book round till the open pages faced the assessor. Grey looked at the lines of neat writing, flicking over the pages till he found the end. He nodded and turned to look at Ant. She had learned to conceal her revulsion, but as he stepped closer, her insides squirmed.

'So. Abigail' – Grey always refused to use her post-fostering nickname – 'what have *you* done today?' His tone had hardened, expecting trouble. He waited for his answer, smile fixed.

'Oh, you'd be surprised.' Ant smiled back.

Dan stepped forward. 'Don't waste the assessor's time, Ant—'

'German verbs,' she said quickly. 'Look.' She turned her work to show Grey, but he ignored it, just kept looking at Ant, his face blank.

'Why don't you tell me?' he said, his voice getting quieter with every word.

'Sure,' said Ant. '*Schlagen, schlug, geschlagen.* That kind of thing.' One of the deputies typed furiously into his tablet, then held up the screen.

'*To hit, I was hitting, I have hit,*' he read from the translation page. 'You have a gift,' he said eventually. 'And a modern languages teacher on hand at all times for the extra vocab.' He glared at Dan. 'How useful . . . And German.' His eyes narrowed. 'Always German.'

'Yes,' said Ant. 'I also know *scheissen*, *schiss* and *geschissen* . . .'

Grey's hand whipped across her face hard, first one way, then the other.

Gina swallowed a cry, Mattie screamed.

The assessor pushed away his deputy's tablet. 'I don't need that translated, you idiot.' He looked at Ant's reddening face, then at Gina and Dan. He smoothed out the roll of his polo-neck. 'You instil some discipline and respect in this girl or you'll *all* be in isolation cells before you know what's hit you.' He leaned forward, his mouth so close to Gina's she could see his stained teeth. 'You should know,' he said, 'that from my observation, eleven-year-olds don't fare too well in the Single Housing Unit.' He turned to Dan. 'And you are allowed to be a *collar* so that you can repay society more quickly. I can stop that. I can also transfer you to Pentonville for a few days if this nonsense carries on.'

Grey swept from the cell, his guards and deputies following behind.

Ant let out a sigh of relief. A smack was a small price to pay, but it could have been so much worse. *Need to be smarter. Quicker.* She glanced at her brother. *More careful.*

Dan put his finger to his lips as they listened to the muffled exchanges in the next cell. 'Just keep on with the German,' he whispered. 'He might not be finished with us.'

'*Abschaum*,' obliged Ant. *Maybe not* that *careful.*

Gina slid in next to her husband and tried to inspect Ant's face, but she pulled away.

'I'm fine.'

Gina mouthed her opinion of the assessor with one word; Ant and Mattie both snorted. Alarmed, Dan made shushing motions, his eyes wide. They all froze, but there was no break in the sound of the assessor's examination of cell 35 no pause to suggest anyone had overheard the stifled laughter from 33.

Eventually, as the sound of footsteps on metal stairs disappeared into the echoey noise of prison life, they felt they could speak. They all spoke at once.

'Where the hell have you been?'

'That was way, way too close.'

'What does *schiss* mean?'

'We'll be separated next!'

'Can't we pay him off like the others?'

The barrage of words was interrupted by the appearance of a small, slight woman dressed in the thin cotton Spike shirt issued to non-working adult strutters. Gina wore one too, but it didn't swamp her the way it did the other woman. Dan called her Frail Mary, and it was easy to see why. Her face was a study in stress – pale skin, deep-set eyes and lined, furrowed forehead. Her grey hair was pulled back from her face and held by a rubber band. She hesitated in the doorway.

'Come in, Mary!' called Gina, and stood as Mary stepped inside. 'What's up?'

Mary sighed heavily before speaking. She held onto the door-frame for support. 'It's not Grey this time – though God knows he's bad enough. No, it's – it's everything else. Out there.' She gestured vaguely in the direction of the Holloway, women-only cells. 'I had to go there this morning.'

'You went to the Castle? said Dan, astonished. 'Thought they didn't allow that any more.'

'It's still the only place to see a dentist,' said Mary. 'Everything was as chaotic as usual – worse if anything –

but it was . . . it was . . .' She searched for the right word. 'It was *seething.* There's big trouble coming, I'm sure of it. Bingo talk everywhere. And if they can't get at the guards, they go for us. If I hadn't had a screw with me, I wouldn't have got out again. I got spat at four times and sworn at by everybody.'

'Won't you sit down?' said Dan. 'You look exhausted . . .' He cleared some of the piles of clothes and towels.

'No, really, I need to lie down,' she said, fingers resting on her strap. 'Damn handle driving me mad in this heat. I was just outside the surgery waiting to go in, and this girl comes over. Didn't look much older than you, Ant. Never seen her before, but she had this look on her face, like she could hardly speak she was so mad. In front of the screw and everyone, she says, "You'd better not be sleeping much now, strutter, 'cos we're coming to get you. Just when you don't expect it. We'll come from here, men will come from there." She pointed in the direction of the Pentonville cells. "We're gonna burn you out, strutter!" That's what she said.' Mary looked at each of them in turn. 'Thought you should know.' She turned to leave, and they heard her mutter, 'Hope I didn't shock the little one,' before she shuffled out.

5

'What's happening?' asked Mattie in a small voice.

'Oh, just the usual stuff,' said Gina, the tension in her voice and the quick glance at Dan suggesting the opposite.

'People don't like us, Mattie, you know that,' said Ant. 'Outside it's because we "got away with it" for so long, because we had this *great* life that we weren't supposed to have. "Stolen money" and all that. It makes them feel better if they can blame us for everything. They used to blame black people, refugees, Jews, immigrants, whoever. Then they ran out of people to point fingers at. So now it's us.'

Standing by the door, Gina called to Dan, 'Need the tally. The bonus boy is coming.'

'And when the big Depression hit,' continued Dan, handing her a small piece of paper, 'so many folk lost their jobs, so many industries went under . . . that was a lot of angry people, Mattie.'

'I know – I watched the official film once.'

'You must have been *very* bored,' said Ant.

'It was called the Hurricane Depression for a reason,' continued Dan. 'It just devastated everything in its path. No country escaped. No one had seen anything like it. There was a lot of anger, a lot of hate and a lot of blame. It was bad before, but when the Hurricane came, everyone stopped thinking. Anyone who was still doing OK was resented, suspected. Everyone kept saying there was a debt to be paid—'

'OK, hush now!' said Gina. 'You can carry on with your history lesson in sixty seconds. We need to pay some bills first.' A bored-looking PO appeared, handing a laptop across the threshold. Gina opened it, entered some figures copied from the paper, then handed it back. Without speaking, the PO walked away.

'And *that's* why they hate us in here,' said Ant, nodding at the departing guard. 'We get special treatment. The cons are jealous of us living in bins not built hundreds of years ago and smelling of piss.'

'Jealous?' said Mattie, disbelieving. 'Of this dump? But it sucks – I hate it. That makes no sense.'

'I know. It's insane. But we pay. Most strutters can afford to pay the screws not to beat them the way they do the cons. And most screws need the money, so they're happy to look the other way; I needed quite a few payments for yesterday. But cons think we're still living in some kind of luxury. So if they hated us on the outside, they *really* hate us when they're inside.'

'Well, it's not that simple—' began Dan, but was interrupted.

'Yes, it kind of is actually,' said Ant. 'And when one of us can't pay – like Lord Whiny upstairs – everyone else chips in. The screws expect it now. If we ever stopped paying . . .' She was silent for a moment. 'We'd be dead basically. We wouldn't last a day.'

'Ant, stop it,' said Dan. 'You're scaring Mattie. We do what we have to do. Given that none of us should be here in the first place, you know that we try anything and everything to keep going.' He smiled at Mattie as reassuringly as he could. 'We'll be OK.'

'But the Noons got put in SHU,' persisted Mattie, 'and when they came out, Jimmy was all bloody. I saw him.'

'They were new here,' said Ant. 'They didn't know. They hadn't paid.'

'So when he was found in the kitchens stealing food,' Dan went on, 'he got treated like any old prisoner. The Noons pay now.'

'And Jimmy doesn't steal stuff any more,' said Gina.

Ant whispered in Mattie's ear, 'Jimmy doesn't get *caught* any more.'

There was a brief knock on the cell wall and a young face appeared through the open door. 'Oh, hi, Daisy,' said Gina. 'Please don't come in. Don't think we could stand even one more.'

'You're way too hot for this 'bin anyway,' said Ant,

smiling, pleased to see her friend. 'Our blood will literally boil if you come any closer.'

'Actually, I was looking for Mary,' said the girl, briefly returning Ant's smile. 'Mum's worried about her, now she's living with us . . .'

'We are too,' said Dan. 'You just missed her. She can't have gone far – she's moving slowly today. Let's see . . .'

The visitor stepped back as Dan and Gina left the cell, followed by Ant and Mattie.

Daisy Raath, with her white-blonde hair, was always the most visible of prisoners. She was two years younger than Ant, but prison seemed to even out age differences; everyone had had to grow up fast.

Dan pointed across the level. 'Mary's in with the Templemans. She's OK there.'

'How was Grey with you?' said Ant, leaning back against the cell.

'Creepy as ever.' Daisy sat down at her feet.

'And he just loves it when Ant speaks German,' said Mattie. Everyone laughed at that.

'You can see the crazed look in his eyes,' said Gina. 'Something's happening he doesn't know about! He doesn't understand! He's not in control!' She did an impression of his stiff, hunched gait and birdlike head movements, and everyone laughed again.

'Actually I don't think he's very bright,' said Dan. 'I'd put him in with my Year Tens. They'd sort him out. Some of them, as I have had the misfortune to find out, are as rough as he is.'

Ant looked down and smiled broadly. Daisy stared at her quizzically, but she shook her head. 'Later,' she mouthed.

Ant had always put Mattie to bed, and prison hadn't changed that. She didn't read to him any more – his reading was as good as hers – but he still liked her to just *be there*. Dan and Gina sat on their bunks at one end while Ant and Mattie followed their routine. This was their catch-up time.

'Do you like Jimmy?' asked Mattie. 'He's always looking at you.'

Ant glanced across the cell, but Dan and Gina were deep in conversation. She sat up. 'What a weird question,' she said quietly. 'He's not bad for a posh boy, I suppose.'

'Do you like him more than Brian?' he tried.

Ant laughed. 'Brian? He's a screw!' She was momentarily flustered. 'Brian's not so bad. He likes to talk sometimes. He hates this place almost as much as we do. I like them both, I suppose, but *you're* the only boy in my life, Mattie,' she said. 'Especially when your hair is all over the place like that!' She tried to flatten it, but he pushed her hands away.

'What do you talk about with a screw then?' He furrowed his brow and stared at his sister. She had always talked to him as though they were the same age, and he was expecting a straight answer.

'Depends. Music sometimes. There's loads of old punk bands he's into. But mainly he talks about this place,' she whispered. 'How badly run it is. How corrupt . . . He sounds more scared of his own side than of us. He says it's chaos . . .'

Mattie's eyebrows shot up. 'Scared of *us*? They're the ones with the weapons . . .'

'He's told me about those too. Skyrockets, cannons, guns, tear gas – that kind of thing. Didn't seem to make him any happier.'

'Skyrockets?' said Mattie.

Ant shrugged. 'No idea.'

'Why did he tell you all this?'

'I think he's lonely, Mattie.'

'Does he fancy you? 'Cos he could always be an idiot, you know.'

Ant laughed and tickled her brother until he begged her to stop. When he had calmed down, he finally asked the question she knew was coming. He beckoned her closer. 'Where did you go this time?' he whispered.

'Dan's school,' she replied.

'Huh?'

'I beat up the two boys who threatened him.'

Mattie gasped in horror. 'But you can't do that, Abi! You'll get—'

And she put her hand over his mouth. 'Mattie, I don't need another lecture. They deserved it. I know you disapprove, but it's done now. I paid. Screws and drones looked away. That's how it is.' He didn't reply. 'OK, I'll consider myself told off.' She kissed his forehead. '*Domì bien*, little man. Sleep well.'

*

She sat on the edge of her bunk, her head full of bin lids, Grey, Mattie's telling-off face, and now Brian MacMillan. The screw she had smoked with, talked old vinyl with, whose security pass was currently under her T-shirt. Until Brian, she had assumed all screws were the same. Then she'd heard him sing. It was her first time in the Special Housing Unit, or SHU (or *solitary*, or *bloc*; prison had many names for separation) and she heard Brian approaching.

'Are you singing?' she had asked as he swung open the steel door.

'Oh. Kind of,' he said, placing a breakfast tray on the small cell table.

'Didn't know POs sang,' she said. 'Ever.'

'We don't,' he replied. 'Singing implies you might be happy. Or enjoy what you do. Or work for nice people. I was attempting "Jail Guitar Doors" by The Clash as it's got lots of *clangs* in it. Sort of fits with all the locking and unlocking I have to do. Though actually I do a better Van Morrison. He's a Belfast boy like me. Next time maybe . . .'

Ant grimaced as she sipped whatever the hot drink was. 'That really sucks,' she said.

'My singing or that tea?'

'Both.'

Brian started to laugh, then checked himself, biting his lip. He blinked a few times, and for a moment Ant thought he was about to burst into tears.

She pushed the tray towards him. 'You want some of

this crappy food you brought me?' Brian shook his head. 'You wanna talk about something?' she tried. He shook his head again. 'You wanna take me out? We could see a movie, get some food . . .'

Brian had left and relocked the cell without replying.

Ant had called after him, 'You know where I am if you change your mind.'

6

My favourite things RIGHT NOW:
Doing word games with Dan, then making up our own. I guessed five of his languages even though he was making it easy. Then I did a word in Czech and he guessed Polish. He had biscuits.

The lights went out at ten. The sudden darkness of lock-down was greeted by shouts of protest that echoed around the prison. Outside on the levels the lights were as fierce as ever, but in the cells, with the doors shut and locked, it was a virtual blackout.

Dan called Ant over. As she knew he would.

'Where were you today?' he whispered. She could see his silhouette; he was sitting up in his bunk. Gina, above him, appeared to be asleep already.

Ant mouthed an expletive, confident he wouldn't see it. *Here we go.*

'In town,' she whispered back.

'You could get us into serious trouble, you know that.'

'I'm careful.'

'No you're not. You're reckless. You know what would happen if anyone found you? Outside prison and not wearing the strap? We'd be in SHU for a month, and I'm not sure Mattie could take it. You need to think of the rest of us.'

She heard his concern but snapped back, 'That's exactly what I *was* thinking, actually.'

'What do you mean?'

Ant sighed. 'I was teaching two stupid boys not to be vile to their French teacher.'

There was a long pause.

'You were *what*?'

'The idiots who messed with you won't do it again. It's not OK to do what they did.'

Apart from the deep breathing coming from Gina and Mattie, there was silence in the cell.

'Oh, Abi,' Dan said quietly. Nowadays he only used her real name when he was cross or upset, and he sounded choked. Ant heard him swallow and clear his throat. 'Wow. I wasn't expecting that . . . It's actually not all bad at school. Not all the time. I know I've been demoted and some pupils like to try it on, but usually it's OK. And I'm touched that you feel so strongly – really I am. But you mustn't try it again, Abi . . .'

'OK, I won't,' she said quickly, and slipped back to her bunk, not wanting to discuss it further.

Above her, Mattie rolled over. 'What did he say?' he whispered.

'You know what he said,' she replied. 'Sleep now.'

Somewhere in the distance they heard a shout, a scream and some yelled curses. Mattie's arm reached down, and Ant, waiting for it, reached up. They both listened for a few seconds.

'Sometimes in the night,' he whispered, 'when there's bad things happening, I remember Mum singing her lullabies. I loved that one about the crab in the gumbo – do you remember that?'

In the darkness Ant smiled. She sang softly:

'Manman ou pa la lalé nan maché
Papa ou pa la l'alé larivyè
Si ou pa dodo krab la va mange'w
Si ou pa dodo krab la va mange'w.'

She laughed. 'I'm amazed I remembered it!'

'What does it mean?' asked Mattie. 'I've forgotten most of it.'

'It means your mama isn't here, she went to the market, your papa isn't here, he went to the river, and if you don't sleep, the crab will eat you.'

'Really?'

'Word for word,' said Ant. 'And when you think about

it, that's pretty much how it turned out for you and me. So she got that right . . .'

She squeezed his hand and held it until the commotion was over and he'd fallen asleep, then rolled over in her bunk. 'You're all I got, Mattie,' she whispered into the dark, her words quieter than his deep, rhythmic breathing. 'And you and me are gonna beat this crab. Somehow we are going to get out and we're gonna beat it.'

Most of the time Mattie seemed to cope just fine with prison life, but tonight he'd seemed really unsettled.

I should lie low for a while, she thought. *No more trips, no more bin lids.*

7

In the early days of her imprisonment, security had been tight. The public mood had been ugly – here were whole families who had grown fat on corruption and crime. Let them suffer! Let them know how much we hate them! Retribution was the order of the day. Images of families behind bars were greeted not with shock and outrage, as they would have been a few years previously, but with satisfaction and pride. 'The Return of the Workhouse!' was celebrated in blogs and newspapers across the country. Ant's behaviour had been correspondingly aggressive; she fought with guards and other prisoners. She was in the bloc as often as she was in her own cell.

But as the vast prison building programme picked up speed and the public's attention shifted, security inside Spike relaxed, chaos and corruption became endemic.

Mistakes were made, IT programs didn't work, prisoners escaped. Sometimes the stories leaked; more usually they were swallowed in the all-encompassing enthusiasm for the new penal code.

But as the newly imprisoned strutters realized they could use their online wealth to bribe the stressed and resentful prison officers, tensions eased. Small but regular payments were made into the bank accounts of any Spike PO who was open to offers – which was most of them. To start with, families made their own arrangements, but now Dan and Gina coordinated the transfers. Ant used this relaxation of the rules to explore. She found her way around the levels, visiting other cells – until she got into a fight with a female inmate who told her to stop prying and to 'do her own time'.

Ant had even talked her way into the control room from where the whole prison was operated; it was from there that she took her first security pass. Its owner only realized it had gone after Ant had discovered the changing rooms and kitchens, helping herself to food on her way through.

Emboldened, she started to make friends with the prison officers. Ant could charm and flatter if she needed to, and many of the – largely male – POs were fascinated by the wild-eyed girl with the shaved head and goose tattoos. Her first visit to Holloway was prompted by a bet: Jimmy Noon had offered her some Pentonville keys he had stolen if she could make it to Holloway and back without being thrown in the bloc. She had returned an hour later with evidence that she had succeeded.

'I was a one-woman invading army!' she declared triumphantly. To Jimmy's amazement, she had persuaded one of the new POs to escort her to the Castle for a medical. A stolen notepad from the surgery was all it had taken to win the Pentonville keys – the tools she needed for her next trip.

However, the arrival of index-finger sensors had stopped most of Ant's excursions. New steel doors had been fitted at the strategic entrances to Holloway and Pentonville. Ant was furious. Like all strutters, she was incensed about her incarceration, but unlike the others she had been able to actually *do* something about it. 'This is my revenge, Mattie,' she said. 'Every small victory keeps me alive.'

Ant had set herself a challenge: *Get Grey*. Get the man who, more than anyone, represented the hated new criminal code that had ruined so many lives. Originally she had hoped merely to set fire to his computer or throw food at him during *Correction*. But it was in his office that she had struck gold. When she slipped inside, she didn't know what she was going to do; she was simply planning to improvise. She knew she wanted to hurt him – it had cost her more in bribes and favours than all her other raids put together. She also wanted the assessor to realize that *he* had been assessed. And that he had failed.

But then she saw the strap-key case. She had scoured the room looking for inspiration, but it was only on her second sweep of Grey's desk that she spotted it. It looked so ordinary – a bit like a brown glasses case – but when she opened it, she found the plastic and steel stapler-style device. *That must be a model*, was her first reaction. But when she picked it up, its heft and intricate steel plug-in told her that this was the real thing. Hands shaking, heart racing, she was looking at the instrument of their torture. This, along with the strap itself, was the implement that had enslaved her, her brother and thousands like her.

With a strap-key, you could lock a strap on and take a strap off. She had only ever seen one in the hands of court officials. The woman who had strapped Gina and her had said nothing, just indicated that they should turn round and lift their shirts. The three-section strap had been held in place against Ant's lower back; then, as the key was twisted, she felt its sections snap together and bite into her skin. There was a skill to it – Ant realized this grim woman must have strapped hundreds of other prisoners, and guessed that if she had wanted to, she could have made it more painful.

Ant had been handed a leaflet outlining strap hygiene, explaining how the GPS technology inside worked, and warning against any tampering. A series of illustrations showed how an attempt at unauthorized removal would cause the end-pieces to snap together, pinching and tearing the skin. In the early days, many had tried to break, melt or snap the device. The photos that went with the subsequent hospitalizations were not for the squeamish.

This key, however, represented Ant's salvation. Standing in Grey's office, she realized that her plans had changed. This wasn't going to be a dramatic demonstration of independence after all; it was going to be better than that. *This will change everything*, she thought. Dropping the key into its case and then her trouser pocket, she knew that she needed to get out, fast. Adrenalin coursing through her body, she raced back to 'bin 33.

It had taken Mattie less than a minute to remove Ant's strap and – under the bed sheets – they had danced with joy. The sensation as it peeled away from her skin like a huge metallic plaster made her giddy. Ant then removed Mattie's, and together they relished the feeling of freedom for as long as they dared. Over a year with a twelve-centimetre plastic and steel band stuck to their backs had left first blisters and sores, then a red strip of toughened skin. Ant had a plastic bottle of water handy; she poured half down her brother's back, then he poured the remainder over her. It had felt wonderful.

But GPS technology showed where each strap was, and they didn't know if they had triggered an alarm by removing it. After a few minutes of delicious freedom, they figured they had pushed their luck as far as they could and used the key to strap up again. They had cried with both the pain and the feeling of enslavement that came with it.

'You have to tell Gina and Dan,' was Mattie's opinion. 'This is way too big for us.'

Ant's original reaction – as usual – was to go it alone, but hiding the key seemed such an enormous task, she soon relented. After gasps of astonishment from Gina and Dan, they had all agreed that absolutely no one else should know what Ant had just acquired. They had toyed with the idea of a mass de-strapping, seeing how many strutters they could release before they were found out. But the truth was, they were still in prison; they would merely be re-strapped and get increased sentences as punishment.

'We'll wait,' said Gina. 'There will come a moment when we'll need it. But until then, we guard it.'

For six months the strap-key had moved from sink u-bend, to light fitting, to shower head. It had been moved in towels, underwear and shoes. The existence of the 'plug', as they referred to it, had remained a secret; in fact its very existence, and the cloak-and-dagger activities needed to keep it hidden, became a symbol of their resistance. Ant found she was less surly with the POs – why bother when she had the plug? Why make Assessor Grey angry when you had his strap-key taped under the toilet seat?

They had been prepared for a security crackdown, but when it came it was unprecedented. The cell and body searches had continued for a week. Everyone knew something had been stolen; only cell 33 knew what and where it was. If Ant hadn't hidden it in a Coke can with a false bottom, her theft would have cost her and her family dear.

Then, after a huge argument with Gina at breakfast, Ant had disappeared. No one saw her for Happy Hour, IR or meals. To start with Gina and Dan had assumed she was just avoiding them. But when they discovered her friends didn't know where she was either, they started to panic. They could report her missing, of course, but that would spell disaster for Ant. It was only after seeing his foster parents' distress that Mattie told them what had happened. In a fit of temper, Ant had recovered the key and demanded Mattie remove her strap, placing it in his clothes drawer. She had disappeared, insisting that he shouldn't follow her.

'Where's she gone, Mattie?' Dan knew he wanted to protect his sister but was as worried as they were.

Mattie shrugged, trying to look casual, but his mouth was tight, his eyes red.

'Might she have tried to leave the prison?' Gina whispered, afraid her voice would betray the fear she felt.

Mattie nodded, his eyes focused on the floor.

'Dear God in heaven,' said Dan, 'she's going to get herself killed.'

'And just how many guards did she need to pay for this little trip?' wondered Gina.

The answer to that was four. It was only when the doors of Holloway and Pentonville had been closed to her that Ant realized that as long as she was back for the assessor's inspection and *Correction*, and as long as the right team were in the control room, she could *actually leave the prison*. She had dismissed the idea as stupidly dangerous but, after the row with Gina, had thrown caution to the wind. It had taken Brian MacMillan half an hour to clear it, but the promises of extra payments worked their usual magic. In the control room the surveillance cameras showed a hooded figure, crouched and running fast, but no one was watching.

'Listen, I know you're mad but hear me out!' Ant had her speech all worked out. She had returned, sweaty and exhilarated, well before the six-o'clock inspection. She launched into her explanation before Gina and Dan had a chance to say anything. She spoke quietly, urgently and fast, taking advantage of their evident relief at her safe return. 'It was brilliant! I sat in a coffee bar for hours – no one cared, no one looked. Then I went to our old house and hid in the trees at the back – that place you made for Mattie to hide in.' She could tell she was about to be interrupted, so spoke louder. 'No one saw me! It looked deserted anyway. I thought about going closer but I didn't, OK? But the best thing was that when I walked, drank, even when I breathed, I could feel my T-shirt moving against the skin on my back – with no strap! It was amazing! I had totally forgotten what it felt like. We *can* get out if we need to! No one has done it before, but it is possible! And if we look after the key, I could do it again!'

'OK, stop right there!' said Gina, her hand raised. She hesitated, torn between horror and admiration. 'Firstly, you're putting everything at risk. They'll separate us for certain if they ever catch you. Secondly, what a waste of your precious strap-key. All that risk for a cup of coffee? And a visit to our old garden? Was it worth your amazing break-in for a hit of caffeine and a nice feeling?'

'Actually—' began Ant, before Gina cut her off again.

'And thirdly, I wish . . . I'd done the same thing.' There was a brief silence.

'Pardon?' said Dan.

'You wish you'd done it?' said Ant. 'Really?'

'Of course. I only hope that if my chance comes, I'll have half the guts you have, Abi. But there's four of us in here and there's Max outside. It's complicated. There are consequences to everything we do. Although it might not seem like it, being sixteen is a whole lot easier than being forty-six.'

'Try being forty-seven,' said Dan.

'You mean it gets worse from here?' asked Ant.

Gina and Dan had laughed, but Ant's only thought had been, *There's no way I'm making it to forty-seven. Who'd even* want *to be forty-seven?*

8

Extra news! My favourite things RIGHT NOW:
Ant's singing(!!!!!!!)

Ant lay awake for what seemed like hours – the heat, noise and her narrow escape taking it in turns to keep her from sleep. She had learned to tune out most of the usual prison din: the constant hum and clatter of the fans, the calls and shouts from the scared and the scary. But tonight it felt different. More babble, more clamour, more tension. Many families were awake and disturbed; above her she could hear her friend Amos yelling at everyone to shut up. The Shahs shouted a lot, but tonight was bad. Beyond them, the hubbub was persistent, nagging and intrusive.

When what sounded like a convoy of sirens passed on the main road outside, Ant sat up in her bunk, resigned to a sleepless night. The cell seemed even more airless than usual and she felt the familiar urge to break out, to run, to feel even the slightest breeze on her face. But she knew she had to stay put and she lay back on the wafer-thin pillow.

In a brief lull, she heard whispers. Ant held her breath. Dan and Gina were having what sounded like an urgent, private conversation.

'. . . which means maybe you shouldn't come back, Dan.'

A pause.

'What do you mean?'

'If it's that bad, disappear. After school. If there's a danger the lid's gonna blow on this place, go and hide in someone's house. You said some of the teachers have offered—'

'Gina, stop it. I'm not leaving you and the kids and you know it.'

'Ant can get out. Maybe she could get us all out.'

'But they'll go for Max if we disappear,' said Dan. 'Someone has to pay – that's all they ever talk about. And he'll be the only one left for them to target. I'll call him from school tomorrow. I need to warn him.'

'He's been ahead of us on that,' said Gina. 'He's always said that if the time ever came, he could disappear via the university system. There's quite an underground movement in Bristol, apparently, and he's had two years to find out how it works.'

'This is desperate talk,' sighed Dan. 'Maybe it'll die down. Jeffrey could have got it wrong, Gina. His information could be false.'

'But he was a politician! In government! He knows!'

'No, he's guessing. Like we all are. And if he was that smart, he wouldn't be in here, would he? He'd have seen the way the mood was running, seen that his voters needed people to blame.'

'But what if he *is* right?' Gina persisted. 'What if Mary's right too? If some of us can get out, shouldn't we at least try?'

Another pause.

He's actually thinking about it, thought Ant. *This must be bad.*

A row suddenly broke out on one of the lower levels. It wasn't close, but it was loud enough to drown out the rest of Gina and Dan's conversation. Ant closed her eyes.

When Mattie crawled into bed alongside her, she thought it was the middle of the night.

Then she saw that all the lights were on, and realized she'd slept in. Not like she used to sleep in – she'd once considered waking at midday as standard – but for prison, 6.30 was unusual.

'Have I missed Dan?' she called, her eyes shut again.

'Yup,' mumbled Gina. 'Collar breakfast at six, you know that.'

Ant cursed loudly.

'Language, Abi,' said Gina, sighing. 'You don't normally speak at all till lunch time. And I think I prefer silence to profanity.'

Ant swore again, but more softly, and Mattie giggled. She dragged herself out of bed, pulled aside the partition curtain and sat on the end of Dan's bunk. 'There's trouble coming, isn't there?'

Gina, now fully awake and pushing her hair into some kind of order, looked at her foster daughter. For a moment she saw her as she had when they first took her in: the fierce electric-blue eyes, furrowed brow and piercing stare. Exactly the face that was studying her now. She'd had wiry brown hair then, and everyone called her Abi or Abigail, but Gina conceded the shaved head suited Ant's finely shaped face. She hadn't minded when the nose piercing appeared, hadn't said anything when Ant revealed her first tattoo. Gina wasn't sure why she'd chosen a flying goose but had decided not to ask. *Presumably it's because they're untameable*, she had told Dan later. More geese arrived later, but nothing was said.

Gina glanced briefly at Mattie, who was getting dressed. She nodded. 'Yes, we think so,' she said quietly.

'Dan's gone to school though . . .'

Another nod. 'Didn't want to, but . . . had no choice, of course,' said Gina. 'Maybe we'll learn more at breakfast. Stick close to Mattie, OK?'

Ant said nothing; just stared at the floor. Gina waited, knowing Ant had more to say. But when Mattie came crashing through the curtain, pulling his T-shirt over his head, the moment had gone. He launched himself up onto Gina's bunk.

'Hey, morning, big guy!' she said, smiling and ruffling his hair, which looked wilder than ever. 'Hungry?'

'When is he not hungry?' asked Ant.

'All the food here tastes disgusting,' said Mattie, wiping sleep out of his eyes, 'but if you go early, it's slightly less disgusting. C'mon, Ant.'

'Wait for us outside please,' said Gina.

'I'll go on—'

'No!' Gina and Ant cried out together. Mattie looked stung by the force of their answer, and Ant softened it with a 'Just not today, Mattie. I'll be one minute, honest. You want me to come down like this?'

He looked at her crumpled shirt and bare legs. 'OK.' He grabbed his journal and pencil from the floor and disappeared behind the curtain.

Ant and Gina dressed quickly. 'Dan's hoping to get back early,' said Gina. 'Your cards still working? They'd get you all the way out of here?'

'Did yesterday,' said Ant.

'Could you take Mattie if you had to?'

'Reckon so.'

'All of us?'

Ant shrugged. 'Could try. Maybe, yeah. Max will hate me even more than he does already.'

Gina looked up, surprised. Ant had barely acknowledged their son. And Max had barely disguised the fact that he blamed Ant and Mattie for his parents' imprisonment. 'You're wrong, Ant. It's true he thinks we wouldn't have got caught if we hadn't fostered you and Mattie. That somehow we'd have got away with it. But Dan and I always knew that our families were well-enough known for someone to tell on us sooner or later.'

'But if we all get out . . .'

'They'll go for him, yes. So we need to warn him. They'll want to put him away, and fast. But I expect Dan will get in touch. And Max will move quickly. He'll know what to do.'

'You'd do all that for us?' Ant said, head down, tying her laces.

Gina straightened her skirt. 'Yes, Abi, we would,' she said softly. 'That's kind of the deal really.'

9

Three years previously

'You're doing *what*?'

'We're thinking of fostering again.'

'Really? After last time? You said never again! This is a joke, right?' Max Norton was aghast. He looked across the table from his mother to his father: they had their we've-been-meaning-to-talk-to-you faces on. It was clear they weren't joking. 'Well, thanks for asking my opinion,' he said. 'Where did this come from?'

His parents had often fostered during his teen years, but after a difficult time with successive children, the family decision had been to stop. Max hadn't minded sharing his house with children who needed a secure and safe house; he'd quite liked some of them. But their complicated, demanding lives had become wearing and now he'd had enough. He thought they'd all had enough.

'We've been talking about it for a while,' began Gina. 'And we've just had the final paperwork through.' She offered Max some pages.

He caught a glimpse of photos amongst the closely typed pages – two unsmiling bi-racial children stared from the sheet – but he shook his head. 'No, Mum, not again.' He stood up, clearing his plate and mug.

Gina and Dan sat at the kitchen table, exchanging nervous glances and watching their seventeen-year-old son pace around the room. They had been concerned about how he'd take the news but assumed that, in the end, he'd understand what they were doing.

'This is about me going to uni, isn't it?' He stopped and faced his parents. 'This is because you're going to have an empty house in September and want to fill it again. I'm right, aren't I?'

His father sighed gently. 'There's an element of that, I suppose. But mainly it's because we've been approached by the agency about an emergency placement.'

'It's always an emergency, Dad! Come on, you know that!'

'Well,' said Dan, 'it's a brother and sister . . .'

'Oh, great,' said Max heavily. 'Because that combination has worked *so* well in the past.'

'You won't have to move out of your room this time, Max . . .' began Gina.

'It's not that. It's just that I thought we'd stopped this

now. Thought we'd helped enough kids. You said it was time for a new start. You wanted to do new things! I'll be eighteen soon. You'll be able to go on an old folks' cruise or something, not tie yourselves down all over again.' He sighed. 'Who are the needy this time?'

'Abigail Turner and her brother Matthew,' said Gina, reading from a sheet of paper in front of her. 'Thirteen and eight. They're in Streatham with emergency foster parents.'

'And?' Max sounded unimpressed.

'And their parents just upped and left one day. Left them alone in their house. The girl kept it going for a few weeks – taking her brother to school, cooking food and so on. But in the end, teachers at the boy's school realized they hadn't seen either parent for a while and alerted Social Services. They were taken into care later that day. The girl put up quite a fight apparently.'

'This just gets better,' muttered Max. 'A stroppy teenage girl and a toddler. Maybe I can go to college early. Give you more room.'

'Max, that's not fair—' began Dan.

'You just announcing it isn't fair, Dad!' said Max, his voice strained. 'Where are the parents anyway? Can't they find them again? You can't just disappear.'

'Well, they have,' said Dan. 'Social Services think they have a . . . gang network.'

'*Gang* network? Is this for real?'

Dan nodded. 'They could be anywhere apparently.'

'Well, that confirms it then,' said Max. 'My vote is no. If you're still interested in my opinion.'

His parents looked at each other, then Gina reached out to her son. His straggly blond hair had fallen over his face but she resisted the urge to tuck it behind his ear.

'OK, a compromise,' she said. 'We'll say we'll take them *in the short term*, but they have to keep looking for long-term foster parents. How's that?' The question was aimed at Dan as much as Max, and her husband nodded.

Eventually her son shrugged his shoulders. 'Maybe. I'll think about it. But one more thing,' he said, 'seeing as we're having a family meeting. I think we should be very worried about this new American law. The heritage crime thing. It's just . . . if that happens here, we'll be the first to get locked up. Everyone knows what your folks got up to.'

Dan and Gina shifted awkwardly in their seats. Dan began what sounded like a speech he'd given before.

'I know the Depression has been bad. Really bad. But the American legal system is nothing to do with the law here. They lock up more of their people than any other country on Earth, they have the death penalty, they love God and guns. We're not the same.'

'Agreed,' said Max, 'but our unemployment is the same, the need for a scapegoat is the same. Plus their tying it to slavery makes it different – makes it harder to argue against. We had a slave trade here; our companies got wealthy like theirs did. They want reparations. Slavery is the original heritage crime, but they're adding more all the time. I don't like it. And the French, Italians and Spanish all seem up for it too. Half of Europe thinks it's a good idea. The European Union might be history, but there are still a few things they seem to agree on.'

Dan shook his head. 'Their legal codes are different to ours—'

'But it's *popular*,' Max persisted. 'In our economics class last week Mr Hogarth was explaining how it got passed in the US, how they'd settled on limiting the guilt to two generations. *Crimine Patrimonio* is already halfway through the Italian parliament, *Crimes Patrimoine* has just been introduced by the French. Then we discussed which of our families would go to prison if it was passed here. Everyone just looked at me. Yesterday I had *Convict* graffitied on my locker.'

Dan and Gina looked horrified.

'Just saying,' said Max.

10

Soon after Abi and Mattie Turner moved into the Nortons' house in North London, heritage crime arrived in the UK. It had been discussed endlessly on news sites and talk shows; some magazines ran articles showing which politicians and celebrities had criminals in their family tree. But for all the analysis of the legal issues at stake, it was a small incident which opened the floodgates. A notorious drug dealer in Southampton was taking part in a community payback scheme: his BMW had been confiscated and sold; now he'd been ordered to help build a local drop-in centre that would benefit the people he had damaged. A small crowd had gathered to watch him begin his punishment when someone noticed that his family were watching from the security of a new Range Rover with tinted windows.

'Make them work too!' shouted a woman, pointing at the car.

'He messed up my whole family,' called another. 'They should get their hands dirty too!' There were shouts of agreement, and a section of the crowd started walking towards the car; everyone heard the sound of the central locking being activated.

'I'd agree if I were you,' said the organizer of the payback scheme, speaking rapidly to the dealer. 'I'll call for back-up, but it would defuse the situation if you just said yes.'

Concerned for the safety of his family, the man agreed. To cheers and applause, his wife and two children, aged fourteen and ten, put on bright orange tunics and began to dig. It was all over social media in minutes. Images of their luxurious house were juxtaposed with the family's 'chain gang' appearance. The response was overwhelming – the public approved and wanted more. Fast.

Within days the community payback scheme saw not only convicted law breakers but their families digging and building, sweating and suffering. The TV crews covered each new work party. Politicians started asking why, if the families of small-time criminals should pay back their debt, the principle wasn't applied on a much bigger scale. Websites sprang up revealing the addresses of 'heritage criminals in your neighbourhood'. Stones were thrown through windows, the police called to disperse crowds outside the houses of the 'offenders'.

★

The Nortons were slow to pick up on what was happening in Southampton.

Dan's office had become a bedroom again; the new arrivals had their statutory bedroom each. All Dan and Gina's attention was on trying to assimilate Abi and Mattie Turner.

For the first week Abi had barely spoken; if she communicated at all, it was through Mattie. Her gaze was fierce, her body language hostile. She refused to go to school, barely ate, and fought off all attempts to get her to wear new clothes or control her shock of brown hair: she tried to attack Gina when she produced scissors. Dan had come between them, but it was Mattie's shouts that had reined his sister in.

Max had kept his distance. He had seen foster kids struggle to settle in before, but none had been as aggressive as this bristling, angry, silent girl.

By contrast, Mattie had attached himself to Max, following him everywhere and talking incessantly.

'Max, what clothes do you like? Max, can I watch you play your computer game? Max, can I sleep in your bed?' The only way to quieten his new fan was to ask about his parents. Mattie clammed up tight.

Then a local news site broke the full story. In lurid detail, with photos, they revealed that the children of criminals had been placed with the offspring of other criminals. BRITAIN'S NUMBER ONE CRIME FAMILY? ran the headline. The national sites weren't far behind.

'Is this true?' stormed Max. He pointed to the

adjoining room where Abi and Mattie were watching videos. 'You mentioned a gang network, but did you know they were *wanted*?'

'Yes,' said Gina. 'That's *why* we took them in. They were the children of crooks, just like Dad and me. We thought we could help. No one else would know what we know: what it feels like to be ashamed of your own parents, to constantly change the subject when someone asks about them. We thought we could be the perfect match.'

There was silence in the kitchen. They all became aware of the muffled sound from the TV.

'Maybe you should give them back,' Max said quietly.

Gina's eyes filled with tears.

Dan reached for her hand but looked as worried as she did. 'What if they come for Abi and Mattie too?' he whispered.

Gina's eyes opened wide, propelling the tears down her cheeks. 'They'd never lock children up, Dan! This is Britain! We don't do that here!'

Max propped up his tablet on the kitchen table. 'Well, you should watch this.'

He played his parents an edited video of all the payback scheme incidents. They watched children and teenagers pulling on fluorescent jackets and, to a chorus of jeers from onlookers, pick up brooms and shovels. Gina and Dan stared at the images, horrified.

'Look at this, though,' said Max, and his parents found themselves holding their breath. 'This is part of a speech from a leading prison reformer. He's a rising star called John Grey.'

'Heard of him,' said Gina. 'Nasty piece of work. Pompous and preachy. A classic moral crusader.'

'That's him.' Max pressed 'play'.

The man in the video stood at a lectern, grasping its sides. Short, well-groomed hair, wire-framed glasses.

'There are those living among us,' he said, partly to the camera, partly to the unseen audience, 'who have come to feel that they are above the law. A culture of impunity has developed whereby they think they can get away with their crimes.' He paused, his lips pressed tightly together. The audience waited. 'And they are right – they *can* get away with it. At the moment. *For now.*' Murmurs of approval could be heard from the crowd. 'While we have all suffered in the greatest Depression anyone has known, there are some who have been untouched, who have done just fine, thank you very much. This is a class of people,' he continued, 'who benefit from the proceeds of crime. Now, the community payback schemes have started to address the problem, but I believe we have say to these people, "Enough! You owe us. And it's time to pay us back."'

Max paused the video. 'That's just the start. This man means business and everyone is listening. I've looked him up. He's hard-core.'

'He's scary,' said Gina.

'Yes, and what did Grandpa do again, Mum? Steal a few million from his own company before disappearing?'

Max turned to Dan. 'And your dad and his partner had a credit-card scam? The family joke about partners in crime isn't going to seem funny any more. I know you guys are great and everything, and how you fell for each other because you were escaping blah blah blah, but this . . .' He pointed at the screen, which had freeze-framed Grey pouting at the camera. 'This means *us.* I know it's sad your dad died and everything, but we got some of his money—'

'Barely anything actually—' began Dan, but Max carried on.

'And, Mum, when your dad had been gone a certain number of years, you got your inheritance, right?'

Gina nodded.

'And insurance?'

She nodded again.

'Did it pay for the house, school fees – that kind of thing?'

'Yes, Max, it did, but—'

'Then we're guilty!' Max was shouting now; he looked frightened. 'Once they start looking for people who need to "pay back", we'll be right there, number one on that list! The press already have our story!'

A thud at the door made them all start. Gina hurriedly wiped her eyes.

'Parcel?' said Dan, getting up.

'I'll get it,' said Max, but Abi and Mattie were there first. They were standing by the open door, staring at a burning, smoking package. The hall was instantly filled with a foul, gut-churning stench and Max hauled them away.

'Dad!' he yelled. 'You need to see this!' He steered Abi and Mattie back into the lounge.

'What's happening, Max?' asked Mattie, holding his nose. 'What's in that parcel? It smells like poo, but why was it on fire?'

Gina hurried in and Max nodded at his mother. 'Mum will explain,' he said, and ran back to join his father.

Gina sat on the sofa, Mattie jumping up and forcing his way under her arm. Abi sat cross-legged on the floor, but her wide eyes were fixed on Gina.

'This is about us, isn't it,' she said.

It wasn't a question but Gina answered it anyway. 'I think so. There are some very sick people out there.'

Mattie nuzzled further into Gina's jumper. 'Are we going to have to go and live somewhere else then?' he said, his voice very small.

'No,' said Gina. She hugged him tightly and met Abi's enquiring stare. 'Whatever happens, we are staying together.'

There were no more stink bombs, but there was no mistaking the new hostility either. After the label of 'Britain's number-one crime family' had stuck, even visiting the shops became a trial. Being ignored or served last every time was upsetting and time-consuming, so they just stopped going. Christmas that year was delivered in a convoy of trucks.

*

With all the children that his parents fostered, Max found that it was birthdays and Christmas that were always particularly stressful. Instead of nervous excitement they were often met with an unhappy, feigned indifference. So it became the Norton Christmas tradition that, for breakfast, you could have any food you wanted. Anything at all. Once Max had explained to the new foster children how it worked, their eyes had lit up. A long list had been written, another delivery booked.

Christmas morning was, therefore, greeted with excitement, tinged with uncertainty.

'You do know what I asked for, don't you?' asked a sceptical Mattie as they went downstairs in their pyjamas.

'Remind me,' said Max.

'Sherbet, toffee marshmallows, cupcakes and chips,' he said.

'Together?'

'Yes, together. You said we could ask for anything!'

'I know,' said Max, 'but that is just weird.'

'And I wanted a cheeseburger with fries, pizza and chocolate cake,' said Abi. 'And fudge.'

Max whistled. 'Hideous. You'll be sick before lunch. Let's see what we've got.'

He opened the kitchen door, and a wave of clashing smells filled their noses. Gina and Dan were already seated, and laughed as they looked at the faces in front of them.

'Happy Christmas!' cried Dan. 'And happy Christmas

breakfast too! Come in, sit down!' The table was laid, and there were place names written on card.

'Wow,' said Mattie as he looked at his plate. Piled high with cupcakes and marshmallows, it had chips arranged around the outside. A side order of sherbet had been poured into a small sugar bowl. 'Abi, look at this!' He beamed. 'I've got everything!'

'Me too,' she said, staring at her three plates.

Gina pointed to each in turn. 'Pepperoni and cheese,' she said. 'A well-done burger with all the extras. And fudge with cake for pudding. Did we forget anything?'

'No, it's amazing!' said Mattie. 'Can we start?'

'Of course!'

'What are you having?' Abi asked Gina through a mouthful of chips.

She pointed to the sizzling frying pan on the stove, where Dan was in charge. 'As many bacon sandwiches as we feel is wise.'

'Which could be about five each!' said Dan, laughing as he prodded and rearranged the rashers. Gina stood alongside him, threading an arm through his.

They had been worried that Abi and Mattie's first Christmas with them would be a tense, awkward affair. Mealtimes were often a flash point, with Max intolerant of Abi's sullenness. Much planning had gone into making the day as stress free as possible.

'Everything considered,' Gina muttered, hoping her words were drowned out by the hissing, spitting fat, 'all good so far.'

Max had found some old-time Christmas music and was trying to get everyone to sing. 'No?' he said. 'Just me then.' And he launched into 'Merry Christmas, Everybody'.

'Best pizza ever,' declared Abi to surprised smiles from everyone. 'Who thought up this whole idea anyway?'

'Well,' said Dan, 'let's just say it's been around . . . a while. Best not delve too much into family history just now.' He saw Gina and Max wince. 'More chips, anyone?'

Day 789
My favourite things RIGHT NOW:
G when she's telling me things.
Not dreaming of ANYTHING.
Everyone stinks at the moment. We need more showers but screws say no (they stink too and need them more than us).
Raced on 4 levels with Daisy. Bin 55 smelled so bad! Actually sick.

Jug up was taken at trestle tables arranged in three rows that ran the length of the levels. Most strutter families had a working parent, a collar, who ate breakfast at 6 a.m.; everyone else ate between 7 and 7.30. Ant and Mattie walked down the levels together. The cavernous annexe filled with the morning noise of cell doors opening, shouted complaints and, below, food being served. The smell of breakfast temporarily broke through the ever-present stench of sweat and mould, and Ant found herself suddenly very hungry indeed.

'Smells like porridge. And toast. And maybe meat of some kind.'

Mattie snorted. 'Might smell like that. Won't taste like it. But just in case it's bacon . . .' Porridge and toast were normally on offer, as was some kind of fruit, usually chopped up in vast bowls. Occasionally they got sausages and, even more occasionally, bacon. Any portable meat disappeared within minutes, some eaten, the rest smuggled out for snacks or trading.

On the steps they were joined by Daisy, her white-blonde hair falling in curtains across her face.

'*Na,* Daisy,' said Ant.

'*Naa,* Ant,' she replied, 'considering the noise last night.' She saw a tall, gangly boy approach them and laid into him immediately. 'What the hell was that all night? I couldn't hear what you were arguing about, but God, you were loud.'

'Really?' said Amos Shah, a fourteen-year-old in an eighteen-year-old body, pushing his black-rimmed glasses further up the bridge of his nose. He moved wearily, spoke sarcastically. 'I think we were arguing about . . . Oh, let me see . . . Oh yeah, pretty much everything really. Don't know if you've noticed but we have to share with the Noons now. Dad doesn't like it much.'

'Yeah, well, next time just hit each other,' she said. 'It'd be quieter.'

A cell door slammed and a tall, broad-shouldered figure came to join them. 'Let me guess,' he said. 'Daisy's complaining about the noise.' Jimmy Noon smiled so widely that all Daisy could do was punch him harmlessly on the arm.

'Can't you and your mum shut them up?' she said, exasperated.

'I know it's bringing the neighbourhood down.' He grinned. 'But what can you do?' He caught up with Ant. 'Busy?'

'I'm going to breakfast, Jimmy,' she said flatly. 'Of course I'm busy.'

'Too busy for company?'

She looked at him, her forehead creased. 'How come you're so annoying?'

'How come you're so difficult?' he said, smiling again. 'So . . . inscrutable?'

She shrugged. 'It comes quite easily actually.'

'You don't say,' said Jimmy. 'See you in Happy Hour? I might be able to fit you in.'

She didn't smile much, but it was enough to make Jimmy laugh.

They all shuffled down the stairs and joined the queue for breakfast.

'More zookeepers around this morning,' said Ant, looking at the number of uniformed guards observing the breakfast routine. Some stared down from the decks, others walked around the tables, all of them stony-faced.

'I've counted twelve,' said Mattie. 'Which is four more than normal.'

'And all of them as ugly as each other,' muttered Jimmy, sitting down. 'Do you think they have to practise to make their expressions that blank?'

'And they're new,' said Amos. 'Not our usual.'

Ant scrutinized the guards near her and nodded. 'You're right. Haven't seen this crowd before. They're not on the payroll. We'll need to break them in . . .' She waited for a white-shirted officer to pass their table, oblivious of everyone holding their breath.

'Where are you lot from then?' she called to a sweating guard.

Apart from quickly narrowed eyes, there was no sign that the man had heard her. He kept walking.

'Rude,' said Ant. She noticed Amos wincing. 'What? You don't trust me?'

He carried on eating. 'No, I'm sure you'll handle it fine,' he said through his porridge.

'Classic Amos,' said Ant. 'Your mouth says one thing, your eyes something else.' She waited for the next screw to approach and tried again. 'Where you lot from then?'

A man with one hand on his belt and the other holding his radio came over to where Ant was sitting. The radio squawked with urgent voices and he paused, then turned the volume down. She saw that his badge said MCTAVISH.

'You trainees or something?'

The PO bent down between Ant and Jimmy. He

smelled of chewing gum. 'We give orders, you obey them. That's the way it works. It doesn't matter where we're from.' His voice was cold, measured.

'You really *are* new,' said Ant.

The guard straightened. 'Stand up,' he said quietly.

'I'm eating my breakfast.'

The man clipped his radio onto his belt so that he had both hands free. 'Stand up, strutter.' His voice was raised and the buzz of conversation died away; everyone recognized a face-off when they saw one.

'My name is Ant. Give me five minutes, Officer.' She took a bite of toast.

'Don't push him, Ant,' muttered Jimmy.

'Abi, just do what he says,' whispered Mattie.

Ant munched some more toast.

The guard's hands were twitching. 'You want me to haul you up by your strap?'

She stopped chewing. 'You wouldn't dare.'

The man beckoned for assistance. 'Last warning, then you're on basic. Stand. Up.'

'Pick on someone else!' said Jimmy.

Someone from another table: 'Leave her alone!'

Another voice: 'Yeah, leave us all alone!'

Then a whole range of voices joined in. '*Dixam pas!*' was the first shout, followed by '*Yeah, bax!*' Then a chorus of '*Bax! Bax! Bax!*' filled the hall.

'Speaking in Spike,' muttered Ant. 'They're gonna love that.'

The sweating officer now joined his colleague. His badge said DENHOLM.

'What are they saying?' shouted McTavish over the noise.

Denholm shrugged.

'She's refusing orders. I've asked her to—'

Ant leaped to her feet and the chanting died away. 'OK, is this better?' she yelled, her face now centimetres from the guard's. 'I'm standing. Hope it helps you understand. All I asked was where you were all from. It's really not a big deal. It's called *conversation* in most places. But hey, why talk when you can beat the crap out of anyone you choose?'

Ant felt her T-shirt being tugged so hard it ripped. She spun round and saw Mattie standing on his chair, eyes blazing. He mouthed some words – so fast Ant couldn't work out what he was saying.

He leaned towards her. 'Passes! Around your neck!' He spoke as loudly as he dared, his tone desperate. And it worked.

It was like a bucket of cold water over her head. Ant couldn't afford a pat down, not with three swipe cards and two passes around her neck. These were Castle or Village POs, or maybe from out of town; they didn't know how things worked in Spike. She turned to face the guard. And smiled.

'I'm sorry, my mistake. I'll shut up now. I was out of order – it's the heat, I think.'

She waited as the man reassessed her. A broad smile had transformed her face; the fierce, challenging eyes were now lit with warmth and sincerity. Eventually the PO grunted and walked away, looking almost disappointed. 'Next time . . .' he said.

'Oh, don't worry, there won't be a next time,' Ant said brightly. 'I've learned my lesson, Officer, really I have.'

12

Ant sat down again. She looked at Mattie and shrugged. 'I forgot!' she said quietly. 'But thanks.'

Gina came over and inspected the T-shirt. 'I'll ask if I can go and get another one,' she said.

'No, really,' said Ant. 'Leave it. It's fine.'

Gina recognized the tone and realized there was no point arguing. She went back to her place.

Flashpoint over, the buzz of conversation rose again. Jimmy leaned in close. 'Well, Miss Norton Turner, that was good shouting,' he said. 'Dangerous, but pretty spectacular.'

Ant shrugged. 'As opposed to you, Jimmy.'

He looked affronted. 'I just thought it could get nasty, Ant. Everything is very tense – it would only take a small spark to set the whole place off. But Master Norton

Turner here might just have saved the day.' Jimmy saluted Mattie with his plastic cup of tea.

Daisy leaned over. 'You really going to leave your strap showing?' she whispered.

'Why not?' said Ant. 'Maybe I'll decorate it while I'm at it. My body. My strap.'

'Did you see the looks on their faces when the chanting started?' said Jimmy. 'They had no idea what was happening!'

'Which is the general idea of having our own words,' said Ant. 'Haven't heard Spiketalk used on new arrivals before though.'

'And if we have new screws,' said Daisy, 'you need to lose the passes. You can't just walk around with them under your shirt. Judging by that shouting match, this new lot aren't very nice. That was a bad one.' She nodded at one of the guards who was still loitering nearby. 'Your sister owes you, Mattie.'

'Like I said, it was the heat,' said Ant. 'That and the Shahs shouting all night.'

'Oh, please . . .' said Amos.

'At least you're not in the same 'bin as them!' said Jimmy. 'I'll swap with *anyone* . . .'

'Plus everything else,' said Daisy. 'All night. The noise. From everywhere. Mum says she thought it was kicking off in Pentonville.'

'I heard the sirens,' said Ant through a mouthful of toast. 'Couldn't tell which prison they were going to though.'

'The screws told her,' said Daisy. 'Said there had been a fire in the gym and a wall had collapsed.' The others had stopped eating and were staring at her, waiting for more information. She shrugged. 'That's all I know.'

'How come your mum gets to hear this stuff?' said Mattie. 'Gina isn't told anything.'

'It's old drug money, Mattie,' said Ant. 'It always works.'

Mattie looked puzzled.

'Basically Daisy's dad ran a drug cartel. Very successfully too. That buys a lot of favours, a lot of info.'

'Did he disappear?' asked Mattie. 'Like our parents?'

'He died,' said Daisy flatly. 'Before he got caught. So I'm out at eighteen, of course. Mum's doing a six – two years more than Amos's dad got, which doesn't seem right to me.'

Without comment or even looking up, Amos picked up his tray and went to sit at the next table.

'You didn't need to say that,' said Jimmy quietly.

'Amos's mum was a bent copper!' said Daisy. 'And did far worse things than your dad ever did. He was just a banker.'

'"Just a banker" is not something I normally hear,' said Jimmy.

'Drug lord, bent copper, banker. What's the difference?' said Ant. 'At least there's only one crook in your cell. There's two in ours. Gina's father was a seriously crooked accountant and Dan's father was a swindler. Plus

Grey hates the fact that our real parents just disappeared. So we're not going anywhere.'

'You don't often mention your folks,' said Daisy. 'You know, your real folks.'

Ant glowered. 'There's no reason to mention them,' she muttered. 'Crap parents anyway.'

13

The rest of their breakfast was eaten in silence.

Eventually Mattie said, 'Gina wants us,' and ran over to where a group of women sat with their heads close together. Sarah Raath and Mishal Noon both made room for him. If they hadn't been in a high-security prison eating porridge at just after 7 a.m., they could have been ladies lunching. Each woman still had the unmistakable air of someone who knew they didn't belong here. Ant knew Gina wasn't like this back in the 'bin and concluded it was a show they put on. For the screws, certainly, and for themselves too.

Ant was watching her brother. 'We ruffle his hair all the time,' she said. 'And it never bothers him. Would drive me crazy.'

'Yeah, well, not much chance of that,' said Jimmy.

'Our dad made us have the same pudding-bowl hair,' said Ant. 'He got some weird, controlling kick out of it. When we went to live with Dan and Gina, we changed. I shaved mine, Mattie grew his. Come on, it'll be Happy Hour in a minute.' She picked up her tray and walked to the slops bucket. As she passed Gina's table, Mattie beckoned her over. 'Sarah says a man died last night. Villager.'

'Told you,' said Daisy.

Ant looked at Sarah Raath; her short blonde hair was going white. She nodded confirmation of the story as Daisy sat next to her.

'Screws say a wall collapsed; Villagers claim he was thrown against it. That's why it collapsed. Load of the cons then set fire to the gym. Cops and fire brigade still swarming all over the place. Village sounds like a bad place at the moment.'

'Don't push it any further with the screws, Ant,' said Gina. 'Reckon that's why they're twitchy and nervous today. Please change your T-shirt.'

'Maybe.' Ant threw her uneaten porridge and toast in a large plastic tub.

'I'll bring Mattie up,' said Gina. 'He's OK with us.'

'You really going to leave your strap uncovered?' called Sarah Raath as Ant and Jimmy walked away.

'We've all got one,' said Ant. 'Might as well flaunt it.'

*

Four years earlier, South London

'Mama, wake up. It's Mattie.' The small boy in school shorts and sweatshirt gently shook his mother's shoulder, but she didn't stir. 'Abi, you try again,' he said. He swapped places with his sister, who had been hovering at his side.

She knelt by the bed so that she was level with her mother's ear.

Please wake up.

'Papa's home,' she said. The words took a few seconds to penetrate whatever level of unconsciousness Shola Murray had achieved, but, spell-like, they worked their magic. She rolled over and forced her eyes open, her gaze flitting between her children.

At last!

'Papa's home,' repeated Abi, more urgently this time. 'We can hear him downstairs.' Mattie started to climb into the bed but his sister pulled him back. 'No. She has to get up. We have to be ready.'

Shola opened her mouth to speak, her lips separating only slowly. '*Pitit mwen*,' she said, her voice still thick with sleep. 'My children . . . OK. We can do this.' She forced a smile, the last of the congealed saliva flaking away, then sat up and pulled back the duvet. 'I just shut my eyes for a second, that's all . . .'

Abi rearranged her mother's skirt. Mattie handed her a glass of water. They all jumped as a crash came from the kitchen downstairs. Shola really was awake now. She reached out and held their hands, talking softly but fast. 'Remember. Speak English to him. Only use Creole if you have to – don't make him mad.'

Heavy steps and humming on the stairs.

When he sounds OK, he's not OK. That's what Mama says.

Abi grabbed a book. 'Read it, Mama. Anything it says, just read.' She pulled her brother down to the floor and they sat together, focusing furiously on what their mother was saying. The bedroom door swung open and Kyle Turner breezed in, a beer in one hand and a mixing bowl in the other. To Abi he looked enormous. Smart as ever, perfumed as ever, but mainly just enormous. She caught him out of the corner of her eye and looked swiftly away.

'What a lovely scene,' he said. 'Though wait a minute . . .' His brow furrowed. 'Who's putting who to bed here?' He looked from his wife to his children and then to the unmade bed. 'A few gins after lunch, Shola? Or before maybe?'

Shola had stopped reading. Apart from her shaking hands, she had stopped moving altogether.

'She wasn't well, Papa,' said Abi.

'I bet she wasn't.' Kyle took a mouthful of beer, swilled it around his mouth and swallowed noisily. 'So who picked you up from school then?'

'I always do it, Papa. I collect Mattie and we walk.'

'Of course. I think you told me that. So . . .' He put his bottle down and hummed again as he busied himself with the contents of the bowl. He tested some hair wax between his fingers, then smoothed it into his hair.

'*Kimbe*,' whispered Shola. (Be strong.)

'*Ou mem tou*,' mouthed Abi. (You too.)

Kyle suddenly stopped humming and held out the bowl. Abi and Mattie could see the long pair of scissors inside. Their father smiled. 'Who wants a haircut?'

Clifton, Bristol. Now

Max Norton was not in the best of moods. Having worked the late shift at the café, he really needed to sleep in. Midday would have been fine, 2 p.m. ideal. Instead, after a sweltering, airless night and his flatmate knocking the bikes over on his way out, he was nursing his first coffee at just after ten o'clock.

The kitchen was already too bright and too hot. He opened the window wide then drew the curtains across. They billowed slightly and he felt the faintest of breezes on his clammy skin. He locked and chained the front door, then flicked open his laptop and began his daily ritual. He logged on to what looked like a chemistry revision site and started to answer the verification questions, eight in all. The last one asked him the name of his current project. He typed 'Complex Cell Evolution' and waited.

His screen went blank, then appeared to reload the same site; this time the answer to the last question was 'Inorganic Chemistry'. Again the screen reappeared and his current project became 'Dark Matter Photons'. Max had drunk half his coffee before the familiar grey screen and black rectangular box appeared, the cursor pulsing, waiting for his sixteen-digit log-in. He gulped the rest of the coffee and typed fast.

Max had been a student for two years and his parents had been in Spike for most of them. He had been so freaked out by heritage crime and the 'New Legal Settlement' that with the university's blessing he had opted to study abroad for a year. Of the courses offered he chose a science option at the Free University of Berlin. Not only did it have a good reputation, but Germany appeared to be the only country immune to the new madness. 'We've done that whole blame thing before,' explained one of his new computer science colleagues. 'We learned from our history. Shame no one else did.'

Max had joined a small team who were setting up sites on the dark web where strutters could communicate freely. The level of encryption they had used made it painstakingly tedious to log on, but it meant that, with patience, it was possible to find out what was happening to imprisoned strutters across Europe. Some of the 'Bug sites', as they became known, enabled affected families to communicate with each other for the first time. Others linked escaped strutters and 'on-the-runs' who had disappeared before they could be arrested.

Not all resistance to heritage crime was underground. A few human rights groups, lawyers and campaigners organized protests and ran online campaigns. But they came up against popular opinion: people were still angry and believed justice was being done.

A clatter from outside made Max jump and he ran to the window. His flatmate wasn't due back till later, but he couldn't risk anyone stumbling into this. He tweaked the curtains. Two floors down he saw the bins being emptied and he exhaled slowly. He was tired and he was jumpy, but being fanatically cautious had quickly become a way of life. There was a small 'Bug group' in Bristol – strutter relatives, friends and supporters – but they usually kept their distance, meeting only rarely. There were too many families in too many countries who would be compromised if anything leaked. Max rattled the security chain, checked the door lock again and returned to the laptop.

The page displayed was simple and in plain text only. Max whistled as he saw the number of messages displayed, and began to scroll down. Usually he would expect a daily update, with four or five reports from the nine UK strutter jails: new prison terms started, new visitors' accounts or smuggled messages from inside the jails. Today he counted twenty-seven reports, all of them from HMP London. He scanned the messages with a growing sense of dread.

Death today in Pentonville. Think it's the Irish guy.

Outrageous.

It's brewing up in Holloway. Could well blow at any time.

. . . mate said he's never known it so bad . . .

. . . that fire in P is way worse than they're saying.

Reckon more died for certain . . .
Medic in Holloway says she's not going in tomorrow.
Too scared. God help us all.

No posts were ever signed or attributed; their authenticity was assumed. Max read each one, then carefully logged out and switched off the laptop.

Then he smashed his coffee cup down on the table.

Spike, HMP London

My favourite things RIGHT NOW:
Daisy thinks I'm cool!!
Amos when he's not being a butt.

Ant and Jimmy were climbing the levels. 'Look, about earlier,' began Jimmy, resting a hand on her shoulder.

'It's fine,' she said. 'I get it. Be careful, don't push it. Smile. Be happy.'

'Ant, that's not fair . . .'

'Nothing in here is fair, Jimmy, in case you hadn't noticed.'

'But going crazy is exactly what they wanted you to do. They wanted a fight.'

'That's true,' Ant conceded, 'and they were about to get one till Mattie saved the day.'

'He's quite good at that,' said Jimmy.

As they arrived on level three, Amos appeared. He looked upset.

'*Na*, Ant. *Na*, Jimmy.'

'*Naa*, Amos, what's up?' said Ant.

'What . . . what you said about my mum was unfair. She—'

'Was it wrong?' interrupted Jimmy.

'She wasn't a bent copper—' began Amos.

'OK,' said Ant, 'she wasn't a bent copper. Point taken. I'm sorry.'

Amos looked at them. 'OK, I get it. I'm dismissed.' He turned, then added, 'Classic Ant. Your mouth says one thing, your eyes say something else.' Then he headed off down the stairs.

'He's got a point there,' said Jimmy. 'About the eyes. Like I said, inscrutable.'

As they approached cell 33, they saw Prison Officer Brian MacMillan pacing outside, and Jimmy groaned.

'What does he want? He's not usually around at this time of day.'

'He looks nervous,' said Ant. 'He wants to tell me something.'

MacMillan stopped pacing as they approached. Instead he glanced around, then disappeared into Ant's cell. Ant and Jimmy looked at each other, then followed him inside.

He had taken off his cap as though visiting a friend's house and was standing uncomfortably in front of Gina's unmade bunk. He was by common consent the least obnoxious of the guards, and not many years older than Ant; she felt the outline of his swipe card under what remained of her T-shirt.

'Morning, Ant, Jimmy.' His accent was Belfast, educated. Seeing Ant's ripped T-shirt, he said, 'Do you need to change, Ant?'

'Who are all these new guards?' she said, ignoring his question.

'And why are you in Ant's 'bin?' asked Jimmy. 'Looking for something?'

'Yes. No. Well, it's just . . . one of our guys got stabbed last night and there's some heavy stuff going down. These new POs are reinforcements. I need—'

'Wait,' said Ant. 'Was this when the lifer got thrown against the wall?'

'You know about that?' MacMillan was sweating; it was considerably hotter inside the cells. He wiped his face with his sleeve, then nodded. 'He had a jammer made from tins he'd got hold of. Stuck it in his cellmate's leg after a fight, then in an officer's ribs after he tried to intervene. He was cornered in the gym.'

They waited for him to continue; when he said nothing, Ant finished the story for him. 'So you killed him.'

'I wasn't there, Ant . . .'

'Doesn't matter. Thrown against the wall maybe? And a few times, just to be sure? Then your shiny boots got to work. And while your colleagues were taking revenge on him, the Villagers who'd seen what was happening started to burn the place down. And it all went bingo from there. How am I doing so far?'

MacMillan fingered his lapel radio cable nervously. 'Listen . . .' he started. Then, lowering his voice, 'Look, yes, that's probably about right. But the point is, I've come to warn you. I obviously shouldn't be here – I'll have to say I was doing a cell search or something. Some of the new guys think we're too tight with you strutters, others are worried about losing their, er . . .'

'Bribes?' suggested Ant.

'Their contributions, yes.'

'Why are you telling us this?' asked Jimmy.

MacMillan hesitated.

'Because,' said Ant, filling in the silence, 'he finds it easier to talk to us than to his fellow officers, most of whom are as corrupt as hell and just counting the days till their pension kicks in.'

He nodded.

Jimmy looked amazed. 'You've talked about this before?'

'And,' said Ant, 'the governor's hardly ever here – too busy dining politicians and intimidating critics – while his deputy is counting his money and covering his arse.'

MacMillan nodded again. 'That's about it.'

'Who's next in command then?' asked Jimmy.

'That'll be Assessor Grey,' he said. 'And God have mercy on us all. It feels like every man for himself at the moment, and that's a very dangerous place to be. Things will be difficult for a while. All the regulars have been drafted in to Holloway and Pentonville – I'm due there in an hour. These officers on duty now come from all over. You can't operate as you have done, Ant. I need my pass back.'

'No chance,' she said. 'Nice try, Brian, but no chance. I need that pass more than you do, and anyway you have a spare. Use that.'

'I need both – I need to account for all my stuff. If they find you with it . . .' He sounded desperate.

'They won't. And if they do, I'll say I stole it.'

'You *did* steal it,' said MacMillan, with more steel in his voice now. 'And I need it back. Seriously. You don't understand.'

'Yes I do,' said Ant. 'And I traded for it, as you well know, so it's mine anyway. So unless you're going to tear it off me . . .'

There was a rapid knock on the door and Daisy burst in. She had an old marker pen in her hand.

'Oh . . .' She looked around. 'I didn't realize . . . What's up?'

Jimmy glanced through the door. 'Gina and Mattie on the way. You'd better start searching the 'bin, Brian, or she'll wonder what's happening.'

MacMillan gave Ant one more exasperated look, then marched out, pulling his cap on as he left.

'I'll be off too,' said Jimmy. 'Check in with my mum before IR starts. Catch you later.' Ant watched him nod at Gina as he hurried away.

'I think he likes you,' said Daisy.

'Everyone likes me,' said Ant. 'Hadn't you noticed?'

Daisy laughed. 'Not at breakfast, they didn't!' She held up the pen. 'You were talking about decoration and it set me thinking. I had this in our 'bin.' She removed the cap and smiled. 'It still works. I reckon a small goose design might look quite good . . .'

Ant's eyes lit up. 'Yes!' she said. 'If you're quick!' She could see Gina talking earnestly a few cells away. 'Do it!' She turned round and lifted her T-shirt. 'Bottom left. Same as the tat.'

Daisy crouched down beside her and began drawing, ink on plastic. In a few strokes she had copied the bird design from Ant's shoulder and neck. 'It looks amazing!' she whispered. 'Can't do the blue feathers though. What kind of goose is this anyway?'

'It's the *Kampfgans*,' said Ant. 'A German fighting goose.'

Daisy smiled. 'Of course. I can see the attraction.'

'And it's got a pretty mixed-up heritage too. Seemed a good fit.'

'It's perfect—' said Daisy.

'And words,' interrupted Ant. 'I want words. I want graffiti. Write . . . *Not to Blame*. As large as you can.'

'Are you sure?' Daisy sounded thrilled and scared in equal measure.

'Yes!' said Ant, eyes still on Gina. 'Quickly. Then I'll do you.'

Daisy finished writing and pulled Ant's T-shirt back down. 'Do me later,' she said. 'I think it's running out of ink anyway . . .'

14

What the prison authorities called Indoor Relief took place every morning for two hours. There were only a few jobs considered suitable for prisoners of all ages, and after experimenting with packing clothes and IT, the governor had decided his prisoners should sort post. A deal had been done with the local post office, and now Spike was one of North London's sorting offices.

Ant, Mattie and Daisy were working alongside a short, round elderly man with a neat white moustache. His prison-issue green uniform – compulsory for adults – had BLAKELY written on the breast pocket. He picked up a package, squinted at the postcode and threw it into one of ten grey plastic sacks that stood in metal stands, waiting to be filled.

'You'd think machines would do this better,' he said

crossly. He wasn't a popular man. This was mainly because he had been an MP and a minister in government, but also because of his constant complaining. Some called him Jeffrey, but most used Lord Whiny.

'Yes, but we're cheaper,' said Ant. 'It's the big plus for slavery – we do it for nothing.'

'Well, aren't we the generous ones,' he muttered. Two POs walked past, deep in conversation. 'And we could be opening and stealing every piece of post for all they know. Morons.'

'Strutters doing IR is not really their concern at the moment,' said Ant, dropping envelopes into the sacks in front of her.

Blakely grunted. Across from them, in the next row of twenty, Gina and Sarah Raath worked through a pile of mail together. Alongside them was Frail Mary and Neil Osborne, former CEO of a large international corporation. Ant knew Gina disliked him, and watched as she focused solely on Mary, reading out the addresses, then handing them to her for sorting.

'I'd be surprised if they had any concern other than their own necks,' said Blakely.

'Sounds sensible to me,' said Ant. 'Look after yourself and your own. That's what I'd do. And anyway, you were a politician – that's exactly what your lot did for years.'

The trundling noise of another full bin arriving interrupted them. Its porter carried himself with a confidence that seemed out of place in a prison.

'Ah, Jimmy Noon!' said Blakely brightly. 'The

banker's boy! Still smiling, I see! You wait till you've clocked your first year in this hell . . .'

'Then I'll be as miserable as you,' said Jimmy. 'I know. You tell me every day.'

'How long you in for again? Remind me.'

'My mum's doing a five, but I'm eighteen next year so I'll be out in May.'

'Well!' said Blakely. 'You may well need every one of those days to win over Miss Norton Turner here.'

'Who says I want to be "won over"?' said Ant, but Blakely had wandered off to talk to an inmate further down the line.

Jimmy glanced around and leaned on his bin. 'The screws here are so distracted! They are basically ignoring us.' He smiled at Mattie. 'Nice work at breakfast.'

Mattie smiled back. 'I was just . . . helping.' He looked up at his sister. 'Sometimes she forgets things, and I remind her. That's all.'

Ant laughed. 'Yeah, like how to stay out of trouble, how to stay out of SHU, that kind of thing. And that we might get out of here one day.'

'Well, it's true,' said Mattie. 'You're out in twenty-one months and two weeks, Ant. There's no point in making things worse. Getting out of here is all that matters.' Then he added, 'When the time is right.'

Jimmy noticed a smile flicker across Ant's face. He looked around quickly. 'I knew it! I knew you could get out of Spike whenever you—'

'No I can't,' Ant interrupted before he could say any more. She fixed Jimmy with a stare. 'It's not true at all. No I can't, and no I won't.'

Jimmy looked from one to the other. 'OK, that's clear,' he said, and went off to get more post.

'Don't think he believes you,' said Mattie.

'I don't think so either,' Ant agreed.

'I like him though.'

'Good for you.'

'And he likes you. He looks at you all the time.'

'Yeah, well he looks at Daisy as well.' Ant smiled. 'And any other female under thirty. Prison limits your options, Mattie. It's no big deal.'

Four years earlier, South London

The clumps of black hair lay in a semicircle on the carpet. Abi hadn't moved for five minutes. No one had moved for five minutes. In the bathroom, the sound of running water and humming.

'It's not as bad as you think it is,' whispered their mother from the bed.

'You said that last time,' muttered Mattie, his shoulders covered in a towel, his head down. He glanced left. His sister's haircut was identical to his.

Abi glanced right. 'And you're wrong, Mum,' she whispered. 'It's worse. We look like monsters. Like freaks.'

She'd stopped crying now. To begin with she couldn't help it, but when she realized the tears seemed to give her father some kind of encouragement, she made sure she stopped.

'This isn't happening again,' she said. 'Not ever. I don't know how you let it start, Mama, but I want it to stop.' She looked at her mother, mostly obscured by the duvet. 'How did it start?' she hissed. 'Why did you let him?'

From the bed, gentle sobbing but no words. When Shola had stopped crying, Mattie whispered, 'How much longer will he be, Mama? How long do we stay here?'

A deep sigh from the bed. 'He likes to take his time.'

They listened to the busy sounds from the bathroom.

'When . . . when it gets bad,' said their mother, 'I like to list my favourite things. It's from a song my mother taught me. There are so many . . .'

'What do you think of?' asked Mattie.

'Lemon sorbet,' she replied. 'That's first. Then hot sunny beaches. Fresh mango, shopping . . .'

'Your children maybe?'

'Obviously, Abi! You and Mattie, always. Of course. What next?'

'Gin and tonic?'

'Shut up!' hissed Mattie. 'That's not fair. I like this game. I'd say playing with my friends, your cakes, Mama, and . . .' He tailed off as the bathroom went quiet.

Mattie and Abi dropped their heads again as the door opened and their father walked back in.

15

My favourite things RIGHT NOW:
Helping Ant to stay out of SHU.
I think Jimmy N is cool. Ant thinks so too but she won't say so. (Why are girls like that?)
Got new pencils in IR (not stolen!). Given 2 away.
JB only pretends to be grumpy. I think he likes it here.
I do sometimes if A's happy and she's actually here.

That evening Dan was first in the jug-up queue. By the time he sat down there was already an expectant crowd of inmates. They knew he would have had access to the Bug sites and were desperate for news. He toyed with his pasta and waited for a guard to pass. Eager faces leaned towards him.

'Haven't got much beyond what we know already – I didn't get a lot of time,' he said, staring at his food. This was partly to avoid looking interesting to the security cameras, but also to shield his mouth from any lip readers the prison might have employed. 'There's definitely big trouble in the Village – you know about the killing; the riot was in the library, I think – but there's only rumours coming from the Castle. Nothing specific. It's difficult and time-consuming to get on most of the sites. The postings suggest there are cons stashing weapons, escape plans being made, that kind of thing. There's a Manchester story about some new strap technology being introduced. Attacks on strutters in Belfast prisons are the worst they've seen. Oh, and more prisons. A *lot* more building, most of it in remote places.' He ate a mouthful of spaghetti. 'That's all I have. The other guys might have gleaned more news . . .' Some of the inmates moved on to other collars who had returned from work, but most stayed where they were.

'Yes, but you're the only one who speaks the language,' said Daisy from behind her hand. 'Was all that stuff you told us in German?'

Dan took a deep breath and checked on the guards. 'This is deep down on the internet, but yes, it is. German is the language of resistance. It's still small-scale, but while the Germans say no to heritage crime, more strutters are learning their language. We don't think the government is onto it yet, but they will be.'

'We should escape to Germany,' said Ant. 'That would be different.'

There were a few muffled laughs, but Dan shook his head. 'Actually, some people have. Getting there isn't easy, but it's definitely happening. Today someone used the phrase *einen dicken Hals haben.* It made me smile. I hadn't heard it before.'

Everyone saw two guards change direction and head towards their table. Without missing a beat, the inmates resumed their eating and made small talk until they had passed. It was a routine they had become familiar with. As soon as it was safe, Dan repeated the phrase. '*Einen dicken Hals haben.* It's an expression of *rage.* It means you're so mad that the veins in your neck are bulging.'

There were smiles around the table and a few tried out the new words, seeing what they sounded like.

'And here's another one. *Aus der—*'

'Dan, it's time to stop,' interrupted Gina, a hand on her husband's leg. They followed her gaze: the two guards were striding back.

'They're breaking us up,' said Gina. 'Someone's got suspicious. Eat up, everybody.'

Heading back to their cell, Dan waited till they were far enough away from anyone and again shielded his mouth. 'Borrowed a phone. Spoke to Max. Says he's ready to go. That's where I got the information from – he checks these sites. He'd heard about the Villager who died, read about the gym. And his old mates in Berlin told him about the strutter refugees.'

Gina put her arm through Dan's. 'How did he sound?'

'He sounded good, Gina. Really. I think he's more prepared than we are . . .'

*

The 800 Bar, Bristol

Max, listen carefully. Those special holiday plans we discussed? You might need to use them. Be ready.

Max Norton remembered the tension in his father's voice; for two years they had been dreading having this conversation. The 'special holiday' meant disappearing. His university life was over.

Max had a job to do. The early evening crowd had drifted away. Theatre, concerts or food had taken many of them, so the staff were working hard to get everything ready for the second wave. Max was serving his last customers – two tables enjoying a noisy family birthday celebration. He had been attentive and friendly, had tolerated their singing, despite the looks of annoyance from other diners. He was hoping for a decent tip, but mainly he was hoping they'd go soon. He needed time to think. He was due a break and it couldn't come quickly enough.

Ever since his father had rung him, Max's head had been spinning. Dan often called from school using a phone lent to him by a sympathetic colleague, and Max was used to his forced cheerfulness. The conversations were usually light-hearted affairs – his father desperate not to worry his son any more than he was already. But not this time.

Whatever was happening at the prison was clearly bad enough for his parents to consider escaping. And if they got out, the law said it would be Max who had to pay the debt; Max who would have to go to jail in their place. They would come for him within hours of any escape.

The birthday party trooped slowly out of the bar. They had left him a decent tip and he stuffed the notes into his pocket. The plates cleared, the manager, Jenny, called him over.

'You and Sara take a break now. Need you back in twenty.'

He didn't point out that he was due thirty minutes; he was just relieved that it was with Sara Hussain. She was at university with him – they'd even dated for a term – and had both hung around for the summer jobs. That was where the similarities ended, however. Her parents lived in Kuwait, his parents lived in Spike. She was one of the few people in Bristol who knew Max's story: they had often discussed the horrors of heritage crime.

'C'mon, I need to talk,' he said. 'Somewhere quiet.'

The bar had a back entrance where the off-duty staff sat. Some smoked, others played cards. Max and Sara pulled their plastic chairs further into the service road for some privacy. They were both wearing the 800 Bar regulation black shirt and jeans, his stained with barbecue sauce, hers miraculously pristine. His blond hair was unkempt and straggly, her long black hair was tied back in a ponytail.

'Here OK?' she said.

'Guess so.'

Sara sat down, exhausted, and waited for Max to tell her what was troubling him. Despite the heat, they both cradled cups of tea in their hands, as though for warmth.

Max leaned against the wall. 'I'm going to have to disappear.'

Sara tried to disguise the gasp. 'Oh, Max, no!' She got up and stood next to him. 'How do you . . . ? What did . . .?'

'I got the call this afternoon.'

'Your father?'

Max nodded.

'Things must be bad,' whispered Sara.

He nodded again.

They stood in silence, both working through what had to happen next. It was a while since anyone had had to disappear, but there were rules and procedures in place. Contacts and addresses needed checking first.

They sipped their tea as some other staff wandered out, their shift completed. 'I need to get back to the flat,' said Max.

'You finish at midnight?'

He shook his head grimly. 'Here till two. Lucky me.'

'You could walk out now if you wanted,' said Sara. 'It's been done before.'

'No, I need to do this properly. Jenny would guess something was up.'

Sara swallowed the last of her tea. 'I'll check who's around.'

He nodded and smiled his thanks. 'When we all sat around that bar in our first year and talked heritage crime, it was the first time I'd found anyone as angry as me. I can't tell you what that meant. There were some who had strutters in the family, but to hear so many on our side was, well . . .' Max realized he was getting choked, so he finished off his drink too. 'But I knew it might come to this one day.'

'Did your dad give you any details?' Sara said, yawning.

'That's all I know,' said Max. '*Correction* is being broadcast soon – maybe someone will say something about the fire, or the death, then.'

'I'll go and make some coffee,' said Sara. 'And then we have a few hundred portions of fries to serve.'

16

'You have ninety seconds to find a seat. Please hurry.'

Assessor Grey stood at the front of a hall that was part gym, part lecture theatre. Two large screens filled most of the wall behind him, six fixed cameras taking it in turns to show their section of the resentful, sullen audience. Grey half glowered, half smiled as the 220 inmates found their places. Families had to sit together, solos in the five rows at the front; everyone knew where to go but took as long about it as they dared.

Ant, Mattie and Gina shuffled past six-year-old Sam Durrow and his eight-year-old sister, Tilly, the youngest inhabitants of the Spike. They were clasping each other so tightly they couldn't be separated.

'We've all told them that their film won't be shown again,' said Ant as they sat down, 'but they don't believe us.'

Gina nodded. 'At least it's the last one this week.'

'I can hardly wait,' said Ant.

Correction was at 7.30 p.m. Monday and Friday, and those were by some distance the most hated and resented hours of the week. It was broadcast online, and had proved a surprise hit with viewers. All prisons that held strutters contributed short films, highlighting the work they were doing 'to correct the mistakes of the past'. No one knew who was going to be featured next.

A large clock on the side wall showed the countdown to 7.30. Those who hadn't yet had their film shown shifted uneasily in their seats. Sam and Tilly Durrow's mother Lena wrapped her arms around her trembling children.

'Poor things,' whispered Gina. 'They were so traumatized by seeing their father's story on screen. I don't think their mum explained that he had taken his own life. They knew he'd stolen loads of money from his customers, but that's all . . .'

Assessor Grey adjusted his glasses, then smoothed his already smooth hair. Resting his hands on the desk in front of him, he inhaled deeply as the lights on the cameras turned red.

'Today we learn again of the consequences of heritage crime, and the justice – appreciated both in this country and elsewhere – of our new criminal code.' He was using his TV voice, warmer and more conciliatory than inmates were used to. 'Your own family's actions have placed you outside our community. But if you, the first heritage criminals to pay the price for your family's crimes, can appreciate the fair-mindedness of our laws, then society will be the better for it.' He smiled broadly. 'We will all be better for it.'

When Ant had heard his speech for the first time, it was at this point that she had heckled him. Two minutes later she had found herself in SHU, and on basic for two weeks. The second time she heard it, she had written a few explicit words of Anglo-Saxon on the seat in front of her. This had cost her a week wiping excrement from the walls of protesting prisoners' cells. She hadn't interrupted him since.

'So . . .' The assessor looked around the hall, pausing only to glance briefly at the camera. When he spoke, he savoured each word. 'The first Freedom Question.' He flashed a pledge card at the camera. 'What have you done today?'

I hate you so much right now, Ant thought.

A second's pause, then a raised hand from the second row. A middle-aged man with grey hair and bad teeth. 'I learned how much my father's crimes have cost us all.' The voice was flat, the words forced. 'The cars he stole belonged to hard-working men and women . . .' There was a pause, as if the man had either forgotten his words or was reluctant to carry on.

'And?' encouraged Grey.

The man sighed. 'And the accident he drove away from cost a woman her life,' he said quietly.

'And so *therefore* . . . ?'

'So I need to pay society back.' His head dropped and he sat with his hands in his lap.

'Correct,' said the assessor, smiling. 'And over the five years of your sentence you will be able to do just that. You will be a better man for it. Who's next?'

The screens cut to a scared-looking girl in a headscarf. The words *Straw Family Prison, Cardiff* scrolled across the bottom.

'Yes?' said Grey into the camera. 'And what have you done today?'

The girl stood up. 'I've learned that my family's business was a money-laundering scheme,' she blurted. 'And that all our wealth is stolen.' She could hardly wait to get the words out. 'I shall try to pay back the debt I owe.'

Even though Ant sat through it twice a week, *Correction* always made her furious. She sat with fists clenched, nails digging into her palms. 'I can't believe anyone watches this garbage,' she muttered. 'Can't they see it's all fake?'

'Shut up, Ant,' said Mattie, head down. 'Just for once, please. It'll be over soon.'

Ant screwed up her face and started counting the number of slats on the heating vent. She had no intention of ending the day back in the bloc and forced herself to calm down.

Most of life in Spike she could cope with. But *Correction* was a humiliation. A ritualistic humiliation. All strutters despised it, but many had learned to cope; Ant wasn't one of them. She looked around. Gina and Dan were zoned out, Daisy was gazing at the ceiling, her mother, Sarah, humming softly to herself.

How weird, thought Ant. *All the cons think we get a cushy deal, but none of them have to sit through this show trial twice a week. Wonder how they'd cope . . .*

Then the films started.

17

‘Freedom Question Four asks us “What are you passing on to your children?”’ Grey looked around at his sullen audience. ‘Well, today we will hear stories from a priest’s family who are atoning for his sins.’

The screens cut to a shocked middle-aged woman holding hands with two teenage girls; they all started crying.

Grey continued, his voice mellow and reasonable. ‘Also from the wife of *another* banker. She lived the high life until he was exposed as a thief and swindler. He disappeared, leaving her to pay the price.’ The screens showed a close-up of a steely-looking woman in her thirties staring unblinkingly back at the camera.

‘That’s more like it,’ muttered Ant. ‘A bit of defiance at last.’

'But we start here in London – with the sorry story of Matthew Norton Turner.'

As the huge screens showed a close-up of Mattie's shocked face, there was a gasp from the inmates. Gina and Dan both shouted 'NO!' and Gina grabbed her foster son, holding him close.

Ant was on her feet. 'You've done us already!' she yelled. 'You've done him! Leave him alone, you bastards! He's eleven years old – what do you—?'

Strong hands – Dan's – hauled Ant back down. 'There's no point, Abi. Let it go.' His words were urgent and delivered behind a cupped hand. 'We have to let it go.'

But she pulled away. 'Letting it go means they just carry on!' she replied, not caring who heard.

'Abi, they'll take you away. Put you in SHU. And we need you with us. *Please.*'

Three prison officers had arrived and were standing in the aisle waiting to see if they needed to intervene. They glanced from Ant to Grey, waiting for instructions.

The cameras cut back to the assessor. His lips were pressed together in the beginnings of a smile. 'Some of our number need to reflect carefully on their actions,' he said, a steely tone to his voice. 'The truth is rarely comfortable. And in the case of your family, Miss Norton Turner, the truth is intolerable. Run the film.'

Ant's fists were balled so tightly, her nails were starting to cut into the skin of her palms.

'*Matthew Turner,*' said the voiceover as a photo of the seven-year-old Mattie appeared on the screens. A scared little boy with wild corkscrew hair stared out. '*Son of gang leaders Kyle Turner and Shola Murray. Wanted for embezzlement, GBH, theft and drug dealing, they disappeared three years ago.*' Old photos of a young, well-dressed white man and a smart black woman faded in over busy, dramatic music. '*While the country suffered, they lived the high life, spending their stolen money on holidays, cars and property. They spent their time in the company of some of Britain's most notorious crooks. But when police closed in, Turner and Murray disappeared, leaving their children, Matthew and Abigail, behind.*'

Gina was hugging Mattie, Dan had his arms around Gina. Ant stared at the screen. She watched as social media footage of family gatherings played; angry and puzzled, she leaned towards Dan.

'They've shown all this before. They've gone through our history. I don't understand . . .'

'They'll have something new,' said Dan. 'Though God knows what . . .'

The film had switched to images of Dan and Gina. Ant saw Dan flinch.

'*Fostered by Dan Norton, son of swindler John Norton, and Gina Norton, daughter of notorious fraudster Ben Hoffman, Matthew continued to live a life of luxury, fuelled with money that had been stolen from hard-working families. And now new evidence has emerged . . .*'

'Here we go,' said Dan. Gina buried Mattie's face in her shoulder.

'*. . . of Matthew's violent past.*'

Dan put his hand firmly over Ant's mouth. She pushed it away but swallowed her rage.

'*Witnesses have reported many occasions when Matthew resorted to the bullying and violent behaviour he had learned from his parents and grown up with.*'

'You have got to be kidding,' said Dan softly.

The film showed a close-up of a skinny man in his forties. He twitched as he spoke. '*My name is Tony Pellow. My son used to play with Matthew Turner. He was a foul-mouthed bully from the start. Vicious, actually. Pushed my kid around and threatened him if he told anyone. Spoiled. That's what he was, spoiled. Like the whole world owed him a living. He deserves to be inside.*'

Gina was sobbing quietly, her head resting on Mattie's. 'But that's not true!' She looked up at her husband. 'Dan, they're just making it all up!'

Now a round woman with long highlighted blonde hair filled the screen. '*I'm Tess Clarke. I had to throw the boy out. Came into my house and just helped himself to my kid's things like he could have anything he chose. When my son tried to stop him, he spat at him. Called him really nasty things. Kids like that need to be taught a lesson.*'

Footage of Mattie working on Indoor Relief was brief, cutting quickly to a live shot from the hall.

'I wonder,' said Assessor Grey, 'if we can see the offender's face?' A wide shot took in Mattie, Gina, Dan and Ant, and the shocked faces of the inmates around them. The camera zoomed in closer.

'Matthew Norton Turner. Look at me please.'

'Stay where you are, Mattie,' hissed Ant.

'Actually, yes,' said Gina. 'Stay where you are.' She looked at Grey, tears streaming down her face. 'That was inexcusable. It was all lies and you know it. Mattie's never hurt anyone.'

Around the hall people stirred as they watched what was for many of them the first act of defiance in *Correction*.

'*Molopaa*,' Ant spat.

'I will choose to ignore your insult, whatever it was. You all know the punishment for denying the truth,' said Grey, flushing slightly under his TV make-up.

And Mattie stood up.

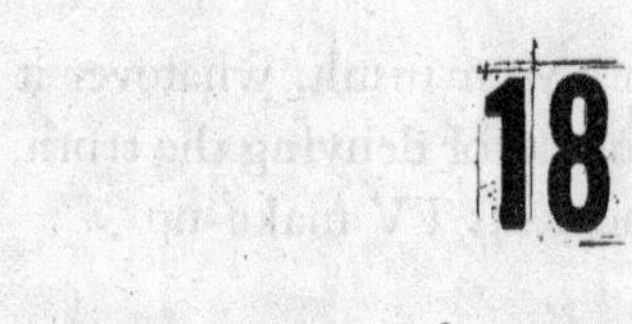

'You don't have to say anything,' Gina whispered as he slid off her lap. He pulled his hand free. The cameras had their close-up; he stared at the floor, then at the assessor.

Grey said, 'You and your sister are here because of the heritage crimes of your foster parents. But given the additional crimes of your real parents, yours is the most crime-ridden family we have found. Anywhere! And now we hear more evidence—'

But before he had finished, Mattie spoke.

'I'm sorry,' he said.

'What?' hissed Ant.

There were gasps of surprise around the hall. Grey cocked his head to one side, eyebrows raised.

'Some of us might have missed that. Could you just repeat what you said – louder this time?'

Mattie lifted his head a little. 'I'm sorry.'

'For your bullying and violent behaviour?'

'Yes. It won't happen again.'

'Mattie, stop!' whispered Ant.

'I think he knows what he's doing,' muttered Dan.

Grey scratched his chin. 'Very well.' His tone suggested he was trying to decide whether to believe Mattie or not. He turned to the cameras. 'We have, I believe, just seen our new criminal justice system in action. Can anyone seriously doubt the wisdom of what we are doing here? Does anyone think we would have got that admission from Norton Turner if he hadn't been confronted with his actions? Prison works!' He beamed at the cameras, then switched to an expression of sad reflection. 'His sister, on the other hand, will need to spend some time on her own this weekend reflecting on her foul-mouthed outburst. And another six months on her sentence.'

As Grey wrapped up the broadcast, Dan reached for Ant's arm. She pushed him away and leaned over to Mattie.

'What was all that?' she exploded. 'What are you sorry for?'

Gina added, 'Mattie, you've never bullied anyone . . .'

Mattie looked at Ant, then Gina, big tears rolling down his face. 'You got another six months, Abi! Why did you shout like that?'

Ant shook her head. 'I don't care about the six months. Someone had to say something. At least people will know we're not all rolling over and taking everything they dump on us. But then you come along and just say sorry . . . everyone will think you did all that stuff.'

Mattie didn't like it when his sister was cross with him and the tears continued to flow. 'I thought if I said sorry they'd leave us alone,' he said. 'If I said it was all untrue, they'd put me in the bloc again. And we need to be together . . . in case.'

'In case what?' asked Gina gently.

Dan stood up. 'Guess you're in trouble, Ant,' he said, nodding at two guards walking briskly towards them.

'Guess I am,' she said. 'MacMillan and Boden. This should be fun.'

Where Brian MacMillan was gangly and awkward, Louise Boden was stocky and confident. She'd clashed with Ant before. Winter or summer, her white shirt-sleeves were always rolled up past her biceps.

'At least Brian's one of ours,' said Gina. 'Never too sure about Boden though. Usually only works for Grey.'

Daisy had clambered over some seats to reach Ant before the guards did. 'Never heard anyone shout like that,' she said quickly. 'Ant, that was amazing! And who were those two jerks telling lies about Mattie?'

'Tony Pellow and Tess Clarke,' said Ant immediately. 'Well, that's who they said they were. Never seen them before. But I'll certainly remember their names.'

Daisy glanced at the two advancing POs. 'How long do you think you'll get in SHU?'

Ant shrugged. 'Depends how vindictive they're feeling.'

'Given that you've just heckled Grey again,' said Dan,

'and on live TV, I'd say they're feeling very vindictive. So, Ant, please don't make it worse. Get out of there as soon as you can. Be humble and charming, if you have to. Tell them what they want to hear. Mattie's right. We need to be together.'

'In case,' said Ant.

'Yeah, in case.'

'*Einen dicken Hals haben?*' said Ant.

Dan nodded. 'Me too.'

The 800 Bar, Bristol

Max burst into the kitchen. He grabbed hold of Sara and tugged at her arm. 'Outside! Now! Please?' His eyes were wide with panic.

He turned to the chef and a waiter who was looking up from his plate of food. 'Just . . . need her . . . for a moment. Won't be long.'

Sara put down a tray of sauces and allowed herself to be steered through the back door. Max pushed it shut behind them and sat on one of the chairs. He motioned for Sara to join him, a phone with a lit screen in his hand.

'This just happened,' he said, his voice a stage-whisper. He played Sara the footage of Mattie and the explosive reaction to it.

'My God,' muttered Sara. 'Your poor parents.'

Max paused the film and leaned in close to her. 'No mention of the fire, or the death of a prisoner!' he said, spitting out his words. 'Just more totally made-up stuff about Mattie! And did you see my poor mum? She was just dying in there . . .' He stood up, knocking his chair over, and paced the short distance to the alley wall and back.

Sara reached for his arm. 'Max, you have to go. Don't wait for the end of your shift. Remember what happened last time Ant was on *Correction*? Reporters came round here for a comment. And given that everyone has just seen your mum and dad too, I reckon they'll go to your flat as well.' She pulled two small keys out of her jeans pocket. 'But no one knows where I live. Take these. Go now – I'll say you were ill or something.'

He took the keys and stared at her, open-mouthed.

'You remember where I live?' she said, and Max nodded.

'Of course.'

'Well, let yourself in and wait for me. I'll get off early if I can.' Max made as if to go back inside but Sara pushed him away. 'I'll bring your stuff. If you leave now, you can go to your flat and get what you need first. If there's anyone hanging around . . .'

'I know, I know.' Max glanced at the back door, and smiled briefly. 'Thanks,' he said. 'See you later.'

He turned, sprinted along the service road, and was gone in seconds.

Two years previously

As soon as she saw Mattie and Max standing together at the school gates, Abi knew what had happened. She always picked Mattie up from his after-school club, and then they ambled home – via the newsagent, if they had the cash. Max was never, ever involved. But here he was, one hand on Mattie's shoulder, standing apart from the usual crowd of parents.

Mattie spotted her first and sprinted over. 'Abi! They've arrested Dan and Gina! We have to go home!' He grabbed her hand and pulled her towards Max.

Abi was aware of turned heads and whispers as they passed the adults. Looking gaunt and angry, Max set off as soon as they were near.

'The police came at lunch time.' His voice sounded tight, close to breaking. He walked fast; Abi and Max jogged to keep up. 'We are the first. Did you know that?' 'The first family to be charged under the new law. Mum and Dad can't leave the house. You have to join them. They were going to send a police car to get you, but Mum persuaded them to let me come instead.' He continued his furious pace.

'Max, slow down,' Abi said. 'Mattie can't keep up.'

But if anything, Max's strides lengthened, and so she stopped. Realizing he was on his own, he turned to see Abi and Mattie staring at him. Ordinarily he would have explained, but not today.

'I can shout this if you want,' he said with a shrug. 'OK, it's your fault. It's your fault because *they noticed us*!' Tears were running down his face, but he seemed oblivious. Other families steered past them in silence, heads down. Max tried to start a new sentence, but couldn't continue. He turned and walked on.

Abi and Mattie followed at their own pace.

'Are we going to prison?' Mattie asked his sister.

'Sounds like it,' she said.

'And Max too?'

'No. He's eighteen. He's grown up. We're not. If Dan and Gina go down, so do we.'

A small hand in hers. 'Is it our fault?'

Abi said nothing.

19

My favourite things RIGHT NOW:
My sister. I messed up. I messed up. I messed up. The film in C was about ME! A went mad and is in SHU AGAIN. I am dumb. Please come back soon A.

Holloway and Pentonville both had their own SHUs – old, austere and spartan. Spike's bloc was a row of underground cells that had originally been storerooms. There were eighteen of them, each with a low bed, toilet and basin. No windows, no decoration, just green walls and a threadbare piece of carpet over a concrete floor. Ant remembered every detail – she had been here before.

'How long am I in for?'

'Till we're told to let you out.' MacMillan swiped a card through the cell door's reader, then turned a key in the lock. As the door swung open, PO Boden pushed Ant inside. The air smelled stale and damp.

'Do you have any contraband, weapons or tobacco on you?' said Boden.

'Sure. Loads. Want to borrow some?'

Neither Boden nor MacMillan smiled.

'Oh, we need the paperwork . . .' said MacMillan.

'On it,' said Boden. As soon as she'd stepped outside, MacMillan whispered urgently, 'It's pat down next! Give me the passes and cards now!'

Ant ignored him and lay on the bed, closing her eyes.

MacMillan was exasperated. 'If she finds them . . .'

'They're not on me,' whispered Ant eventually, her eyes still shut.

Boden strode back in with a sheaf of papers. 'An IP98. I'd forgotten how long it is. Pat down first.' She passed the papers to MacMillan. 'Against the wall, Ant.'

For a moment she considered refusing, but then remembered the strip search she had endured last time she resisted. And Dan's plea that she get out as soon as possible.

'I haven't got anything hidden. Honest.'

'Against the wall,' repeated Boden. 'You know what happens next if you refuse. It's so much easier this way.'

'And I get to keep my knickers on.'

'Like I said, it's easier if you just let me do it. Then we can leave you alone.' The guard waited, arms folded.

Ant got up and stood against the wall. 'Tess Clarke.

Tony Pellow. Tess Clarke. Tony Pellow,' she muttered as Boden's hands worked their way briskly over her body.

'What are you saying?' asked MacMillan.

'I'm remembering.'

'She's clean,' said Boden.

'Like I said.'

MacMillan shrugged. 'Whatever. Jug up at six. We'll let you know how long you're in for when we know.' Both guards headed for the door. 'And if you remember anything you think I should know . . .'

'Go away, Brian,' said Ant, and the cell door clicked shut behind them.

Although no sunlight ever found its way into the bloc, the heat was oppressive. Ant paced the cell, walking in laps. It was eleven square metres; eighteen steps to walk around all of it.

Another six months.

Her outburst had cost her another six months in Spike, and who knew how long in the bloc.

'Nice work, Ant, really well done,' she said out loud. She punched the wall as she walked.

But someone has to shout, someone has to protest. It's just that it's always me.

She turned and walked the other way round the cell, each lap taking her over her bed. The thin blanket scrunched up as she trod on it; Ant barely noticed. Her mood was grim: she didn't have her cards or passes, there were new guards she didn't know, and Dan thought there was trouble brewing. She punched the wall again.

But anyone watching online would have seen that we are fighters, wouldn't they?

Even as she asked the question, Ant wasn't sure of the answer. But how many others had shown any kind of dissent? She couldn't remember any.

With little support outside, and cut off from her friends and family inside, Ant suddenly felt very lonely. Her thoughts returned to her brother, and she punched the wall again.

20

It was a few seconds before Ant realized she had company.

Her head was heavy with hard-won sleep and her cell was dark, but she knew there was someone there. In a cell this tiny, any change, however small, triggered an inmate's internal alarm system. She sat bolt upright, then jumped into a crouch. The adrenalin was waking her fast.

The room was too dark. The door's outside shutter had been closed, the light from the corridor's fierce neons blocked. No passer-by would see her trespasser. Ant's heart was beating like a hammer. The suddenness of her waking seemed to heighten her senses; she could hear the intruder breathing, smell his sweat. She balanced on the balls of her feet, ready for an attack.

'Ant, calm down,' came a whisper from the corner. Belfast accent. Brian.

'What the hell, Brian?' Ant exhaled deeply and sat down on her bed. 'What are you doing? Why's—?'

A hand over her mouth. The guard had moved quickly, surprising her, and instinctively she punched him hard.

MacMillan fell to the floor. 'No, you've got it wrong!' he said in a frantic whisper. 'I'm here to help! Listen to me – I haven't got long.' He scrambled to his feet and sat gingerly on the low bed, holding his chin. 'Bloody hell, Ant, I'm trying to help,' he said, sounding as though his mouth had been anaesthetized.

'How are you helping by creeping around my cell in the middle of the night?' she hissed, still on her guard.

'Listen, Ant, just for once,' he said. 'How many "trips" have you made to Holloway and Pentonville?'

The question surprised Ant and she took a moment to answer. 'Three to the Castle, one to the Village. None for a while. Why?'

There was a long pause and she wondered whether he had heard her. Eventually he took a deep breath and whispered, 'Those names you were repeating earlier . . . Pellow and Clarke. After pat down, on the way back to the levels, Boden said the names sounded familiar. We checked the rolls. Tony Pellow is in Pentonville – armed robbery; Theresa Clarke is in Holloway – GBH.'

Ant's heart rate picked up again. The liars who had been filmed making stuff up about Mattie. The liars who had got her another six months. Both in HMP London. Both within a few hundred metres of where she was now.

'But that doesn't make sense! Why would they get

involved? I've never met them, never even heard of them,' said Ant, her voice tight.

'Boden said they volunteered. That's all I know.'

Another pause.

'Why are you telling me this, Brian?'

The PO drew another deep breath. 'Pellow and Clarke think they're untouchable. They're both members of the Cloverwell gang.'

Ant shrugged. 'I've heard of it. But we don't do gangs in Spike – there aren't really enough of us.'

'I know most of you guys stick together,' said MacMillan. 'But there are gang contacts here. Some families had dealings with them on the outside – and they still know how it all works. The Shahs, for example. Your friend Amos and his dad. They're pretty well-informed, if you ask me. Well connected. And in the other prisons they most certainly "do gangs". The Cloverwells and the Fords run most of the crime around here. Drugs, prostitution, trafficking. A lot of it pretty hard-core. Pellow and Clarke are right in there. Some of us in the prison service fear for our families if we take them down. There have been, er, messages left at some of our homes . . .'

'What sort of messages?'

'Parcels of dog faeces in the post, that kind of thing. Messages on Facebook, threats to our kids . . .'

'Go on,' said Ant.

'We thought you might help.'

'Me?' Her eyes had adjusted enough to see that the guard was nodding. 'Brian . . . I'm in SHU, I'm wearing a strap. There's a thousand metres of locked doors and security systems between me and them. In case you hadn't noticed.'

'We can do something about that,' MacMillan said.

'Brian, you were here for pat down. You saw. I don't have my passes. Any of them.'

'You won't need them.'

'You what?'

'You won't need the passes. If you want to get even with Pellow and Clarke, we can . . . allow that to happen.'

'Don't tell me,' said Ant. 'You can open doors.'

'That's one of the things we can do, yes.'

'And the fingerprint ones?'

'The ones that stopped your trips? We can open those too.'

'Yeah, well, I'm not doing it. Break into two prisons? That's crazy talk. If you want to smack them around a bit, go ahead. Give them one for me. But that's a suicide mission – if I got caught, they'd rip me apart. You know what they think of people like me. Why should I do your dirty work anyway? God knows, you've got enough vicious thugs on your side.'

'It has to be prisoner-on-prisoner,' said MacMillan. 'It's pretty explosive in there at the moment and if an officer got involved, it could light the bonfire.'

'More reasons why I should stay out then . . .'

'Maybe. But you know, they're not going to stop, Ant.' MacMillan's voice was more urgent now. 'Boden says they've got more stuff on your brother.'

'They *what*?'

'And the next one is even nastier,' he said.

'Don't tell me. He's a warlord this time?'

'Ant, this is serious. And then they're coming for you too.'

'But they've done me, done Mattie, done Dan and done Gina!' said Ant. 'What are they trying to do, Brian?'

He shrugged.

Dan had said to get out soon, and she *wanted* to get out soon, but she also needed to pay Pellow and Clarke a visit too. She turned to face MacMillan. 'I want to be back in my 'bin by tomorrow.'

'OK,' he said cautiously.

'Who's in the control room?'

'Friends,' he said, and listed the names on the rota.

Ant nodded. It was three on for nights, four for days. She knew tonight's POs, and knew too that their bank balances were much healthier than they should be. 'Strap monitors?'

'It's sorted. They know what's happening, Ant. They'll watch you.'

'I still want my passes.'

'But I've told you, you don't need them.' MacMillan sounded exasperated.

'Yes, Brian, you have. But guess what? *I don't actually trust you.* Isn't that odd in a girl who's been locked up for things she never did? You might be a pretty decent screw, but you're still a screw. It's quite possible you'll abandon me in there. But if I have those sweet cards with

"B. MacMillan" on them, I stand more of a chance of getting out. I'm sure you understand. Anyway, that's the deal.'

MacMillan eased himself to his feet, still rubbing his jaw. 'Where are they?'

'In a number of places. Scattered . . .'

'OK, give me a moment,' he said, and left the cell. Ant heard him relaying her terms on his radio. She pulled on her trainers. She knew they'd accept her terms, whoever 'they' were. Pellow and Clarke needed to be taught a lesson, and she wanted to be able to do it.

Hey, Pellow! Hey, Clarke! It's payback time. Don't think that locked door's going to work tonight . . .

MacMillan was back, lanyard swaying from his hand. 'I'm giving you my new card. It'll work in all major doors, gates and cells. My pass code is *8B 3S 2C3*. Anything it doesn't cover should be open when you get there.'

Ant took the pass and hung it round her neck, tucking the card under her T-shirt. '*8B 3S 2C3*,' she repeated, and MacMillan nodded.

'It's my magic code.'

'And what if the gates are shut?' asked Ant.

'They'll be open. And you'll need these.' MacMillan handed over two small slim booklets, both pink. 'New POs get them. An idiot's guide to Holloway – Clarke's cell is A283. That's A283. And one for Pentonville – Pellow's cell is D177. That's D177. They've been moved to cells you should find easily enough – Clarke's on the ground floor, Pellow's on the first.'

Ant tucked them into her waistband. 'I should get going then,' she said. 'Tell whoever you need to tell.'

While MacMillan radioed the message, she checked and tightened her laces. She bounced on her heels. She pulled at her T-shirt. She patted the pass underneath. Pulse racing, she waited for the green light. The expectation, the anticipation. The grinning.

'What will you do to them?' asked MacMillan nervously.

'Something memorable,' said Ant.

She counted to four, and ran.

21

As though it had caged her for twenty years, not twenty seconds, Ant tore out of the lift as soon as its doors finally lumbered open. The twisting corridor that led to Pentonville opened up on her right, but she sprinted left; the 'tube' to Holloway was on the far side of the building.

Without phone or watch, she had no idea of the time but guessed it was after 1.30 a.m. Prison was never quiet, but this was usually the quietest time; only the very young and the really distressed were shouting. It seemed quieter than normal; her rubber soles squeaked on the lino floor. Even though she knew she was being 'allowed' to come here, Ant moved as quietly as possible, keeping to the shadows where she could.

Two POs appeared. Walking the levels continued all night, and they jumped, startled at the sight of a sprinting prisoner. Ant didn't miss a stride; she recognized the officers – and carried on running. She glanced over her shoulder. Both men had quickly resumed their conversation – it was as if she wasn't there.

This might even work . . .

The entrance to the Holloway tunnel came into view. This was the first of the fingerprint sensor-operated doors and always had a PO stationed on either side. Now, it was deserted and the steel door was open; Ant shot through the narrow gap. She paused briefly, breathing heavily. Behind her the door swung back and clicked shut. Beads of sweat ran down her face. Exhilarated and terrified in equal measure, she gazed down the thousand-metre tunnel that led straight to Holloway Prison. Low-ceilinged and whitewashed, it stretched out like something from a horror movie. There were security cameras every fifty metres and metal gates every hundred. They looked closed.

She allowed herself only a few seconds' rest, then sprinted for the first gate: it was unlocked. She pushed through and ran on, getting into a rhythm like a hurdler: twenty paces, kick the gate, twenty paces, kick the gate.

A guard's station was positioned at what appeared to be the halfway point of the tunnel. It was only a small booth, where a PO could watch all the comings and goings, but behind it Ant spotted an unmarked door. She slowed her run, jumped the booth and jabbed MacMillan's ID card into a box on the wall. The door clicked and swung open. A changing room, six lockers and a toilet. No security cameras.

Ant guessed her detour would have been observed on the monitors and wondered how long before they'd want to know what she was up to. Two minutes maybe? She needed to change. Whatever had been 'arranged' in Holloway and Pentonville, she was still obviously a convict on the run. If she came across anyone MacMillan hadn't spoken to, anyone who wasn't part of the game, she was in big trouble. She kicked the lockers hard. The fourth one buckled and she succeeded in bending the top down far enough to see inside.

'Get in!' she shouted.

Uniform. Reaching inside, she pulled out the regulation jacket, trousers, shirt and hat. They were too big, of course, but they were still better than her T-shirt and joggers. It took her ninety seconds to dress like a PO. The badge on one breast pocket said HATTON. In the other she found a pen and a phone; she checked the battery – 40%.

She rolled up sleeves and trouser legs, then butchered the belt with the locker door mechanism and pulled the trousers as tight around her waist as she could. One more feel around the locker – and Ant found contraband from heaven. Three items. She took them out one by one and laid them on the floor. Pepper spray, handcuffs and a steel baton. It was standard issue for a PO at HMP London, but for a prisoner to have them – and a strutter at that – it felt like revolution.

A prisoner with weapons.

Ant fixed all three to her belt. Seeing her trousers sag, she put the pepper spray in her jacket pocket. She retrieved the 'idiot' guide books MacMillan had given her and tried on the remaining piece of kit. At least the cap fitted, and she saluted herself in the mirror. She'd been powerless for two years, institutionalized and useless. Now something had shifted and it felt good.

The tunnel end was marked by another set of steel doors. On the other side was Holloway. She slowed her run to check the Holloway book.

'A283?' she said. 'Visitor incoming.'

22

The lights on the doors switched from red to green as she approached. *So they* are *watching.* Ant took a moment to remember her route on the other side, then the doors began to hum. She bounced nervously on the balls of her feet, felt for the pass under her shirt and briefly touched the handcuffs, pepper spray and baton.

'Come on, Castle, open up,' she muttered.

As soon as the slowly moving doors offered a gap, Ant slid through. Her eyes darted everywhere. Seeing no one, hearing nothing, she took a few steps forward. Every part of her wanted to finish the job and get out as soon as possible, but she forced herself to go slow. *There's always a chance Brian has screwed me over,* she thought. *Or someone has screwed Brian.* Her hand rested lightly on her baton. *But I'm not going back now . . .*

The map in the guide showed A Wing as the first block, downhill from where she stood. MacMillan had said 283 was on the ground floor. She remembered from her previous visit that Holloway had been built on a hill and had expanded both uphill to her left and downhill to her right. She guessed that 283 was two minutes maximum from where she stood now. She'd stick to the POs' corridors and walk rather than run. Maybe three minutes . . .

OK, enough with the caution. Let's go.

Ant pushed through the swing doors to her right. Another new-build, low-ceilinged, windowless corridor. More doors thirty metres ahead, more signs. More silence.

Why so quiet? Twelve hundred prisoners and no noise?

Ant started to jog. She finally heard echoing voices as she passed a stairwell: POs walking and cursing. She slowed to a swift walk, her heart pounding. The voices behind her were getting louder. They would be in the corridor before she reached the next set of doors; they would see her, no question. She could make out the voices now – two, maybe three women and one man. Ant was three metres from the doors when the POs appeared, their conversation dying away.

'Hey, Officer!' The challenge was loud and unmistakable.

Ant hesitated, then stopped and turned round.

OK, Brian, let's see how good your plan is then.

Four guards were strung across the corridor, all in the regulation black trousers and white shirt but without ties or jackets. Their conversation had ceased – Ant knew she had their full attention. She saw them looking her over; the ill-fitting man's uniform was enough to raise concern but her trainers sealed it. She had hoped her outfit would get her some distance into Holloway without a challenge; she'd covered about a hundred metres.

She was *obviously* not a prison officer; she was *obviously* a prisoner on the run. And she had weapons. And she had the high, straight walk of a strutter. The chances were that she was about to get a kicking.

The male guard turned to his colleagues and they all conferred. Ant saw some nodding before they faced her again.

'You new?' The question came from the lead PO, a powerful-looking woman of around forty, her hand resting on her baton. She had started to walk towards Ant, the other guards falling in behind.

Ant saw no point in pretending. 'You know who I am.'

'Do we?' The guard was still walking, still closing on her. 'Do we really? Don't think we've seen you before. Certainly no one dressed . . . like this.' She unclipped her baton and pointed it at Ant's feet. 'Is this a new guard fashion in Spike? *Another* privilege?'

Ant desperately wanted to run. She wanted to take her chances; she was considerably faster than any of the POs facing her now – they looked exhausted as well as overweight. But it was their prison, and if she was to get to Clarke, it would have to be with their tacit permission. She stood still, her heart hammering in her chest.

'I need to find cell A283.'

'We know,' said the woman behind the lead officer. 'We know what's going on.'

Relief flooded through Ant's body. She almost smiled.

'But you shouldn't be dressed like us,' said the squat man; he looked like a bulldog. 'And you certainly shouldn't have any of that kit.' He stared at Ant's pepper spray. 'Where did you get it?'

Ant glanced at the badge on her jacket. 'Mr Hatton didn't seem to need it for a while.'

He cursed loudly. 'You'll need to give us the uniform and kit back, then you can go,' he said. 'Can't have strutters with weapons.'

Ant forced a smile that momentarily disarmed them.

'You're right, of course, Officer . . . It really is just for the . . . mission. Why don't you escort me to A283? There's four of you. I could be back in Spike in five minutes.'

'You could,' said the lead PO. 'But you could do that dressed as a prisoner too.'

'I don't have a uniform,' said Ant. 'I'm only sixteen.'

'Well, we'll sort that,' she replied. 'You can be eighteen for the night.'

The squat man laughed at that and Ant twitched. *You so need a punch in the face. Maybe before I go . . .*

'I'll get you a suit,' he said, and went back through the swing doors. Ant and the other guards stared at each other. A stand-off. The POs stood there, batons drawn, their stance suggesting they thought Ant might charge them at any minute.

So instead, she took off her cap and sat cross-legged on the stone floor. 'Why's everything so quiet in here?' she asked. 'In Spike you can hardly hear yourself think.' Ant noticed swift glances between the three of them, but none of them replied. 'Ah, the stony-faced look . . . The let's-make-sure-we-don't-treat-anyone-like-a-human-being look. You guys are all the same.'

The doors opened and the man reappeared carrying a blue jumpsuit, the compulsory Holloway uniform for the last four years. He threw it at Ant and it slid across the floor. 'Put it on, strutter.'

'My name is Ant,' she said, her muscles tensed.

'Your name is what I say it is,' he said. 'Put it on. And then slide the kit over. Slowly.'

Ant looked up at the guards, their arms folded, impassive. Turning her back, she used the misdirection of removing her trousers to palm the phone from the jacket pocket. Still hiding it in her hand, she pulled on the stiff cotton jumpsuit and slipped the phone into one of the pockets. Spending some years in the same house as crooks – she could hardly call it an upbringing – did have its advantages. She had learned some unusual skills. She kept the white shirt on, the pass still hidden underneath.

She turned round, tucking the shirt into the waistband. She felt the pass – sticky but safe – underneath, then forced her feet back into her trainers. She remembered to retrieve the small notebooks MacMillan had given her.

'I need the cuffs,' said Ant matter-of-factly as she slid the baton and pepper spray across the floor. 'They're only for Clarke. You'll see. You can watch if you want. Let's go.'

The words were bold, the guards surprised. Ant led the way through the doors, half expecting to be hauled back to Spike. Or worse. But behind her, she heard the doors open again and four sets of heavy PO boots following her. A loud voice barked, 'Two more doors, first left.'

I'm actually being escorted.

She went through an open security door. Three long corridors fanned out from a central hub where two guards sat looking at computer screens. She paused for a moment, realizing that her escort had disappeared. This was obviously where she needed to be. The POs did not look up. They knew she was there, Ant was sure of it. A shaven-headed, blue-uniformed prisoner, on her own in the middle of the night, doesn't get ignored unless she is supposed to be ignored. The two men were typing furiously as Ant walked slowly past their desks – a ghost again – then chose the middle corridor.

The main lights appeared to be off; short florescent bulbs provided just enough illumination for Ant to see the doors; *A200* inked in large letters on the first. A small box with two orange lights was fixed where the handle would have been. She began to jog, guessing that A283 would be about halfway along this row.

A209. More orange lights. Ant felt for the handcuffs. She knew they were there: she could feel them against her leg; hear them jangle as she ran. The clash of the steel links and clasps reassured her.

A238. Orange lights. *How many to a cell? Would Clarke be on her own? What am I going to do anyway?*

A257. Orange lights. Ant pulled the phone out of her pocket: 33% battery. *Should be enough.*

A272. Orange lights. She pictured Clarke's face as she had appeared on the *Correction* screen. Puffy. Dyed blonde hair. Overweight. And a liar. A filthy liar who had made Mattie cry.

A283. Orange lights. Which clicked to green.

Wake-up call.

Ant almost kicked the door in. Foot raised, centimetres from the metal, she pulled away. Breathing hard, adrenalin pumping, she'd nearly forgotten. She made herself count to four.

En.

De.

Twa.

Kat.

She exhaled deeply, then pushed. As the door opened, she slipped silently inside, shutting it behind her. A smell of alcohol filled the room.

Home brew? Really?

Three nightlights lit a room big enough for two prisoners. Ant counted: it was sleeping six. Two sets of bunks had been squeezed tightly together; the third ran across at right angles. As Ant opened the door, it barely cleared the corner of the first bunk. She dropped to a crouch, pushing the door closed behind her.

Six of them! Which is Clarke?

Ant saw that she was being watched. Two eyes and a shock of short white hair had appeared on the top bunk furthest away from her. Ant put a finger to her lips, then drew it across her neck in a cut-throat gesture. The old woman got the message and retreated back under her blankets. Ant had to find where Clarke was before the room woke up and turned against the intruder.

She checked the sleepers. Bottom bunk, nearest to her – snoring, dark-haired, twenty-ish. Not her. Top bunk – long blonde hair covered the sleeper's face. Ant lifted a handful.

Got her.

She reached for the handcuffs, then climbed a rung of the ladder and snapped one cuff around a wrist that was poking out from the bedclothes. She climbed another rung and locked the other cuff around a bar of the metal bedstead.

Got you.

Ant climbed onto the bunk and straddled the still sleeping Tess Clarke. Leaning over, she placed a hand over Clarke's mouth and the woman woke with a start. Seeing Ant's face so close, then realizing that she was pinned to her bed, Clarke panicked. She writhed and kicked, but Ant held her down.

'Listen carefully,' she hissed. 'You're cuffed to your bed. And drunk, by the smell of you. Stop struggling.

Make no noise and I won't hurt you.' The terrified Clarke nodded quickly. 'You are a filthy, stinking liar,' spat Ant. 'You made up lies about my brother. *Kids like him need to be taught a lesson*, remember?' Clarke nodded again. 'Well, this is *your* lesson . . .' Ant removed the phone and selected the film option. 'You say your name. And you say you are a liar and a cheat. And that Mattie Norton never did any of the things you said. And you don't wake anyone up while you're saying it. Go.'

Hurry up, Ant.

'My name is Tess Clarke.' The woman swallowed hard. 'I am a liar and a cheat. That boy I talked about . . . the one in *Correction* . . . ? He never did them things I said he did. I've never even heard of him. They just said if . . .' She tailed off. A final glance at Ant. 'So . . . sorry.' She squeezed her eyes shut as though expecting a beating.

Ant leaned over her and, removing the pen from her shirt pocket, wrote *Liar* on the wall above Clarke's head. 'Open your eyes,' she demanded. 'They said what?'

Clarke looked blank.

'Who told you to say that stuff?' said Ant.

This is all taking too long.

Movement from one of the beds. A face appeared in the bunk next to the old woman. Dark skin, braided hair. The woman blinked twice and looked over at Ant, poised above Clarke – pen in one hand, phone in the other.

'Hey . . .'

'Clarke!' said Ant urgently. 'Look at me! Who told you to say that about Mattie?'

But now the two lower bunks were stirring.

'We have an intruder!' shouted a voice. 'Intruder!'

OK, time's up.

Now the white-haired prisoner sat up again. 'Intruder!' she echoed.

Ant sat back on her haunches, took a photo of Clarke and the recently daubed graffiti and vaulted off the bunk. As she landed, a woman launched herself off the lower bed. She tackled Ant round the waist and they both collapsed onto the floor. Ant felt the woman's hands find her strap, then recoil.

'God, she's a strutter!' she shrieked, and leaped back to her feet. 'Strutter in the cell!'

Ant jumped back up and sprang for the door. She didn't fancy six against one, even if one was shackled and one looked like she was a hundred years old.

'Cell's open!' cried the white-haired prisoner in alarm, pointing at the crack of light from the corridor. Everyone froze except Ant. While her attacker's attention was diverted, she rammed her forehead into the woman's chest. It was a move she had tried a few times; it had always poleaxed her victims. But as her head made contact with the woman's ribcage, Ant felt layers of padding under the T-shirt. Her victim staggered backwards but stayed on her feet. Ant didn't wait to find out any more – she had to get out of cell A283 before it became a scrum.

Her fingers found the door edge and pulled. As light flooded in, she heard more shrieks and cries of 'Shut it!' She sprinted down the corridor, expecting to hear a small cohort of angry women chasing after her; glancing over her shoulder, she saw nothing more threatening than scared faces peering through the doorway.

She ran past the guards – faces still studiously buried in paperwork – and into the corridor where she had last seen her escort. And there they were, waiting for her. This time, however, they had back-up. The whole corridor was lined with baton-holding prison officers. As Ant appeared, some straightened, others flipped their batons from hand to hand.

She stopped abruptly.

'Everyone wanted to see you,' said the squat PO, smirking. 'Haven't had a strutter in the Castle for quite a while. We forget what you lot look like.'

'We look better than you,' said Ant.

Shut up and run.

She looked along the lines of guards. They were ready for a fight – she could sense it.

Don't give them the excuse.

She set off again, raising her hands above her head as she ran. 'No weapons!' she shouted. 'No weapons! Going back to Spike!'

One officer started banging his baton against the wall and his colleagues followed suit. The sound of steel on brick filled Ant's ears as she ran the gauntlet.

'No weapons!'

Then the abuse started:

'Strutter scum.'

'Mutt.'

'Hapa.'

'Slut.'

One woman spat at Ant as she passed. Others joined in, and her face was soon splattered with phlegm. She knew she was being provoked, she knew they were desperate for a fight. She had seen it before. Violence was good for officer morale. 'Letting off steam' was part of the deal. These guards looked as though they had a cauldron of it.

But still Ant stopped.

Run.

Brushing the spit off her face, she turned to a red-haired, thin-lipped man who was still wiping his lips.

Run now.

'Nasty habit you got there, Officer . . .' And slowly, deliberately, she cleaned her hand on his sleeve. The mucus smeared over a surprisingly large area, streaking his jacket from shoulder to elbow. *Too late.* For such a large man, the guard moved surprisingly quickly. His forehead dipped and cracked into Ant's skull, just above her left eye. She fell to her knees, her vision swimming.

'Leave her! Back off!' The tone was urgent, authoritative. 'Back off *now*!' It was the lead officer's voice. 'Get up,' she said to Ant.

Still on her knees, Ant wiped blood from her face. 'I *was* up. Until your bullying ginger friend got involved.'

'Just get up and go,' the woman said sharply. 'You've got a minute to get back to Spike, then you're on your own. And the Castle's not good for anyone on their own.'

'No kidding,' said Ant, getting to her feet.

'No one touch her!' called the PO. 'She's got one minute.'

Now run.

Ant spotted the squat officer and ran over. 'Just wanted to thank you for all your help with the uniform,' she said pleasantly. 'See you around.'

She had sprinted fifty metres before a bellow of rage told her that he had noticed the blood she had smeared over his shirt. She raised her middle finger in salute and headed for the tunnel.

The surveillance cameras by the steel door picked up a bloodied prisoner as she eased her way through. She appeared to be grinning.

24

Ant crashed back into the mid-tunnel guard station. She needed two things fast: water and wifi. The white PO shirt was plastered to her skin, the jumpsuit dark with moisture. In the changing room she put her head under the tap and gulped mouthfuls of warm water, smearing it over her face and – more gingerly – her scalp. Instantly the basin turned red as blood from her wound was washed away. She grabbed some toilet paper and winced as she held it firmly over the gash. With her free hand she retrieved the phone and held it up. Most telecommunication in prison was jammed, so small pockets of wifi became obvious; wherever you saw a guard checking a phone, you knew there was a hotspot. Ant had assumed that all guard stations had wifi, and here in the Holloway tunnel, 500 metres from Spike, she was proved correct.

Within seconds the video of Tess Clarke had uploaded and Ant set it for release in two hours.

Should be back in Spike by then.

She smiled at the thought of Clarke and Pellow being exposed as liars, and Mattie's face when he heard he was in the clear. She caught sight of herself in the mirror above the sink. A badly fitting Holloway uniform covered in spit. A guard's shirt wet with sweat and stained with blood. A head wound that now had bits of toilet paper stuck to it.

Not good.

Back in Spike, the SHU cell door was open, the tall PO standing where he had woken Ant barely ninety minutes earlier.

'I need a Pentonville uniform,' she said, breathless.

MacMillan looked at her blankly.

'Like *now*?' said Ant.

'You want to change?'

'Do I look like I'll blend in there?'

'Not really,' said MacMillan. 'I'll find one.' He left the cell unlocked.

'Don't suppose Pentonville uniforms come in a size eight,' she said to the empty room.

By the time MacMillan returned with the grey cotton trousers and shirt, Ant had made up her mind.

'You're coming with me,' she announced.

'I'm *what*?' he said.

'I can't do it without you.'

'That wasn't the deal.'

'Then the deal's off,' said Ant. 'Think about it. The Castle was weird. Silent. Something's brewing there, you can just tell. And they just killed a man in the Village, remember? And started a fire. If you escort me – get me a beanie hat maybe – I might pass as a Villager. Otherwise forget it. I won't stand a chance.'

'I've been assured that the same rules apply in Pentonville. You got to Clarke. You'll get to Pellow.' MacMillan was trying to sound convincing but it wasn't working.

Ant stared at him. She was still buzzing, bouncing from one foot to the other. She felt like she was in charge. It was still prisoner-versus-prison officer, but there was no doubting the power shift.

The answer wasn't long coming.

'OK, you're right. I'll sort it.'

The tunnel that led to Pentonville was very similar to the Holloway one. It had the same paint, the same fierce lighting and the same steel, fingerprint-sensitive door at each end. Ant and PO MacMillan walked it, handcuffed, in four minutes.

The Pentonville grey uniform fitted better than the Holloway one-piece and it was loose enough to hide Ant's strap. It had a washed-out name tape that said CZEZNY. MacMillan had indeed found a beanie; Ant had pulled it down as far as she could.

'What's our story?' she asked. 'In case we need one.'

'New prisoner. Emergency alcohol rehab,' replied MacMillan. 'They specialize in it here.'

'In the middle of the night?'

He pushed her into one of the guards' rooms – an exact copy of the one she had found on the way to Holloway. 'No cameras. Drink this.' He passed her a miniature bottle of whisky. 'Drink it, spit it out, pour it down your shirt, whatever. If you stink of it, it'll help.'

Ant studied the label. 'You have a supply of these ready to go?'

'Pretty much. It's all confiscated, all contraband. Just putting it to good use . . .'

She unscrewed the cap, rinsed her mouth and spat the whisky over her shirt. She poured the rest down her trousers. 'I smell like a tramp,' she said as she inhaled the pungent fumes. 'Good enough?'

The PO nodded.

Pentonville Prison was old school. There were sections that had been modernized, and rapid expansion was evident everywhere. But the heart of the prison was still the Victorian central hall with five radiating wings. The tunnel brought them to the right of D Wing.

Prison officer and prisoner had to have a certain choreography about the way they walked; Macmillan now strode purposefully through the steel door, while Ant shuffled, trying to disguise her usual gait. Some strutters were always obvious, others adapted. She saw no reason to advertise that she was from Spike. She felt the stretch and pull at the base of her spine.

The smell of the fire hit them immediately; it seemed to fill the whole prison.

'Maybe no one will notice that I stink after all,' said Ant.

MacMillan waved at six officers standing beside a wide desk; one of them acknowledged him, the others just stared.

'Am I supposed to act drunk?' muttered Ant. 'I'm not a good actor.'

'Don't worry about it,' said MacMillan in a tone which suggested that was the least of their troubles.

Ahead, two POs appeared at the other end of a walkway, heading towards them. Ant felt MacMiillan tense. The officers straightened as they saw the unexpected sight of a prisoner being moved along their corridor.

'Here we go . . .'

25

The oncoming guards slowed their pace; MacMillan did too. Heart thumping hard, Ant realized that she would, after all, need to act. She closed her eyes and allowed herself to trip slightly, bouncing off the wall. She opened her eyes wide – took in the gaze of two suspicious-looking guards – and shut them tight again. Their faces were smudged and grimy, the smell of the fire clung to their clothes.

'Drunk as a skunk,' said MacMillan. 'Found him with a bottle in Remand.'

'How did that get in there?' asked one of the guards, his voice hoarse. *A firefighter*, thought Ant.

'No idea,' said MacMillan. 'Dropping him off in Rehab anyway.'

'It's full,' said the second guard. 'Has been for days.

Everyone wants to be in there – like it's some kind of holiday camp. Thought everyone knew that.'

Ant leaned her face against the wall and tried to look as though she was falling asleep.

They're not buying it.

'I'm in Spike normally,' admitted MacMillan. 'Just brought in to help tonight. You guys had it bad.'

'We've taken out the last of them,' said the second PO. He spoke with grim satisfaction. 'Whole place has been itching for a fight for months. Well, they just had their moment. It was fun while it lasted – we got to kick a lot of heads.'

'We could kick this guy too,' said the hoarse-sounding PO, pointing at Ant. 'We can do pretty much what we want tonight. Surveillance cameras have "broken", apparently.'

Ant heard the smile in his voice and hoped her shudder wasn't noticed.

MacMillan looked at his prisoner. 'Nah, wouldn't bother. He'd only puke on your shoes.'

Nice one, Brian.

'Who is he anyway?' The guards were staring at Ant's name tag.

A beat's pause, nothing more.

'Can't pronounce his name. But he's eighteen – possession and dealing. That's all I know.'

'Barely looks old enough,' said the first guard. 'Sure he doesn't belong in Spike?'

Ant held her breath but the other officer laughed. 'Cons looking younger by the day. Time to quit, old man!'

They all laughed, and Ant felt herself being pulled away from the wall. She opened her eyes wide, then staggered after MacMillan as he led her past the POs.

'Thought you said you couldn't act?' he muttered.

At the end of the walkway they took a winding iron staircase to the next floor.

'It's as quiet as Holloway,' whispered Ant.

'I think that might be fear we're listening to,' said MacMillan quietly.

At the top of the steps, on a closed-off landing, he stopped and took the handcuffs off, then looked nervously at his prisoner.

'You were right about coming here on your own. You would have got nowhere. And most likely got your head busted. But I'll be gone in sixty seconds. I can't hang around, and neither can you. You don't want to be on your own in here.'

'You reckon?' said Ant. 'You think a sixteen-year-old female strutter with brown skin who had broken into a male prison wouldn't be treated properly?'

'You know what I mean,' he said. 'D177 is the first through the doors. It's key operated. I'll unlock it and wait one minute here. The cell should have three inmates. You remember what Pellow looked like?'

Ant nodded. The image of his thin, twitchy face had been etched firmly into her mind since he'd appeared on the *Correction* screen. 'You bet. He called Mattie a spoiled, foul-mouthed bully.'

'OK.'

'Thought I'd do some foul-mouthed bullying of my own.'

'I don't need to know,' he said, and stepped out onto the second-floor walkway. Ant didn't look any further than the cell door in front of her. Bigger, older than those in Holloway, it had one large silver-coloured keyhole. MacMillan leaned in front of her, selected a long key from his chain, inserted it into the lock and twisted it through 360 degrees. They heard the tumblers fall.

'Go!' he said, and stepped swiftly back onto the landing.

Heart thumping fast, Ant pushed the cell door open. It was heavy and swung slowly. She stepped inside. The cell was dark, but the light from the walkway showed her all she needed. D177 was empty. Three empty bunks. No bedding, no prisoners. No Pellow.

She didn't need to go into the cell, but she did anyway. There was no sign of life. It smelled of cleaning fluid and floor polish. If Pellow had been in this cell, it wasn't recently.

She was back on the landing in seconds. 'He's gone. It's empty.'

MacMillan was aghast. 'Really? But I was told that was his cell!' They stared at each other briefly before he took out his cuffs again. 'Well, we can't go looking for him. There's obviously been a cock-up. Let's get back to Spike. Sort it from there.' He cuffed her and they retraced their steps down the stairs and onto the first-floor walkway.

Failed. Clarke dealt with but Pellow gets away. Ant cursed under her breath. 'I'm coming back,' she said.

'We need to get out first,' replied MacMillan. 'And that just got trickier.'

Ahead, the hoarse-voiced officer was back, this time with two colleagues. This was no night-shift patrol – there was a purpose to their stride.

'Officer MacMillan!' the guard called, reading his lapel tape again. 'Turns out Remand don't know anything about any drunk. We just called them.' Ant's stomach tightened. 'So my colleagues here will deal with him. I'll take you up to G Wing. Lots of work there.'

Not good at all. Do something, Brian.

MacMillan forced a smile. 'No, I signed the paper-work. Let me—'

A thick-set man pushed his way forward. 'You don't understand how it works here, MacMillan. Unlock him.'

MacMillan bent down and unlocked Ant's cuffs. Their eyes met for only the briefest moment before they both looked away. Ant knew that this was now a whole new ball game. These were rough and aggressive men – she had met their type before. They were prison officers and her experience was with criminals, but in her opinion there wasn't a lot of difference.

Clifton, Bristol

It was gone 1 a.m. when Sara Hussain tapped gently on her own front door. Max ushered her inside, glancing briefly up and down the street. They edged past the bikes in the hall and into her flat. He waited while she chained and bolted the door.

'I followed the rules getting here.' Max spoke fast as she entered the room. 'No taxis. Two bags.' He indicated the two rucksacks on her sofa. 'You keep the green one.'

Sara scooped it up. 'Laptop. Phone. Keys. Documents?' she said.

'Yes,' said Max, his voice strained.

'Trackers disabled?' asked Sara.

'Yes, did that.'

'Any sign of journalists?'

He shook his head. 'None.'

Sara was poised, her tone efficient. 'Let's be quick.' She handed him a small jiffy bag. 'New cold phone, some cash. There'll be more when you get to the next house.'

'And what—?' began Max.

Sara put her finger to his lips. 'I hope your folks get out. Really I do. But right now, Max, you just need to disappear. We've rehearsed this enough times – we know what happens if there's a delay. You've memorized everything you need. Is there anything else?'

Max stared at her, his eyes glistening. 'I don't feel very brave, you know,' he said quietly.

She wrapped her arms around him and pulled him close, pushing some hair away from his ear. 'We're not doing this because we're brave,' she whispered. 'We are doing this because it's right. And because it'll keep you out of prison.'

They stood silently in the middle of the room, both aware of the other's racing heart. Eventually Max sighed deeply. 'We've vanished three people in three years and only one had a happy ending.'

She pulled away now, but took his hands in hers. 'Max, stop. We've learned how to do this the hard way, it's true. Disappearing is difficult, but it can be done. There are woods and quarries where you can stay for months. And anyway, one in three is better than most of the Bug groups I know of. And those odds will worsen the longer you stay here.' She smiled at him, running her fingers down his cheek. 'It's lovely to have you round here again, but now you have to go.'

He dropped her hands. 'I never wanted Mum and Dad to start fostering again. Always thought it was a mistake . . .'

'I know,' said Sara. 'I also know that your parents are amazing. What they do for their foster kids is amazing. And their son is pretty amazing too.'

Max grinned awkwardly. 'Thanks.' He ran both hands through his unkempt hair. 'I suppose everyone on the course will guess what's happening . . .'

Sara nodded. 'The university will announce that you dropped out. No one will say anything. No one will have to.' She reached down for the green rucksack, hoisting it onto her back. 'And now I have to take this out of harm's way. I'm locking up.' She took his face in her hands and kissed him on the mouth. 'Good luck, Max Norton. Stay safe. Come back to us.'

26

My fourth 'bin of the night. Way to go, Ant.

The Remand cell in Pentonville held six bunks in a stark, brightly lit box of a room. Three apparently sleeping inmates occupied the two berths to her left and one in front. She walked over to the right-hand, bottom bunk and sat down briefly before keeling over and hitting the pillow. Pulling a blanket over her, she closed her eyes. She heard the guard leave and the door beep twice as it locked.

Ant normally slept facing the wall, but she had no idea who was in the cell with her; she needed to be watchful. And she had never been more aware of the plastic and metal strap attached to her back. In Spike, everyone had one. When she'd gone outside, she'd removed it. Now she was the only strutter in a place full of cons and hunchies. She was behind enemy lines. If they found out who she was, she'd have the whole prison – guards and inmates – chasing her. She had to stay alert.

But as she lay down, Ant felt waves of tiredness flow over her. The seemingly endless supply of adrenalin that had kept her wired through the night was being overpowered by exhaustion. Even though there was extreme danger in the cell, she pulled the beanie low and allowed her eyes to close.

Just two minutes . . .

Ant woke with a start. Shouting filled the cell and she opened her eyes. The men in the bunks opposite her were arguing – something about men not turning up, though the accents were strong. A podgy, shirtless man – Glaswegian, Ant guessed – was kicking out at a skinny man in the bunk above him. A third man crouched on the floor, clearly desperate to join in. He seemed to be waiting for orders.

The Scot rolled off his bunk and jabbed his finger at the man above him. 'If you had done your job,' he yelled, 'we wouldn't be here.' He gestured around the cell and, seemingly for the first time, noticed they had company. 'And we wouldn't be sharing our space with the likes of him.' He pointed at Ant and they all turned to look.

She didn't move, just returned their stare. She felt the adrenalin kick in, her stomach lurching, but she remained motionless. Her best hope was to stay as silent and still as possible. The beanie covered some of her face, the blanket covered most of her body. There was no need to panic.

The men glanced at her, then looked away as the skinny man on the top bunk spoke.

'They'd have come, Mr Campbell. Honest. But they were . . . scared off.' He glanced nervously at the man standing by his bunk, who had started punching the frame, seemingly for fun.

'Scared off?' Campbell said. 'Really? By my good friend Treves here?' He pointed at the crouching man. 'Cuddly and safe Day Treves?' He laughed, but the man on the bunk nodded hard and fast.

The cell fell silent. Ant sensed the danger.

If they fight, it's nothing to do with me.

'So you *knew* we would fail? You *knew* the others weren't coming?' His voice was quiet, barely a low rumble, but the menace was clear.

The skinny man fidgeted with his bedding. 'Well, I hoped—' he began.

Campbell held up his hand. 'Enough. Treves? You're on.'

This is nothing to do with me.

As Day Treves leaped up towards the bunk, Ant saw that he was smiling. His watery eyes didn't change, the rest of his face didn't move, but his mouth twisted.

Campbell spoke to Ant. It was almost a whisper. 'You – face the wall.'

Suits me.

She turned and faced the wall.

The sounds were terrifying enough. She heard a strangled gasp. She heard body blows. Fists on flesh. She heard someone collapse onto the floor. Grunting. Muffled screams.

This is getting close. Still not my fight. Still not moving.

Silence.

Then a crashing weight landed on Ant's legs. She swallowed her shout and turned to see a man sprawled across her bunk. He was cut above both eyes, the wounds bleeding freely. He wasn't moving. Treves was crouched, one hand touching the floor, ready to go again.

'I said, *face the wall*,' Campbell spat. Ant thought hard. Was it conceivable that she could keep her identity hidden for much longer? Was it likely she could just slip out unnoticed? She thought not. And she remembered the noise the door had made.

It's my fight now.

Ant didn't face the wall. Instead she pushed the skinny man's body off her legs, then sat up.

'I can get you out,' she said.

27

The effect of Ant's voice in the Remand cell was electrifying. Campbell and Day Treves stood frozen to the spot. The skinny man lay bleeding, forgotten, sprawled over Ant's bunk. She knew she wouldn't have the advantage for very long.

'I can get you out,' she repeated. 'If you want. You might rather stay here, of course. But it sounds like you have unfinished business.' Her voice was steady, controlled – and clearly female.

It was Campbell who found his voice first. 'But you're a girl,' he said, the astonishment in his voice matched by the open mouth of Treves.

'It's a long story,' she said. 'Do you want to get out or not?' She needed to keep the conversation where she wanted it; they had think of her as an escape route, not as a woman.

'And how would that happen then?' said Campbell. 'You're just a kid.'

'But a kid who knows what she's doing. Do you want to get out of here or not?'

Make them answer that question.

They were still frozen to the spot, struck dumb by her words. Skinny man coughed, then spat blood onto Ant's bedding. It broke the spell.

'Day,' said Campbell. 'Sort him.'

Treves reluctantly walked over to Ant's bunk, only tearing his eyes away from her at the last minute. He hauled the barely conscious man to his feet, then dragged him over to the other bottom bunk, dropping him as quickly as he could.

Treves had come a few steps closer to Ant. His smile was back. 'Nice smell,' he whispered.

Ant returned his stare. 'Oh, the whisky?' she said. 'Yeah, it's a bit strong.'

Campbell shook his head. 'No, he means you.'

Two more steps and Treves was sitting next to her. Ant didn't move, forcing herself to focus on Campbell – he was the power in the room. Nothing would happen here that he didn't allow.

'You haven't answered my question,' she said.

'OK,' he said. 'Yes, I'd like to get out of here. Yes, I have unfinished business. But no, I don't think you can help. And I'd say you have about twenty seconds to convince me otherwise.'

Treves edged closer.

'Wrong,' said Ant. 'I'll tell you when this friend of yours is back on his bunk.'

Stay fierce.

Campbell was intrigued. No one had spoken to him like this in years. He sauntered over to where Ant sat and dropped to his haunches. 'Sweetheart, let me explain something to you. You're a wee girl in a small room with three cons. A drug dealer, a psycho and me. That's not a good place to be. If you think you're in charge . . .'

Hemmed in by Treves to her left and Campbell in front, Ant was sweating again. 'Obviously you're in charge,' she said, 'so tell this creep here to back off.' She had no doubt that the 'psycho' he'd mentioned was Treves. He smelled of smoke, sweat and urine. And his leg was touching hers.

'He likes dancing girls, you see,' said Campbell. 'That's what he's hoping for.'

Ant edged away, but she was now up against the bunk frame. She glanced at the cell door and, set into the wall next to it, a small plastic box with a red light.

'Can we talk about getting out of here?' she tried. 'There's a PO coming for me in—'

'I think *you* should dance,' said Campbell, smiling. 'Then we'll listen to your plan. If you keep Treves here happy, everything will be so much . . . easier.'

Ant cursed. 'Do I look like the sort of person who *dances*?' she spat.

'I have to say, honey, I think you do.'

Outside the cell door, the piercing wail of the general alarm made them all start.

Treves glanced at Campbell. 'It's starting again. And without us,' he said.

The Scot lashed out, punching the wall in frustration. 'We should be out there!' he yelled. They heard shouts and running feet. 'Your PO that's coming for you,' he said. 'That's your plan? That's how you can get us out?'

Ant nodded.

'Well, here's mine.' Campbell took a running kick at his bunk; it bent where his trainer made contact. Treves joined in and the bunks started to sag under the assault.

They're going to trash the cell. And trash me with it. Change of plan.

'OK, I'll dance.'

You sure about this?

For the second time in two minutes, Ant had stopped the men in their tracks. They spun round.

Keep the advantage.

'I'll dance. You sit here.' She stood up. 'I'll dance, then we can all smash the place up. By then my PO should have come . . .' She tried her best smile.

And it worked. She knew she was playing a very dangerous game, but she had just the one card to play and she had to play it now.

'When you're sitting comfortably, I can get started . . .' Ant moved till she was standing near the door; they sat down on her bunk. Treves's mouth was open.

'This had better be good,' said Campbell. 'If it isn't . . .'

Ant put a finger in front of her lips. 'Why don't you stop talking and watch?' she said.

Both men smiled.

Outside, the alarm stopped. The shouting from the other cells continued, but inside Remand cell 9, there was silence. Ant calculated Campbell and Treves were four metres away from her; the skinny man still facing the wall. The cell door and its security box a metre to her right. Ant's pulse, already high, ticked up a few beats.

Have you even thought what you are doing?

'Ready?' she said. They nodded like schoolboys. She played the plan through in her head.

You have one chance, Ant. Maybe not even that.

28

She'd never danced. Not really. Never saw the point. But she did know how to attract their attention. Ant turned her back on the men and started to shift her weight from one leg to the other. Her hips moved from side to side and she started to unbutton her shirt. The men behind her cheered in surprise just as her fingers found the lanyard plastered to her skin. She tugged at the cord and, hidden from her audience, MacMillan's security pass popped into her hand.

'Come on, love, let's see some action here! Keep the troops happy!' called Campbell, and started clapping.

She needed to unhook the pass from the cord – and quickly – but it was fiddly. 'Just undoing this button!' she said, and the clapping got louder.

The pass came free. Ant's hips swayed more. A step to the right. A bigger step to the left. Half a metre from the door. She palmed the pass in her left hand, turned and continued her half-dance, half-hustle. She forced a smile as she placed both hands behind her back; one hand pulled out her shirt, the other tucked the pass into her waistband.

The panicked, gasping sound was delayed by only a second. But as Ant moved the card, she realized that someone else had been watching.

The skinny man's shout was a loud one. 'Oh my God, guys! She's got a strap!'

Now she really *was* in trouble.

Ant dived for the door. Card in hand, she sliced it through the security box before anyone had moved. She stabbed MacMillan's code into the keypad just as Treves got to his feet. The red light on the box changed to green and the door clicked open – just as Treves grabbed her shoulder. She dipped left and swung the door inwards, smashing it into his forehead. Treves fell to the floor, howling in pain.

She had taken two steps out of the cell when Campbell rugby-tackled her. Ant crashed down, but was up first and kicked him hard between the legs. Now Treves was up again, and by the time she had disabled Campbell, he was on her. Head down, he charged into her and they tumbled to the floor. A hand grabbed her throat and started to squeeze. Lying on her back, she kicked out, but Treves had long arms – she couldn't reach.

'You nasty little strutter filth,' he spat. 'You're going to die.'

Ant's vision was already blurring. She heard groans and

more shouts, then – with a deafening clatter – the alarm again. There was a momentary hesitation in the grip around her throat, and with all the energy she had left, Ant twisted round, tearing herself away. She gasped for air. On her knees, she saw Treves look straight past her, distracted by a PO who was now advancing, baton in hand, yelling into his radio for help.

Treves pointed at Ant. 'She's a strutter! I just felt her strap!'

The guard glanced at her. When he'd locked her up, she'd been a drunk man called Czezny.

Ant tried to speak. 'They attacked me! They're thugs.' Her voice was husky enough to keep the guard's attention on Treves. Campbell was recovering. He'd be on his feet in seconds, but now had a PO between him and Ant.

'Back in the cell! Get back in the cell!' shouted the guard, his pepper-spray can now aimed at Treves's face.

Ant had seen enough. Reinforcements would be on their way; it was time to go. She needed to take advantage of whatever chaos was out there. She turned to run, then stopped as PO Brian MacMillan, his head bleeding now, came crashing through the doors in the corridor.

He grabbed her by the wrist. 'Spike!' he said. 'Now!' He pulled her back through the doors and led her along a maze of empty passages. 'Short cut to the tunnel. I'll explain.' His breathing was laboured and he was clutching his left side.

'Where is everyone?' Ant managed, her breath coming in short bursts.

'There's another fire. B Wing. They're all there.'

'*Another* fire?'

'Yup. I started it,' said MacMillan matter-of-factly.

Ant's mouth dropped open. 'You what?'

'Let's get to the tunnel.'

'And the alarm?'

'Started that too.' MacMillan removed his jacket as they ran, then, wincing, threw it at Ant. 'Put this on. It might confuse people for a few seconds. We're gonna need a lucky run here.'

She gasped as she saw his blood-soaked shirt. 'Brian, you're injured!'

'I'll get it sorted in Spike,' he rasped.

They burst through more doors, and Ant realized they were entering D Wing, just a few metres from the tunnel entrance.

'What's happening, Brian? You said this would be straightforward, but everything's gone wrong. What happened to you?'

'What's my pass code?' he said, ignoring the question.

'You've forgotten?' said Ant, concerned.

'Tell me,' he said, his words slurring. 'It's important.'

'8B 3S 2C3.'

MacMillan glanced across at her. 'Good. Keep a record of them. Keep. A. Record. You got that? Grey's gonna go crazy, but they'll get you out OK. Then they'll change your life.'

She was puzzled by his choice of words, but they were approaching the fingerprint-activated door.

MacMillan rammed his finger onto the sensor – the lights stayed red. 'My God, they've locked us out,' he muttered.

Ant took his hand and wiped his index finger on her shirt. 'Too much sweat and blood,' she said. 'Try again.'

He placed his finger on the pad again. There was a heart-stopping pause, then the light turned green and the door swung open. As soon as the gap was wide enough they squeezed through.

Ninety seconds to Spike. It was Ant who led the way, glancing back to make sure MacMillan was keeping up. He ran with one hand pressed to his side. He looked wiped out, his face white, eyes bloodshot.

What happened to you?

29

They reached the first gate in the tunnel. Ant was about to kick and run as she had before, but it was shut. And locked.

'Keys!' she shouted, and stepped aside as MacMillan pulled the bunch of keys from his belt. 'And why is it shut anyway?' She looked anxiously down the tunnel to the second gate – it appeared to be open.

MacMillan was trying to single out the key he needed when a screeching metal-on-metal sound filled the tunnel. They spun round to see what appeared to be a large grey piece of piping forcing its way between the steel door and its frame. The motor was still trying to close it, grinding and pushing without effect – the door was stuck open.

MacMillan cursed. 'Who the hell is doing that?'

'I've got a good idea,' said Ant, her voice tight. 'Just find the key. Then we go through and lock it again. But you have to hurry.' He slowly fingered the keys. 'Brian, which one is it? Tell me and I'll do it!' But the more urgent her voice, the slower MacMillan became. When he dropped the keys altogether, she dived for them. 'Describe it!' she yelled as she spread out the keys.

MacMillan closed his eyes, forcing the words out. 'Silver. Short. Wide bow,' he whispered.

From the steel door behind them came the sound of screeching metal, followed by the groan of the dying motor. As the broken door swung open, two men stepped into the tunnel entrance. Campbell and Treves. Campbell still held the two-metre pipe he'd used as a crowbar, Treves brandished a knife. They saw Ant and MacMillan, and a bloodcurdling yell echoed down the tunnel. Both men sprinted towards them, eyes fixed on Ant.

'Silver. Short. Wide bow . . .' she repeated, sifting frantically. 'This one!' She found the key and glanced over her shoulder; her pursuers had closed to three hundred metres. She rammed the key home and twisted, pushing the door open. She was about to go through when MacMillan slumped against the bars.

'Brian! We have to go!' She pulled him to his feet. She knew she was faster than the other two, but with MacMillan she'd be caught within seconds.

Leave him. He's a screw. Save yourself.

Two hundred metres.

'Brian, focus! We have to run! Please!'

He stumbled towards the gate and leaned against the metal frame, reaching for his belt.

With an increasing sense of hopelessness, Ant tugged at him, pulling him through. 'Brian! We have to close the gate!'

Leave him. He's a screw. He'll be fine.

One hundred metres.

The advancing men were shouting. She could still make it to Spike, she thought, but without MacMillan. He was still groping around his waist.

But he came back for me.

And she suddenly realized what he was trying to do.

MacMillan leaned back against the bars, and Ant, propping him up, stood behind him. Campbell and Treves were fifty metres away; she could hear every breath, every step, every curse. Campbell had the pole in one hand, Treves had the knife – he smiled as he ran. In the harsh lighting, Ant saw that the ten-centimetre serrated blade was already covered in blood.

She waited until the last minute. With one hand she held MacMillan against the bars, in the other was his can of pepper spray. 'Shut your eyes and hold your breath,' she whispered.

As the men reached the gate, they slowed and Ant stepped out from behind the guard. With two swift sweeps of her arm, she sprayed the chemicals directly into their faces. She knew from the screams and the clang of the dropped pole that it had worked, but she had already turned and was dragging MacMillan towards the next gate. The spray had been effective, but she needed to get away from the oleoresin capsicum she had released into the tunnel; she could already feel her eyes and throat prickling. With any luck, the full effect of the gas – tears, pain and temporary blindness – would keep the two cons out of action till she was back in Spike.

MacMillan was capable of walking if Ant led him. A hundred metres on, she allowed herself to look back. Campbell was rolling around, his hands over his face; Treves had pulled himself up onto his knees. Wiping his eyes with his sleeve, he was trying to focus.

She rattled the can. 'You want some more of that?' she yelled at him. 'You want some more of that? Want to cry some more?'

Treves kept his distance.

'I think he *will* be back for more. Let's pick this up, Brian.'

It was only when they were going through the open second gate that Ant realized her mistake. She paused, the blood draining from her face.

'The keys,' she muttered. She glanced back down the tunnel at the first gate. In her panic, she had left them in the lock. 'Brian, your keys are still in the gate. What could they open with them?'

Her tone had been as flat as she could manage, but his reaction told her all she needed to know. He spun round, eyes wide, mouth open, and swallowed twice before he spoke. 'This gate. A lot of Spike.' He gulped again. 'Some parts of Holloway and Pentonville, not sure where exactly. Never needed to find out.'

'My bad,' said Ant. 'I need to get them back.'

MacMillan grabbed her before she could move. 'No, we need to get out. Now, while we can.'

They both looked at Campbell. He was getting onto his hands and knees, still coughing and retching. Treves was approaching now.

'OK, you're right. Let's go.'

Ant pushed, pulled and encouraged MacMillan towards the steel door at the end of the tunnel. One hand was still firmly pressed against his ribs, the blood seeping through his fingers. He tried to run but could only manage a lop-sided shuffle. Ant knew it wasn't fast enough.

'Bigger steps, Brian! We need bigger steps!'

A cry from behind them; Ant spun round, holding onto MacMillan and running backwards. Treves was coming towards them in a low crouch, pole in one hand, knife in the other.

She waved the pepper-spray can. 'Ready when you are!' she yelled.

Treves grinned.

She turned to MacMillan. 'We're going to have to fight,' she said.

Her breaths were coming in short gasps now, MacMillan's in rasping heaves. Ten metres from the tunnel end, she took his hand and wiped it on her shirt again.

'Brian, get ready! Every second counts. Get that door open!' She steered him to the control pad and guided his finger onto the sensor. The lights changed and she heard the gears of the door start to move. Turning to face

Treves, she raised the can of pepper spray just as the pole hit her in the stomach. She crumpled, dropping the spray, the wind knocked out of her. White lights bursting in her vision, she scrabbled for the pole. She could hear Treves's victory cry as her fingers closed around the metal tube. She pulled it towards her, then raised it, stabbing upwards. It caught Treves on the shoulder and he spun away, bouncing off the corridor wall.

Ant scooped an arm around MacMillan's waist and hauled him towards the slowly opening space between the tunnel and Spike. Ten seconds and they'd be through.

'Oi, strutter!' yelled Treves.

Ant and MacMillan saw the knife flash as he lined up the throw. As they backed into the gap, shoulder to shoulder, squeezing through, Ant raised the pole – it was the only defence she had. It wasn't enough.

When the knife hit MacMillan, Ant felt his whole body judder. It sliced into his ribs just below his heart – he managed a huge gasp of breath before collapsing.

With a shout, Treves ran forward, but only Ant was armed now. With as much strength as she could muster, she threw the pole. He tried to swerve, but the bar hit him on the knee and he fell. Ant grabbed the prostrate MacMillan and hauled him towards the slowly opening door. The gap was wide enough for one, but with the guard bent double, she had to pause. Two more seconds and they'd both be through. Ant glanced into Spike, but there was no help there. And Treves was on his feet again, metres away, reaching to reclaim his knife from MacMillan's chest, when Ant felt herself being pushed backwards. Surprised, she staggered a few steps into Spike.

'Brian!'

In the same movement, MacMillan rolled back into the tunnel, away from the door, landing at Treves's feet. Just as the prisoner bent to retrieve his blade, MacMillan's boots found the door and pushed. To Ant's horror, it shuddered, then started to close. It took Treves valuable seconds to realize what had happened and he lunged for the door, his fingers finding the locking mechanism.

Torn between helping MacMillan and fighting Treves, Ant froze. MacMillan was pushing, Treves was pulling. She made her mind up. She kicked Treves's fingers away. Free of resistance now, the steel door closed the last few centimetres.

The lights on the door turned red.

30

Now she heard the sirens. Now she saw the flashing lights. Collapsing against the steel door, Ant wanted to scream. She wanted a phalanx of armed POs to come storming round the corner, but that didn't happen. Instead she lay stunned and unmoving against the steel door, her clothes soaked in blood. That it was MacMillan's blood, livid and sticky, made its dampness all the more shocking. She started to shake.

Brian's dead. He has to be. And he pushed the door shut. And he saved me. And he's dead. And he saved me.

She tried to wipe her face with her hands, but merely succeeded in smearing the blood and tears further.

And I need Mattie.

Now the guards came. Ant didn't count them, but

there weren't enough. Batons in hand, they ran to where she was sprawled. All the voices shouted together:

'Where's MacMillan?'

'What have you done with him?'

'What's happened to MacMillan? Whose blood is that?'

She crawled away from the door. 'He's on the other side,' she said, her voice barely audible above the prison's emergency siren. 'Couldn't you guys see? Weren't you watching? We needed you in the tunnel . . .' The familiar rattle of handcuffs followed by the coldness of the steel on her wrist made her start. 'Are you kidding?' she shouted. 'Try helping your mate before sorting me out – he's bleeding to death through there! Trust me, I'm actually pleased to see you.'

There were six of them, none she recognized. One shouted into his radio, then went to place his finger on the scanner.

'No!' came the shouted command. 'Wait!' It was the assessor. Everyone turned to watch Grey stride towards the door. 'We have a hostage situation. You know the Riot Control Plan. Hats and bats, gentlemen, hats and bats. Back here in two.'

The officers ran off, leaving the one who was cuffed to Ant awkwardly waiting for his orders.

Ant couldn't help herself. 'You have to help!' she cried. 'We were attacked! MacMillan's dead, I think, and they have keys and—'

'Give me your baton,' interrupted Grey. The guard,

surprised, slowly passed his stick to the assessor, who snatched it greedily.

'A nightstick!' he said. 'Just like the old days . . .' It had a short side handle, and Grey spun it round in his fist. He knelt down in front of Ant, then stabbed the baton under her chin and lifted. 'I don't need to help anyone,' he said, his voice in its quietest, most dangerous register. 'You really have messed up – I could send you away for ever for this, you know.' His voice became quiet, almost confidential, as though sharing a secret. 'Escape. Sabotage. Murder . . . The murder of a prison guard. That sentence of yours just got *so* much longer.'

'You've got the cameras,' said Ant. 'You know that's not true.'

'The security tapes will show nothing. For now you're back in your cell – SHU is full. It seems rather popular tonight. But when I've sorted this' – he waved the baton at the steel door – 'I'm coming back for you and your criminal family. You always were trouble.'

Ant glanced up at the guard who was chained to her. He was looking at the ceiling.

Grey used the baton to push her head down again. 'He can't hear us over the siren. Barely speaks English anyway.' He jabbed the baton into the bruise on Ant's head, pinning her to the wall. She swallowed her howl of pain. 'The thing is, Abigail – you don't mind if I use your real name, do you? No, of course not. The thing is, you and I both know that this prison is a shambles. Hopeless failures being looked after by hopeless failures. And thanks to you, this whole storage unit is now falling apart. But at least there's someone who can pick up the pieces.' He removed the baton, wiped it on his trousers before handing it back to the guard. 'You see? You need me now. Everyone needs me now.' He stood up and brushed his hands together. 'Cell thirty-three,' he said.

Bloodied and exhausted, Ant spent more than an hour explaining where she had been and what she had done. She told them everything. Propped up in her bunk, she fought the sleep that was threatening to overwhelm her. Mattie was tucked in beside his sister, Dan and Gina sat on the floor. By the time she had finished, they were all done with expressions of anger and gasps of surprise; they just sat there in stunned silence. Gina's hands were over her mouth, tears running down her face.

'Did he die?' asked Mattie, a small voice from under a sheet.

'Don't know,' said Ant. 'But probably.'

'He came back for you,' he said.

'He did.'

'Is it my fault?' A smaller voice now.

'Shh now. Of course not.'

'*Sèten?*' (Certain?)

'*Sèten.*' (Certain.)

'And you have his pass?' said Gina.

'8B 3S 2C3,' said Ant. 'That's Brian's code. He said Grey would go mad if he found out I knew. Then he said those numbers would change my life.'

'Well, they got you out of that cell,' said Mattie.

There was a silence before Dan spoke. 'And the crazy guy has the keys.'

Ant nodded. 'I guess so. There's always a chance that they're so stupid they'll miss them. But it's not likely.'

Dan and Gina both sighed deeply.

'OK. We stay together as much as we can. Abi and Mattie – you need to be *stuck* together, you understand?'

In the bunk, Mattie squeezed Ant tightly.

'Dan, you're frightening Mattie,' chided Gina.

Dan nodded. 'Maybe. And maybe that's a good thing. This is going to be tough. When does that video you posted go live?'

'What's the time?' asked Ant.

Gina checked her watch. 'Five thirty-five.'

'Thirty-five minutes ago then.'

'I know why you did it, Abi,' said Gina. 'But that's a *humiliation* right there. And a humiliation committed by a strutter too. If that Clarke woman is in the Cloverwell gang, we'll know about it soon enough.'

Ant fell asleep just before six, Mattie – still in his sister's bunk – soon after. Dan and Gina dressed in silence, then waited for the unlocking. As soon as the door to the cell buzzed open, they stepped outside. The air was cooler there, but not by much; within seconds their clothes were damp with sweat. They spoke in urgent whispers.

'I'll stay here,' said Dan. 'Get as much food as you can and tell as many folk as you can.'

Gina nodded. 'I'll wait till there's a decent crowd, then go. I don't want to hang around too long.'

But it seemed the whole prison was hungry. Jug up was busy within minutes, and when they spotted the Raaths, the Noons and the Durrows all queuing, Gina gave Dan a kiss on the cheek and disappeared down the steps. Dan watched as she moved along the lines waiting for food, then amongst the tables, spending no more than a minute with any group. As word spread from family to family, he saw them gather as much breakfast as they could carry, then hurry back to their cells. Gina emerged slowly from the steps, her arms full.

'Nice work.' Dan smiled as he saw the bread, fruit and sausages that Gina had scooped up.

'Told everyone, I think,' she said, glancing down at the emptying tables. 'Reckon the whole of Spike knows it now. Kids OK?'

Dan managed a smile. 'I haven't checked. You were only gone fifteen minutes. But I have been standing here, sentry-like, getting hungry. Let's store what we can.'

As they stepped inside their cell, the siren fired again.

Day 790
My favourite things RIGHT NOW:
Bacon.
Ant being safe.
Brian going back for A.
Maybe he'll still be OK?
D and G look bad. Everyone worried about the crazy guy and the keys.
A is the bravest.

A Wing, Holloway

The women of cell 283 went to breakfast together. They rolled in, queued up for their food, then found a table in the far side of a half-empty hall.

'Will everyone know?' whispered a haunted-looking prisoner, spooning cereal into her mouth as though it might disappear at any second. 'Will everyone know about what happened to Tess?' She gave a quick glance at Tess Clarke, who was sitting beside her.

'Given that we had to get a screw to unlock her handcuffs,' said another, 'and given that screws never keep their mouths shut, I'd say yes. And here comes the proof. Hold tight, everyone, we've a mad witch incoming.'

The six women looked up and then swiftly down again as a thin-faced woman with wild black hair marched up to them. Tess Clarke made space for her, but she didn't need much. Grace Chang was one of the Cloverwell gang leaders; her reputation for casual, unthinking violence had been well-earned.

Clarke handed her a mug. 'Here, have mine. Not touched it yet.'

'I've seen the video,' said Chang, ignoring her. 'Outside, *everyone* will see the video.' Her lips pursed with controlled disappointment. 'How did it happen?'

Everyone around the table looked at everyone else.

'Tess should tell you,' said the white-haired woman. 'She's one of yours, isn't she?'

Chang turned to face Clarke, who disguised her shaking hands by shoving them deep in her pockets.

'She just broke in somehow,' Clarke blurted. 'I was asleep. Next minute she was on top of me! And threatening me and . . .'

Chang raised her hand and the words trailed away. 'Who broke in? Who did this? No one just *walks* into another cell like that.'

'She's the boy's sister. From the *Correction* film,' said Clarke, and stopped.

Chang looked puzzled. 'She's here? In Holloway?'

There was a long pause as Clarke hesitated, then said, 'She's a strutter. She came from Spike.'

Chang hurled the mug down with such force that it smashed into hundreds of ceramic shards, showering the table with cheap china and hot tea.

Pentonville

It had happened so quickly that the much-vaunted Riot Control Plan hadn't even been ordered, never mind executed. With the keys left behind by MacMillan, Treves had opened eighteen cells before any guards arrived. Swiftly overpowered, they now faced every prison officer's worst nightmare. Trembling, the guards sat together, then cried out as the blows came. Years of grievances – real and imagined – were being satisfied, each strike delivered with a name or an insult attached.

In front of them Treves and Campbell sifted newly liberated keys and passes.

'Who knows where we can get from here,' said Campbell, stuffing three cards into his pocket. 'If they've any sense, they'll have shut the prison down. All the passes will be useless. The keys are obviously still good . . .'

'We need weapons,' said Treves. 'They'll come at us hard. And soon.'

'We have C Wing,' said Campbell, 'some offices, access to the tunnel and, as many of our friends are discovering, the pharmacy.'

Treves grinned. 'This is going to be the biggest party ever.'

Spike

The speakers squawked to life, killing the siren. In cell 33 everyone jumped and then froze, waiting for the message. Then the words came. The male voice was clipped and tense.

'*There is a temporary security issue. Your cells are secured and locked until further notice.*'

'Well, that's one way of putting it,' said Gina.

'And let's see how temporary it is,' muttered Ant drowsily.

The siren fired up again. Mattie was waving at the Evanses and the Claytons in 31. Their twelve-year-old daughter waved back briefly, then disappeared from view. Ant had given up on sleep but was still lying on her bunk. Images of Brian filled her head. The sound the knife had made as it struck him, a fearful thud, filled her ears. *Your stupid bloody plan, Brian! Why did I ever agree . . . ?* The tears came fast now. *My God, what have we started?*

Gina and Dan were talking in brief shouts to compete

with the siren. Mattie was lookout; with the cell doors locked, it was the only way to find out what was happening outside.

'Where's the strap-key now?' asked Gina.

Ant realized that the question was for her. 'The first fan on the fifth level,' she said. 'There's a small flap by the cable. Small beans tin. In there.'

Dan whistled. 'We *will* need it today, I'm sure of it. But everyone's way too twitchy . . .'

'They're going to be twitchy all day,' said Gina. 'If we need it, we need it. When the alarm stops . . . maybe then.'

'And what if it doesn't stop?' asked Dan.

Ant pulled MacMillan's pass from under her shirt and got off her bunk. 'Could be worth a try,' she said.

'Will it still work when we're all in lockdown?'

'One way to find out,' said Ant, and walked towards the door.

She was about to swipe her pass through the security box when Gina exclaimed, 'No, stop! Wait . . .' Ant hesitated, her hand poised with the card above the box. 'They'll know it's you,' said Gina.

'What?'

'They'll know it's you. MacMillan is . . . in the tunnel . . .'

Ant nodded. 'Good point.'

'Whatever happened,' said Gina, 'everyone knows he won't be opening cell thirty-three, so if they're monitoring their screens and see his pass being used here, they'll know it's you. And they'll cancel it.'

Ant looked at the pass – Brian's startled face staring right back. 'So I can use it just once more?'

'That sounds about right,' said Gina.

Ant tucked the card back under her shirt.

Holloway

Following the smashing of the mug, the hall had quickly emptied. As the inmates headed for the cells, shouts of alarm rang out around the tables.

'This is it! It's starting, get out of here!'

Four POs who had been lounging around the edges of the hall came striding towards Chang, pushing against the crowd. In the rush to leave, one officer was barged into a table, crashing heavily into the crockery and half-eaten food. Dazed, he rolled onto the floor. Three inmates made sure they stamped on him as they hurried past.

It happened so quickly, none of the other POs were sure what had happened. But they had a man down – a wounded and unconscious man – and they knew what they had to do. Batons drawn, they chased after the running inmates, catching two stragglers before they could leave the hall. Flung to the floor, both women received a flurry of blows; their howls and screams rang out down the corridors.

The women of 283 got to their feet as the prison siren fired up.

'We didn't start this, OK?' said Chang. 'What happened last night was a strutter takeover. The screws *allowed* it, the governor *allowed* it. We are on our own!'

More inmates ran back into the hall, alerted by the screams. A few had brought weapons – blades and bludgeons visible at fingertips and inside shirts.

'If they've let one strutter in, there *will* be others.' Chang suddenly sounded as if she was addressing a political meeting. 'If we don't put a stop to this, there'll be more tonight. We'll be overwhelmed.'

'But we're in trouble now,' said a scared voice. 'We'll be put in SHU. All of us. Can't we go back to our cells?'

Chang smiled. 'No one is going to get punished,' she said. 'Trust me. We now have the best security a prison can offer.' She pointed at the now cuffed and prone guards. 'We have hostages.'

Spike

Silence. The quietist a prison can be. The scariest a prison can be. Everyone in their cells, everyone straining for the first sounds of danger. Ant and Mattie looked out of one cell window, Dan and Gina peered out of the other. They caught occasional glimpses of running POs and hammered unsuccessfully to attract their attention. As the morning progressed and the temperature inside the cells rose, there was no sign of anyone in a uniform. There hadn't been a tannoy message for an hour.

'What's happening? Where are the screws?' muttered Dan.

'You've said that a hundred times,' said Gina. 'Same answer: no idea.'

'Have they run away?' asked Mattie. 'Are we on our own?'

Ant put her arm around him. 'Don't worry, little brother. *Tout pral pase byen.*'

But he shook his head. '*Non. Tout pap pase byen.*'

Dan and Gina exchanged a brief glance. Over the years they had learned the meaning of only a few of the Haitian words Ant and Mattie spoke to each other. They had learned to keep out; it was a private language from their old life. But this phrase they understood. 'All will go well,' is what Ant had said. Mattie was unconvinced.

The siren started up again. Everyone jumped. Gina took advantage of the cover and leaned in close to Dan. 'I don't think I could honestly say to Mattie that all will be fine.'

Dan nodded his agreement. Across the level, in cell 31, he could see the young Evans girl, her face pressed up against the window. She was crying hysterically.

Holloway

The cafeteria had filled swiftly. The mood was ugly. With access to the kitchen, scores were being settled. The inmates attacked the guards, then they attacked each other.

Chang climbed onto a table. She was shouting but had to wait a long time before she could be heard. 'Leave the guards alone. We need them to bargain with – we have hostages, we have power. There's a first-aid kit in the kitchen . . .' One of the gang members ran to find it. 'Let's patch them up and get them awake.'

A cry from a lookout. 'We got company! Governor's here!'

Chang ran over and stood by the door, gang members following in her wake. 'Stay there, Burridge!' she yelled. 'We have four hostages. You try and take us and they won't last five seconds.'

'I'm not trying to "take you", nor will anyone else,' said the governor of Holloway. 'I just need to talk . . .'

'No, you just need to run a prison properly,' shouted Chang. 'You allowed a strutter to break in and assault us. Now she's back in Spike and we want to find her. That's all. Can you help us or not?' Shouts of support and applause came from the cafeteria, but Chang told them to be quiet.

There was only the briefest of pauses before Jan Burridge replied. 'Can I see how my guards are?' she asked. 'Can we get them medical help?'

'How about how your *prisoners* are?' called one woman. 'We're only treating them the way they treat us.' Raucous support greeted that remark.

'The answer to your question,' shouted Chang, 'is that one of your men is losing blood fast. We'll swap him for you if you want.'

Within a minute the suited figure of Governor Jan Burridge walked into the cafeteria. 'My medics are outside. Can they come in and get him?'

'If you stay,' said Chang.

Burridge called back through the door, and two anxious men with a stretcher ran to the bleeding guard, their eyes fixed straight ahead. Everyone watched as the unconscious PO was carried out of the room. When the door swung closed, Burridge turned to Chang. 'Now can we talk?'

'Sure,' said Chang. 'We want to get into Spike.'

The governor smiled. 'I'm sorry I can't help you with that,' she said, and returned Chang's stare.

'Oh, you'd be surprised,' said Chang, and punched Burridge in the throat.

Pentonville

The inmates were effectively in control of half of C Wing, some ransacked offices and a plundered pharmacy. A man in a bandana made from a ripped white shirt came running up to Campbell carrying three phones and a black box the size of a small suitcase.

'What's with the box?' asked Campbell, his attention on the hostages.

'It's the blocker,' came the reply. 'This is what blocks all phone calls.'

Campbell smiled. 'And you've switched it off?'

'I've smashed it up a bit.'

'Good,' said Campbell. 'Hand out the phones. Let's film this.'

Five hostages were dragged over and dumped at his feet; all five lay there motionless.

He stood on a chair, glanced at the inmates, then at the security cameras. 'Listen up,' he said down the lens, 'and listen well. I have some requests. My friends you can see behind me, and they have requests too. Some are easy for you to sort, some not. But if you say no to any of them, any at all, we kill a hostage.'

Huge cheers from the inmates; they closed in around him.

'You also know that somehow a video of the executions will end up online. And I'm sure none of us want that to happen. So . . .' He smiled briefly. 'There is a prisoner in Spike who was here just recently. She paid us a visit. You know who she is. We'd like her back, please.' Loud cheers were again silenced by Campbell. 'I have a phone you can call me on – it's one of yours anyway, so don't worry about the bill.' He read out its number. 'Call me in ten minutes. Or, if you don't, we could always come and get her . . .'

The men behind him pushed forward in their desperation to be let loose.

Campbell shouted at the camera, 'I don't think they're feeling very patient!'

33

Spike

The tannoy again.

'*The security situation is ongoing. Cells will remain locked. Police are assisting us with . . . events.*'

Ant, Mattie, Dan and Gina stared at each other. Now they all looked scared.

'The police?' said Dan.

'The screws have lost control, haven't they?' said Gina. 'Whatever they think they're dealing with, they need help.'

Mattie was at the window again. 'The police are here. Well, I think they are . . .' Everyone crowded around. Six men with helmets and shields were at the windows of cell 31.

'No, they're screws, Mattie. It's hats and bats time,

that's all. They're counting us,' said Gina.

Within seconds they were at 33, Mattie exclaiming in alarm as they came right up to the window. Visors up, three urgent faces peered in, checking names and faces. Satisfied that the numbers tallied, one of the men managed a thumbs-up before disappearing.

'Oh well, at least we're all here,' said Ant. 'They must be relieved.'

'It is safer in here, isn't it?' said Mattie.

Ant shook her head. 'That's exactly the point. I don't think so. When have they ever cared what happens to us? We have to make this call ourselves. And we can move when we need to.' She waved her pass again.

'Ant's right,' said Gina. 'We have to be ready to make this our decision, not theirs.'

HMP London control room

The usual eight had been supplemented by four emergency staff, their leave cancelled at the last minute. Calls were taken, radios shouted into; it sounded more like a trading floor than a prison control room. In the middle stood Assessor Grey and HMP London Governor Ernest Gaunt.

The screens showed the growing pandemonium in Holloway and Pentonville. Some had images of the lockdown in Spike: deserted halls and levels, cells full of scared inmates staring out. The resolution was good enough to see the sweat pouring from their faces.

There was perspiration on Gaunt's forehead too, and he wiped it with his shirt sleeve. 'Will someone explain,' he said, his words slow with controlled anger, 'how I can watch images from the rioters *on my phone*? On my phone, for God's sake!'

'I understand,' said Grey, 'that the phone-jamming signal comes from the Pentonville medics' office, next to the pharmacy. It was out of sight, but the rioters found it and smashed it up. As a result all phones and internet work as normal. There's wifi in the medics' room too. They found some work phones . . .' He shrugged. 'The rest was easy. That's what you're watching.'

Gaunt ran his hand through his hair. 'So if – God forbid – they kill a hostage, the whole world will be watching.'

Grey nodded.

'Can you see Jan?' asked Gaunt wearily.

One of the screen watchers looked up at him. 'Not at the moment, sir. She was attacked soon after she walked into the cafeteria.'

'We need to get her and the other hostages out,' said Gaunt. 'But we follow procedure. What do the rioters want, Assessor? What can we give them before we send in the troops?'

'They want Abigail Norton Turner from Spike. I'm afraid she broke into Holloway, then Pentonville – with the help of a guard. Caused a lot of trouble.'

There was a silence as Gaunt waited. When nothing more was forthcoming, he said, 'Is that it? They want a *strutter*?'

'That appears to be the case, yes,' said Grey.

Gaunt breathed heavily. 'How many rioters are we talking about? Top figure.'

'About ninety in Holloway. And it looks like eighty in Pentonville. They also have the Pentonville tunnel door wedged open.'

Whatever blood was in Gaunt's face drained from it now. 'So they have access to the tunnel?'

'I'm not worried on that score,' said Grey. 'The system is designed to cope with a breach. Your prisons are still secure.'

'But they both have hostages?'

A nod from Grey. Silence from Gaunt.

'A thought, Governor?' said Grey. 'Let them get to the tunnels and deal with them there. Take out the cameras first – it's probably best if it's only us watching. Procedure states that deadly physical force is acceptable to prevent arson or escape. I think both are in play here.'

Gaunt looked aghast. '*Deadly force*? But what about the hostages? Jan is down there!'

'Obviously we save as many as we can,' said Grey flatly.

The governor shook his head. 'No. We're not there yet. We negotiate, we compromise, we stall. In ninety minutes we should have the troops we need to cover all eventualities. We keep them talking.'

There was no reply – Grey had already left the control room.

Holloway

Grace Chang held Deputy Governor Jan Burridge's radio in her hand. She pressed the TALK button. 'Who am I speaking to?' she said. 'Who's there?' For a few seconds there was the sound of rustling and whispering before a man's voice said, 'This is Ernest Gaunt. I'm the Governor of HMP London.'

'I know who you are,' said Chang. 'I have Burridge here, and three other hostages too. We want the strutter who broke into Holloway. And we want her here. Are you prepared to do that?'

'Do you know who she is?' said Gaunt pleasantly.

'She's the sister of the kid in that *Correction* film. He is Matthew Norton Taylor, she's Abigail Norton Taylor. Shaved head, looks like a boy. Shouldn't take you long to find her.'

'OK,' said Gaunt. 'I need to see Jan Burridge, please. I can see the other hostages but I can't see Jan.'

'No.'

'Why?'

'She's busy. Listening to complaints.'

'Let me see her.' A moment's pause.

'OK. If you insist.' Chang walked to the kitchen, Tess Clarke at her side. Jan Burridge was sprawled on the floor, her face cut and bruised.

'You're coming with me,' Chang said.

The governor gave a muffled cry as Chang turned and

dragged her through to the cafeteria. As they came within range of the security cameras, Chang dropped Burridge, pulled the gag from her mouth and turned to the lens.

She pressed the TALK button again. 'Now you can talk to her.'

Spike

In cell 33 Dan and Gina were sharing out the last of the food from their breakfast takeaway. The bacon had gone first, then the fruit. Only the bread rolls were left.

'I'd been hoping to save these for later . . .' said Gina. 'But maybe now is a good time.' She handed them round and they ate in silence.

'What would you do first,' asked Mattie, staring through the window, 'if we ever got out of here? What would you do, where would you go?'

Dan looked up in surprise at the question, then managed a smile. 'Think I'd call up some old friends and, if they still remembered me, go for a run with them. A long run – then a few iced beers and a chicken Jalfrezi. Extra hot, extra poppadums. What about you, Mattie?'

'Swim in the sea,' he said immediately. 'Roll in the sand, eat chips and then swim again. All day. And when you called me in, I'd take at least an hour to hear what you said.'

'Fair enough.' Gina smiled, her mouth still full. 'Sounds like you got it all planned!' He nodded. 'But just to be clear,' she said, 'is this once we're released? Or have we escaped?'

He shrugged. 'Dunno. Either. Whichever you like.'

'OK,' said Gina. 'I'll go running with Dan, swimming with Mattie, and then . . . go dancing. And camping. And eat outdoors – fresh food I've bought from the market.' Her eyes were closed now. 'And get some decent clothes, go to the cinema, order pizza . . .'

'No pizza in the cinema,' said Dan, smiling.

'Live dangerously, Dan,' said Ant. 'Go crazy. I'm off backpacking. But I'm only going to countries who never backed heritage crime.'

'Which narrows it down a little,' said Gina.

'Agreed,' said Ant. 'But then I'm buying a wrecking ball.' Dan and Gina looked quizzical but Mattie grinned. 'I'm gonna knock down some prisons.'

Pentonville

The fire started in the pharmacy. The combination of cigarettes and surgical spirit proved explosive, and two inmates ran into the main hall, their hair and clothes on fire. The rest of the drugs caught quickly; the inmates' slowness in responding, a direct result of the sheer volume of medicines they had already swallowed.

No one took control of firefighting. The fire alarms kicked in, followed by high-pressure sprinklers, but without any coordinated effort the blaze started to spread.

'We move now!' shouted Campbell. 'We either head for the other wings or the tunnel.'

The inmates had decided already. They ran for the

tunnel entrance. Some had phones strapped to their heads, the red 'record' icon already flashing. A few sported stolen PO caps.

'Bring the hostages!' ordered Campbell. 'They'll get us out the other end.'

Still hooded, the POs were herded together. As they stumbled towards the tunnel, they whispered encouragement to each other.

'Has anyone ever wanted to visit Spike?' Campbell yelled. Cries of laughter and applause. 'Has anyone ever wanted to show strutters just what we think of them?'

In the enclosed tunnel the noise was deafening.

34

Control room

Panic.

'They're in the tunnel!'

'Put that fire out!'

'If they're all in the tunnel, just seal it off!'

'Fire brigade ready. Riot Squad here in three!'

Governor Gaunt watched images of the inmates running for the tunnel. 'Campbell just took the hostages with him,' he shouted to his staff. 'He can use their fingerprints to get into Spike. We need to remove names from the database. How long will that take?'

'Not too long, but there is a procedure . . .' shouted a woman in front of a bank of screens. 'Give me the names! How many am I looking for?'

'There's five,' he said over the woman's shoulder. 'Darcy is one. I can see Mangan. Who else is down there, people? Need this fast!'

As the security data was accessed, more names were shouted, then some disputed.

'They had bags over their heads, for God's sake – it was hard to be certain!'

'Get me pictures from the tunnel!'

Some keys were punched and images from the security camera nearest the tunnel exit flickered onto the screen.

'God, there's hundreds of them.'

'Who can we see of our people? Shout out their names!'

Everyone in the control room scoured the screens for friends and colleagues.

'Piercy was down there, I'm sure. Was that Norris with him?'

The governor was getting desperate. 'Who was on *that* wing in *this* shift? It's in the logs, people. Thirty seconds! And I need everyone to the tunnel entrance now. Everything we have. Use all force necessary!'

The woman at the keyboard yelled, 'Darcy and Mangan deleted. Piercy and Norris deleted. If in doubt, shout them out.' More names were shouted, all mixing into an incomprehensible noise.

'Theresa,' said Gaunt gently, 'can you take out the whole shift? Remove all their security clearances? We can't risk forgetting a name.'

The woman shook her head. 'Not as far as I know.

It's the way it's programmed.'

Gaunt nodded. 'OK. Get ready to type faster than you've ever typed before.'

Pentonville

The inmates arrived at the steel entrance to Spike in swift order, running down the tunnel, exhilarated by their own noise and speed. When Campbell reached them, knife in hand, he pushed the first hostage towards the control pad. 'Get us in,' he spat.

The crowd quietened as Mangan, his face covered in blood, pressed his finger to the sensor. The light stayed red. He wiped his shaking hand on his under-pants and tried again. The red light flashed twice, then stayed red.

'You did that on purpose!' shouted Treves.

Mangan turned to protest, but Campbell slammed his head into the steel door. The guard fell to the floor, hands over his face.

'You're next, Darcy. Don't make us mad.' The bat-tered guard stumbled towards the sensor but needed Campbell's hand to steady her shaking arm. He forced her finger onto the sensor. Red light.

He cursed, then punched her, casting her aside. 'Bring the other three. Now.'

The other POs were shoved to the front. Campbell removed the hoods. The terrified officers glanced from their captors to each other. When they saw Mangan and

Darcy lying face down by the door, they cried out.

'They couldn't get us in,' said Campbell. 'I'm sure you'll do better.' He offered them each in turn a corner of his shirt. 'Wipe your hands, particularly your index finger. Let it dry, get us in. Like your lives depended on it.'

Control room

All eyes studied the screens. As the hoods came off, the names came fast.

'OK, that's Goldman at the front! John Goldman!'

'And Jordan Harris behind him!'

For a moment the third hostage was obscured by an inmate; then he moved slightly.

'Kahn! It's Sid Kahn! He's only been here three weeks, poor lad.'

'Go, Theresa!'

They had the names; now all they had to do was remove them from the security file. Theresa's hands flew over the keyboard as they watched Goldman being shoved towards the sensor. She hit 'delete' just before his finger touched the pad. In the control room, a small sigh of relief was quickly followed by a shout of alarm as the guard was struck on the head. Goldman fell next to Mangan, and already Harris was in position. His finger made contact at exactly the same time as the 'delete' order was executed. A moment's pause before he too was assaulted by three inmates, then dragged away.

'Last one!' shouted Gaunt. He watched the screen as

Campbell grabbed Sid Kahn, then suddenly paused. He stared up at the security camera.

'He's just realized what we're doing,' said a voice in the control room. The only other sound was Theresa's frantic typing. She hit one final key.

'That's it! Kahn's deleted!' she cried triumphantly. On the screen they watched as Campbell stepped behind the rookie PO, glanced briefly back at the camera and, with one swift pull of the knife, slit his throat.

Screams in the control room. Two men were sick; a tight-lipped, swaying Gaunt gripped the back of a chair, knuckles white. 'God help us,' he muttered.

Only Theresa, hands still on the keyboard, heard him. 'Amen,' she mouthed, eyes on her slain colleague.

Looking at the screens, they saw that the cons had turned on the other hostages.

'Turn it off!' cried an anguished voice, but the screens continued to beam their terror into the control room.

The governor's words sounded unnaturally loud. 'We have lost a brother officer. We'll mourn in due course and we will have justice for our colleagues. But first we have two riots to sort. Theresa will remove all the Pentonville shift from the security-access file, then the tunnel will be secure.'

He walked over to a different bank of screens which showed Holloway's Governor Burridge being marched along a corridor. Behind her, brawling inmates were brandishing weapons and smashing anything within reach.

'Why doesn't someone stop them?' called a voice, but Gaunt shook his head.

''Cos they've seen what happened to Sid Kahn, that's why. Remember, they're beaming this stuff out to anyone who wants to watch.' He pointed to other screens showing deserted posts, empty desks and unmanned exits. 'My God, they've actually run away . . . Get the Spike Riot Squad into the Holloway tunnel. Close it behind them. Let's stop this now . . .'

'Governor!'

The cry from someone watching the Pentonville screens was shrill and panicky. All around the room hands were covering mouths. Gaunt ended his call and ran over; now it was his turn to feel sick. He was watching the body of PO Brian MacMillan being hauled out of a cupboard. It was taking two, then three, then four inmates to move him, but there was no doubting where they were headed.

'Great God in heaven,' muttered Gaunt. 'We are dealing with savages.'

'Take MacMillan off the list!' someone shouted.

Theresa's fingers were working fast but she had started to sob. 'He's on the Spike list!' she said, shaking her head. 'It's arranged differently . . . it's not easy . . . I'm not in yet.' She hit more keys. 'Come on! Come on!'

Everyone had stopped what they were doing; around the control room conversations were halted, heads turned. Eyes flicked from Theresa to the screens. The inmates seemed to be taking it in turns to hold MacMillan's hand – ten seconds maximum before the next one took over.

'Governor . . . ?'

'The sensor needs heat,' he said flatly. 'Not much, but some. They're ahead of us . . .'

Theresa shouted, 'I'm in!' and eyes switched back to her. 'Governor, you need to override!' She slid sideways as Gaunt entered his command code, then back again as he stepped aside. They now watched the grotesque comedy as the inmates positioned the dead man's hand over the sensor.

Theresa spluttered, 'Nearly got it!'

Staff names were scrolling down the screen.

'Might he have been taken off already?' someone suggested.

'No, there he is!'

MacMillan, Brian Donald Hester. Staff number e382184p. Age 23. 31C Penn Gardens N7 89P.

Everyone in the control room wanted to yell. No one said a word.

On the screen: inmates everywhere, obscuring the camera's view.

Theresa highlighted MacMillan's name.

The crowd parted; MacMillan's finger was on the sensor.

Theresa began to type her command order.

The red light went off. Three people screamed.

The sensor light turned to green.

The tunnel door was open.

The governor turned to his staff. 'We evacuate the prison.'

35

When the siren stopped, everyone in cell 33 looked up. They had become accustomed to the wail – its disappearance filled the prison with an eerie silence. Ears still ringing, Ant stepped over to the window that looked across the level – everywhere, nervous faces peered out, eyes darting up and down, left and right. She had just opened her mouth to speak when the siren started again. But this was different. Unlike the single high note they had got used to, this was a series of short blasts. Deeper, louder, more chilling.

'Something's changed!' shouted Gina. Ant's stomach flipped. It felt as though this marked the end of something. Gina and Dan exchanged glances.

'OK, I think this is it,' said Dan. 'Ant, you should go and get the strap-key.'

Gina nodded.

'Use the pass?' said Ant.

'Use the pass,' agreed Dan.

'Why don't I let everyone out? Might as well . . .'

Dan shook his head. 'No, wait till you have the key. You need that first. Then – assuming the pass still works – unlock everything you can.'

Ant pulled the pass out from under her T-shirt, then felt her hand being grabbed fiercely.

'I'm going too,' said Mattie. 'You said we had to stick together. Well, that just started.'

A second's hesitation before Gina nodded. 'You're right, we did say that.' Another hesitation. 'OK, do it together.' She glanced at Ant, who nodded and stepped towards the door, her pass in one hand, her brother holding onto the other.

Ant's heart rate was in overdrive but her head was clear. 'We won't be long,' she said, and swiped the card through the small box. The door buzzed and clicked, then, after Ant's tentative push, swung open. She stepped outside, Mattie waving briefly at Gina and Dan as he followed her.

'See you later,' whispered Gina, eyes brimming with tears.

The door clicked and locked again.

Outside on the levels the staccato blasts of the siren were deafening. Ant and Mattie ran to the railings. She felt better out of the cell. *At least I'm doing something.* Lines of POs in riot gear were running towards the Pentonville tunnel entrance; behind them ran police, some with helmets, all with batons. In the brief gaps between the siren bursts, new sounds: the fury and panic of a pitched battle.

Ant pulled her brother down into a crouch, held his face in her hands.

'Mattie, you know this is bad,' she said. He nodded, his eyes not leaving his sister's for a second. Hers were everywhere, looking for danger from the steps, from the railings, from the other cells. Ant wiped the sweat from her face. Heart racing, she struggled to keep her voice calm. 'We get the strap-key, we escape.'

'And get Dan and Gina out?' he said, his voice urgent, his eyes pleading.

She nodded. 'Everyone we can. If this still works.' She tapped her pass, now swinging free around her neck.

He pointed up at the security cameras. 'And those?'

'I reckon the screws are all too busy to care at the moment,' she said. 'But we mustn't take the straps off till later. We can't. The fact that we have a key *has* to stay a secret for as long as possible.' More shouting from below, then a man screaming. 'Ready?'

Mattie nodded and grabbed her hand again. They ran, crouching, for the steps. Taking them two or three at a time, they passed the fourth level in seconds; the cells apparently quiet, the open spaces deserted.

'Five!' shouted Mattie as they got there. Each level had the same layout: eight cabins around the outside, two running down the middle. Four high-powered fans blew the hot air about, the nearest just a few metres away.

Ant knelt in front of its control panel, shielding it from the camera above. 'In there,' she said, pointing at a hinged flap by the power cable. 'In an old rusty tin.'

Mattie squeezed in front of her and pushed his hand inside the fan. He nodded as his fingers found the tin; he pulled it out and, tipping it slightly, let the strap-key – still in its case – slide into his other hand. He swiftly offered it to Ant, aware of the treasure he was holding. She smiled briefly, kissed it and pushed it deep into her pocket.

'That was easy!' Mattie beamed.

'I think it gets harder,' said Ant. 'Look.'

Around the level, from the six cells that could see them, desperate, imploring faces stared out. There was banging and calling too, noise they had somehow missed earlier.

'Let's see if Brian can still help us,' said Ant. She sprinted towards cell 50, then checked, ran back and grabbed Mattie. They reached the cabin together, and Ant sliced the card through the box control by the door.

36

Green light.

'It still works!' yelled Ant. There were cheers from inside, but she had already moved on.

'Fast as we can!' she shouted. 'Before anyone notices what's happening! 'Bin fifty-one, here we come.' Another swipe, another cell open. Ant and Mattie opened all ten in under two minutes. By the time they had finished the circuit, the whole level was teeming with released prisoners.

'Where do we go?' shouted Lena Durrow, holding onto a clearly terrified Sam and Tilly. 'They've just said they're evacuating the prison! Came over the speakers . . .'

'Do they come and get us?' asked Jeffrey Blakely, his whole body shaking.

Ant shrugged. 'No idea. Didn't know about it.'

As most of level five moved to the railings to see what was happening, Ant and Mattie headed for the stairs.

'Gina and Dan!' said Mattie. 'Let's get them out next!'

'We're getting there!' said Ant. 'Let's do level four while we're here – Daisy will be going crazy.'

Sure enough, the Raaths in 48 spilled out gratefully, crying and applauding. Ant and Mattie were enveloped in hugs and kisses.

'I thought I was going to die in there!' cried Daisy. 'Mum was going seriously crazy!' She pointed to Sarah Raath, who was weeping on Frail Mary's shoulder. 'What do we do now?' She turned and looked expectantly at Ant – but Ant and Mattie had gone.

As they reached the steps, the noise from below suddenly surged in volume. Ant and Mattie peered cautiously over the fourth-floor railings and it was Ant who exclaimed the loudest. Under a barrage of missiles, followed up by a fearsome array of knives and cudgels, the POs and police were losing to the rioting prisoners from Pentonville. As they watched, two more guards lost their footing and tumbled to the ground, and then Ant saw Treves and Campbell. Before she was spotted she dropped to the floor, pulling Mattie on top of her.

'Who are they, Abi?' he whispered.

Ant could feel his body trembling and held him tight until he stopped. 'Real bad guys from next door,' she said. 'From Pentonville.'

'Do you know them?'

'I recognize some of them.'

'What do they want?'

She inhaled deeply and, for the first time, smelled fire. Now she really *was* scared. 'Revenge, Mattie. They want revenge. Revenge on the guards for being locked up, and revenge on strutters for everything else. But mainly they want me. Two of them chased me out of Pentonville—'

'The ones who killed Brian?' said Mattie with a sharp intake of breath.

'Yes. I fooled them. I beat them. They lost to a strutter. And a strutter who's a girl and a mutt. Doesn't get much worse for them. So I think they want revenge.' She felt Mattie's sinewy arms tighten around her and they were still for a few moments.

'We need to get Gina and Dan,' he said.

'Let's look,' Ant replied, and they both peered through the railings.

Two lines of riot police or prison officers – in the melee it was impossible to tell the difference – had fallen back to the level's entrance. Batons drawn, shields high, they were waiting for the next assault. They didn't have to wait long.

When the rioters spotted the released strutters on levels four and five, they surged forward. The line of POs and police had started to buckle when the roar of an engine made heads turn. A mobile water cannon careered into view. Compact and tank-like, it sent prisoners scattering. Two women fell under its wheels as they tried to flee. Then its two barrels swivelled, the vehicle trembled and water blasted into the rioters, knocking them down like skittles.

The guards and police advanced, batons swinging, catching many of the stunned and soaked prisoners before they could pick themselves up.

For a moment it looked as though the advantage had shifted to the POs, but then some of the rioters regrouped. While the water gushed left and right, enraged prisoners rushed the cannon. Momentarily unprotected, it was soon overwhelmed by screaming men and women. The barrels swung to and fro, but they hung on, jumping up and down on the turret, causing the whole vehicle to rock.

Then petrol bombs started to rain down, sending out flames as they smashed. The water cannon stuttered, swerved and jolted as the driver tried to free it, but, blinded by smoke, he only succeeded in crashing into the ground-floor level, scattering guards as it went. It shook as the rioters renewed their attack.

'This is a disaster,' muttered Ant.

Twenty metres below, the turret opened, and the cannon fired a single shot before many hands reached in and pulled out the unfortunate driver. Ant turned Mattie's head away.

Three men now fought to get into the cannon. The winner disappeared inside the smoking vehicle. Ant looked along the railings and saw three spectators transfixed by the battle.

She felt a tug on her lanyard. 'Now!' said Mattie. 'Dan and Gina! We can do it!'

Maybe they could. Maybe this was their last chance . . .

They had only taken a few steps before water burst out of one of the barrels. In a few seconds it had found its range. The three watching strutters on level four took the brunt of the blast; they were torn from the railings and thrown against a cell wall with astonishing force. Before they had time to react, Mattie was hit, then Ant. Stung by a wall of water, they crashed in a heap at the foot of cell 46. Mattie clung onto his sister, dazed but still conscious, as the funfair-like hosing of strutters continued.

They crawled out of range, then, bedraggled and bruised, climbed up a couple of levels to the sixth.

Ant hated being thwarted. 'We'll try again, Mattie. Soon as the cannon's stopped.' They were still recovering when Jimmy Noon appeared at Ant's shoulder. Eyes darting around, he spoke rapidly. 'You OK? The cannon won't get you here, but the cons have started climbing!'

Ant wiped her face. 'We need to let everyone out. Looks like we're going to need all the help we can get. If the screws can't defend us, we're going to have to do it ourselves. Eventually they'll send in troops, but it seems it's just us for now.'

'You're right. But we'll need weapons,' said Jimmy.

Ant nodded. 'Then we're going to have smash the place up a bit,' she said.

The three of them started running from cell to cell. Ant did the releasing, Jimmy the explaining. Soon the sounds of breaking glass and splintering wood could be heard from every 'bin. They were joined by the Raaths and Amos Shah, and it was he who noticed that a group of rioters had peeled away from the main pack.

'Watch them!' shouted Jimmy. They were running in an arc around the levels, then veering sharp left. 'Where are they heading?'

'There's the chapel,' said Ant. 'There's the toilets. And . . .' She swallowed hard. 'And the Holloway tunnel. I think the riot is about to get a whole lot bigger.'

37

The women of Holloway emerged into Spike with their governor walking on the end of a rope. With Jan Burridge a hostage, the Riot Squad had fallen back, unwilling to provoke the rioters further. There were just too many of them. Attacked head-on by the women and from the flank by the men, they were overwhelmed in minutes. They fired off some rubber bullets – one took out a man's eye – but when they lost their guns, it was all over. Burridge was pushed forward, a trophy prisoner.

Gripping the railing on level six, Ant spotted Tess Clarke. The woman she had last seen chained to her bunk now aimed a shotgun straight into Burridge's bloody face.

'Ant, there's two more levels up here.' Mattie was tugging his sister away from the railing. 'We need more on our side. Let's get everyone out.'

Ant tore herself away and followed him to the steps. They ran past strutters armed with splintered planks of wood, pieces of glass and broken tiles. Inside the cells the destruction continued.

From the steps, they stared down the levels. Black smoke billowed from the many small fires that were beginning to find each other; with no one putting them out, the flames were catching and taking hold. Great curtains of smoke hung in the roof. Spike had been hot before; now, as they looked around at the chaos, the whole place shimmered with heat haze.

Jimmy had been right. The rioters – Ant guessed two hundred, maybe more – had taken over the ground level and had started to climb to the first. Ant, Mattie, Amos, Jimmy and the Raaths led the way to level seven, their breathing becoming laboured. She was about to start opening cells there when they heard a buzzing noise. She pulled up short; everyone froze. As they watched, all ten cabins hummed, then the doors popped open.

Strutters poured out, relieved and terrified in equal measure. Each was quickly briefed about the need for weapons, and the smashing began again.

Cries from above. Level eight had also released its prisoners; they appeared at the railings above them. Jimmy Noon and others ran up to explain what was happening.

'How did that happen?' asked Mattie.

Ant looked up at the security cameras. 'Someone's watching,' she said. 'Who knows what their game is, but for the moment they're helping.'

'But if they're all open, Dan and Gina will be out!' cried Mattie.

'No, I think they're still shut. Look.' Ant pointed down at the rioters. 'They're still looking up at us. If the lower floors were open, they'd be looking at them.' She squeezed his hand. 'Maybe it's safer that way. They would have come out straight into the arms of that mob.'

Mattie swallowed but said nothing.

'Where's the fire brigade?' asked Jimmy. 'Where are the police? Army – anyone? How can it be like this? Prisoners versus prisoners!'

Jeffrey Blakely appeared on the stairs. 'Because this is how they want it, young man, don't you see? *This is being allowed to happen.*'

'Well, that's certainly how it feels,' said Ant.

Jimmy Noon looked at her. 'We need to escape then,' he said. 'If we can beat this lot, we should keep running. We need to get out of here.'

Ant absent-mindedly felt for the strap-key. And her heart stopped. It wasn't there. She plunged her hand deep into her pocket. Nothing. She only had one pocket it would fit into, but she tried all of them anyway. Nothing.

'Lost something?' said Jimmy.

Ant shook her head, but Mattie had understood in an instant. His eyes wide, he held up four fingers. He mouthed 'fourth level', and she knew he was right. The case must have fallen out when the water cannon blasted them against cell 46.

They looked at each other, horrified. Ever since Ant

had stolen Grey's strap-key, it had been the focus of all their escape plans. There was no point in breaking out if everyone knew where they were. Why go on the run if the strap was beaming their location to anyone with a tracking device? They needed it back.

She felt Mattie's hand in hers and knew they had to do this together. There wasn't time to protest; there wasn't time to find a 'safer' place for him – Ant doubted one even existed. So they pushed their way down the steps, past terrified families moving in the opposite direction. Those who noticed Ant and Mattie looked aghast.

'Wrong way, kid!' yelled one. 'They're coming this way – turn round!'

Between the sixth and the fifth they came face to face with one of Gina's 'lunch' friends. She was brandishing three rudimentary spears: splintered lengths of plywood, a broken tile tied to one, splintered glass to the others.

'Ant, it's bad down there,' she said. 'You want me to take Mattie?'

Ant ignored her, pushing past and pulling her brother closer. She heard the woman call after them, 'OK, take one of these!' Ant turned just in time to catch one of the spears. She nodded her thanks, then, holding it high above her head, forced her way down.

Level four was emptying. They both crouched like sprinters on the landing, Mattie tucked in behind Ant, the spear gripped in her hand. She took as deep a breath as her smoky lungs allowed. *Find the key, free Dan and Gina. That's all. We can do it.*

They scanned the floor, then shifted their gaze to the nearest fan, twenty metres away. Black smoke was drifting up from below then dispersing but Ant and Mattie weren't watching. They only had eyes for a silhouetted object that lay hidden under its base. If you were walking past you'd have missed it, but viewed from ground level there was no mistaking the outline of Grey's strap-key case.

They glanced at each other, then, with no time for caution, sprinted for the fan.

Mattie dived first. 'Got it!' he shouted.

He pulled his hand out, fingers wrapped tightly around the case. He checked its contents – the key was safe. It looked like nothing at all, but now, everything was possible again.

'*Kle!*' he said, and slapped it in Ant's hand. She shoved it as deep as her pocket would allow.

Mattie crawled over to the railings and briefly peered down. 'Looks like they're fighting on level one now. There's too many of them, Abi!'

She clasped his shoulder. 'OK. We'll be quick then,' she said. 'And invisible.'

Alone on the stairs, they ran down to level three. Cells 30 to 39 . . . They knew the cell layout by heart, knew everyone still locked inside; as they crawled to the corner of cell 30, Ant looked along towards the cabin they had lived in for the last two years. She gasped and grabbed her brother's shoulder: Gina and Dan were hammering on the window, trying to attract their attention. They were shouting too, but their words were lost, muffled by the cell walls and obliterated altogether by the fighting below. It took Ant and Mattie a second to realize what they meant, then they spun round together.

The rioters had climbed to level three. One had scrambled over the railings and was in the process of helping two more. Through the railings, Ant saw that one of the new arrivals was grinning. She recognized Treves in an instant, and her blood ran cold.

'Go!' yelled Ant. They ran past the staring faces of their distressed neighbours; the panic-stricken banging was all around but they kept on running.

They closed on cell 33. Framed in the window, Dan and Gina were waving frantically, imploring them to put some distance between them and their pursuers.

'Do it, Ant!' yelled Mattie. 'Swipe them out!'

Ant glanced round. Treves was now climbing over the railings. 'OK!' she said, and they headed for the cell door.

She checked Treves again. He had one hand pointing straight at her, the other cupped around his mouth. Above the din she heard him yell, 'She's here! The girl is *here*!'

A volley of well-aimed missiles fell from above – chunks of a cell wall by the look of them – and crashed into Treves.

As he stumbled, Ant swiped the pass through the entry pad of cell 33.

38

The red light stayed red.

'No!' she yelled. 'Open! Please God, open!' She tried again. Twice, three times more. No clicks, no buzz. The door remained locked. Ant stabbed the card through faster and faster, each time with the same result. The red light stayed red.

'Again!' cried Mattie. 'Try again!'

'It's dead,' said Ant. 'It finally stopped working.' She held it up to the window, her face grim.

'No!' wailed Mattie. 'It *must* work!'

Now Gina, face pressed up against the glass, was shouting. Her voice was indistinct but her meaning clear. 'Go on!' she was mouthing. 'You. Must. Go.' She pointed to the spirals.

Now Dan joined in. 'We'll be safe! Just run!'

Ant tore Mattie away. 'Maybe they're safer in there,' she said as they hit the steps. She knew he didn't believe her. She didn't believe herself.

They had reached the fourth level before they looked back. There was no sign of Treves now, but they could see cons swarming to the railings like sailors to rigging.

'We should join the rest of the crowd,' said Ant, breathing deeply.

'Then what?' said Mattie.

'Then we fight, Mattie. We have no choice!'

They joined a throng of strutters running up the spirals, screams and shouts echoing around them. On level seven Lena Durrow smiled quickly at Ant, then turned to reassure her children. The exodus continued. Level eight next.

With nothing above it save the prison's metal roof, its cameras and its maze of pipes, it looked like the end of the line. A few prisoners liked it on the eighth and referred to their cell as a 'ghetto penthouse', but most found it too high and too hot.

Now it was rammed with all the strutters in Spike – the only ones missing were those still stuck in their cells on levels one, two and three. A few stood in huddles, unsure of what to do next; others issued panicky instructions and waited for someone to listen. But now the Shahs were getting things organized. The railings were lined with spotters crying, 'Two here . . .' 'Three climbing round your side . . .' Lena was applying makeshift bandages and splints.

Then came the droppers. Piles of ammunition were being passed along human chains. Jeffrey Blakely and Neil Osbourne sorted out the missiles. Anything would do – just so long as it could knock a rioter off the levels. Smashed furniture, broken windows, stolen cutlery, shoes, mugs and mirrors, all rained down as fast as those on level eight could find them. Jimmy Noon's aim seemed to be truest, each throw accompanied by a volley of abuse aimed at the prisoner below.

The last cabin to be looted was cell 87. Ant, Mattie and Daisy were frantically kicking at a wardrobe. Eventually it collapsed under the combined assault and, armed with impromptu weapons, they ran to rejoin the battle.

Between cells 84 and 85 five rioters had, by sheer force of numbers, made it over the railings. They slashed and swiped, trying to keep the strutters at bay. Ant hurled a piece of wardrobe at the nearest man, hitting him in the stomach. As he doubled over, he was attacked with pieces of wood.

Now the strutters rushed the remaining rioters. As many left their posts to join in, a solitary figure climbed over the railing and into the gap between cells 86 and 87. Unseen, he produced a small gun. Until recently it had belonged to HMP London, part of the armoury of the water-cannon operator. Now it belonged to Day Treves. He checked the bullets and stepped out of the shadows. He took six paces towards the fight and shot Neil Osbourne in the head.

39

The gunshot stopped the fighting. Everyone turned. Some saw Osbourne's body slump to the floor, the top of his head blown away; others had to be told. There was a convulsion of shock and anger, but before anyone moved, Treves grabbed Daisy. Arm tightly around her neck, he placed the gun to her head. Her mother screamed, and had to be restrained. He stepped backwards, pulling a terrified Daisy with him.

'Well, well, I believe I have your attention!' he bellowed. 'Listen very carefully!' There was still fighting below, but on level eight everything had stopped. 'Trust me when I say I will do to this pretty little girl what I have just done to that ugly fat man. It really would be quite easy. Maybe I'll just do it anyway!' He pushed the barrel of the gun hard into Daisy's temple and she cried out.

'Do something, Abi!' said Mattie, his voice a mere whisper. He wasn't expecting a reply and he didn't get one. Ant was scouring the floor for a weapon – something, anything to help Daisy.

Treves, his face stuck in a rictus grin, was enjoying himself. 'I could shoot her. I could shoot anyone really.' He pointed the gun at random. Some ducked, a few screamed. 'But I only want to shoot one person. I think you know her. Shaved head. Goose tattoos. Bad attitude.' Involuntarily, those around Ant turned to look at her. Treves followed their gaze. 'And there she is! The girl who started this whole party! You do all know that she *invaded* happy Holloway and then peaceful Pentonville? Upset a lot of people, you know.' As he spoke, more puzzled faces turned towards Ant.

'You started this?' said one strutter.

'Don't be so pathetic,' spat Mattie.

The man backed off, but the glances continued.

'I'll trade this girl' – Treves shook Daisy hard – 'for the goose girl. In fact, if we can take her, we'll all go away. And pretend none of this' – he indicated all the chaos around him and laughed – 'ever happened. Seriously. All this will stop. We just need *her*,' and he pointed to Ant. 'You can carry on fighting if you want. But just below, there's a small army equipped with the finest weapons these prisons can offer. And trust me, they would *love* a piece of the action up here.'

Ant knew that many strutters would trade if they had to. She hadn't exactly gone out of her way to make friends in Spike – who would stand up for her now? If it was a choice between saving themselves and handing her over, Ant didn't fancy her chances. She felt Mattie's grip tighten.

'You're not going anywhere,' he said.

'I might have to,' she muttered.

From below there was a shout of 'Coming up!' and Treves dragged Daisy over to the railings. His eyes dipped over the side.

'Aha! A friend at last.' He pointed the gun at the spotters and they backed away as a man hauled himself over the railing. Campbell, his face covered with blood and soot, jumped to the ground. Sporting a blood-stained bandana with a camera still stuck in its folds, he went to stand beside Day Treves.

Using his gun hand, Treves pointed through the crowd to Ant. 'Either you come here now,' he said, 'or your friend here dies in five seconds. One . . .'

There was never any doubt in Ant's mind: she would have to go. It was Mattie who was the issue.

'Two . . .'

He solved it for her. 'We are together. We are stuck like glue, remember?'

'They just want me, Mattie . . .'

'Three . . .'

'Shut up, Abi, and walk.'

So hand in hand, Ant and Mattie headed through the crowd of strutters. Amos gave them a funny little salute as they passed.

'And I never even got to four,' said Treves. 'Shame. I was quite looking forward to wasting this one.' He kept his grip on Daisy as tight as ever.

Ant stopped. 'Let her go!' she shouted, her voice louder than she was expecting.

Campbell was twitching, edgy, excited. Eyes still fixed on Ant, he prised Treves's hands off Daisy. She ran over to her mother and they embraced, sobbing. Campbell then took Treves's gun, aimed it straight at Ant and flicked it upwards, beckoning her forward.

Ant and Mattie came to stand in front of him and Treves. A shout from the steps, and three women staggered through. Ant swore viciously as Tess Clarke and Grace Chang – both armed with knives – came over.

'Holloway's finest,' she muttered.

Mattie jumped up, his arms clinging round Ant's neck, his legs round her waist.

'Lose the boy,' called Chang.

Ant hadn't seen the woman with the crazy hair before, but she seemed to be in charge. *Gang leader*, she thought. *I might as well go for it.*

'Hi,' she said. 'This is my brother. This is Mattie. But then, Tess Clarke, you know all about him because he's the boy you made up all that stuff about for the *Correction* film.' Clarke shifted her weight awkwardly but still glared at Ant. Ant turned to Chang. 'I was just standing up for family honour. I'm sure you understand. And when I was in the Village, I was looking for a scumbag called Pellow, who told lies like Clarke did. Instead, I found you two—'

'Family honour?' laughed Campbell. 'You're in Spike! You're a *strutter*! We've seen your strap, remember? Your family has no honour. You're leeches. You're scum.'

The women cons nodded.

Mattie put his mouth to Ant's ear. 'Look at the cameras.'

Ant flicked her eyes to the ceiling. The security cameras had moved. They were all pointing at her.

'Lose the boy,' said Chang again. 'Last time.'

Ant looked down. Shook her head.

'At home,' the woman went on, 'we have a saying. *Hum kah chan*. It means "death to your family". It is rarely invoked these days. We try to avoid it if we can. Many wars have started this way. But sometimes it is necessary . . .' She stepped forward, knife raised; Campbell's gun still pointed at Ant's head.

Mattie whispered again. 'There are lights coming on in the pipes,' he said.

Another glance at the ceiling. Sure enough, a large triangle of blue and orange lights was flashing. It was about a metre long, and as Ant watched, the lights seemed to flash faster. It wasn't the only triangle either – Ant could count three other sets, their coloured lights blinking.

'Skyrocket?' whispered Mattie.

And suddenly Ant understood. Mattie was right. This is what Brian had told her about, so many conversations ago. The prison's final line of defence.

How long before it goes bang?

40

Head pounding, heart hammering in her ribcage, Ant looked at her tormentors. Treves, Clarke and Chang had surrounded them, knives at the ready. Campbell faced the crowd, gun poised, daring anyone to challenge him. With Mattie clasped in her arms, Ant started to turn, trying to keep her eyes on the knives. She needed to act fast.

'OK!' she shouted. 'You were right! I'll lose the boy!' She eased Mattie to the floor, whispered swift instructions in his ear, and he ran towards the crowd. None of the cons noticed or cared; it was Ant they wanted.

'You should have stayed in Spike,' said Chang.

'You should have minded your own business,' said Campbell.

'You should never have broken into our room,' added Clarke, and she lunged forward, slashing at Ant.

The blade cut through her shirt, slicing a three-centimetre gash in her stomach. She pressed her hand hard against the wound, felt the blood seep through her fingers. If this was how they wanted to play it, she wouldn't last long.

Then the shouting began. From all over level eight voices were raised: support for Ant, abuse for the cons. Then one voice, higher and clearer than the others. It was Mattie. And only one other person understood him,

'*De triyang limyè, de flache!*'

Mattie, you're a genius. Two triangles of light were solid, two flashing. Not long. Maybe seconds.

As her attackers jabbed at her, Ant feinted and dodged. But when she avoided one attack, another found her. Most of the cuts weren't deep, but Ant reckoned they were just warming up. They certainly seemed to be enjoying themselves.

Mattie's voice again, high and shrill: '*Twa triyang limyè!*'

Three triangles lit. When all four were on, would they fire immediately? Who was the operator? Why had they waited this long anyway?

'*Kat! Kat! Kat!* Now, now, now!'

As Ant spun round again, her eyes flashed to the roof. Four lit triangles; four primed skyrockets.

Time to go.

Tess Clarke lunged forward once more. Ant leaned left, then grabbed her knife arm in both hands, twisted and pushed up hard. Clarke howled as her shoulder dislocated, and dropped the knife. Ant had picked it up before any of the others could react. She wanted to stay and fight but knew she had to run.

She heard a whine start in the pipes above her – loud enough for the others to glance up – and that was her cue. Ducking behind Treves and Chang, she headed for the crowd. Campbell, tracking her, was lining up his shot when the ceiling exploded.

Night coach between Bristol and Bath

Only one passenger on the night coach was awake, his face lit by a small screen. Max's new phone was better than his old one; the images were sharper and the wifi pickup was instant. He had been staring in horror at the live stream from Spike; the picture was shaky, the camera lurching all over the place, but he had spotted Ant and Mattie as soon as they stepped out of the crowd. Max had cried out when Ant was attacked, then again as he watched her run.

The woman in the next seat woke up and peered blearily at him, then at his screen.

'Can't you watch something else?' she said, and shut her eyes again. 'Something less scary maybe . . .'

By the time he looked back, the screen was blank, the picture lost. Frantically he tried some news sites, but they had lost the signal too. He killed the screen and sat staring through the window. The woman sat up and sighed heavily.

'Well, that's me awake,' she said.

'Sorry,' muttered Max, and she looked at his reflection in the glass.

'You OK?'

'Fine.'

'You said fine like my kids say fine. Usually means anything *but* fine.'

'I said I was sorry . . .'

The woman smiled. 'Don't worry about it. Never sleep much on coaches anyway. Was it a film?'

'Was what a film?'

'The thing that scared you.'

'No, it was . . . the news.'

'Oh, that. Was it bad?'

A pause, then Max said, 'Just some riot. Looked bad, that's all. Probably nothing.' He carried on staring at the darkness outside, his body language suggesting he hoped she'd fall asleep again soon.

'What was it about?' the woman persisted.

Max shrugged. 'What are they ever about?'

She thought for a moment. 'Well. Usually some people think that something bad has happened. So they go on a march and wave banners.'

'No, it wasn't really like that.'

'Do you know anyone . . . ?'

'No,' said Max, more loudly than he had intended. 'I don't know anyone involved.'

She got the message. After a few seconds she closed her eyes again.

41

'Gas! Gas! Gas!' screamed Ant. She flew across the level as first glass and metal fragments, then great clouds of tear gas, were blasted from the roof. She had a few seconds' advantage at most. She ignored the pain from her wound. She didn't look up. She didn't look back. Ant leaped through crowds of bewildered strutters, all staring at the rapidly expanding shroud of gas.

'Inside!' she shouted as she passed, but no one was moving. She took a sharp left past the middle cells and glanced over her shoulder. The spot where she had been standing was enveloped in a thick, white, churning pall of gas. Expanding rapidly but forced into the narrow space between level eight and the ceiling, it was moving fast. Ahead she saw Mattie in the doorway of cell 87, his eyes flicking between her and the cloud.

'Run, Abi, run!' he yelled.

Suddenly everyone was running for the smashed-up cells, criss-crossing in front of her, slowing her down. She hurdled a man who had fallen, and felt a rush of blood from her wound. A column of gas tumbled between the middle cells, coming straight for her. Ant had no option. She took a deep breath, closed her eyes and ran faster. A few steps, Mattie's call of, 'Abi, here!' and she was through.

She vaulted into the cell and collapsed on the floor as Mattie and Jimmy Noon slammed the door shut.

'Barricade!' she shouted. 'No one gets in now! No one!' She turned to see who else Mattie had persuaded to take cover – it wasn't many. Daisy was there, Jeffrey Blakely, Amos Shah and the three Durrows, Lena, Tilly and Sam.

'No one else would come . . .' began Mattie.

'Doesn't matter now,' Ant said, embracing him. 'Nice work anyway.'

'That's a bad cut, Ant.' Jimmy was staring at the blood seeping through her shirt.

Lena Durrow passed over a strip of bed sheet. 'We have a few left . . .' she said, and Jimmy folded it in four. Ant peeled her shirt away from the wound.

'I should clean it—' began Jimmy.

'Just stop the bleeding!' snapped Ant. He nodded and gently placed the makeshift gauze on her stomach. 'Push harder,' she said. 'I'll tell you if it's too much.' He pressed until she winced, then eased off. 'Fine.' Ant replaced his hand with hers and breathed deeply. 'And thanks.' He nodded, wiping Ant's blood off his hands onto his trousers.

Daisy came next. 'Thanks, Ant,' she whispered in her ear. 'Sorry he got me like that . . .'

Ant shook her head. 'Daisy, he'd have killed you,' she said. 'Then he'd have killed someone else.' She shrugged. 'He'd have seen me sooner or later.' She changed the subject. 'We need the cell to be as secure as possible. Whatever is left in here – which isn't much – we need against the door.'

'Are the walls damaged?' wondered Jimmy. 'We don't want that stuff to get in.' Outside, the gas cloud had enveloped the cell; visibility was reduced to just a few metres.

Everyone inspected the patch of cell 87 that was nearest to them, looking for any crack or hole. Cries of, 'OK here!' 'All fine,' and 'Think we're OK,' eased the tension.

'Everyone look out,' Jimmy ordered. 'We need to know if anyone is coming.'

'Can we let in friends?' The tiny voice belonged to Sam Durrow, and Lena hugged him closer.

'We'd be letting the gas in—'

'What does the gas do?' interrupted Tilly.

'It makes you cough and cry. A lot,' said Lena.

'It makes you blind, makes you vomit,' interrupted Ant. 'We need to keep the door shut.'

'Too harsh,' whispered Mattie.

'They need to know . . .'

'Too harsh,' he repeated.

Ant turned and eased herself down onto the floor,

kneeling next to the Durrows. 'We need to stay well,' she said. 'If we open the door, we'll get sick. Very sick. OK?' Sam and Tilly nodded, their eyes wide.

'You think the rioters will still come for us?' asked Daisy.

'If the gas is everywhere,' said Jimmy, 'maybe we'll be OK for a while . . .'

'Did you know about the gas, Ant?' asked Lena, arms tightly wrapped around her children.

Ant considered her answer. 'Well, Brian MacMillan told me that Spike had a final line of defence against "the mob", as he called it.'

'*Mob* is exactly right,' muttered Blakely.

Ant ignored him. 'And he mentioned "skyrockets", and I think – if I thought about it at all – I assumed they'd be fired from the ground. Like that useless water cannon they tried. He said something about it being a "show-stopper", so my guess is the whole of Spike is gassed up.'

'That's good, isn't it?' said Daisy, linking arms with her.

'It's better than being killed by Villagers and Ladies high on whatever they've stolen, yeah,' said Ant. 'But it was Mattie who saw the lights in the ceiling. He said "skyrocket". Suddenly it made sense.'

'Why didn't they use it sooner?' growled Blakely. 'How many had to die before they decided to take pity on us?' There were murmurs of agreement.

'Who knows?' said Lena. 'Maybe poor Neil was the last straw . . .' Her words tailed away and they worked in silence as they remembered seeing Osbourne being executed. Most of them had jumped over his body to get to the cell.

'Well, everyone will know what's happened,' said Jimmy eventually. 'Loads of cons had phones. I saw one stuck in a headband. If they were streaming pictures, then the whole world knows about the riot. And if that Scottish guy's phone was working, they'll have seen the attack on Ant. And the gas.'

'Good,' said Daisy. 'Maybe they'll be on our side for once.'

'Are you kidding?' said Amos. 'They wouldn't care if we all burned to death. If anything, they'd have been on the side of the fire.'

When the cell had been stripped for the barricade, the door still looked far from secure. Jimmy took half a space back and pulled a face. Four bent table legs, some beaten-up drawers and two mattresses were rammed against the door; it wasn't enough.

'I'm staying here in case,' he said, finding a space where he could lean against the door. 'We'll need some more muscle if it comes to a contest.' He slid down till he hit the floor, then rearranged the drawers and table legs behind him.

Daisy shouted, 'There's someone coming! Straight ahead!'

Everyone but the Durrows and Jimmy ran to the main window. Through the billowing clouds of gas, four figures were staggering towards cell 87.

42

One of the approaching men collapsed on the floor; the other three carried on, not bothering to help him up.

'More on the door now!' shouted Jimmy. Amos joined him, throwing himself against the barricade as though they were already under siege.

Outside, the three floundered through the gas like zombies through fog, rags tied around their mouths and noses. They tottered closer, makeshift masks slipping. Cell 87 filled with cries of alarm and revulsion. Daisy stifled a scream as three faces pressed up against the glass, swollen red eyes trying to focus. Streams of mucus flowed from their noses, smearing across the window as they moved. One of them mouthed some words, a long stream of phlegm falling from his mouth.

'What's happening?' called Jimmy.

'They want to be let in,' said Daisy quietly. 'They're saying, "Help us".'

'Look away,' said Ant. 'It'll pass. It won't kill them.'

There were a few feeble bangs on the door.

'Loads more coming now!' said Amos. Through the window they could see scores of figures, some on their knees, others lurching and vomiting.

'How long do the effects last?' asked Lena, suddenly nervous again. 'Anyone know?'

'It's a riot-control weapon,' said Jimmy. 'Maybe twenty minutes?'

'Is that all?' wondered Amos.

A brief silence, then from somewhere in Spike – it was impossible to tell where – the sound of shouting. Not the yells of rioting prisoners, but the disciplined, staccato orders of a military operation.

'There's your answer, Amos,' said Blakely. 'The riot's over. We should lie low. This could get nasty.'

On level eight the prisoners lay waiting for rescue and medical help. In cell 87 Amos was at one window, Daisy at the other, with Ant and Mattie at her feet.

'They're here!' cried Daisy and Amos at the same time. Everyone crowded round the windows. From both sides, gas-masked soldiers appeared, medics following close behind. One by one the sick were treated as the army searched for rioters. A masked face suddenly appeared at Daisy's window; she recoiled as the soldier counted the faces staring back at him.

'Show him straps!' said Ant. 'Just so he knows!'

Shirts were raised; then the soldier nodded and headed back into the haze. The sick had been taken away on stretchers; now fire crew, army, police and POs were all rushing to finish the evacuation.

'They're moving fast,' said Ant. 'I reckon that's smoke, not gas. The place must still be burning.'

Jimmy tugged at her arm. 'Watch that PO by cell eighty-four – the one talking to the army guys.'

They stared through the glass at an animated conversation between three people, two in combat fatigues, one in prison riot gear. Suddenly the PO took off his gas mask, wiped his face with his sleeve, said a few more words, then replaced it.

'He's done that three times now,' said Jimmy. 'The air might still be bad, but it's not so bad you can't survive without a mask for a short time.'

'Want to test your theory?'

Without a word, Jimmy began removing the barricade from the cell door. Amos and Daisy joined in and Jimmy explained to the others what he was doing. When the door was clear, Daisy checked the windows.

'Quickly,' she said. 'Try now.'

Everyone involuntarily held their breath. Jimmy had the door open and closed in under a second. Daisy gave a commentary for those who weren't at the window.

'He's opened his eyes. He's breathing a bit. Blinking a lot. Bigger breaths . . .'

The door quickly opened and closed again. Jimmy's eyes were watering but he smiled, excited. 'We can breathe out there. The gas is clearing all the time. But the smoke smells bad.'

'Why are you telling us this?' said Blakely. 'We're waiting till they come for us. Aren't we?'

Jimmy turned to Ant. 'Tell them, Ant,' he said. 'Tell them now.'

'Tell them what?' she asked.

'About the key.'

Ant's eyes were wide. She was also furious. 'You *knew* . . . ?'

He nodded. 'I guessed. Tell them.'

She looked at Mattie.

'Go for it,' he said.

43

Ant reached deep into her pocket. 'I have a strap-key,' she said, opening the case and holding it in front of them. There were cries of astonishment, but she continued, knowing she didn't have long. 'Which means I can take off your strap. If we can get out of Spike, we *could* disappear. There was no point in telling anyone before, because what's the point of losing your strap if you can't escape? And what's the point of escaping if your strap gives you away? It is just possible that we could make a run for it. Most of us have family we'll be leaving behind but this is our best chance. It's our *only* chance. But you have to decide now.'

Furious calculations registered in the faces in front of her.

'I'm in!' whispered Daisy.

'Me too,' said Amos, looking around.

It was clear that Lena was struggling.

Ant broke the silence. 'Sorry, Lena. It's now or never.'

'What are we deciding, Mum?' asked Tilly.

'You can take their straps off?' asked Lena, tears running down her face. Ant handed her the key. She lifted her daughter's T-shirt and, with trembling hands, tried to slot the key into the strap across Tilly's spine.

Ant stepped forward. 'We should wait in case—'

'Take it off,' said Lena, gripping her arm. 'I need to see this. You do it. Please.'

Ant knelt down, placed the key under the strap's arched bridge and twisted. There was a double click, the two clamps retracted and Tilly Durrow's strap fell to the floor. Tilly and Lena burst into tears.

'Troops running!' called Jimmy, on window duty. 'Last casualties being cleared, by the look of it.'

'In which case,' said Ant, 'this is it. Take Tilly's strap, Lena. I don't suppose anyone is monitoring us, but just in case, keep it with you for now.'

'I want my strap off,' said Sam, staring at his sister.

'I'll take them all off,' said Ant. 'I promise. But we need to get out first.'

'Too late!' cried Jimmy, a fraction of a second before the cell door was kicked open. Three gas-masked, camouflaged soldiers burst in, hand guns raised. Screams and yells filled the room. One of the soldiers slammed the door shut again.

'We're strutters!' shouted Jimmy, moving fast as everyone ducked, cowering.

'There are rioters everywhere!' shouted one soldier; his voice was muffled but almost panicky. He and his colleagues scoured the cell. 'We need to evacuate, but strutters only. Let's go!' He pointed his gun at Amos, who stood up slowly.

'But we've got no masks!' he said.

The man lifted his gas mask. 'It's a thirty-second run to the bridge. You cross it and you're in the guards' quarters. The air is normal there. There isn't time to wait for masks. Hold your breath, if you can. When we start running, we don't stop. We run together. If we see rioters, they'll be dealt with.' He pulled on his mask again and his colleague opened the door.

Ant stood with Mattie and the Durrows. 'We'll run together,' she said to Lena. 'Mattie, stay close. Close your eyes,' she told Tilly and Sam, 'and see how long you can hold your breath! It's not far.'

The two children screwed their eyes shut and inhaled deeply. Ant felt for the gauze on her stomach and left a protective hand there as she ran out.

Through narrowed eyes she saw Amos already jogging past cell 85. Within a few steps, she felt her chest tighten and her eyes start to water. She glanced up at the roof; clouds of rolling, churning black smoke were edging lower.

The soldiers were right, they didn't have long.

44

No one spoke. It seemed a waste of air. The level was clear. Everyone had been taken away. *We're the last ones here*, thought Ant.

The high gates that marked the ends of the bridge were open. They ran into the POs' corridor. It stretched for maybe fifty metres, numbered rooms on either side. Cold air from somewhere! Cold, uncontaminated air, and Ant, taking a lungful, began to cough. More soldiers, more shouting. 'Keep going! Straight ahead!' Behind them they heard doors slamming shut; ahead, raised voices. They ran through a fire door into a stairwell, the source of the voices and the cold air.

Like passengers waiting to board a plane, long lines of strutters were being herded down the stairs. Many were suffering from the effects of smoke or gas, others from wounds, but there was no let-up in the shouted instructions.

'Down the stairs! Get in the coach! Take the first seat!'

Ahead of her Ant heard a man shout, 'What's down there? Where are we going?'

'Prison transport! They're putting us in coaches!' came the reply.

Mattie was jumping up and down, straining for a decent view of the descending crowd. 'Gina! Dan!' he shouted, but his voice was lost in the hubbub.

Ant's turn. 'Who's out from one, two and three?' she yelled. 'Anyone from levels one, two and three?'

'I'm looking for the Toselands from cell twelve,' someone shouted further down the stairs.

'And the Hapgoods? Are they here?' cried a tearful voice. There was a murmuring and shaking of heads. No one, it seemed, had seen anyone.

'Maybe they're evacuating the first three floors somewhere else,' said Ant.

Mattie looked at her blankly. 'Yeah, maybe.'

A breeze had started blowing up the stairs. After the smoke- and fume-filled oven that Spike had become, it made Ant feel light-headed, almost dizzy.

Mattie had noticed too. 'That smells sweet,' he said. 'That's my first fresh air for two years.'

Pushing past some of the injured, they caught up with Daisy. Jimmy and Lena were just ahead, carrying Sam and Tilly. Tilly waved and Mattie waved back. All around them there was a sense of elation at having escaped the riot, fear for those unaccounted for, and fury at what they had been put through.

'I can't see Mum anywhere!' said Daisy, fear pushing her voice higher.

'Some coaches have already gone!' came a voice, and her face relaxed a little.

'Well, maybe she's in one of those,' she said. 'Jimmy can't find his mum, and Amos is searching for his dad. Everyone's looking for someone, I suppose.' Daisy's hands were shaking and Ant took them in hers.

At the bottom of the stairs Ant recognized a PO waiting to lock the doors behind them. It was Denholm, the sweating officer she had shouted at during jug up yesterday. He looked wrecked, beaten and very twitchy. Ant thought she'd risk it. 'We the last?' she said casually.

The guard shrugged. 'Who knows?' he said, his voice hoarse.

'What happened on one, two and three?'

He shrugged again and said nothing. The queue was moving forward. Ant and Mattie hesitated, then headed away from the stairwell. They'd caught up with the others when they were aware of heavy footsteps behind them. It was Denholm, his head bleeding profusely.

'Some got out. I know that,' he said, eyes fixed on the middle distance.

Ant offered him what was left of her gauze. He looked taken aback, then took the dressing.

'So some didn't?' said Mattie. He nodded. Mattie held out his bottle. 'Would you like some water?'

The guard gulped down a few mouthfuls before handing it back. 'They're saying you killed MacMillan,' he said, staring at Ant.

'You mean Grey says I killed him,' she said. 'And he's lying. Treves killed him. Brian was trying to save me.'

Denholm's eyes flicked between Ant and Mattie. 'Thanks for the water,' he said, 'and the dressing.' They watched him head back into the stairwell, locking the doors behind him.

Ant and Mattie climbed into the coach. It wasn't a high-security transporter – there were no restraints on the seats; it was used to move HMP London's employees between prisons. There was room for forty passengers, and Ant and Mattie found two spaces in front of Jimmy. Four police officers took up positions along the aisle.

Ant sat there glumly as the coach picked up speed. There was an unshiftable knot in her stomach, eating away at her. It was grief, terror and remorse all in one.

What a catastrophic day. What a disaster. And my fault. And Dan and Gina? Surely they got out . . . But so many dead . . . Who knows how many . . . ? MacMillan certainly, Osbourne certainly. And all those bodies . . .

She became aware that Jimmy was trying to attract her attention. 'Ant, this is it!' he said.

'This is what?' Ant turned to face him – his expression was animated.

Jimmy had leaned forward as far as he could and spoke in an urgent whisper. 'What you said inside! If we don't try to get out now, we'll be inside for years. We need to find a way to get off the coach. *We're outside, Ant – look*!'

Through the glass, they saw a supermarket, a pub, estate agents, coffee shops, beggars, drunks and shoppers. Ordinary life. An almost-forgotten life.

'I thought we could have got out of Spike in all that chaos,' she said. She indicated the police. 'It's less chaotic now.'

'So we need to create some chaos,' said Jimmy.

Ant twisted in her seat as far as her wound and her strap allowed. 'Jimmy Noon, you're smiling,' she said. 'You must have an idea.'

He nodded.

'It had better be good.'

'It's the best,' said Jimmy. 'And actually, it's yours.'

45

Bug safe house, Bath

Max was given the top room. It was small, dark and sparsely decorated. It was also exactly what he had been hoping for. Max felt hidden. The bedding was musty and the carpet worn, but he didn't care. After leaving university and watching what was happening in London, all he wanted was a hole to bury himself in. Not for long – he knew there was work to be done – but for now this suited him fine.

The street was noisy; the middle-aged couple who were his hosts were noisy too – radios seemed to blast from every room – but Max was reassured. Life was carrying on around him. Life was carrying on *without* him. He could hear creaking floorboards, conversations and ringing phones but knew he could ignore it all. Only the doorbell had made him jump, but it was nothing. He watched a supermarket delivery van drive away, then lay back on his bed, clutching his rucksack. Inside was his new phone, a hundred and twenty pounds and a change of clothes. It was everything he had.

Max had taken the memorized route from the coach station to the safe house. He had knocked once and the door swung open to reveal a smiling woman in jeans and dusty black shirt.

'Top of the house,' she said quietly as the door closed behind him.

That had been a few hours ago. Since then, an endless supply of tea and cake had been deposited outside his door. He had eaten what he could, but the truth was, he had lost his appetite. He removed his new phone from the rucksack and stared at the screen. Sara had said it was 'cold', so he assumed that all data he sent or received would be encrypted. Desperate for information but terrified of what he would find, he stalled. His fingers hovered above the keys. He started to type in the site address, only to stop and delete it. For a moment he even considered asking the woman downstairs to find out for him.

'Don't be ridiculous,' he said to the room. 'Don't be an idiot, Max. Just . . . Just do it.' His throat was bone dry and he gulped down some water. He took a deep breath, then typed in the address of his dark-web contact site. This time he hit 'enter'. Deeper and deeper he went, answering the familiar questions – until finally he keyed in his sixteen-digit code. He hit 'enter' and waited for the pages to load, his hands trembling slightly.

'Please let them be alive,' he whispered.

Prison coach, Archway, North London

The shouting began on the back row. It was a woman who started it.

'Cons!' she yelled. 'We've got cons on board!' Heads turned; other voices exclaimed in alarm. The woman then launched herself at a couple sitting in front of her who were wearing hoodies; soon fists were flying. All three fell onto the floor before the first policeman reached them.

'They don't have straps!' shouted a man on the back row.

'Cons trying to escape!' shouted another.

Strutters stood up to see what was happening, pushing their way into the aisle. The other policemen were now caught up in the crowd; one ordered the driver to pull over immediately.

There was no mistaking the fury in the coach. Ant, Mattie and Jimmy were sitting quietly, but around them people were itching for a fight.

'The police need to get this under control soon or there'll be a lynching,' muttered Jimmy.

'I'll go to the front with Daisy,' said Ant. 'Do some talking.'

'I'll take Blakely.'

They stumbled as the coach swerved, changing lanes.

Ant grabbed a woman sitting nearby. 'This is an escape. Tell everyone.'

Horns blasted, cars braked and swerved around them, but on the coach all eyes were on the fight.

The two suspected cons weren't going quietly, but six strutters now pinned them against the back window, their faces forced against the glass. The police had now reached the melee; one had raised a sidearm.

'Stand down! Stand down! Let them go! Move away!'

But the woman who had led the attack now hauled her captives' shirts up as high as she could. Two pale, bruised but strap-free backs produced howls of anger and the crowd surged forward, shouting, 'Murderers!'

The coach came to a sudden stop. Bracing themselves, the police kept their balance while around them everyone staggered. Two officers grabbed the pair of 'cons', then frog-marched them down the aisle; another walked in front, clearing a path, the fourth walking backwards behind them, gun raised, aiming at the outraged passengers.

Ant watched as the prisoners were pushed past her. She made eye contact with the first, nodding her head slightly as he was bundled away.

The doors hissed open as the police escort car pulled up in front, lights flashing, siren wailing. The prisoners, now in handcuffs, were pushed out of the coach. They stumbled and fell onto the pavement. Immediately they were surrounded by police.

Ant leaped to her feet. 'Now!' she said.

From the back of the coach, Mattie shouted, 'Catch!'

He threw two lengths of metal, the first caught by Ant, the second by Jimmy. They sprinted to the front and jabbed them hard into the back of the driver.

'Stay silent,' said Jimmy, leaning in close. 'Get off the coach. You've got two seconds.'

The man started, half turned, then froze.

'One second,' said Ant, pushing the still-warm strap harder into the folds of flesh. He didn't need telling twice; he leaped off the coach.

'Blakely, you're up!' Jimmy called.

The driver's seat was instantly occupied, and Blakely punched the button that operated the doors. Outside, the police were still bundling their newly acquired prisoners into the car, but they all turned as they heard the hiss of compressed air. The nearest officer was just metres from the coach, and as he turned, he levelled his gun at Blakely.

46

The coach started forward. As Blakely found the controls, he steered it straight into the police car. The officers leaped clear, their vehicle propelled into a lamp post. The bonnet buckled, the windscreen smashed, and as the coach pulled into traffic, it caught the police car again. There was a screech of tearing metal as the car was spun through 180 degrees, one of its wings spinning across the road.

'Get down! Everybody down!' yelled Jimmy as he ran along the aisle. Some, too stunned to move, were pulled to the floor. Ant found Sam and Tilly Durrow under one of the seats, Lena lying flat next to them. The first bullets smashed the rear window, showering glass over the back six rows. There were screams followed by more gunfire, louder this time. With the window shattered, the *crack-crack-crack* from the police guns sounded closer.

The Durrows looked petrified. 'What's happening, Ant?' asked Lena, struggling to keep her voice steady.

Mattie scuttled along the aisle and handed Ant the strap-key. He was grinning. It was the biggest smile any of them had seen for days. 'Worked a treat,' he said.

Ant ruffled his hair. 'Sure did. We're going to get off this coach, Lena. Soon as Lord Whiny up front can find somewhere to pull off the road. Somewhere safe.'

'Safe?' Lena sounded incredulous.

'OK,' said Ant, 'maybe not safe. This coach is too big. And the tech in the straps pinpoints exactly where we are. As soon as we've put enough distance between us and those coppers, we'll park up and I'll unstrap everyone. Hopefully most of the police are tied up with the riot. Might give us a few minutes. But that's it. We leave the straps on the coach, maybe hide them somewhere if there's time.'

'Then what?'

Ant shrugged. 'Haven't worked that bit out yet. But we'll be *free strutters*, Lena! The first ever!'

Lena smiled but still looked sad. 'Then we just have to *stay* free.'

Ant nodded. 'That's about it, yes. But first we need to get these straps off. Might as well start here . . . You first, Lena.'

There was a flash of panic in Lena's eyes; then she sat

up and lifted her top. Ant dug the key into the centre of the strap and twisted. Lena bit back a cry as the clamps sprang back, the handle dropping to the floor. Her hands rubbed the place where the strap had been. 'Thank you.'

'Didn't you use to be a nurse?' said Ant.

'Yes. Seems ages ago now . . . but yes.'

'If you could help with some of these strap sores . . .'

'Of course. I've only got a few dressings left, but I'll follow you round till they run out,' she said.

'Thanks,' said Ant. 'OK, Sam, you're next.'

The coach braked, turned, then accelerated. The gunfire had stopped, the screaming replaced by volleys of questions and comments.

'Where are we going?'

'Who were those cons?'

'Looked like the Pearsons from forty-one, but they had no straps . . .'

'It *was* the Pearsons . . .'

Ant shouted, 'Jimmy, tell everyone what's happening! I've started already!'

Jimmy Noon crouched at the front of the coach, facing the strutters. Through the shattered back window he saw that they were climbing past a hospital and a football stadium; beyond them was the burning prison.

'OK, listen up! We haven't much time. Who knows how long it'll take for the cops to get a fix on us and send a helicopter? We're pulling off the road ASAP. Ant has a strap-key – that's how we got the Pearsons' straps off – and she'll take off every strap before we stop. We leave the straps here and lose the Spike shirts. We disappear. If anyone doesn't want their strap off, you can just wait for the screws to come and get you. Take you back inside. Though inside where is anyone's guess.'

'What's the deal with the Pearsons?' came a shout from under a seat near the front.

'They didn't want to escape,' said Jimmy. 'I persuaded them to help everyone else. They can say they were threatened, but I saw them run off when the shooting started.'

There was a sudden burst of car horns and the transporter swerved left. Blakely laughed. 'Everyone's getting out of our way! We're heading for Hampstead Heath. Possible exit point in two minutes, ladies and gents. Hope you're enjoying the ride!'

In the distance they heard a wail of sirens. Through the smashed back window it was difficult to judge numbers, but it was enough to produce a wave of nervous glances.

Ant had moved on from the Durrows. She had unfastened four more straps, hurling them aside, cursing each one as it bounced on the floor.

'Be ready!' she shouted. 'We've got no time!' She was getting quicker at it, but it was a delicate operation. In a few cases a strutter's skin came away with the strap and Lena had to step in.

Ant was working anti-clockwise around the coach. As the strutters watched her work, and the shifting, rolling collection of straps got bigger, the questioning and shouting died away. Everyone waited for their turn, desperate to lose the cursed strap, but scared too.

Ant had stopped looking at faces. She saw spines and she saw straps.

Insert, twist, release.

Insert, twist, release.

Then she hit trouble.

47

As soon as she saw them, Ant realized the straps were different. An elderly couple were kneeling on the floor holding onto a seat with one hand, holding up their shirts with the other. The straps were at the base of the spine, but the locking device was different. Instead of being in the middle of the handle, the holes had shifted to the left. Ant had never seen one like this. Two years in Spike, hundreds of straps, all the same.

Her hand hovered above the woman's strap; then she tentatively inserted the key. The pins went into the handle, but when she tried to twist, nothing moved. She tried again, twisting harder.

'Get on with it then,' snapped the woman.

Mattie appeared at Ant's shoulder. 'Different strap,' he said.

Now the woman swivelled round and glared at Mattie, then Ant. 'What do you mean, different strap?'

Ant shrugged. 'It doesn't fit. Sorry. Haven't seen it before. And your friend has one too – look.' She inserted the key into the old man's strap and twisted. Nothing happened.

The woman had grabbed Ant's arm now. 'But everyone's the same, aren't they? All the others have come off – why are ours different?'

'No idea,' said Ant. 'They just are. You're going to have to stay on the coach.'

'But we want to be with our friends,' said the old man.

Daisy crawled her way over. 'What's up?' she said. 'Why have you stopped? I need you to get my strap off!'

'These people have different ones,' said Mattie. 'The key doesn't work on them.'

More people had noticed the hold-up; hearing Mattie's explanation, they felt instinctively for their strap.

'Maybe the key is broken?' shouted one.

'Are you doing it wrong, Ant?'

'Let me try!'

Ant grabbed the nearest seat and hauled herself up. 'OK. I am not doing it wrong!' she shouted. 'And the key isn't broken, it's the straps – there are different versions and the key doesn't unlock them. If you have one of those, you can't escape, and you can't come with us. They'll find us all in seconds if you do.'

'Try me again!' pleaded the woman, but Ant had moved on. Everyone had suddenly fallen silent. Ant released Daisy, then three women. 'Thank you,' they whispered.

Behind them, more sirens had joined the police chorus. Ant had visions of a vast posse streaming up the hill towards the Heath, but despite the noise she couldn't see a single flashing light.

'Everything depends on what "evacuation of the prison" means.'

Frail Mary was next in the line and she read Ant's mind perfectly. 'If it includes the techies, you might get away with it. If they're all at their posts and watching us on the radar . . . well, you may not be so lucky.'

'*You* may not be lucky?' queried Ant. 'Don't you mean *we*?'

Mary smiled but shook her head. 'No I don't, dear,' she said. 'Think I'll sit this one out. I'm not running anywhere. I'll just serve my time and annoy them when I can.' She smiled weakly. 'Sorry, pet.' Ant started to protest but Mary waved her away. 'Get on with your job. You haven't long. Anyway, it won't just be me, will it?'

Ant nodded as Amos hurried up to her. 'Ant!' he said urgently. 'Why don't we throw the straps out of the window? That way we'd slow the police because they would think we were escaping, a few at a time. It might slow them down . . .'

'I was thinking about that,' she said. 'But it wouldn't slow them for more than a few seconds. And then they'd realize we had a strap-key. I want them to think we are all here, in one place, for as long as possible.'

'One minute, folks!' shouted Blakely. 'There are smaller roads on this part of the Heath. Turning onto the first one we find!' There was a nervous murmuring around the coach, and some of the freed strutters moved towards the doors. The coach had slowed in heavy traffic and they were eager to jump.

'Can't we go now?' called a red-faced woman with dyed blonde hair.

'No reason we should wait!' said the man next to her, nervously feeling his spine. The question was aimed at everybody, but it was Blakely who answered. He punched the door button again and the doors folded open.

'No reason at all! Jump when it's safe! God speed!'

Outside, there were now woods on both sides. It was a busy summer afternoon, the pavements and secluded paths bursting with joggers, picnickers and dog walkers. As the coach slowed, the first two strutters jumped. There was no cheering, no applause, just anxious eyes watching them disappear into the crowd.

'Hurry up, Ant!' shouted Blakely.

She said nothing. She knew what was at stake. If your strap wasn't off in the next few minutes, you were going back inside.

'Mattie, you next,' she said, pulling up his T-shirt.

'At least we know ours come off,' he said.

Insert, twist, release.

'Nice one,' he said. 'I'll do yours.'

Ant held her stomach as Mattie took the key. She felt the tug, the rotation, and then it was gone. The procedure was almost routine now – but it thrilled her anyway. She smiled at her brother. 'We might actually make it, you know.' He held up her strap so she could see the small goose and the graffiti. 'Nice work by Daisy!' she said. 'But throw it with the others.'

Eight more to release. Then Jimmy, then Blakely. The coach was slowing again, and four more strutters jumped, landing awkwardly but then scampering away. Fifty metres further on, another six. Ant saw that the Durrows, Daisy and Amos were hanging back. Daisy anticipated Ant's question.

'Because we're waiting for you, that's why. We'll go together.'

Insert, twist, release.

Insert, twist, release.

Insert, twist, release.

'She means thank you,' said Mattie.

'I know,' said Daisy.

The coach was emptying fast. More thick woodland was appearing on the right, and Blakely pointed through the windscreen. The sirens sounded louder now.

'That's the turning! Gonna park this beast up! Ready with that key, Ant!'

More jumpers.

It was Jimmy who replied. 'You're next, after me. Take it off, Ant.' He lifted his shirt and waited. 'Ant?' He turned. She had one hand on the key, the other over her mouth.

'It won't fit,' she said quietly. 'You've got one of the

old ones. Or the new ones. Whatever. It won't work.' She pushed the key in and tried to twist.

The coach lurched to a halt. Blakely came over. Almost absentmindedly, Ant released his strap and it fell to the floor. He kissed Ant on the cheek and leaped out of the coach without a word. The sirens were closing fast now.

'Well, I'll have to stay then,' said Jimmy quietly. 'I'll be fine. You better go!' He turned and headed back along the aisle towards Mary.

'He's right,' said Mattie. 'We've only got seconds, Ant—' Flashing lights appeared through the trees.

'We go,' she said, interrupting. 'Of course we go.' She put the strap-key back in her pocket, and glanced briefly at the small group they were leaving behind.

'I'll watch over him,' called Mary.

Ant, Mattie, Daisy, Amos, Sam, Tilly and Lena jumped from the coach. Sprinting into the woods they ran along the first pathway they came to. It twisted its way into a shaded, cooler, more densely wooded area. Ant led the way, Amos had Sam, Lena had Tilly, Mattie and Daisy ran together. Anyone who saw them coming dived out of the way; anyone who didn't ended up sprawling in the dirt.

They ran in silence. Behind them they heard sirens, shouts, radio chatter and then, chillingly, the sound of a helicopter. They struggled through brambles and jumped over fallen trees. The sun-drenched open parkland was only two hundred metres away now, but Ant knew they needed cover: ahead she saw a copse arranged in a rough semicircle. The undergrowth was dense and shielded from the paths.

Behind her Ant could hear rapid breathing and pounding footsteps – the occasional whimper from Tilly, a muttered curse from Amos – but the overwhelming noise was of police cars, police radios, slamming doors and shouted orders.

She led them off the path, crashing in amongst the trees. But they weren't the first there. Standing between two of the trees, chest heaving and sweat pouring from his face, was Jimmy Noon.

Ant was furious. 'What the hell are you doing?' she spat. 'They'll know precisely where we are now!'

He held up his hand, and she saw that he had a knife. 'Cut it out,' he said. 'Cut my strap out. Do it now.'

There wasn't time to argue. Lena took the knife from him – a jammer; a crude weapon made from what looked like a ruler and a razor blade. 'Lie down,' she said. As he did so, she sat on his legs and reached for a stick. 'Bite on this,' she told him. As soon as it was in his mouth, she sliced into his back, and his whole body went rigid. The first cut was angled under the right clamp; blood poured from the wound. The second cut was more difficult – under the handle and meeting the first, completing the V incision.

No one said a word. They could all hear the police, hear the confusion, hear the approaching helicopter, but they were watching Lena cutting into Jimmy. She wiped the pooling blood away with her hand, pushing it down his back and away from the strap. Two more swift cuts under the left clamp, then Lena gripped the handle.

And pulled.

Jimmy bit clean through the stick.

'Sam, take off your T-shirt.' Sam pulled it over his head and, bewildered, handed it to his mother. The strap had come away, but there were two deep holes in Jimmy's back. Lena folded the shirt and held it over the wounds. It turned red almost immediately.

'Keep it there if you can, Jimmy,' she said. 'Though you'll need a proper dressing.' She stood up and grabbed Sam and Tilly's hands. 'Ant, we love you but we'll go it alone. It's best this way.' She kissed Ant, and they ran. Tilly and Sam looked back briefly, but then they were gone.

'Right, we split up,' said Ant. 'There's enough people out there for us to vanish. Try and stay in sight if possible.'

They fanned out, taking different paths to the open heath. Ant and Mattie headed left, Daisy straight on, Amos right. Jimmy insisted on going last, clutching his back with both hands. 'I'm too slow,' he said. 'I'll follow.'

The police chatter was getting louder. The helicopter was definitely closer. At full sprint, they headed for the light.

'Mattie!' said Ant. 'See that football match?' There was an impromptu game going on about a hundred metres away. A small crowd had stopped to watch.

'Yes, I see it!'

'Aim for that!'

The undergrowth and trees were thinning; they could now feel the heat of the sun. Even the damp-earth smell was changing to scorched grass.

In a few steps they'd be out. This is what Ant had dreamed of. Through all the misery of the years in Spike, this was the moment she had hoped for. She counted them into the light. Without thinking, she used a different language.

The language of freedom.

Eins!

Zwei!

Drei!

Vier!

Ant realized she was crying.

Bug safe house, Bath

The messages on Max's screen finally appeared. His hands were shaking so much he had to put the phone down to read them.

> *It was carnage in there. So many dead. Saw mainly cons but POs too.*
> *Fire engines still there. I counted at least 10.*
> *Full evac going on!*
> *Anyone else watching these scenes from Spike? Where are the army, for God's sake?*

He read on, swiping the screen for new messages, each one adding to his sense of dread. Three times he had to dry his fingers on his T-shirt.

spotted my sammy and ellie. hope they're still safe.
Why is the fire still burning? What are they doing in there?

And then something that made him sit up straight.

There are on-the-runs. Escaped from one of the coaches. Police everywhere.

Max scrolled down, scanning the messages for more details. He found this exchange:

man here said the coach was empty when the cops found it.
how many would be on a coach?
dunno. 20 maybe.

There was more to read, but he got paranoid about being online for too long, even if this was a 'cold' phone. He hesitated, then typed.

Who's on for the holiday then? Thanks a million.

The holiday was a reference to his last conversation with Dan; 'thanks a million' was a joke family name for Maximilian. Only his parents and Ant would understand it. Memories of their first Christmas together flooded back and his eyes glistened. Ant had read out a label on a present from his aunt. *To Maximilian, Happy Christmas, love from Aunty Milly.* Ant had mispronounced his name, and Max had fallen about laughing. 'It's like "thanks a million",' Dan said, and for the next few days, that's what Max had been called.

Max logged off from the site, shut down the phone and threw it on the end of his bed as though it was infected. He fell back against the pillows, his head spinning. Everyone suddenly seemed a long, long way away. His safe house felt like a coward's retreat. How could he be lying here when his parents were in such danger? He knew why he had been sent here, but now he felt ashamed of his comfort and safety.

He grabbed his phone, shoving it deep into his bag, and headed out of the room.

Hampstead Heath, London

The shed had been stiflingly hot when they first crammed in. Now, with five people inside, the temperature was unbearable. Mattie, Jimmy and Daisy were crouched amongst garden implements and pots of old paint. Amos and Ant were sitting on a ladder staring skywards through dirty, cracked windows.

'Let's at least leave the door open,' said Daisy, her voice croaky. 'Just a little bit? Surely the drone won't see that.'

'It stays shut,' said Ant. 'A locked shed looks normal, not worth investigating. Soon as it moves on, we can too.'

The police drone was hovering over the edge of the Heath, a few houses away. Bright blue, a metre wide and revolving slowly, it had arrived just after they found the shed.

'Did it see us?' whispered Mattie.

'Don't think so,' said Amos, rummaging through an old tool box. 'I think it's just patrolling. Looking around.'

'Haven't seen a pol-drone like that before,' whispered Daisy.

'You've been in prison,' Ant pointed out.

'Do we need to whisper?' said Mattie. 'Can it hear us?'

'They're new,' muttered Jimmy. 'They'd just come out when me and Dad got done. They're just cameras, but very high def.' He winced, and Ant knelt down beside him, gently lifting his blood-soaked shirt. Lena's improvised dressing had done its job but was now stuck to his back. 'Assuming we can find some proper medicine soon, I think we should leave this, Jimmy. I don't want to start the bleeding again without the right kit. Sorry. Can you last a bit longer?'

'I'll be OK,' said Jimmy, trying to smile. 'I'm sorry I'm holding you guys up. If—'

'OK, shut up,' said Daisy. 'That's not helping.'

'Try these.' Amos threw a small packet of tablets onto the floor in front of Jimmy. 'I picked up a sports bag on the Heath. Thought it might help.'

And could have got us caught within minutes, thought Ant, but it wasn't the moment to protest. Jimmy quickly swallowed the painkillers.

For a moment they were all quiet. Ant could still hear the buzz of the drone and shouts from the Heath, but was mostly aware of her heart hammering in her chest. She looked around at her exhausted, terrified and exhilarated friends.

'We actually escaped,' she said quietly.

'We actually did,' whispered Jimmy. 'I hope Dad's safe. And Dan and Gina. Hope all our folks got out OK.'

'How do we find out?' asked Mattie.

'There are sites we look on which will know,' said Ant, her eyes still fixed skywards. 'But while that drone is sitting on top of us, we can't really do anything.'

The police drones had been late to the search. By the time they had been scrambled, the prison coach was empty and the strutters, with the exception of Frail Mary and the unreleased, gone. In the confusion of the evacuation and the escape, it took more than an hour for the police to work out who was accounted for and who wasn't. By the time they knew who they were looking for, the strutters had fled.

The police had charged through the trees, emerging onto the Heath, but then had to pull up short. They were faced with hundreds of people sunbathing, picnicking and playing ball games. There was no one to chase. The escaped strutters were strap-less and, for the moment, undetectable. The police could demand to inspect everyone's backs, but they didn't have the resources. Not yet.

If they'd been able to identify the escapees, they would

have spotted Ant and Mattie watching football, Daisy and Jimmy 'sunbathing' and Amos sitting on a bench reading a paper. Disappearing down a path, the Durrows would have looked like any other family out for a stroll. Lena had lost her Spike shirt, a swiftly stolen football top draped over her. She now looked like one of the many sun-worshippers. On the edge of a group of tourists, a shirtless Jeffrey Blakely, hands carefully placed behind his back, appeared to be taking in the sights.

Ant had been smiling and applauding a goal scored between two rucksacks. As the players congratulated each other, she and Mattie had turned as nonchalantly as they could and walked further onto the Heath. Eyes everywhere, they saw Daisy help Jimmy to his feet and Amos put down his paper.

If a pol-drone had spotted them, it would have shown five figures spread out over many hundreds of metres, walking in a v-formation like migrating birds. It would also have noted the changes in their appearance. Three were wearing stolen hats, one had helped himself to new shirt and sunglasses, and another, the smallest, was kicking a football as he went.

Strung out across the parkland, the five walked steadily away from the woods and the empty coach. They were watching each other, looking for cops and listening for drones. By the time the first fingers pointed skywards, each of the five was virtually invisible, swallowed up by bigger groups.

They had ended up near a series of large ponds. There

were people paddling and splashing, and Ant took a chance. With the four drones moving away, she took Mattie's hand, mouthed 'Follow me,' and approached Amos.

'We need to get out of here before all the cops in London arrive. They'll have our pictures soon, if they haven't already. And Jimmy will need medical attention . . .' She glanced across the pond: he was pretending to watch the swimmers, but she could see him wince every time he moved.

'This is my patch,' said Amos. 'I know these streets. If we need to disappear, our best chance is an empty house. And those' – he nodded towards the corner of the Heath – 'have always been second homes. Or third homes. Either way, they're usually empty. I bet nothing's changed. And see the overgrown gardens? That's good. Big alarm system, but no people. Usually.'

Ant had glanced up again. The nearest drone was hovering above trees two hundred metres away. 'Do it. We'll watch and follow. Don't run.'

He nodded. 'Watch the fence,' he said, and began weaving his way through the crowd.

Amos had left the Heath with a large group of French students, and within minutes Ant had seen movement. Knowing the others were watching her, she strolled down the hill. The wooden fencing ran down to the bottom of the Heath, but some houses appeared to have cut a private gate in it. One of these now stood ajar. With one final glance heavenwards, Ant stepped over an unscrewed lock and into a private garden.

She had hurried into the shed, closely followed by Mattie – 'I couldn't make myself go any slower!' Then came Jimmy, who had collapsed on the floor, then Daisy, who had helped herself to someone's sandwiches – 'They were unattended,' she explained as she swigged from a water bottle. Amos had gone to screw the lock back on the garden door, but had been forced to forget about it when he heard the whine of a pol-drone.

It had hovered above them, forcing them to take some thinking time in the shed.

'We absolutely can't stay here,' said Ant, 'or in the house. Even if it is empty and we can break in, the cops will be all over it once they've got their act together.'

'But we might find food and medicine,' protested Amos. 'There's bound to be stuff we could use—'

'We need to get away, Amos. If Jimmy can cope, we should hide in a crowd again and get off the Heath.'

'So, like, are you in charge now?' said Amos, turning to face Ant. 'Just 'cos you say something doesn't mean we have to do it.'

She stared back at him. 'No, of course I'm not in charge. I'm just saying we should get away as soon as that drone moves on.'

Daisy stood up and held out her hands to help Jimmy. 'We wouldn't have escaped without Ant, so maybe you should just shut up for a while, Amos,' she said.

'Wouldn't have been a riot without Ant either,' he muttered.

Jimmy, now back on his feet, grabbed Amos by the

arm and squeezed hard. 'Don't be a dick, Amos. You know Ant's right. But you want a vote? Fine. Anyone want to stay here?' There was silence in the shed. Jimmy kept hold of Amos. 'Seems to me like we're moving.'

Amos pulled his arm away just as Mattie pointed skywards. 'Drone's gone,' Mattie said.

'OK, so we leave,' said Amos. 'Then what? The Tube stations are bound to have police and CCTV . . .'

'We get on the first bus we see,' said Ant. 'Wherever it's going, it'll be away from here.' She glanced at Amos. 'If that's all right with everyone?'

'Buses have CCTV too,' he said.

'We'll risk it,' she said. 'By the time they realize what they're looking at, we won't be there any more.'

49

With the drone gone, they gathered round the garden gate. Daisy peered out.

'Looks like we've cleared the place,' she said. 'Loads of people are leaving.'

'Drones above your picnic is like sharks off the beach,' said Jimmy. 'Word spreads. No one is going to hang around. So let's get out of here. One every ten seconds. And remember to move like hunchies too. We're all walking too straight.'

'Force of habit,' said Daisy. 'It'll take time to be normal.'

'Agreed,' said Jimmy as they all tried to slouch. 'There'll be police around, but let's pray they don't know who we are just yet. Amos, you wanna go first? Not that I'm in charge or anything . . .'

Amos pulled a sarcastic smile and pushed his way through the gate.

'Mattie and I'll go last,' said Ant. 'Go, Daisy!'

Daisy nodded, swallowed hard and headed out.

Jimmy looked left, right and up, then turned. 'Stay close!' he said, his eyes darting between Ant and Mattie. They nodded, and he was gone.

'You next, Mattie,' said Ant. 'We'll be OK. I'm right behind you. Go.'

She knew he was terrified – she could see it in the fierce concentration and wide eyes. She pulled his stolen beanie lower, and then he was back on the Heath. She couldn't wait ten seconds – her count was, as usual, to four.

Amos was already on the path that led to the nearest gate, moving with the crowd. *He might just take off,* thought Ant. *We might never see him again.* Daisy, Jimmy, Mattie and finally Ant joined the throng.

She had her own baseball cap pulled low, but people were glancing at her goose tattoos. *They might just remember those later.* She kept walking, avoiding eye contact, pushing where she dared, holding back if necessary. It was surely obvious to everyone that she was an escaped strutter. The strap was more than a plastic and steel tag, it was a brand. It said *guilty*, and even though hers was now gone, she still felt her back burning.

As they had expected, there were flashing blue lights ahead – she saw Mattie recoil. *Ignore them*, she urged him mentally. *Just keep going!* Then she saw why: two policemen were filming the crowd as they headed away from the Heath. *They might not know who they're looking for now, but when they do, this will be the film they release.* A few people chanced a wave or a rude gesture at the cameras, then laughed at their own daring. Ant fought the temptation.

Amos had reached the exit; he was walking straight towards the cameras, then took a sharp right. She watched Daisy, Jimmy and Mattie follow, and at last it was her turn. She didn't know whether to ignore the camera pointed at her or stare straight into it. At the last minute she opted for a pretend conversation with the stranger next to her; Ant wondered whether her words would be picked up by any lip readers the police employed.

Mattie had crossed the road, following Jimmy, so Ant stayed on her side, behind Daisy. Amos was already out of sight. It was a swift pace – she guessed the fastest they could manage without drawing attention to themselves.

There must be loads of buses near here – but where are they?

Turning onto a busy main road, Ant saw Amos, with Daisy twenty metres behind. On the other side it was Jimmy setting the pace and Mattie half running to keep up. The pavements were busy here, and Ant kept as close to other people as she dared. Her friends had done the same, but all five had eyes everywhere, heads constantly turning.

We look like we're army, she thought. *Like we're soldiers patrolling the dangerous streets of a foreign country.*

A sudden cacophony of sirens was followed seconds

later by three police cars screeching into view. Mattie glanced over his shoulder at regular intervals, checking that Ant was still there. Each time she nodded, and each time she wished he'd stop. He was the most noticeable of them all. Even with the beanie, his black curls bounced as he walked and she held her breath whenever he passed a pedestrian.

Someone's gonna spot you soon.

Bus stop. Amos was looking up at the illuminated scrolling timetable. Ant watched as he nodded and joined the waiting crowd. *A bus must be coming soon*, she thought, *or he'd have kept walking.* She glanced over her shoulder – a large red double-decker was a hundred metres away. She hurried over.

'How do we pay?' asked Daisy.

'We don't!' said Amos.

When the bus's entrance and exit doors hissed open, instead of joining the queue swiping their cards, he forced his way through those getting off, then turned and waved the others on.

Mattie looked alarmed. 'If the driver reports us . . .' he said.

'If he complains, we'll just get off,' Ant said. 'Come on.'

They jumped onto the bus just as the doors hissed shut. Amos was standing on the stairs to the upper deck, and when he was sure they were all aboard, he shot up the remaining steps.

They crashed in the rear seats. As Amos had warned them, a single CCTV camera was sited at the front;

instinctively, they all slouched and slid below the windows. No one said anything, but they all exchanged rapid glances. When no one seemed remotely interested in the new passengers, the worried faces relaxed. Amos even smiled.

'No one pays for the bus,' he said. 'No one I know anyway.'

The bus pulled away and edged into traffic. Mattie leaned in close to Ant. 'We left them behind,' he said, his voice shaky. Ant closed her eyes. She replayed the images of Dan and Gina waving them away, telling them to run.

'I know.' She was about to add that maybe they had escaped, maybe they taken another coach. But she had said that already, and saying it again wouldn't make it sound any more convincing.

'I hope they're OK,' he whispered.

'Me too,' she whispered back.

Daisy had moved to the edge of her seat. 'This is all so slow,' she muttered, her legs jiggling with frustration.

'But no one's watching us,' said Ant. 'A bus is an unlikely getaway vehicle.'

'And where are we going anyway?' asked Amos. 'Now we're here, what's your plan, great leader?'

She ignored the barb and glanced at Jimmy, who was curled up on a seat. The back of his shirt was soaked in blood. 'We need shelter, money and the internet. But medicine first. Better painkillers and bandages.'

'I could get them easy,' said Amos. 'There'll be a chemist soon . . .'

'We need to get stuff *without stealing it*,' Ant told him. 'It's too risky, Amos. Let's not get caught because of some first aid.'

'Does Jimmy need this stuff fast or not?' he said, his anger causing heads to turn.

In the silence that followed Mattie stood up and whispered into Ant's ear.

She smiled. 'Yeah, say it.'

'There is somewhere else we could go,' he said.

50

Day 0
We owe you:
1 football
4 hats
5 bus fares

You owe us:
Everything

My favourite things RIGHT NOW: No strap!! Sunshine. Smells. Thinking that D and G escaped. But we don't know anything. Sometimes feels scarier out of Spike. J is bad but A says he should be OK (she's guessing).

Highbury Fields, North London

It had taken a bus change and a lot of arguing, but they were finally in position. Amos and Daisy had thought it was too dangerous, but the prospect of a debit card and a phone had swung it. They were standing in a deserted service road with lock-up garages on one side and high wooden fencing on the other. Three of the planks in the fence were hinged halfway up, creating a hidden gate. Even though there was no one around, they were all uneasy standing together. Jimmy was leaning against a concrete pillar, his eyes closed.

'We lost the house when we got sent to Spike,' said Ant, speaking fast. 'Don't know who bought it. Dan built this entrance for Mattie, when he was smaller. It still works. My cards are in a tin buried in the garden. It should take me thirty seconds.'

'Do it,' said Daisy. 'Then let's get poor Jimmy sorted.'

Ant pushed the fence and the three planks tipped inwards like a cat flap. Protecting her stomach with one hand, she used the other to crawl commando-style, hauling herself into what had once been her garden. Tall trees and thick bushes masked most of the house, but she froze anyway, listening for activity. She heard distant traffic and birdsong, but nothing else.

She crawled towards the small wooden hut where she and Mattie used to hold 'secret meetings', pretending they were in a plane, flying off to foreign countries where there were no adults. For reasons that were forgotten, she always chose Australia, he always chose Iceland. Their meetings always finished with one of them saying, 'We'll be fine' – the only time they ever referred to their father. There was just enough space inside for Ant to crouch down and tug at the wooden flooring.

She pushed her hand into the earth and pulled out a small biscuit tin. She prised it open and removed a phone and charger, a fake ID and a debit card. She replaced the tin and the plank, and was about to leave when she noticed the 'spy hole' that Dan had drilled in the front of the hut. Through it she could see most of the three-storey Victorian house she and Mattie had lived in for a year. The upstairs curtains were drawn; downstairs the shutters were closed. Between Ant and the house, twenty metres of uncut lawn. *There's no one here*, she thought. *No sign of life*. An empty house, she was sure of it.

She was about to scuttle back to the others when Mattie came crawling through the fence.

'It's Jimmy,' he said as soon as he was close. 'We need to get him to a hospital – the bleeding is really bad.'

'There's no one here, Mattie. Must be on holiday,' Ant said. 'There'll be first aid inside – maybe in the same place we had. Remember the alarm code?'

Mattie hesitated. 'We're breaking in?'

Ant nodded. 'Remember the code?' she repeated.

'Of course,' he said warily. 'But they'll have changed it, won't they?'

She smiled. 'Remember the master code?' He nodded but looked uncomfortable.

'You said we'd never do this again, Abi.'

'This is different . . .'

'Is it?' he said. 'It's not our house any more, you know that—'

Ant interrupted. 'No, but it should be! And anyway, they'll have drugs for Jimmy! We need to do this, Mattie! You can put it in your book if you like, but we need to go.'

'Isn't our old house the worst place to be?' he said.

'Maybe. Dunno. But Jimmy needs help *now* – let's get it for him. We don't need to stay long.'

Within minutes the five were hidden in the garden. Mattie had been right: Jimmy was very pale, his T-shirt a blood-drenched red. He lay on the ground; the crawl through the fence seemed to have taken most of his strength.

'Mattie and I can be inside in seconds, Jimmy. We'll fix you up,' said Ant. He managed the briefest of nods.

'And if there's nothing, we get him to hospital?' said Daisy.

'If we need to, I can call 999,' said Ant, waving her phone. 'Then we need to be out of here. But we're not giving him up, Daisy, not unless we have to.'

Daisy nodded grimly.

'Are we just going to break the windows?' asked Mattie.

'Guess we'll have to,' said Ant.

Amos rummaged in his pockets. 'Would these help?' he said, and held out three screwdrivers and a utility knife. 'They were in that garden shed. I know you don't like my ideas much, but I thought they might come in useful.'

Ant beamed as she pocketed the tools. 'Perfect! Amos, you're a genius after all.'

'So what happens now?' asked Daisy.

'What happens now,' said Ant with a hint of a grin, 'is you realizing that me and Mattie were brought up very badly.'

'What's the date?' said Mattie.

'Pardon me?' said Daisy. 'Why?'

'What's the date?' repeated Ant. 'Anyone know?'

Amos checked his watch. 'The fourteenth. July.' He looked quizzical, but got nothing back from either of them.

'The window's a latch, the shutter's a blade,' Ant said to Mattie.

He nodded. 'I remember,' he said.

'The alarm?' said Daisy.

'Shouldn't be attached to the windows,' said Ant. 'We had a motion detector in the room.'

'And if you're wrong?'

'We'll be fine,' Ant said, exchanging a glance with Mattie.

'Your stomach OK?'

'I'm fine.'

'OK, go,' said Daisy.

Ant and Mattie sprinted the length of the garden. Mattie jumped onto the window ledge, then disappeared behind the dense, overgrown ivy that curtained half of it.

Ant, crouching underneath, glanced up at the latch of the sash window.

'Old wood, Mattie,' she said in an urgent whisper. 'Thinnest, widest screwdriver should do it.'

'Already got it,' he said, a ten-centimetre metal shaft protruding from his clenched hand. 'Ready?'

Ant nodded. Mattie jabbed the screwdriver up through the two wooden frames and waited. Ant jumped onto the ledge and they both clasped the handle, tensing for the final push.

They counted together. '*En, de, twa, kat*,' then rammed the shaft against the locking mechanism. The ancient brass ball-and-socket came apart, pieces flying against the glass before clattering somewhere out of sight.

Ant reached up and pulled the top sash down, Mattie sliced a knife between the shutters, and they swung inwards.

Watching from the hut, Daisy whistled softly. 'I think they might have done this before,' she said.

51

Mattie jumped and rolled into the house, sending a plume of dust into the now sun-filled room; Ant climbed down, feeling her way with care. They hesitated only briefly before closing the window and folding the shutters back into place, then looked around the darkened room that had once been Dan's office, now redesigned as a lounge. It was musty and hot, the air thick with the smell of cats.

Mattie wrinkled his nose. 'Disgusting,' he said.

Ant checked the small, flashing white boxes on the ceiling. 'When we move past that table the alarm will be triggered,' she said. 'We'll have thirty seconds to enter the code.'

'What if they've moved the console?'

'They won't have. Ready?'

Mattie nodded, and they sprinted across the room.

As they passed the table, they heard a high, loud whine from the cupboard under the stairs. Ant pulled the door open and Mattie dived in, throwing shoes and old coats out of the way.

'About twenty seconds!' called Ant. 'Reverse date! Code one!'

'They've changed the console!' cried Mattie. 'There's extra keys with room numbers!' The box continued to emit its warning signal. 'I need to put in a number, Abi!' he said.

There was a pencilled diagram drawn on the inside of the cupboard door. Rooms and numbers. A long thin 3. A wide 1.

'It's two!' shouted Ant. 'Try two!' A flurry of beeps came from the cupboard. 'Five seconds!' She hit the wall in frustration, and was about to haul Mattie out – when everything went quiet.

'I did it!' came the muffled but triumphant voice from under the stairs.

'Nice work!' said Ant, exhaling deeply. 'Now let's check for medicine and get back to the others. Kitchen first.'

They headed straight for the cupboard above the microwave, which contained only cat food.

'It was worth a try,' said Ant. 'OK, upstairs next.' They took the steps two at a time, making for the bathroom. If there wasn't anything here, their search could well be a long one. Ant opened the mirrored medicine cabinet.

'Yes!' said Mattie as they saw a large metal tin with a red cross on it. Inside there were ointments, plasters, bandages, painkillers and scissors.

'You beauty,' said Ant, replacing the lid. 'Let's get this to Jimmy!' They jumped the stairs four at a time. Through the kitchen in seconds, they stood by the back door. 'Keys where they always were!' said Ant.

'On the hook I put in!' said Mattie, pointing at a cup hook screwed into the door jamb. Two keys on a brass ring hung from it. The top and bottom locks were undone in seconds, and Ant pushed the handle down. The back door swung open and they looked out across an apparently deserted garden. Then Amos and Daisy appeared from behind the hut, waving them over.

'Jimmy isn't going anywhere,' Daisy told them. 'We either take him inside or we call an ambulance now.'

'Then we take him inside,' said Ant, kneeling down. 'Amos, help me.' They both put an arm under each of Jimmy's and pulled him slowly to his feet. He winced and cried out as his back straightened.

'Just make it to the kitchen,' she said to him. 'We'll get you cleaned up in no time.' *My God, I'm sounding like Gina*, she thought. Ant wondered again about the fate of her foster mother as she guided Jimmy inside.

Once in the kitchen, Daisy pointed at Ant's stomach. 'You're bleeding again too. Me and Amos'll sort Jimmy, you clean yourself up.'

The shower was cold but Ant needed it anyway. She gingerly eased herself out of her clothes and stepped into the shower cubicle. She watched the dirt and blood wash away, and saw the cut on her stomach clearly for the first time. It stung as the water hit, but she decided she had seen worse. They had a first-aid kit. It had antiseptic cream and bandages – she'd be fine. Her back stung too but she let the water wash over the blistered skin; she wondered how long it would be before she lost the marks of a strutter. Did they ever go?

The euphoria of escape hadn't lasted long – pain and exhaustion had seen to that. When she stepped out of the shower, the temptation to crawl straight into her old bedroom was almost overpowering. But she forced herself back into her filthy, sweaty clothes because she knew – had known ever since they broke into the house – that they would have to move on.

As she was pulling on her T-shirt, she heard a gentle tapping on the bathroom door. Through the frosted glass she saw a shirtless Jimmy and opened the door.

'You're up!' Ant said. 'I thought Amos and Daisy—'

He tried a smile but it turned into a painful grimace. 'I'd rather it was you fixing me . . .' In one hand he was holding the first-aid box; the other clamped Sam Durrow's T-shirt to his back. It was now a blood-soaked sponge. Ant peeled it away and the two wounds started bleeding again.

'You need to lie on the floor,' she said, taking the box. As he eased his way down, Ant staunched the flow with the cloth and pressed hard. He tensed but said nothing, holding his breath.

'I'm no expert, but I think Lena did a good job,' Ant said. 'Under the circumstances.' She knelt by Jimmy's side and lifted the makeshift dressing. 'You didn't need to go through this, you know,' she said. 'I'm glad you're with us, Jimmy, but you'd have been fine with Frail Mary and the others. You would have hooked up with your mum again. Now you're wanted like the rest of us *and* your strap's been gouged off.'

Jimmy exhaled, then cleared his throat. 'I didn't think too deeply about it, Ant. But when you all jumped, I realized that, more than anything else, I wanted to jump too. I'm not going back to prison – not after all this.' There was a silence before he added, 'And anyway, prison without you wouldn't be any fun.' He felt the pressure ease slightly as Ant hesitated.

'Yeah, right,' said Ant. She smiled at him. 'Always the smooth-talking banker boy.'

OK, where's this going?

'No, Ant, it's true. I'd rather . . . I'd rather be with you than anyone.' He winced, then kept his eyes screwed shut. 'See, that wasn't very smooth, was it?' He grimaced. 'And I'm not the banker boy. Just Jimmy Noon.'

Ant relieved the pressure. 'OK, Jimmy Noon. Point taken. And thanks.'

He changed the subject. 'That was a neat trick with the windows back there, by the way,' he said.

She smiled. 'Yeah, our parents taught us some unusual life skills.' Her hands had stayed on his back. *I guess this counts as an intimate moment*, she thought. *And actually it feels good.*

'You did some jobs with them?' he said.

'One or two,' said Ant. 'A long time ago.' She wiped away the blood that had seeped through the shirt.

'Did you get the phone?'

'Yes. And the cards.'

'So we can move on?'

'When you're ready,' said Ant. 'But this needs to be done first or you'll leave a trail of blood. Hold still, this might hurt.' She opened the box, then applied the cream and a large gauze dressing. Again she pressed.

'You're good,' he said, wincing again.

'Gina taught me,' she said, and they were both silent. Ant made herself focus. 'Sit up.' She kept her hand on the dressing and straddled his legs to strap the bandage around his waist. She lapped it four times, then tied it off. 'Tight enough?'

'I've lost all feeling in my legs,' he said with a smile, 'so yes.'

She surveyed her work. 'Of course, you should lie still for forty-eight hours now.'

'Great. I'll bear that in mind. What about your cut? That was pretty bad . . .'

'It'll be OK. It's not so deep.' She lifted her T-shirt to show him the gash across her stomach.

'Ouch,' he said.

'Yeah, well. I'll sort it soon. But we should go.' She stood up and reached for his hand. He took it, his other hand holding onto the door for support. When he was standing, she kept hold of his hand.

Enough misery. Enough terror. Enough pain.

'Thank you . . .' was all he managed before she kissed him.

52

Downstairs Ant joined the others slumped around the kitchen table. Mattie was explaining their burglar-alarm trick, while everyone ate cornflakes and biscuits.

'I was never supposed to tell anyone,' he said. 'But you type in a staff number, then reverse the day's date. The guy who designed the system worked for our parents. He used it as an emergency back door into the system. The staff numbers don't change much – he gave us some that are always used.'

'And you remembered?' asked Amos, amazed.

Mattie nodded.

'Quite the thief,' said Daisy. 'You should be locked up!'

Everyone but Mattie laughed. 'I'm only doing it because I have to,' he said, his face serious. 'Where's Jimmy?'

'In my old bedroom,' said Ant. 'It's all fancy and vile but he's crashed for a bit.'

'There's some frozen pizzas,' said Mattie, 'but maybe we're not staying?'

'We could lie low here for a couple of hours,' suggested Daisy. 'Eat pizza and sleep?'

'Agreed,' said Amos.

'But we have to be invisible,' said Ant. 'Doors, windows, shutters – all closed. No lights on. I'm sure whoever lives here is on holiday. The hot water's off and there's no food. So this house has to look empty. If anyone comes to check – which they will – it's dark and locked.' She pushed the back door shut and turned the key. 'Assume we're being watched all the time.'

They cooked the three small pizzas from the freezer, then made some toast with some long-forgotten, frozen sliced white bread. With half-full stomachs, their attention turned to the phone, which was now charging. With the kitchen blinds down, its screen was the brightest light in the room.

Ant typed in the name of her encryption browser. She had accessed the dark web on only two previous occasions, but Dan had taken her through the many levels of security and told her how to access the information she needed. She had remembered every password and every code number. She hit 'enter'. Her screen went blank and she glanced at the others. 'I don't know what we'll find,' she said quietly.

'Don't worry,' said Daisy. 'Just do it.' Amos and Mattie craned their necks to see.

At last the oblong box and the pulsing cursor appeared. Swallowing hard, Ant typed more letters and numbers, hit 'enter' again, and she was in. In its characteristic plain white text on a black background, Ant's screen filled with information from Spike. Survivors, casualties, reactions from Bug sites around the world. She scrolled down as fast as she could, looking for names she knew. Dan Norton. Gina Norton. Ahmet Shah. Sarah Raath. Mishal Noon.

'Must be something somewhere,' she muttered. 'Where have you all gone?'

She scrolled back more slowly, and found a stream of comments about their escape, and then felt a shot of adrenalin kick into her system. She read the post five times.

Who's on for the holiday then? Thanks a million.

'It's Max!' she whispered. '"Thanks a million" was a Dan rhyme for Maximilian.'

Ant entered her code again and typed:

Hey TAM. Me and my bro need a holiday. And our friends. Come and get us.

She paused. Should she be more obvious? Could she trust the site? She decided to leave one more line.

We don't know about D and G. How can we talk/meet? Is it safe to leave number?

She hesitated, hoping for a moment he'd post straight back. When nothing appeared, she logged out.

'News sites?' suggested Daisy, and Ant nodded, typing again. There were four gasps when the first headline loaded.

LONDON PRISON ESCAPE: THE MOST WANTED

Beneath was a row of photos. The two largest were of Ant and Mattie. They read fast, Ant scrolling down the story.

'Five confirmed deaths?' said Amos. 'We saw more than that . . .'

'But fifteen escapers sounds about right,' said Daisy.

'*Biggest police manhunt in years*,' read Ant, and looked up. 'They're definitely going to check this house. We have to be ready.'

'But where will we go?' asked Daisy. 'Where is safe?'

'That's the point,' said Ant. 'Nowhere. So we stay here. We clear everything away. Make it look like it did when we got here. Mattie, can we fix the window? Put the bolt back?' She pointed at the lounge window they had forced.

'I think so,' he said, picking up the brass lock from the floor.

'And reset the alarm?' asked Daisy.

He nodded.

Everyone seemed relieved to have a plan. Ant began opening the shutters so that Mattie could get to the window, and caught her reflection – gaunt, tired eyes and hair three days longer than it had been in ages. She blinked her mind clear.

'OK, we stay here,' she said, 'and if anyone comes looking, we are invisible.'

The A4, just outside Marlborough, Wiltshire

Another window, another gaunt reflection. Max hardly recognized himself – the shaved head and sunken eyes staring back at him belonged to someone he'd have avoided in the past. He wondered what Sara would think of his new look, how his parents would react, what Ant would say. He smiled at that last thought; all he needed were some goose tattoos and he'd look like her. He hadn't seen her for two years – his visits had always been to his parents – but he didn't imagine she'd changed much.

His new look was the idea of the woman who ran the safe house. She had it all planned. A complete change of image – different, smarter clothes – and Max could pass for an off-duty soldier or policeman. She had driven him fifty miles to the coach so that he could avoid the police at the railway station. He would be in London in two and a half hours.

The news sites now listed all the escaped strutters – his parents weren't mentioned.

Ant had written *Me and my bro need a holiday.* Then *Come and get us.* He couldn't imagine the circumstances under which she had written that message. Ant and Mattie were clearly on-the-runs and hiding out somewhere. And his parents weren't with them. *We don't know about D and* G. He ran those words over and over. They could mean anything. The Bug sites had nothing, the news sites had nothing. Why the silence? All he knew was that he had to get close to where his parents might be. And that the knot of fear in his stomach felt like it would never leave.

Ant had signed off *How can we talk/meet*? And he had no idea. He picked up his phone for the third time in ten minutes, entered the multi-layered world of the dark web and checked the Bug sites for messages – any mention of Dan and Gina Norton. Nothing. He had already left a *Tell me where you are* message for Ant, but now he added, *Believe this site is safe. Leave a contact number or address if you can.* He added his new phone's number and exited the site.

Max closed his eyes. The images of the Spike fire filled his head again and he balled his fists. It had taken most of his time in Bristol for him to accept that Ant wasn't responsible for his parents' incarceration. A combination of Sara's gentle persuasion and his mum and dad's more urgent arguments that they'd have been arrested sooner or later had persuaded him not to blame her for everything. But the truth was, he did resent their fondness for Ant and Mattie, resented their time together, and *really* resented his new fugitive status.

But he was also convinced that ending heritage crime was a war that had to be fought. And that right now, finding his foster sister and brother was the first battle.

53

My favourite things RIGHT NOW:
Pizza!
Thinking D and G might have escaped, but don't think A thinks they have.

Highbury Fields, North London

Ant had wanted her old room back, even if it was for just one night. But Jimmy was still sprawled across the bed, so she was sharing the main bedroom with Daisy. Amos had opted for the couch in the lounge, while Mattie got his room and had shown them the best hiding places if the house was searched. It would, thought Ant, be the grimmest game of hide-and-seek, with the losers getting re-strapped and sent back to prison. She had absolutely no intention of giving Assessor Grey the satisfaction of seeing her captured. She hadn't given him a thought for many hours, but, reaching under the duvet, could feel his strap-key in her pocket.

And that means you lost.

She cursed him in German, she swore at him in Haitian Creole, then in Anglo-Saxon. Then felt better.

'Thought you were asleep,' said Daisy. 'Who are you talking to?' She was standing by the curtains, peering through a small crack onto the street. It was her watch, and she was pacing across the darkened room between the front and back windows.

'Grey,' said Ant from the bed. 'I'm telling him a few things he needs to hear.'

Daisy chuckled. 'Say them from me too.'

'I did. He knows.'

'You took a long time fixing Jimmy's dressing earlier.'

Ant heard the smile in her voice. 'You think?'

'I think, yeah.'

'It was more fun than fixing a bandage should be, I suppose . . .'

'Ha! I knew it. Well, if you can, you should sleep, Ant. It'll be your shift next.'

'I know, I know.' Ant's head was spinning with tiredness and pain, but the tablets she'd taken were beginning to work. The room was hot but the bed was cool and soft and the tiredness was overwhelming. She was about to say that she'd be up in a minute when someone jumped on the bed.

Ant sat bolt upright. Daisy had disappeared; she heard running feet downstairs and muffled voices nearby. It was a few seconds before she realized where she was and that she had, however briefly, slept. The room was pitch black, but she could just see the outline of Mattie's hair, inches from her face.

He spoke in an urgent whisper. 'Hide! They're here!'

He pulled her out of bed and into the small office across the landing. It had a deep ornate cupboard that ran the length of one wall – their chosen hiding place.

'Where did Daisy—?' began Ant, but Mattie put his hand over her mouth.

'Everyone's where they need to be,' he whispered, 'apart from Jimmy. I couldn't wake him.'

'What?' said Ant. 'So we're not all hidden, then, are we?'

She pushed her way into the cupboard, clearing files and boxes as she went. Mattie followed and pulled the door shut behind them. 'Well, I didn't know what to do!' he said.

'OK. Who saw what?' she said into the silence.

'I saw someone in the garden,' said Mattie. 'At the back, by the hut.'

'Just the one?'

'I think so.'

'I wonder . . .' Ant pulled her phone out of her back pocket. She hit the buttons that took her through the security and encryption of the dark web, then logged onto the Bug site and found what she was looking for. She climbed out of the cupboard.

'What are you doing?' hissed Mattie.

'Follow me,' she said, heading for the back window.

'Ant!' came Mattie's nervous cry.

'Watch!' she said.

They went into the main bedroom, taking up position by the curtains. The large wardrobe creaked, then opened.

'What's happening? Why aren't you hiding?' said Daisy from behind a rail of dresses.

Ant was hitting the phone again. 'Watch,' she said, and hit CALL.

She drew back a corner of the curtain and they peered into the dark garden. The London sky was bright enough for them to make out some grass and flowerbeds close by, but beyond that everything was blurred shapes and shadows.

'What am I looking for?' whispered Daisy.

As if on cue, a light shone through the trees at the end of the garden. It was bright enough to reveal hands, a jacket, then the side of a face. A man on a phone.

'That,' said Ant, and held her phone to her ear. The figure was suddenly crouching, shielding the light from the screen. They saw him glance up at the house. In the bedroom, everyone heard the nervous whispered, 'Hello?'

'Hi, Max,' said Ant. 'We'll let you in.'

Mattie was downstairs first, Amos joining him on his way to the kitchen.

'What? He's . . . ? How did he find us?'

'I left him a message,' said Ant, unhooking the back-door keys.

'You did what?'

'Calm down, Amos,' she said. 'He's on our side.' She unlocked the door and pulled it open. A tall figure appeared in the doorway, then hesitated.

'Max!' said Mattie in a half-whisper, half-shout, and ran towards him. Max came into the dark kitchen just as Mattie collided with his waist.

Max laughed, a low chuckle. 'Mattie? But you're enormous!' He dropped his rucksack and ruffled the boy's hair. Behind him, Ant pushed the door shut and locked it.

'Hey,' she said.

'Hey.'

They stared at each other. It was just light enough to make out faces and shapes. Neither of them were smiling.

'Nice haircut,' said Ant.

'What happened to my mum and dad?' said Max.

Ant looked away. 'We don't know. None of us do,' she said. 'There are three others here; none of them know what happened to their families either.'

Max peered into the kitchen.

'Hi, I'm Daisy.'

Max saw white blonde hair and an upheld palm. 'Hi.'

'Amos,' said a voice from the shadows.

'Hi, Amos.'

Mattie pulled Max over to the table, where he slumped

onto a chair. 'Amos's dad Ahmet is missing,' said Mattie. 'Daisy's mum is Sarah. We don't know where she is either.'

'You said there's five of you . . .'

'Jimmy Noon,' said Ant. 'We had to cut off his strap. He's upstairs, sleeping. His mum is missing.'

'You cut off his strap?'

'I didn't, Lena did. She escaped too. She did a good job – I think he'll be OK.'

There was so much to say that no one said anything. Eventually Max looked around and whistled softly. 'This is so weird,' he said.

He made tea and found some porridge oats. He sat opposite Ant – across their old kitchen table – eating hungrily. Mattie had fallen asleep in an armchair, Amos and Daisy had wandered off, presumably to their beds.

Ant began to talk. Starting with the disastrous *Correction*, she told him the story of the last forty-eight hours: Brian MacMillan's plan for getting her revenge, her run into Holloway, finding Tess Clarke, disguising herself as a man in Pentonville and not finding Pellow. Then her escape and Brian's death. Max listened in silence, but as she paused, knowing that the riot and the fire were next, he interrupted.

'He did all that for you? Why did he sacrifice himself like that? Were you guys a thing or something?'

'No, not really,' said Ant. 'We were just friends – he was way too old anyway.'

'And a PO,' added Max.

She sighed. 'Yeah, and that. I think he felt responsible. The double raid was his idea . . .'

'Was it?' said Max? 'Sure about that? Sounded like he'd been chosen to ask you.'

She shrugged. 'Maybe . . .'

'And what were those numbers he gave you? The ones he said would change your life?'

Ant closed her eyes, remembering. '8B 3S 2C3.'

'So why would they change your life?'

She shrugged again. 'Because they got me out of Pentonville? I don't know. It did sound weird at the time, though . . .'

Max reached for his phone. As he hit the keys, the screen lit up; he squinted at the sudden brightness. She saw his face was gaunt, the cropped hair accentuating the ridges of his skull.

You're as tired as we are.

Max frowned. 'Nothing here. Just getting maths questions and algebra.' He scrolled down. 'What were Brian's exact words?' He looked up at Ant, his face illuminated from below as though he was holding a torch and they were playing at horror films.

'Something like . . .' She screwed up her face. 'He got me to repeat the numbers. Then said something like, "Keep a record. They'll get you out. Grey will go mad. Then they'll change your life."'

'*Then* they'll change your life?' whispered Max. '*After* you get out. He was trying to tell you something, Ant! Have you looked them up?'

'Just got the phone, Max. Not a lot of research time so far.'

'OK, OK, fair enough,' he said, getting up and pacing the kitchen. He read out the numbers and letters again. 'A staff number? A tax code?'

'No idea,' said Ant.

'It must be something he thought you'd get,' said Max. 'Something you'd understand. What did you talk about when you were . . . not being a thing?'

'Mainly how terrible life was for everyone. He hated Grey, hated his job, hated the system.'

There was a creak from the armchair. 'You said he was into music,' said Mattie, his voice slurred with sleep. 'He liked loads of bands.'

'You been listening to all this?' said Ant.

'Nope. Just the last bit about Brian.'

'Did *you* like him?' asked Max.

'He was OK,' said Mattie. 'Better than the rest, I s'pose . . .'

There was silence in the kitchen before Max spoke again. 'And how long between Brian dying and the riot starting?'

'Not that long,' said Ant, taking time with each word. She took the next silence to mean that he was waiting for the rest of the story, and she figured she owed him that. She described the invasion from Holloway and Pentonville, the fire that followed, the last time she saw Dan and Gina.

Max rubbed his head with his hands. 'What are the chances they got out alive?' he asked, his voice flat.

'We don't know, Max,' she said quietly. 'They waved us away! We couldn't get them out – the card had stopped working—' She broke off. Mattie got up and came to stand beside her.

Max paced some more. 'Would it be fair to say that you and Brian started the riot?' he said softly.

'No, it wouldn't,' said Ant. 'It would be a stupid thing to say. And ignorant. And dangerous.' She was on her feet now. Mattie tried to take her arm, but she shook him off. 'I know you hate me, and I know you blame me for what happened to Dan and Gina.' She walked to within a few centimetres of Max. 'But I went into Holloway and Pentonville to stop all the shit they were talking in the *Correction* films. It was all lies and there was more coming. I might have stirred it up a bit, but the whole prison was ready to blow anyway.' She was bouncing on the balls of her feet and Mattie recognized the danger.

'Let's go, Abi,' he said.

'You have no idea what you're talking about, Max,' she said loudly. 'I don't even know why you're here. We escaped without you, we'll cope without you!'

Max had heard enough. They stood shaved head to shaved head, seeing the anger and fear in each other's eyes. 'Yes, I'm sure you'll cope without me,' he said. 'You started the riot without me, started the fire without me, got my—' He broke off.

'Go on, finish the sentence,' Ant said, ignoring Mattie, who was tugging at her arm. '*Got my parents killed without me*? Is that what you were going to say? You came all this way to accuse me and Mattie of killing Dan and Gina? Really?'

A voice from the shadows. 'What the hell . . . ? Who are you?'

Ant and Max turned to see Jimmy coming into the kitchen, followed by Daisy. Amos was standing in the doorway. They all stared at each other – it was Mattie who broke the silence.

'This is Max, Dan and Gina's son,' he said.

'Great,' said Jimmy drily. 'Are you trying to get us caught? Because I'm pretty dosed up at the moment, but you sure woke *me* up. You see everything is dark in here? It's because we don't want to go back to prison. So if you can help, great. Otherwise go back to wherever you came from. And – Ant? For God's sake, calm down.' He turned and headed back upstairs. Daisy and Amos melted away too.

'Is that the guy who had his strap cut out?' asked Max, the spell broken.

'Yes,' said Mattie.

Ant hesitated, looked from Max to Mattie, then turned for the door. 'I'm going back to bed,' she said.

Max hadn't moved; he was still standing in the middle of the room. Mattie approached him warily. 'We didn't kill Dan and Gina,' he said, his voice tiny. 'We tried to save them.'

Max sighed heavily. 'I'm sure you did, Mattie, I'm sure you did.'

'And you should separate the numbers and letters.'

'What?' Max said.

'Gina taught me algebra,' said Mattie. 'The code that Brian gave Ant . . . She mentioned it before, but we haven't really talked about it till now. But you mentioned algebra . . . and I think you should separate the numbers and letters. Try that.'

After Mattie had gone, Max did try that. By the light of his phone he scribbled down different combinations of numbers and letters using 8B 3S 2C3. Then he typed them into his phone, searching for any combination that might give him a lead. It was a long list, and eventually he gave up. Maths wasn't his subject, but even he knew there must be thousands of variations. *Then they'll change your life* was what Ant had said. She was the key, he was sure of it. This prison officer must have assumed that he had given her all the information she required. He needed Ant to decode it, but after that row, they might not be speaking for a while.

'We haven't got time to tiptoe around this,' he said aloud. 'Need to sort it now.'

He hadn't even got as far as the landing before flashing blue lights filled the house.

54

'Police!' yelled Max. He crouched down on the landing. 'At least two! Front and back!' Amos flew across the hall and dived under the stairs. Jimmy peered from behind a door, then disappeared again. Mattie burst out of the spare room and tore across the landing. 'You need a space!' he hissed as he passed Max. Ant and Daisy had tumbled from the bed, both looking dazed. Daisy's hair was a white curtain in front of her face as she climbed into the wardrobe. Max and Ant were pulled by Mattie into the spare room, then pushed into the cupboard.

'Did you clear your stuff up?' said Mattie as Max disappeared into the jumble of boxes. It was clear from Max's face that he hadn't. From outside, the sound of low conversation and squawked radio chatter.

'Too late!' said Ant. 'Get in, Mattie!'

There was room, just.

'Did you fix the window lock?' said Ant, sitting on cupboard's cluttered floor, her voice deadened by the closed door.

'Yes, best I could,' said Mattie from somewhere above her. They sat in the dark and in silence. When the doorbell rang, they all jumped. When it was followed by rapid, loud knocks, they all held their breath. They heard voices, then doors being rattled, their locks tested.

'What if they break in?' whispered Mattie. The others didn't reply – the answer seemed obvious.

We go back to prison.

The tapping, knocking and radio chatter moved round the house as every window and door was examined. Ant's heart was beating so hard and fast that, in the close confines of the cupboard, she was convinced Mattie and Max would hear it.

The noises subsided, silence returned. They waited.

'How do we know when it's safe?' said Mattie.

'We don't,' said Ant. 'We just stay here.'

'I should go and clear up my stuff in the kitchen—' said Max.

'Yes, you should,' interrupted Ant, 'but you shouldn't have left it out in the first place.'

'I know. That was a mistake, but—'

There was the sound of movement in the hall downstairs; Amos had stepped out of his hiding place and they all listened hard. They heard him walk, pause then curse.

'Cops are with the neighbours!' he half whispered, half shouted. 'Looks like they're getting keys!'

Now it was Ant and Max's turn to curse.

In the cupboard, Mattie crawled over Ant and pushed the door open. 'Mattie?' said Ant.

'Setting the alarm,' he said. 'If they open the door and the alarm goes off, they'll know there's no one here, right?'

'Can you do that?' Max sounded doubtful, but Ant followed Mattie, then turned to Max.

'We have seconds. Tell Daisy what's happening.' Max leaped out of the cupboard.

By the time Ant had told Jimmy, Mattie was down the stairs. She paused only to glance through the window above the front door; a number of police were walking their way. A neighbour was looking on.

'They're coming! Amos, we're setting the alarm,' she called. 'Stay put. We'll turn it off when they're gone.'

Rapid beeps came from the alarm unit, followed by a single tone.

'Twenty seconds!' she called. 'Mattie, get out of there!'

The flashing blue light shone through the stained glass of the front door, filling the hall with deep, moving colours. Ant and Mattie saw dark shapes approaching and sprinted up the stairs. The doorbell rang as they reached the landing, the shout through the letterbox came as they entered the spare room. They heard a key in the door as they jumped into the cupboard.

First lock undone. Second lock undone. Mattie gripped Ant's hand, then the alarm countdown was triggered.

They heard the single tone and then the series of beeps. Heavy footsteps in the hall. Shouting. Radio squawking. Orders given. Then silence.

Upstairs no one breathed, no one moved. From the hall, more shouting, a slammed door, and then the sounds of an urgent conversation; three voices? Four? Ant wasn't sure.

'They know the code too,' whispered Mattie.

'They're so close to Amos . . .' breathed Ant.

Then a clear voice from the hall. Authoritative – in command. 'If the alarm's set, they're not here. Reset it and move out.'

More boots in the hall, more beeping from the alarm unit, then the slam of the door. The click of two locks. In the darkness, Ant and Mattie high-fived.

'Are we sure they're gone?' said Max.

'Amos will tell us,' said Ant, pushing the door open.

Sure enough, after a minute a muffled voice came from downstairs. 'They're gone! All clear! Shout out the code!'

They all stumbled across the landing, Mattie calling out the security code. As they slowly went downstairs, they saw Amos standing in the hall, looking dazed. 'My ears are ringing . . .'

Daisy quickly covered his mouth with her hand. 'Too loud!' she whispered. 'They haven't gone far!'

Max positioned himself on the stairs so he could just see the road out front. 'Police cars gone,' he said.

When they were sure they were on their own, they all returned to the kitchen and sat around the table. The only light came from the gas hob that was heating a kettle.

Max held his phone in his hand. 'We should go on the Bug sites. Tell them what's happened.'

'Agreed,' Ant said. 'There might be other on-the-runs posting. How much should we say?'

'I think it's important—' began Max.

'I wasn't actually asking *you*,' she snapped.

Amos leaned in. 'And anyway, Max, honestly? We don't care what you think. You say "we", but you haven't been in Spike, you haven't had a strap stuck to your spine for years and you know *nothing* about us.' He sat back, face like thunder.

'That's true,' said Max. 'Fair enough. But I'm here because you guys busted out.' He pointed at Ant and Mattie. 'And I would have been thrown in prison instead. And *my* parents are missing too. In case you'd forgotten.'

There was a challenge in his voice, but Amos didn't back down. He looked from Max to Ant and back again. 'What is it with you guys?' he said. 'One of you always thinks you're in charge. You're some family . . .'

'We're not family,' said Ant and Max together. Daisy and Jimmy smiled, Mattie looked away. Then everyone except Amos laughed.

Jimmy said, 'I think we should log on and tell everyone we got out. That we are still out and intend to stay out. Anyone object?'

Everyone looked at Amos, who shrugged. 'Sure. Why not?'

Ant and Max both started the logon process. Max was

in first. 'There's a post here saying there are record numbers of strutter transfers going on. All the strutters who were moved after the fire are being moved again. Plus strutters from other prisons.'

'Where to?' asked Daisy.

'Doesn't say,' he replied, 'but all heading west. Parts of their routes have been posted. The transporters from around here all go along the Heath. If it's accurate, that's where you all escaped.'

Apart from Ant's typing, there was a thoughtful silence.

'We could do something about that,' said Jimmy.

'Like what?' asked Daisy, sceptical.

He shrugged. 'Don't know. Just saying. Depends what we want to do.' He looked at the faces around the table. 'Are we going to hide? Keep on running? Or do we . . . do something? Strike back in some way?'

'You mean, attack a prison van?' said Daisy, aghast. 'Are you mad?'

'Yeah, going back inside seems like a really stupid idea.' Amos was dismissive.

'Apparently they're still using ordinary coaches,' said Max. 'There can't be enough proper transporters to move everyone.'

'Why would they be moving so many?' queried Mattie.

'How about this . . . ?' said Max quietly. 'We—' He corrected himself. '*You* see a coach with strutters on – maybe you guys recognize some of them – and it is stopped at the lights. Do you walk past? Do you let it go? That's the question.'

'I'd let it go,' said Amos. 'We'd just get ourselves killed.'

'Think I agree with Amos,' said Daisy.

'I like the attitude,' said Ant, 'but not if it means going straight back to Spike. Or wherever. Which is what we'd be doing.' She returned to her screen. 'OK, I'm in.' She spoke as she typed. '*We are escaped strutters from HMP London. We are safe for now, a few injuries. Any others out here?*' She looked up. 'That OK?' Everyone nodded. She hit 'send'.

'Now what?' asked Daisy.

'Wait and see,' said Max. 'Think you'll be surprised.'

'At four in the morning?'

Max was right. Within seconds, messages appeared under Ant's post. She held up the screen for everyone to see.

Thrilling news! Stay safe.

Go Brits! Best news in a terrible week.

Wir sind in Deutschland begeistert.

Mattie translated. 'We are thrilled in Germany.'

Was this your strap message? Brilliant! Not to blame! Nicht schuld!

Attached to this post was a photo of a pile of discarded straps – the top one clearly marked with *Not to Blame!*

'My God, that's my writing,' said Daisy. 'Those are from the coach!'

'Probably a close-up from a police photo,' said Max. 'I wonder if they knew what they were doing . . .'

For the next half-hour they sat and watched as messages of support from all over the world filled the screen, many adding *Not to Blame* as a sign-off. Then a video was attached to a post and they all leaned in closer. The message on it said:

This is out there now. God speed.

'That's the Heath!' said Amos. The still showed a crowd of people filing out of one of the exits.

Ant, suddenly nervous, hit the 'play' icon.

It was footage from one of the police cameras; a time-code scrolled in the top left corner.

'This is going to be us, isn't it?' said Mattie.

Amos was first into view, and immediately a red box graphic surrounded his head and stayed with him as he walked. Daisy and Jimmy got the same treatment. Three red boxes moved towards the exit. Only Jimmy's was still visible when Mattie and then Ant appeared. Immediately the film slowed. Mattie's beanie hat and Ant's baseball cap gave them some disguise but not enough. A digital zoom showed Ant turning to a woman next to her. Another zoom, closer still, Ant's goose tattoos clearly visible as she spoke. A maximum close-up showed her mouth moving.

'*Not . . . to . . . blame*,' lip-read Daisy.

The words had been written in crude graphics across the bottom – clearly a doctored version of the police original. When the video finished, they sat in silence.

Eventually Jimmy said, 'Staying hidden is going to be tough. Everyone knows us now. Max, can you drive?'

'Sure.'

'Could you hire a van with that fake ID and debit card, Ant? Those drop-off car rental sites don't ask too many questions. Ant?'

Ant wasn't listening. She had her hands over her mouth.

'Ant, what's the matter?' said Jimmy, standing. She held up the screen again. Once more it was full of messages, but these were very different.

Oh you poor things. So sad.

Vicious bastards. Sympathies from Glasgow.

What terrible news! We are all crying here.

Stay hidden young ones. RIP.

Ant's heart was thumping in her chest, her hands shaking.

'What do they mean, *RIP*?' said Daisy, barely audible.

Ant clicked through to a news site and dropped the phone on the table. Everyone could read the headline.

TWELVE MORE RIOT DEATHS ANNOUNCED AT HMP LONDON

And below:

The deaths have been announced of twelve more prisoners held in the family annexe of HMP London, scene of one of the UK's worst ever prison riots.

The names that followed were in alphabetical order, but only five made an impression:

Mishal Noon . . . Dan and Gina Norton . . . Sarah Raath . . . Ahmet Shah . . . all died as fire and vicious fighting swept through the prison.

Mattie ran to his sister as howling and grief filled the kitchen. She held him tight while he sobbed uncontrollably. Ant's eyes were wide but dry, her mouth open but mute. She felt as though she had shut down, her system unable to cope with what she'd read.

She remembered Dan and Gina meeting her for the first time, Dan and Gina saying goodbye to Max, then Dan and Gina frantically waving her and Mattie away from their cell. She knew she should cry – everyone else was – but nothing came.

Max embraced them both, tears streaming down his face. Daisy, Jimmy and Amos huddled together nearby.

As the first wave of grief subsided, Ant's numbness began to thaw. She pulled the strap-key out of her pocket and placed it on the table.

'I've changed my mind,' she said, her voice tight with barely restrained fury. 'Let's go free some prisoners.'

55

Day 1
We owe you:
tools from shed
a window frame
first-aid kit
3 pizzas
porridge oats
bread
tea
wifi usage

You owe us:
Everything

My favourite things RIGHT NOW:

MAX!
Our old house! I like M more than anyone else. Even if he shouted at A. In fact everyone is shouting and stressed. Found some of my old books and felt sad. D read them to me all the time.

Hampstead Heath, London

A sudden, surprise summer thunderstorm. The old coach was travelling more slowly than usual as the driver, a grey-haired retired PO, stared doggedly through the smeared windscreen. He cursed the wipers, which struggled to cope with the volume of rain; they, like him, had seen better days. The roads were slippery, the cloud was low and he was nervous. Called back into service in the aftermath of the riot, he wasn't sure he was up to the job of long-distance prisoner transfer.

He took the notoriously tight bend at The Spaniards at ten m.p.h. – any faster seemed reckless. A narrow, straight road lay ahead where the Heath opened up and ran down towards the city; by legend the haunt of many a seventeenth-century highwayman.

The driver had just started to accelerate when he heard a sharp bang. The coach's sudden drop and tilt to the left told him that it was the rear kerbside wheel; he braked and cursed at the same time. In his mirrors he saw three darting figures flit from the trees, cross the road and disappear behind the coach. His stomach lurched. This did not feel good. Some of his prisoners woke up and started shouting. The two POs on board told them to calm down, but they were up and pacing the aisle nevertheless.

The driver was reaching for his radio when two figures jumped in front of the windscreen. He exclaimed loudly as he braked, then stared through the glass, the wipers still failing to keep the screen clear. What he could see – intermittently – looked like two boys – no, one girl and one boy – both glaring at him with the most ferocious faces he had ever seen. The boy had light brown skin, a pile of black hair and blue eyes that were on fire. The girl was terrifying: shaved head, the same wide, electric eyes, a tattooed neck that was visibly pulsing. The torrential rain lashed against them but they seemed oblivious to it; water ran in rivers down the girl's face but her stare was unblinking. The driver wiped the windscreen with his sleeve and saw that the girl's lips were parted. For one ridiculous moment he thought she was about to smile; then he realized she was about to attack.

As the remaining tyres blew – Amos, Jimmy, Daisy and Max stabbing ferociously at the thick rubber – Ant leaped onto the kerb. 'By me, now!' she yelled, running halfway along the coach. In seconds the others had lined up behind her and she reached for the handle marked FOR EMERGENCY USE ONLY. She pulled hard, and a door panel popped unlocked, triggering the on-board alarm. Four pairs of hands yanked it open. Howling like banshees, Max and Daisy leaped in, Jimmy and Amos close behind. The two guards attacked with their batons but they were no defence against grief-fuelled rage. Max had one PO cuffed to a seat in seconds, blood oozing from a gash in his forehead. Jimmy and Amos had the other face down in the aisle, one of the prisoners getting in a well-aimed kick as he fell. There was cheering and foot-stamping from all around the vehicle.

Ant ran up to the driver, grabbing the fallen PO's baton as she went. 'Cuff yourself to the wheel!' she yelled, pointing the stick between the man's terrified eyes. He didn't need telling twice: he grabbed the handcuffs from his belt and fastened them around his wrist and then to the steering wheel. Ant took the keys from his belt. 'Which one?' she asked, and he pointed to a small black one. She unhooked it and threw it to Mattie. 'OK, fast as you can! Be ready to run.'

Ant climbed on a seat. 'I have a strap-key!' she yelled above the alarm. 'We'll release who we can!' She registered the gasps, the shouts and the anxious glances through the windows, but she had a job to do. Jimmy and Max were unlocking handcuffs with the other liberated keys, and soon there was a queue forming in front of Ant.

A father and daughter were first. 'You can take off straps?' The man was incredulous.

'Most of them, yes,' she said.

His daughter, a fragile-looking girl of around fourteen, pulled up her T-shirt.

Insert, twist, release.

The strap fell away and the girl burst into tears. Her father cried out then laughed – his was off next. 'Thank you, thank you, thank you!' he whispered.

'Where were they taking you?' said Ant, kicking his strap away.

'Bodmin, they said.'

'Really? Why Bodmin?'

The man was desperate to leave, but he owed this strange girl an answer.

'Big new strutter jail,' he said. 'The old ones aren't safe any more so they're putting us all in one place.'

'But not you,' said Ant. 'Not now.' She smiled at the girl, who ran forward and kissed her.

'That was from me too,' said her father, and they left the coach.

Seeing what had happened, the others surged forward – more than twenty strutters, each realizing that the police would be there in a matter of minutes. They crowded around Ant as she worked.

'Faster! For God's sake, speed up! Please!'

'Do me next!'

'Please help my son!'

She ignored them. They had discussed it in the hire van (if you could call the sorrow- and anger-fuelled shouting a discussion). She would de-strap until they heard sirens. They wanted to strike back, to hurt the system that had just murdered their parents. Jimmy, Daisy, Max and Amos were outside keeping watch. She was working as fast as she could.

Two women, then a man – free strutters – jumped down from the coach, running towards the sodden Heath. Next in the queue, a father pushing his son towards Ant.

'Go on, son,' he said encouragingly.

'Turn round,' said Ant.

The boy, who couldn't have been more than eight, lifted his shirt. She took one look and swallowed hard. She'd known this was likely to happen, just hoped it wouldn't be like this.

'I'm sorry,' she said. 'The key won't fit. You have a different strap.' She looked at the father. 'Would you like me to try yours?'

'What do you mean—?' he began.

'There isn't time to explain. I can try yours if you like . . .'

The boy pulled his father towards Ant. 'Go on, Dad,' he said softly. 'I'll be fine. You should get out if you can.'

But his father scooped him up, carrying him to the nearest seat. Ant heard him say, 'No chance. I'd rather stay with you. It'll be that new strap you had fitted, I reckon . . .'

Then a cry from the road. 'Drone coming up fast!' Ant crouched low just as a blue pol-drone took up position high above them.

Amos appeared on the steps. 'We should go now!'

'Are there sirens?' she said.

Insert, twist, release.

'Forget the sirens, Ant! We'll need all the time we can get!' He sounded desperate, scared. Mattie appeared at his side and she knew he agreed.

Insert, twist, release.

'I'm nearly done!' she called.

But there never were sirens. The police arrived unannounced, three cars at high speed. They burned rubber as they braked twenty metres from the transporter, skidding to a halt on the wet road.

'Cops!' shrieked Daisy.

'Ant, run!' cried Jimmy.

She glanced up at the remaining strutters. 'Sorry,' she said, and jumped. So did everyone else. Unable to resist the open doors, the strapped and the de-strapped all leaped from the coach. A few ran for the woods but many charged straight towards the police cars, splashing through the newly formed lakes of water. Six officers fought fifteen prisoners . . . The first pair to climb from their vehicle were surprised by the charge, stumbling in the wet, then falling and losing their tasers. With both stun guns now pointed at the fallen policemen, a stand-off quickly developed.

The rain was getting heavier still, the whole Heath swathed in mist. The pol-drone was now nowhere to be seen.

Ant had hesitated, torn between escape and joining in the fight.

'Let's go!' said Max. 'We can fight another day. Let's get to the van!'

'No!' said Amos. 'I'm not taking orders from you. I'm staying.'

'Me too,' said Jimmy, and they ran to join the prisoners.

'Jimmy, you can't!' Ant shouted after him. She felt Mattie take one hand, Daisy the other.

Max was desperate. 'Ant, we have to escape now or it'll be too late!'

The two policemen looked up. Recognizing Ant, they broke the stalemate. Ignoring the shouted threats from the taser-armed prisoners, the policemen charged. Two dart-like electrodes fired; the policemen fell, stunned.

But one shot was all the prisoners had. Each taser had to be reloaded and the prisoners had no ammunition left. The four standing officers, by contrast, had plenty, and they fired at will. Four prisoners collapsed. While two policemen reloaded, the other two drew their batons. Still the prisoners fought, but they were dropping in numbers.

'Ant!' cried Max again.

'We can't leave them, Max! We have to help!'

But now the police had a clear shot at Ant. One officer dropped to his knee.

'No!' yelled Daisy, and ran across his line of fire. The dart hit her in the shoulder, and Ant saw her shudder, then crumple. She lay face down in the mud.

'Daisy, no!' She started to run towards her, but Max and Mattie pulled her back. Another policeman took aim; this time Jimmy launched himself at the officer. As they both fell to the ground, there was a muffled explosion. Both men lay still for a moment, then it was the policeman who got up. It was Jimmy who lay motionless.

Ant cried out again, but Max had seen enough. He pushed her and Mattie away from the coach. Then the smell of pepper spray hit their nostrils, and they ran.

56

'But we've left Amos!' shouted Mattie.

'Get to the van!' said Ant.

'But we've actually left him behind!'

'We'll circle round and find him!' said Max.

The hire van had been parked as close to the Heath as they dared. Ant, Mattie and Max had made it through the woods when they heard sprinting footsteps behind them. Max turned just as Amos hit him full on the mouth, the running punch sending him sprawling into the road.

'That's for leaving us,' Amos spat at him.

Ant pulled him away. 'In the van,' she hissed. 'We'll sort it in the van, not here.' She pulled Max to his feet and they ran on. 'As soon as we're inside, we've disappeared,' she said. 'Then we talk.'

Spitting blood, Max staggered the final few paces.

He hit the key fob and the van's lights flashed twice. They flung the doors open and dived in; Max and Ant in the front, Amos and Mattie in the back.

Max fired the engine and pulled away from the kerb. 'Everybody down!' he shouted. 'You can hit me again later, Amos, but let's get out of here now!'

Mattie was sobbing. Ant reached behind to squeeze his hand and then they all slid to the floor.

'I can't believe you just left us,' said Amos from behind the driver's seat. 'Daisy was down, Jimmy was down, and you just . . . ran away.' The disgust in his voice couldn't have been clearer. 'I was still fighting some copper and you' – he managed to kick Max's seat – 'you disappeared.'

'Amos, I'm sorry,' said Max, carefully keeping under the speed limit. 'We were all about to be caught. There seemed no point—'

'No point in helping?' Amos interrupted. 'You're a coward. From a family of cowards.'

Ant bit back her retort; their situation was bad enough already. 'We messed up,' she said. 'We're sorry.' There was silence in the van, which was a forgiveness of sorts. 'We're all upset. We all make mistakes.'

At each set of lights, each junction, Max looked around nervously. 'There's loads of police, but they're not looking at us,' he said.

'That's because they don't know what they're looking for,' said Ant, still on the floor. 'The van's not stolen, my debit card works, my fake ID is cool and you can drive. Unless we get a puncture or something . . .'

'Don't,' said Max. 'Just don't. We need to hide. Actually, more than hide – we need to disappear.'

'Keep driving,' she said. 'For now, even not being in London would be something.'

After a few minutes a small voice came from the back. 'How do we know they're telling the truth?' said Mattie slowly.

'What?'

'When they said that . . . Dan and Gina . . . and the others . . . well, is it true?'

Amos shifted behind the driver's seat. 'Actually, yeah,' he said, sitting up. 'Maybe they're lying, maybe it isn't true . . .' He was incredulous and hopeful at the same time. 'But why would they make that up?'

'To flush us out?' suggested Max. 'To make us do something stupid?'

'I don't think it was stupid,' said Ant. 'I think it was brilliant. Right up to the point when we lost Daisy and Jimmy . . .'

'Which makes it stupid,' snapped Amos.

'We need the Bug sites on this,' said Max. 'They're the only eyes and ears we have. Tell them what's happened. I suppose it's possible that the prison released false information . . .'

Mattie was sitting up now. 'So you do think Dan and Gina might still be alive?' Everyone heard the yearning in his voice.

'Maybe.' Ant was back on her phone, logging on.

'Why don't you post a video on the site, Ant?' said

Max. 'You're the *Not to Blame* girl. Tell them what's happened.'

'Isn't that risky?' she said.

'The site is the most secure I've seen. We made it that way.'

'You OK with that, Amos?' Ant turned, and he shrugged.

She propped the phone up on the dashboard, stared at the screen and started to record:

'*My name is Ant. Me and my friends are the strutters who busted out of Spike. Today we stopped a prison coach and took a few straps off. Freed some people. But we lost two of our friends – they were hit by tasers. We don't know what's happened to them.*'

She looked away from the camera for a moment.

'*And none of us know about our parents. The news sites say that Sarah Raath, Ahmet Shah, Mishal Noon, Dan Norton and Gina Norton are all dead, but we don't know if this true. If anyone can help, then please let us know.*'

She stopped recording and there was ironic applause from the back.

'Quite the TV star,' muttered Amos.

'Ignore him,' said Max.

'Like you ignored me back on the Heath,' he replied. 'This is getting boring.'

57

They lapsed into a heavy silence, Max driving, Ant, Mattie and Amos still slumped out of site. Ant's head was full of Jimmy, tasers, Daisy, rain, storming the coach, taking off straps, Dan and Gina.

What a mess. What a total, hideous mess, Ant thought. *Why couldn't I save any of them? How come I always lose everyone?* She reached behind to hold Mattie's hand.

'*Nou pral dwe OK*,' she said. She felt him squeeze her hand, then noticed Max glancing over. 'What?'

'I'd forgotten,' he replied. 'How you speak to each other. Your secret language.'

She shook her head. She hadn't realized. 'That's just stupid,' she said. 'It just comes out that way sometimes.'

'What did you say?' asked Max.

'In my "secret language"?'

Max hit the radio button and the van filled with classical music. He changed stations till he found something with a guitar in it. 'Anything's better than silence,' he muttered.

'I said, *We'll be OK*,' said Ant, relenting, and he nodded.

'Thanks.'

Eventually Mattie asked, 'Where are we going?'

'I'm heading south-west,' Max said. 'I know my way around there. Unless anyone has any other ideas . . .'

'Fine,' said Ant. 'Actually we should head for Cornwall.'

'Really? Why?'

'It's Bodmin Prison,' said Amos; it was the first time he had spoken for a while. 'I spoke to one of the strutters.'

'Yeah,' said Ant, pleased he'd joined in. 'Seems like everyone's being put in one place. In which case Jimmy and Daisy will be there.'

'And if my dad's alive . . .' said Amos.

'Yeah, but why?' persisted Max.

'Because we *should*,' said Ant. 'I know it sounds useless, but if every strutter is being taken there, then we need to be there too. No one else wants to help. Maybe there are some coaches to storm, more strutters to free. I don't want to go back to Spike, but we can't just do nothing.'

'Revenge,' said Amos.

'Call it justice,' said Max.

Amos snorted. 'If it makes college boy feel happier, sure. We'll call it justice.'

The clouds and the rain had vanished, and by noon the heat was back. The van's air-con had broken so Max drove with his window open. The M4 became the M5, and everyone but him fell asleep. No one noticed him looking forlornly at the signs to Bristol; he wondered what Sara was doing, what she would say to him. Were his mum and dad *really* dead? Images of the riot filled his head and he pushed them away. No one actually knew anything, so driving to where his parents *might* be seemed like a plan.

He remembered Sara talking about 'disappearing' people. Three students had needed to vanish and had gone what she had called 'stealth camping'. One had pitched a tent in some woods; the others hid in a disused quarry. The key, so she said, was finding a safe space, but as it turned out, the quarry was used by quad bikers. They reported seeing gas canisters, uncollected rubbish and tents – the students were soon arrested.

'We need a safe space,' he muttered, assuming everyone was still asleep.

'We need a what?' said Ant, stirring.

'We need to hide. Bodmin Moor isn't huge, but it's big enough. And we need to hide this van too.'

'Are we going to live in this van?' asked Mattie.

'Might have to,' said Ant.

They refuelled and Max used Ant's card to stock up on

provisions. The gloom in the van was un-shiftable but lack of food and drink had been making everything worse.

'I nearly drove into a service station while you were asleep,' said Max, 'but there were cops there. This will keep us going for a bit.'

They ate tacos, sandwiches and chocolate as the road twisted and narrowed. On either side of them the moor rolled out as far as they could see. Apart from a few rocky outcrops, it seemed featureless, almost desolate.

'What a boring place,' Mattie groaned. 'I don't want to live here.'

'A bit of boring would be fine,' said Max. 'I'd settle for that.' He explained about stealth camping. 'We go off the grid. To all intents and purposes, we disappear. Wait for everything to die down.'

'It's not going to die down,' muttered Amos. 'It's never going to die down. We're going to have to disappear for a long time.'

'Well, it's better than Spike,' said Mattie.

'And some people can disappear for years,' Max went on. 'They just don't want to "join in" with anything any more. So they come to places like this. Run their own lives.'

'Great,' said Amos. 'Good for them. But I can't do that. *We* can't do that. I want to know about my dad. I need to find out what happened.'

The winding road had forced Max to slow down. '*Bodmin two miles*,' read Ant from a road sign. 'How close do we want to be?'

The question was left unanswered, but when a small dirt track opened up ahead of them, Max took it. 'How about this?'

The track was narrow, with concrete posts and a wire fence on either side, and they bounced along over the potholes. Max steered round rusting furniture and piles of scattered engine parts.

'Where is this?' muttered Amos. The fencing had given way to a roughly made, three-metre-high wall, its granite stones topped off with corrugated iron sheets and barbed wire. Looking up from the van, they could see the tops of roofs, but nothing else. Even the padlocked gates had sight screens attached.

'Friendly neighbourhood,' said Ant. 'Let's keep going.' The buildings fell away to scrubland but the track continued onto the moor, the van bouncing and rolling on the turf.

'If anyone sees us, we should keep going.'

'It's not like that here,' said Max, steering around granite rocks. 'If you're living on the moor, you don't watch the news. And you certainly don't go calling the police. It would just draw attention. Everyone wants to be invisible. Left alone.' Ahead was woodland, the trees wide enough apart to allow them to drive in. 'Let's try here.' Max headed into a clearing, coming to a stop when he couldn't go any further.

They tumbled from the van, stretching and yawning, taco and sandwich crumbs falling to the ground. Ant looked around and almost smiled. Mattie said out loud what she was thinking: 'It's like everything has disappeared.' From where they stood, all they could see were trees and moorland.

'But the van is still white,' Ant pointed out. 'Let's do some camouflaging.'

She and Mattie walked deeper into the woods, picking up branches as they went. It felt good to be out of the van but still invisible to the outside world.

'Hey, Mattie, look at that,' whispered Ant. She pointed at a deserted caravan wedged between tree trunks. The door was hanging off its hinges, the windows missing altogether. They approached cautiously, but a brief glance inside told them all they needed to know. The floor had given way, tall grass pushing its way inside.

'On balance, I think our van is better,' said Ant, and they moved on, picking up more camouflage as they went.

When their arms were full, they turned back, but pulled up short, hearing the sound of running water.

'There was a river on the satnav,' said Ant, 'and we're seriously filthy. When was the last time you swam, Mattie?'

'Before Spike,' he said. 'Dan took me.' He paused, and Ant guessed what was coming next. 'Do you think they're alive, Abi?'

'You know I don't know,' she said, 'but we'll find out. Let's go for a swim.'

He looked unconvinced but followed her anyway. There was no path – they climbed over fallen trees and squeezed through dense bracken. A crunching noise underfoot revealed a sea of rusting tin cans and discarded rubbish.

'This is like a tip,' said Mattie. Now piles of bundled newspapers appeared, like stepping stones across the wood. 'Abi, this isn't safe . . .' He stopped. 'We're following the sound of the river but it's like we're really following a trail. And we don't know what's at the end of it.'

She walked back to where Mattie had stopped. He was looking at a shopping trolley half buried in the undergrowth, flowers blooming under its wire basket.

'I don't think we're alone here,' he said.

They both heard the precision *click* of a gun being loaded. From behind it came a growling West Country voice.

'You got that right, kid.'

58

My favourite things RIGHT NOW:
Not being in Spike.
Seeing sheep and foxes.
Thinking D and G might be OK.

Ant and Mattie walked slowly into the clearing.

Amos and Max looked up and their expressions changed immediately. Max's face drained of colour. A shirtless Amos cursed loudly. Ant and Mattie joined them in the line-up, backs to the van. The shotgun was in the hands of a portly, balding man with frizzy tufts of hair around his ears. His skin was weather-beaten and lined, his eyes narrowed.

'It's my wood,' he growled. 'Has been for years. There's no room for the likes of you.'

Ant exchanged nervous glances with the others. 'What do you mean, *the likes of us*?'

'Ha!' he said. 'You know what I mean.' He waved the barrel of the gun at them. 'You're a curse, the lot of you.'

'Why are we a curse?' asked Amos.

Max was conciliatory. 'We honestly didn't realize this was your wood. We can go somewhere else.'

A brief look of confusion passed over the man's face. 'You all speak English?'

'Of course,' said Mattie nervously. 'Why wouldn't we?'

''Cos you normally only speak Lithuanian. Or Latvian or something. 'S where you fruit pickers normally come from.'

The four relaxed immediately. 'We're not fruit pickers!' Max would have laughed if there hadn't been a gun pointing at him. 'We're just . . . on a gap year. On holiday.'

The man stabbed the gun in Mattie's direction. '*He's* on a gap year? Don't make me laugh.' Mattie took Ant's hand.

Amos whispered, 'Max, the water!'

'Oh, yeah,' said Max. 'We were making tea, on the other side of the van. I should turn off the gas . . .'

The man walked round the van to check, then sat down, the shotgun discarded. 'White. Three sugars,' he said.

Now Max did laugh. 'What? Can we stay then?'

'Depends on the tea,' said the man. 'White, three sugars,' he repeated.

Ant looked at the saucepan and the portable barbecue it sat on. 'Got them at the petrol station!' Max said. He brewed the tea and handed an oil-company-sponsored mug to the stranger.

The man blew on it twice, sipped it twice and said, 'I'm Henry.'

More glances between the four, followed by shrugs.

'Max,' said Max.

'How do you do,' said Henry. 'Your friend there used to be a strutter.' He pointed at Amos. 'S'pose you knew that though.'

Amos reached inside the van for his T-shirt and pulled it back on. He looked furious.

'Yes, we knew,' agreed Max.

Henry drank his tea. 'You OK with that?' There was caution and surprise in his voice.

'Sure,' said Ant, her tone matter-of-fact.

'Are you *all* strutters then?' Henry sounded incredulous.

'We should go . . .' Ant was heading towards the van.

'Agreed,' said Max, kicking earth into the barbecue tray. 'Sorry to trouble you, Henry. If you could keep quiet about us . . .'

The stranger found that funny. 'I've been in this wood a long time,' he said. 'You're the first English speakers I've come across. I don't have too many folk to "keep quiet" to. And anyway . . .' He paused. Something in his tone made Ant turn to hear what was coming next. The man looked at each of them in turn. 'Truth is, I should be a strutter too.' They glanced at each other. 'I would have been in prison, but I chose to come here. To disappear.'

Ant and Max sat down next to Henry; Mattie glanced around nervously.

'Ten years ago my old man ran a cowboy building firm. He was very good at it too – till one of his houses collapsed. Killed an old couple, injured loads. Dad died before his trial. When they passed the new laws, I knew they'd come for me. I've got no family, so disappearing was the obvious thing to do. I remembered the moorland from holidays we had around here . . . I tried some other places but it didn't work out.'

'Why not?' asked Mattie.

'Oh, many reasons. Who wants people like me living nearby? And anyway, most of the best places were taken.'

'Really?' said Amos.

'Yeah, there's quite a lot of us, as it turns out,' said Henry. 'Faced with either prison or disappearing, we all chose to disappear. It's not bad here. The river's good for washing, and there's even a phone signal there sometimes—'

'Hang on,' said Mattie. 'There are *others* like you?'

'We're classified as "on-the-runs", though actually we try to stay put, if we can. You're more invisible that way. Let me show you . . .' Henry picked up his gun and headed off into the woods. They followed a few metres behind, stepping carefully over bracken and bin liners. He parted some curtain-like branches and waved them through. 'I'm guessing it's not what you expected,' he said.

'You got that right,' said Amos.

Henry's home was a shipping container. About six metres long and nearly two metres high, it had clearly once been blue but was now mainly browns, greens and rust.

'Managed to paint it a bit,' he muttered as he pulled on a metal bar, releasing a door in the end wall. Inside it was dark and, they all realized together, revoltingly smelly. Piles of papers and heaps of magazines littered the opening. They all hovered at the container's entrance. 'Wind- and waterproof,' said Henry proudly, 'and I've changed the door mechanics so I can lock it from the inside.' He pushed a few tottering stacks of paper to one side. 'Though I wasn't expecting visitors . . .'

Ant saw that all the papers had completed crossword puzzles.

'Any chance of you losing the gun, Henry?' asked Max. 'Makes me nervous.'

'It's supposed to make you nervous!' he said, irritated. 'Are you stupid or something? Prison rot your brain?'

'Oh, *he* wasn't in prison,' said Amos. 'He was at *university*.' He managed to make it sound like an insult.

'I'm an on-the-run too,' said Max. 'It's a long story.'

'They always are.' Henry emerged from the gloom at the back of the container. He had lost the gun and was holding a vinyl album sleeve. Quiet music started to play, and he sat on old car seat propped against the metal wall.

'Van Morrison,' he said, holding up the record sleeve. 'You won't know him, but he was a genius.'

'Actually I *have* heard of him,' said Ant. 'He was from Belfast, wasn't he? One of our POs liked his stuff . . .'

'Where's your power from?' asked Mattie, changing the subject.

'Oh, some car batteries I wired together. It's not perfect, runs a bit slow, but even at the wrong speed, music stops me from going totally mad. It doesn't go any louder than this.' He closed his eyes and conducted along for a few bars. 'But it's enough. You'll need to keep everything you do quiet. Attract no attention.' He read something on the record sleeve. 'What are you going to do?'

Amos got in first. 'We think all the strutters are being brought to Bodmin Prison. There was a fire at ours and . . . we don't know if our parents are alive or not . . . and we were sort of heading this way . . .'

'Not exactly a plan of action,' said Henry, nibbling at a fingernail, 'but you're right about one thing. Bodmin is the new strutter prison. They've been doing the place up ever since I got here. It wasn't used for a hundred years – became a hideous tourist attraction with waxworks and everything. But now it's state-of-the-art. It's not finished, but word is they're filling it with strutters.'

There was silence for a moment. 'So Bodmin Moor is where you go if you want to hide, to disappear—' said Ant.

'It's *one* of the places . . .' interrupted Henry.

'But Bodmin Prison is where you end up if you're caught,' she concluded.

He nodded. 'That's about it, yes.'

'Can you get near the prison?' asked Amos.

'You can if you want to,' said Henry. 'There's a high

fence around most of it, but it's in the town – you can walk past it. Not sure why you'd want to though. If you're hiding, stay here. If you want to get caught, take a trip to Bodmin.'

'What if we drove through?' said Max.

'Is the van stolen?'

Max shook his head. 'Nope. Hired.'

Henry shrugged, then got up and went back into the container. They heard him rummaging and cursing, before he reappeared with some number plates in his hand. 'My last visitors didn't, er, seem to need them,' he said by way of explanation. 'Lithuanian number plates. Everyone will assume you're here for the harvest. Put them on and you really will disappear.'

They hadn't discussed it, but Ant was sure that they were all thinking the same thing: *they needed to see the prison.* If all the strutters were being taken there, then Jimmy and Daisy would be there too. If Gina and Dan had survived – if any of the adults had survived – they would be inside Bodmin Prison.

Whether it was revenge or justice, it had to start there.

59

Day 2
We owe you:
A busted coach

You owe us:
Jimmy
Daisy
Everyone else
Everything else

Mattie declared it the worst night ever. Initially they refused Henry's offer of bedding on the grounds that it stank of Henry, but the hard metal floor of the van had forced them to reconsider; finally they accepted a threadbare sleeping bag and three mouldy cushions.

Max and Ant had argued with each other, then they had argued with Amos. When anyone moved, the whole van shook. When anyone made even the slightest noise, the van seemed to amplify it. Sleep eventually came, but the respite was brief; a heavy storm was followed by sunrise just before five. As the borrowed bedding heated up, the smell became unbearable. Breakfast was biscuits, but the fresh air tasted good. Ant and Mattie stood together in a pool of early morning sunlight and breathed deeply.

'Thank God that's over,' muttered Ant.

'Grass. Wood. Flowers. Earth. And the river,' Mattie said, inhaling again. 'So many nice things at once.'

'Certainly beats Spike first thing in the morning,' said Ant, stretching. Then she paused, listening. 'Can you hear music?'

Mattie nodded. 'Henry's up.' They heard shuffling feet and turned.

'Henry is indeed up,' said Henry, 'and offering you tea. If you fancy it.' Without waiting for an answer, he turned and headed back towards his container.

Ant and Mattie exchanged 'why not' shrugs, and followed. They sat on piles of newspaper, and Henry handed them a mug each. A slow, delicate piano solo drifted out from the container.

Henry sipped. 'It's some Bill Evans,' he said. 'You know him?' They both shook their heads. 'It's my morning tune. Play it every day.' He waited for a few more chords, his free hand playing air piano. 'I know every note.' He held up the record sleeve, which showed a bearded middle-aged man sitting hunched at a piano. 'People said we looked alike. Long time ago. What do you think?'

Ant shook her head. 'Can't see it, Henry – sorry.'

He passed it to Mattie.

Ant sifted through some of the newspapers at her feet. All were folded to the crossword, each clue completed. 'You're good,' she said. 'Our foster dad did them. Think you're better than him though.'

Henry shifted his weight on the makeshift seat. 'You think he may have died? Your friend seemed to be suggesting . . .'

'Yeah, maybe . . .' she said, glancing at Mattie.

Henry cleared his throat. 'I always was good with words,' he said, changing the subject. 'Loved playing with letters. Fitting it all together. Some puzzles take me a while but' – he gestured around – 'I have plenty of time.'

'What about numbers?' asked Mattie.

'How do you mean?'

'Are you good with number puzzles too?'

Mattie and Ant exchanged glances. 'Good call,' she muttered.

'Not bad, I s'pose,' Henry said. 'Why do you ask?'

Ant took her cue. 'Just before he died, a prison officer who helped me – his name was Brian . . . anyway, he told me that the code he used for his security pass would not just get me out but change my life. I think it means something but—'

'What's the code?'

'8B 3S 2C3.'

Henry repeated the numbers and letters back a few times. 'No idea. But I'll work on it if you like?'

Max appeared and nodded at him. 'Thought I heard voices,' he said. Then, to Ant and Mattie, 'We should go to Bodmin.'

Ant finished her tea; Mattie poured his dregs onto the ground and said, 'See you later, Henry.'

They followed Max back to the van and told Amos what they planned to do.

Mattie looked at Ant. 'You know Brian said to keep a record of the numbers and letters?' he asked her.

'He said something like that, yes,' she replied. 'There was a lot going on . . .'

'Well, did you? Did you write them down ever?'

'No. No way. Seemed too dangerous. Why, Mattie?'

He shrugged. 'Just seems a weird thing to say, that's all.'

After removing the bedding from the van, they set off. Max headed past the fenced-off houses and back onto the road.

'About five minutes to the prison,' he said. 'That's what Henry says anyway.'

Ant's nerves started to jangle; now she really was awake. She scrolled through the Bug sites; she had tried to log on the previous night but got no signal in the woods. Here it was strong, and she called out the posted comments as she found them.

'*Sorry, guys, no information here . . . Big sympathies, no sightings* . . . Oh, hang on!' She read a new post to herself, and everyone turned to face her. 'Someone called Ally67 says she's heard of a possible sighting of Sarah Raath. And someone else says they heard of some escaped strutters getting recaptured. And that's all.'

'No it isn't.' Amos grabbed the phone. He'd been looking over her shoulder and noticed a whole stream of comments that Ant hadn't mentioned. Mattie tried to snatch it back, but Amos read from the screen. '*Goose girl is right. We need more like her . . . What do those geese mean? . . . Good messages from the goose girl . . . "Not to Blame" needs to be shouted from the rooftops . . . Want more videos, goose girl . . .*' He threw the phone back to her. 'You're getting famous,' he said, with mock enthusiasm.

'Well, feel free to post the next message,' she said, shrugging. 'It doesn't really matter.'

Max braked, interrupting the argument. 'OK, we're here!' he called, and they all stared through the windscreen. 'This is Bodmin – prison's off to the left, I think.'

Houses and small stores lined the road. There was little traffic about.

'Where is everyone?' wondered Mattie.

'In bed. It's still only seven o'clock. Wonder if we stand out, driving around so early . . .'

'We've got the foreign plates on,' said Amos. 'Didn't Henry say we'd be invisible?'

'He did,' said Max. 'And we have to remember we're Lithuanian harvesters if anyone speaks to us.' It seemed so ridiculous, everyone laughed.

'What do Lithuanians sound like?' asked Mattie.

'Vaguely German, I think. Hang on, guys – look at this.' Ahead, two large white vehicles had stopped at some traffic lights; it was clear what was happening.

'Oh my God,' said Ant. 'Prison transporters.'

'And proper ones this time,' added Amos. 'The kind we can't attack.'

Max drove closer, waiting for the lights to change. Rather than pulling up alongside them, he tucked the van in behind the second transporter. It was white and polished steel, a tinted window set in its rear door.

'Can they see us?' asked Mattie. 'Should we be hiding?'

Before anyone could answer, a truck trundled past them towards the junction. '*Cable Broadcast and TV Services*,' Mattie read from the painted logo. The driver blasted his horn at the prison transporter, which replied in kind. There followed some shouted greetings across the tarmac.

'Old friends apparently,' said Max.

Amos frowned. 'That's not good.'

'Not good at all,' agreed Ant. 'TV and prison means *Correction*. They must be planning on filming here.' She felt her flesh creep.

The prison vehicles and television truck moved away. Max waited briefly, then followed at a distance. They drove down a steep hill, a few more vehicles providing some cover, and then a large rectangular tower appeared above the rooftops. Max slowed as the rest of the prison came into view. From Henry's description, Ant had expected a modern building, but what she saw was something from a distant age. Ancient and forbidding, its vast brick walls rose castle-like into the sky, tiny windows arranged at regular intervals. Ivy covered whole sections of the wing that was closest to them; here there were larger, patterned windows with ornate surrounds, and bright, modern lighting shone from inside. Ant saw movement and a face appeared in the window, pausing momentarily before moving away.

'Don't stop! Don't stop!' she said, her voice urgent. 'Keep going! That was Grey! Oh my God, he's here!'

Max spun round; Amos twisted in his seat; Mattie grabbed Ant's arm.

'You've got to be kidding me,' breathed Amos.

'The assessor guy from Spike? You sure?' asked Max.

'No,' said Ant, 'I'm not. I can't be. But I know how he stands. How he looks. How he breathes. And that sure looked like him.'

Max had swerved back into the lane.

'God, I hate him,' Ant muttered.

'Whether Dad's alive or not,' said Amos, still staring at the window, 'I want to see Grey *punished*. I want to see him *hurt*.'

'OK, guys, calm down,' said Max. 'If that *is* Grey, does it make a difference to where I'm driving? The road follows the security fence – I can do a lap . . .'

Steel barricades and six-metre-high concrete blocks encircled the prison; security cameras every fifty metres. The building might be gothic but the security was brand new.

'No, no, no, it's too risky,' said Ant. 'Why would anyone do a lap of a prison? Pull away, Max.'

He turned left and started the climb back into the town.

Ant's head was buzzing. 'If that *was* Grey, and if those TV trucks *are* for *Correction*, we are right back in it here,' she said.

'Is that a good thing?' asked Mattie. 'Do we want to be "right back in it"?'

'What can the four of us do against all that?' Amos pointed at the prison tower, still visible over the rooftops.

'We can cause trouble,' said Ant. 'At the very least, we can cause trouble.'

They drove in silence for a while; then Max slowed right down. 'How about here?'

The road sign said ARMCHAIR CORNER; the houses were small, neat and modern, but as the van stopped, they saw the view. Max had looped round, ending up behind the prison but much closer than before. This housing estate, built when the prison was just a ruin, looked straight into its courtyards.

An overgrown brick-and-wood fence gave them cover, and they piled out of the van. Ant hoisted Mattie up in front of her and they peered over the top. She guessed the prison's exterior walls had been kept because it was a listed building, but it could just have been because they were terrifying. The dread she felt was, she thought, just what she was supposed to feel.

'There are the transporters.' Mattie pointed to a walled area in front of an arched gatehouse. The two prison vehicles and the CB&TV truck were parked alongside each other, prison officers and technicians milling around them.

'You think this is for *Correction*?' said Max. 'That wouldn't be till tonight – they seem extremely busy for seven forty-five in the morning.' The TV technicians were setting up small spotlights and switching them on.

'No,' Ant said slowly, 'this is happening *right now*,' and she pulled her phone out of her pocket. 'There's something they want to show us.' The fear in Mattie's eyes mirrored her own. She found one of the morning news shows and held out her phone for them all to see. Along the bottom of the screen ran a caption: *News Alert – Live statement from HMP Bodmin.* Ant propped the phone against a tall clump of weeds and her eyes switched from screen to courtyard.

From Armchair Corner they watched a woman in a suit appear in front of the lights, a cameraman poised and ready. Both then turned as a stooped man in a black suit emerged from the prison building.

Ant inhaled sharply. 'It *is* him. It actually *is* him. The bastard is here.'

They all took it in turns to curse Grey as he shook hands with the reporter, then patted his hair.

'Anyone got a rocket launcher?' said Amos. He mimed the action of firing into the courtyard.

Grey and the reporter stood together, the POs behind them; they all seemed to be waiting for something.

'What's happening?' asked Mattie.

'The eight o'clock news,' said Max. 'Maximum coverage, highest viewing figures. That's what's happening. And here come the drones.'

They instinctively ducked as four prison surveillance drones appeared above the courtyard, two dipping and moving further away, two hovering thirty metres above the transporters.

'Great,' said Ant. 'Right at our eye level. Thanks for nothing.'

They all slid to the ground, sitting with their backs to the fence, and stared at her phone.

'I have a terrible feeling we're going to know whoever's in that transporter,' said Max.

61

'*You're watching Breakfast News . . .*' A suntanned, slightly puffy-faced man smiled into the camera. '*As you know, we've been expecting a statement from Bodmin Prison about some of the recently escaped prisoners from HMP London. Our reporter Vic Ladysmith is there. Vic, what can you tell us?*'

The view switched to the walled courtyard, where a thin-faced woman with big hair and stretched skin nodded. '*That's right, Eammon. Here at Bodmin Prison we've been waiting to hear from their new governor, John Grey, and he's with me now.*' The shot widened to reveal not just the black-suited Grey but also the two transporters. '*Governor,*' continued the reporter, '*I believe you have news of some of the escaped London prisoners.*'

Grey smiled and nodded. '*Yes, Victoria. Following the*

shocking violence at HMP London, many heritage criminals regrettably managed to escape. We have mounted an unprecedented security operation to recapture these dangerous men and women.'

He glanced over at the first transporter, where handcuffed prisoners were starting to emerge, POs leading them past the camera towards the prison.

'*The message this sends, Victoria, is that the rule of law holds firm. Heritage crime needs to be tackled, and here at Bodmin we will lead that fight. Every prisoner here is a so-called strutter. They will pay the debt they owe. These criminals*' – he gestured to the line of shuffling men and women behind him – '*tried to run away. And they failed . . .*'

Four hundred metres away, behind the fence in Armchair Corner, Ant, Mattie, Max and Amos crowded around the phone, trying to identify the strutters.

'There's Blakely!' cried Ant. 'They got him! Poor man . . .'

'And the Pearsons,' added Amos. 'Plus loads from our coach . . .' The camera caught dejected faces and a two-fingered salute from Jeffrey Blakely.

'Maybe we'll see Dan and Gina,' whispered Mattie to Ant.

She put her arm round him and pulled him close.

The second transporter was emptying now.

'We all know what's about to happen, don't we?' muttered Amos. On screen, they saw Grey glancing from the strutters to the reporter. 'He's waiting, isn't he?' said Amos. 'He knows exactly who's left.'

And then Daisy appeared, wrists tied together, face covered in bruises.

'Oh, Daisy, what have they done to you?' whispered Ant.

She was followed by Jimmy, who had to be helped down the step by a PO.

'He can barely walk,' said Amos.

Despite the drones, they all stood up and peered hesitantly over the fence. They were just in time to see the subdued figures of their friends disappearing through the prison doors.

From Ant's phone they heard Grey's voice conclude the interview. '*There will of course have to be a re-strapping for all those who escaped. This will be done in public, as part of our next Correction. Thank you for coming, Victoria.*'

They had seen enough.

'Time to go,' said Ant. 'And those drones are looking busy.' One had positioned itself above the prison tower, the other three had started patrolling the security fence. The van pulled away just as one appeared at the end of Armchair Corner.

The mood in the van was grim.

'A public re-strapping?' said Amos, now in the front passenger seat. 'How barbaric can you get?'

'Has that ever been done before?' asked Max.

'No,' said Ant from the back. 'That's just Grey's sadistic twist. Re-strapping, yes – particularly in the early days when some straps just got ripped off. It's a pretty horrible experience . . .'

They drove out of Bodmin, back towards the woods.

'You said we were going to cause trouble,' Mattie said to Amos. 'What sort of trouble?'

'Because now might be good,' added Max.

'Yes, yes, yes, but what with?' said Amos. 'Look at us. We're four kids. What can we do against all of them?'

'Well, we can do something or we can do nothing,' said Ant.

'But our "something" will get us caught and re-strapped,' said Amos. 'We need help. That's the truth. We need help.'

'That would be great,' said Max. 'Of course we need help. Who did you have in mind?' Ant could tell he was struggling to keep the scepticism out of his voice.

'The Cloverwells would help.' Amos spoke boldly, his words hanging in the van.

Ant and Mattie exchanged astonished glances. 'You'd bring the gangs in, Amos? Are you totally mental? You'd ask the most vicious London gang down here to help us? You do know they made up all that stuff about Mattie, don't you?'

'Yes, I do. I know all that,' he said. 'But it might work. The way I see it, we can fail on our own or we can succeed – maybe – with the gangs. They're probably here already anyway – we'd just have to ask. But if you're squeamish—'

Max banged the steering wheel angrily. 'Squeamish?

I'm not squeamish about them, I'm *disgusted*. You would seriously get the people responsible for the riot that maybe killed our parents . . . you'd ask them to help . . . *here*?'

Amos turned to face Max, his face flushed. 'If it meant getting inside that prison and releasing anyone we can, then yes, I would. What is your plan? Go on, use that expensive education of yours and tell me.' He leaned over till his face was centimetres from Max's. 'If we don't bring in the Clovers, how do we get Daisy and Jimmy out?'

'But why would they help us?' said Max, staring at the road. 'And what do you even know about them anyway?'

'Oh, he knows lots,' said Ant. 'Don't you, Amos?' Now it was her turn to lean forward; their heads were nearly touching. 'You and your family always were pretty tight with the criminals. On the take for years. Your mum was the gangs' favourite copper, wasn't she?'

Mattie's urgent, 'Back off, Abi!' came too late. Amos's forehead suddenly crashed into Ant's, and she fell back.

Max and Mattie both started yelling; Max brought the van to a screeching halt. He jumped out, ran round to the passenger side and hauled Amos out of his seat, throwing him onto the ground. Checking for passers-by, he opened the back door.

'Is she OK, Mattie?' he shouted.

Ant eased herself out of the van, holding her head. Her fingers and forehead were bloody and she winced. Mattie jumped out behind her. 'You shouldn't have said that, Abi,' he said.

'Maybe,' she muttered as she walked over to the prone Amos. 'Hey, Max, I can fight my own battles here.' She reached out to pull Amos to his feet but he shook his head. Kept his hands on the ground.

'You deserved that.'

'OK, maybe I did,' said Ant, 'but we need to decide this now. If we tell the Cloverwells – or any gang – where we are, it'll end badly for us—'

'Might end badly for *you*,' interrupted Amos, 'but then, you started the riot.'

'Shut up, Amos,' said Mattie. 'You know that's not fair.'

'Enough,' said Max. 'Let's vote. If you want to call in the gangs, raise your hand.'

'This is a sham,' muttered Amos. 'You know it.'

'And if you think working with murderers, thieves and traffickers is like committing suicide,' continued Max, 'raise your hand.' He looked around. 'Three to one. You lost, Amos. Now get in the van and let's work out what to do.'

Amos didn't move. 'No thanks.'

'You what?' said Ant.

'I'm fine. You left me before, you can leave me again. I'll find my own way back. You go and make your little plans. Which will fail. See you later.'

They stood staring at him for a few seconds, then Ant shrugged. 'OK, see you later.'

They climbed into the van, slamming the doors behind them.

'Are we really leaving him?' asked Mattie.

'Sure looks like it,' said Max, and headed back onto the road.

'This isn't good,' said Mattie. No one said anything. 'Do you think he'll come back?'

Max nodded. 'Once he's cooled off, yes.'

'Once he's stopped being an idiot,' said Ant.

62

Back in the wood, they sat around the van eating dry cornflakes. Henry offered them some jam to go with them, but they declined. It was late in the afternoon before Amos appeared, walking slowly towards the wood. Hands in pockets, head down, he headed straight for the van. No words, no eye contact; he climbed in and slammed the door behind him.

'Still mad then?' said Ant.

'My guess is that if he could think of anywhere else to go, he would have gone,' said Max. 'For now, we're all he's got.'

'He looked very red,' said Mattie. 'Maybe he was just lying in the road all this time.'

'Maybe he's embarrassed at being such a dork,' said

Ant, standing up. 'I need a phone signal. Henry said it was better by the river. Gonna check the Bug sites.'

She pushed her way through the bracken and nettles towards the sound of the river. While waiting for Amos they had decided to ask the site users for help. Who knew how many supporters were out there? Maybe Bodmin was home to many other Henrys. If they were saying no to the gangs, maybe they could form their own?

The woods ran all the way down to the river. It was fast-running, swollen by last night's storm, and Ant sat on the bank, legs in the water, while she began the logon. Henry was right about the signal, but it was weak and the connection was slow.

The water felt thrillingly cold, and suddenly Ant felt filthy. Her shower in their old house seemed like weeks ago, and her skin was encrusted with sweat and grime. Swiftly glancing around, she put down her phone, stripped off and plunged into the river. Ant gasped as the freezing water hit her, losing her footing on the slippery soil bed. Submerged briefly, she regained her balance and struck out for the opposite bank, reaching it in a few strokes. Her whole body felt electrified with the cold and she paused there as she caught her breath.

With only her head above the water, the loudest sound was the churning, bubbling river. But now there was something else. Ant was increasingly aware of a humming, whining noise that seemed to be all around her. Feeling suddenly vulnerable, she took a breath and sank deeper below the surface. Her first thought was bees or wasps, but then, with a feeling of dread in her stomach, she realized she knew exactly what it was.

A drone.

Frantically she looked around. Guessing that it was following the river, she stayed as low in the water as she could, glancing first downstream, then up.

She missed it at first, her eyes adjusting to the bright, sparkling water, but then it moved and she had it. Thirty metres away – a small, black, four-rotor machine hovering a metre above the river. She recognized the model, and she recognized the high-def camera on top of its shell too. Ant thought it unlikely that she'd been spotted but she couldn't be sure. She took a deep breath, then disappeared below the surface of the water. She had no idea how long she could hold her breath, but she had to stay under until the drone passed. Her hands held onto to some submerged tree roots as she floated below the surface.

Please God, keep the boys away, she thought. *For loads of reasons . . .*

Ant's eyes were open, straining against the current and the dazzling brightness, but there was no doubting the drone when it came. The water acted as a fractured magnifying glass. She was numb with cold, but Ant shivered anyway as the giant bug-like apparition came into view. Her lungs were already bursting when the drone stopped right above her. Ant could see the four eddies caused by its rotors and watched as they moved through 360 degrees.

Move on. Go away. Please go away.

Ant knew she had only seconds left before her lungs gave out. Still the drone didn't move. What was it looking at?

It must have seen a path in the woods. Or Mattie. Oh God.

Lights beginning to pop in her eyes, she realized she couldn't hold on any longer. With as much control as she could muster from her aching, trembling arms, she let herself rise a few centimetres. Head back, her mouth broke the surface. She gulped in lungfuls of air and, still clinging on to the roots, held her position long enough to eyeball the drone. Gold solar panels, black plastic shell, no microphone. Its camera, set on the central hub, was moving but aimed away from her, into the woods. It was within arm's reach, and she was briefly tempted to pull it down – but that really would give the game away.

Then, just as she started to sink again, Ant saw what the drone had seen. Her phone. Her clothes. And, clearly protruding from her pocket, the strap-key. She cursed herself silently. She hadn't thought to hide them – why would she? Now whoever had sent the drone had all the evidence they needed. It couldn't be worse.

Slowly she pulled herself back under.

How can I warn the others when I can't shout out?

With the new oxygen, her head was buzzing. She couldn't risk luring them into danger, but somehow she had to let them know. If the drone now found her route through the woods, she knew she'd have to take her chances.

And then it moved on. Surprised, Ant watched it

continue its journey downriver. She resisted the overwhelming urge to strike out immediately for the other bank; the river ran straight for twenty metres and the camera could be pointing anywhere.

OK. Enough. En, de, twa, kat.

She resurfaced. The drone was gone. She was across the river in seconds. She grabbed her clothes and phone, then ran, dressed and shouted all at once.

'Drone! Drone! Drone!' she yelled as she crashed along the path. Henry emerged from his container looking puzzled, but she ran straight past him. 'Drone on the river!' Mattie and Max were on their feet as she burst into the clearing. 'It came along the river. It knows we're here! We should get out now!'

'But how—?' began Max.

'It doesn't matter. Van. Now.'

Henry had appeared, a large stick in his hand. 'You're too late, I'm afraid. If it saw you, then it'll be finding a way in now. There are little paths—'

And suddenly the drone was there. Hovering at around two metres, it was approaching the van from the far side.

'To me!' shouted Henry. 'Trust me!' He turned and ran. Ant, Mattie and Max followed. He stood next to his container, ushering them inside. 'Climb in! As far as you can!'

'What's he doing?' asked Mattie, sliding over an old armchair.

'I think we're bait,' said Max.

They stood as far back in the container as the accumulated rubbish would allow. Within seconds the drone was framed in the container's open doorway.

It dipped almost to ground level to see where its prey had gone.

'It's too dark in here for it to see us,' said Ant.

'Can it hear?' asked Mattie.

'Don't think so. Couldn't see a mic.'

'Where's Amos?'

'Good question,' said Max.

The drone edged closer. They could hear the rotors and the hum of its engine. The camera lens stared straight at them. They could read the drone's logo – STAMPER 1.0 – arranged around the hub's gold panels.

'Oh, I get it,' said Max – just as Henry appeared, smashing his stick into the drone. It hit the ground, and before it could recover, Henry picked it up, threw it into the container and slammed the door shut. The sudden darkness seemed total, but as their eyes adjusted, they noticed a few tiny beams of light, presumably where corrosion had begun to eat away at the metal.

'It's solar powered,' shouted Max, his words bouncing off the walls. 'We can kill it here.'

Henry was banging on the side. 'Just cover the lens while it's dark! It's not hard!'

They could hear it, the whine of the motors still trying to get it flying.

'We can't wait for the batteries to die,' said Ant. Arms stretched in front of her, she felt her way forward. Her hands found what felt like one of Henry's disgusting blankets. She picked it up, pushing aside any thoughts of where it had been.

'Does the drone have weapons?' whispered Mattie.

'Too small,' said Max.

Led by the sound and its flashing green light, Ant inched her way forward till it was centimetres away. She removed her phone and, holding it in her left hand, pressed a key. The screen lit.

In the pitch-black container, it revealed everything – Max and Mattie wide-eyed at the back, lines of graffiti on the walls, and a Stamper 1.0 drone at her feet. In that instant she saw the drone's camera respond to her phone light, spinning in its hub. Ant resisted the urge to stamp it to bits and dropped the blanket. It covered the drone completely, and after a few feeble attempts at taking off, the whirring stopped.

Ant banged on the wall. 'All sorted, Henry. Door open please – it stinks in here.'

The container flooded with light as he opened the door. Max peered under the blanket and disconnected the drone's power source; its pulsing light died instantly.

'And we need to start running again,' he said. 'Whoever sent that drone knows where we are. We'll have visitors soon enough.'

My favourite things RIGHT NOW:
Killing drones!
Henry's cool container hut.
Henry's old vinyl records.

They all knew it was Amos. The timing was just too much of a coincidence. Henry pulled the door open and they hurried out of the container.

'You might be too late . . .' he called as they ran past him and through the woods.

'He called his gang friends anyway!' shouted Max as they burst into the clearing, before braking rapidly.

'You have to be kidding . . .' said Ant.

Their van was leaning precariously at the foot of a tree, its front wheels deeply enmeshed in the tangle of roots. The driver's door was open, the van empty. Running to the edge of the wood, they saw Amos disappearing in the direction of the main road.

'Amos!' shouted Max, but he was gone.

'Great, just great,' said Ant bitterly, kicking the nearest tree.

'Why did he run away?' asked Mattie.

'I think he's scared,' said Max. 'Called in his gang friends, then, when the drone appeared, he panicked.'

'Or he was trying to escape with the van. And crashed because he can't drive. And he's still an idiot.'

They went back to find Henry waiting for them. 'You didn't see it, did you?' he said.

'See what?' asked Max.

'In the container. And outside the container actually.'

'We were a little busy with the drone,' said Ant.

'Of course,' said Henry. 'So come. I know you'll want to go, but you have to see this first.'

'We should be trying to get the van out, Henry, to be honest. Someone will have been piloting that drone . . .' said Max. 'Thanks for the help, by the way . . .'

Henry shook his head. 'It's not that.' He stared at Ant. 'I've got something to show you.'

'OK, let's make this quick,' said Max irritably.

They followed Henry towards his container, then stopped dead in their tracks. The outside walls were covered in numbers and letters.

'That's Brian's code . . .' gasped Max.

'We told him,' said Mattie. 'He does crosswords.'

Ant ran inside and looked around. 'I thought this was graffiti, but it's not, is it?'

'Different combinations of 8B 3S 2C3. I filled these walls, then, when I ran out of space, moved outside.'

They filed back outside. Henry led them to the back wall. A few minutes earlier their backs had been pressed against the other side, facing the drone. Now they stared at hundreds of different combinations of Brian's code. In the container's top corner he had circled some figures.

'Look, it could be anything really. Any one of these combinations could be the secret. But I was looking for patterns – anything that looked *familiar* . . . and then I saw it.'

'We haven't really got time for games, Henry,' said Max.

'You know that music I played yesterday?' he persisted. 'Van Morrison?'

'Yeah,' said Ant. 'I said Brian talked about him.'

'So he liked music?'

'Old stuff mainly. But yeah.'

'Then it might be one of these sets you need.' He pointed at the encircled numbers and letters.

'CBS 2328, CBS 3382, CBS 2833,' read Ant, following the list. She turned to Henry, puzzled. 'Why these combos?'

'Mattie, quick – pick up that record sleeve.' The jazz album lay where he had left it that morning. 'Top right,' said Henry, 'what do you see?'

'Letters and numbers,' said Mattie, excited. 'MPS 44782.'

'Exactly. It's a catalogue number. All records had one. If your PO was a music fan, the letters will be CBS. The Columbia Broadcasting System. It was a huge record label. The numbers, in one of these combinations, will be a record. A whole album, or maybe just one song. Find that and you might find your message.'

Ant was buzzing now. 'Wait! Henry, you call it a *record* sleeve. With a *record* number—'

Mattie interrupted, 'And Brian said to keep a *record*.'

Ant, Mattie and Max looked at each other, each of them making the same calculation; each coming to the same conclusion.

'We've got no signal and we've got no time to check this out,' said Ant, taking a photo of Henry's circled numbers. 'Let's get the van going now, or whoever was flying the drone will be here. If it's not the police, it'll be the Cloverwells.'

With Max back in the driving seat, they tried to bounce the van free, but the front wheels were caught on the strong tree roots. Henry produced a pocket knife and threw it to Ant. She was about to start hacking when Mattie grabbed her shoulder. She followed his gaze and felt her stomach flip. A black car with tinted windows had appeared at the edge of the distant field, a cloud of dust in its wake.

'Max, look at this!' she said, her voice sounding

suddenly breathless. He jumped out of the van and came to look.

'What do we do?' whispered Mattie.

'Is there another way out, Henry?' asked Max.

'Across the river, maybe,' he said, 'but it's just fields.'

The car started to move. Slowly, it began to navigate its way across the field, and they ran. Single file, they tore through the woods, brambles whipping at their legs.

'Where are we going?' shouted Ant, leading.

'Away from the car,' said Max. 'Head for the river!'

They could hear the car's engine now; it revved, then slowed again.

'We can't get across in time!' yelled Ant as they ran past the container.

'Can't we hide?' yelled Mattie.

We're running because we don't know what else to do, thought Ant. *This is just panic.*

They were within sight of the river when they heard the unmistakable sound of a gunshot.

That made them stop.

Mattie grabbed Ant's hand. 'The container,' he said, panting. 'You can lock it from the inside, remember?'

There was only the briefest hesitation. Ant and Max nodded. 'Go!' she said.

They turned back. Running *towards* the danger filled her with fear, but if they could just get to the container, maybe they could summon some help. They still had their phones, even if they had no one to call. The numbers and letters scrawled on the container's end wall came into view as they heard a car door slam.

'Faster!' screamed Ant. Ahead, Max reached the open door and was already pulling it shut as Mattie, then Ant threw themselves inside. As they turned to slam the locking mechanism shut, they had the briefest glimpse of a figure in the woods, and then it went black.

The container filled with the sounds of rapid, frantic breathing. Ant felt Mattie clutch her hand. 'Who *is* that?' he whispered. 'Did he shoot Henry?'

She didn't answer. She didn't know. They stood rooted to the spot, not daring to move. Ears straining, they heard shuffling, casual footsteps, the sound of someone in control and taking his time. Something hit the side of the container – the gun maybe – and, slowly, was dragged along one side. It bounced over every dent and blemish, causing the container to ring like a bell. The clanging of metal on metal continued along all four sides. Only the momentary darkening of the tiny beams of light showed the visitor's precise location.

Their ears were ringing, but when the silence came, when the gun-dragging was over, the waiting was as terrifying as the noise. In the darkness Mattie grasped hold of Ant. Ant, without realizing, grasped hold of Max.

Then, from maybe ten metres away, came the sound of a man humming. It was tuneful, slow and soft, some notes barely audible. Ant and Mattie felt each other shift, their heads moving to catch the sounds better. Outside, the man – it was definitely a man – took a breath and started up again. Something inside Ant stirred. Memories fired. Images crashed.

She knew the tune.

She knew the voice.

She knew the man.

It was their father.

Ant vomited where she stood. If she hadn't been holding onto Max and Mattie, she would have collapsed. They eased her down onto the ground, Mattie urgent, terrified in her ear.

'Abi, what is it, what's the matter?'

She groaned, spat, then wiped her mouth on her sleeve. She held his hand and reached for his hair, flattening and stroking where she could.

'*Il se Papa*,' she whispered. Ant felt him go rigid, saw the whites of his eyes.

His voice was a tiny croak. 'Papa? Here?'

'W-w-wait a minute,' stammered Max. 'That's your actual dad out there? The guy who disappeared?'

Ant nodded.

'Are you sure?'

'I recognize that hymn.' She could still barely talk.

'What does he want?' whispered Mattie.

'Nothing good,' said Ant. 'It was never anything good.'

Stones started hitting the container. Every few seconds another sharp crack would reverberate around the walls. Mattie put his fingers in his ears.

Suddenly the voice was at the door. A London growl, the words slurred. 'Seems like you might know who this is out here.'

Ant started to shake. Everything came back in a rush: the control, the fights, the lessons, the drinking, the hair-cutting and the beatings. She forced herself onto her feet.

Max held her steady. 'There's three of us, remember,' he said.

'Yeah, but he's got a gun,' she said. 'I remember that.'

The metal bar rattled; a boot thumped against the panel. 'Time to come out, kids. Abi? Mattie?'

Ant heard Mattie whisper, 'Please go away,' just as they heard another kick on the door. They all jumped and Mattie started to cry.

'Little kids, little kids, let me come in . . .'

'This guy sounds like a real jerk,' said Max. 'What's his name?'

Ant took a deep breath. They were words she hadn't said out loud for a long time. 'Kyle Turner,' she said. 'Though our mama usually called him *Bata.*'

'I won't ask. You want me to talk to him?'

'Why not?'

Max took a step towards the container door. 'There's no one here who wants to talk to you,' he shouted.

Kyle Turner laughed long and loud. 'No, I reckon that's right,' he said. 'Quite a few birthdays I missed. But I just need a look around, that's all. You've got something I need. Something that doesn't actually belong to you. Something you *stole*. And you know what I taught you about stealing.' He laughed again.

'What's that about, Ant?' asked Max.

'He must mean the strap-key,' she whispered. 'The drone saw it when I was in the river.'

'Why would he want that?' said Mattie.

'Money,' she said. 'Same as everything. Must be worth a fortune.' She didn't need to check she still had it: she could feel its weight in her back pocket, but her fingers traced the familiar outline anyway. 'But he won't just want that. He wants *us* . . .'

Another kick against the door. 'Little kids, little kids, let me come in . . .'

'Is he drunk?' whispered Max.

'You can never tell,' said Ant. 'His voice is always slurred. Just assume he's dangerous.'

'That's exactly what I am doing.'

The voice came again. 'You should know, Abi, Mattie and the other guy doing the speaking, that there's only me here. For now. But my friends aren't far away, and they aren't exactly patient. They called me when they knew where you were. So here I am! Back in your lives after all these years!'

Max pulled Ant and Mattie close to him. 'We are going to have to deal with him somehow. He's right, there'll be others nearby. Amos's friends have moved fast. So we have to do something *now*.'

There was movement outside and they heard another gunshot. Again they jumped; again Mattie held onto his sister.

'Getting impatient, kids . . .'

Stones started hitting the container once more. Every few seconds another sharp crack would echo around its walls. Mattie put his fingers in his ears.

Ant closed her eyes. For a brief moment she could smell her father's sweat, tobacco and hair gel again and knew she would do anything to keep him away. Away from her. Away from Mattie.

She walked silently to the door and put her eye to one of the tiny holes. She couldn't see much – just a few leaves, a piece of grass and that was it. Then her father walked past and she recoiled, flinching as though she'd been hit across the face. *Just like the old days.*

She turned back to the others. 'I want to take him out.' She heard the new hardness in her voice and expected a reprimand from Mattie, but none came. 'We'll wait till he's right in front of the door,' she whispered. 'And you're right, Max, there *are* three of us, but we might only get the one go with those odds.' She returned to the spy hole.

'Can you see Henry?' asked Mattie.

'No.'

'Can you see . . . ? Can you see Papa?'

'No.'

Then the stones started up again, this time hurled with force. With *anger.*

'He's walking around us,' said Max, turning clockwise, following the sounds of rock on metal.

Ant steered Mattie towards the largest rust-hole. 'If you see him, put your hand up. If he's in front of the door, *right* in front of the door, drop it.'

'But I don't want to see him,' said Mattie, pushing back.

'OK, me neither,' said Ant. 'But if we do this right, it'll be the last time.'

Mattie took a breath, nodded, then stood on tiptoe, eye pressed to the hole. As the stones continued to hit, Ant swiftly cleared a path to the door. Hands on the horizontal bar Henry had fitted, she counted back six paces. Ant and Max stood together on their mark.

'Last time, Mattie. Guaranteed,' she hissed.

It appeared that Kyle had almost completed a circuit, each clanging stone marking his progress. Ant and Max crouched like sprinters before the gun. They saw Mattie stiffen; then his hand shot up in the air. Heart racing, blood hammering in her head, Ant was desperate to be unleashed. Silently she started her own silent count. '*En. De. Twa . . .*

Then his voice again. Up close. 'Little kids . . .'

Mattie's hand dropped. Ant and Max charged.

Kat!

Ant and Max hit the door-release bar together. The door burst open, hitting Turner with such force that he was poleaxed. As he collapsed on the ground, his gun went flying. Ant jumped on his chest, pummelling him with her fists. She landed blow after blow, each one accompanied with a flurry of words. It was a while before Mattie and Max could hear what she was saying.

'This is for Mama . . . This is for Mattie . . . This is for me . . .'

Mattie wanted her to stop. 'Abi, enough!'

'This is for Mama—'

Max grabbed her shoulder. 'Ant, that's enough.'

She turned on him. 'No, it's not enough – it'll never be enough. And what do you know anyway . . . ?'

Max held up his hands in surrender. 'No, that's not what I'm saying.' He was doing his best to sound calm and reassuring. 'You have every right to say all that stuff. But we need him to go back to the Cloverwells or whoever sent him. *And* we need to give him the strap-key.'

'What? Are you mad?'

'Because if we don't,' he continued, 'we'll be fighting the gangs as well as the prison system, the police and the law. Pick your battles. Pay them off. One fight at a time.'

Breathing heavily, sweat pouring from her, Ant forced herself to calm down. There was a logic to Max's argument. She hated his sweet reason, but he was right. She wiped the sweat out of her eyes.

'I need some rope or wire then,' she said, her voice hoarse but calmer.

Mattie grabbed the electric cable from Henry's record player and Ant had it around Turner's wrists in seconds. She stared at him; she remembered him as taller, stronger, more stylish. He seemed diminished. Sure, his clothes were expensive, but they were worn, even threadbare in places. His face was gaunt, unshaven, with dark circles around both eyes But mainly it was bleeding: the container door had left deep cuts in his temple and cheek.

'Don't think you'll be forgetting me again,' she said.

Turner stirred beneath her and she jumped up. Max threw a pan of Henry's water over him and he spluttered, opening his eyes and then wincing in pain.

'Hi,' said Ant coldly. 'I'm your daughter; this is your son. We are now going to tell you what's about to happen.'

He blinked and tried to sit up, but she put her foot on his chest. 'When we say so, you're going to walk out of here. Straight back to where you came from. We'll even give you the strap-key so that you can show your gangster buddies how brilliant you are. How does that sound?'

Turner nodded his agreement, then lay still.

'And your gun's in the river,' said Max. 'Save you looking for it.' He bent down and pulled Turner to his feet. 'And my other helpful tip,' he went on, 'is this. You should get some stitches in your face. Just saying.'

The blood was dripping from Turner's chin onto his shirt and he wiped it with his arm. 'When do I get the strap-key?' he growled.

Max and Mattie looked at Ant. She took a deep breath and pulled it out of her pocket.

Turner eyed it greedily, then his brow furrowed. 'Is that it?'

'That's it,' said Ant.

'Does it come with anything?'

Max screwed his face up. 'What kind of a question is that? What do you want it to "come with"? Fries?'

'Like a case or something.'

Ant poked the strap-key into her father's chest. 'You take the key. You run away. We *never* see you again. That's the deal.'

Turner smiled. 'I said you'd be fine.'

Suddenly Max was in his face. 'How can you say that? How can you actually not care about your own children?'

'Because,' said Turner, eyes darting between Ant and Mattie, 'with their mother, I was never sure that they *were* mine.'

The first to react was Mattie. He charged, head down, crunching into Turner's groin. Doubled up, his father fell to the ground, pain rendering him speechless. Ant and Max pulled Mattie away.

'OK, that's it! shouted Ant. 'He's not worth it, Mattie. Let's get rid of him.' She hauled Kyle to his feet, spun him round and pushed. 'Walk. When you get to the field, you get the key.'

Turner limped and stumbled through the woods, Ant, Mattie and Max a few steps behind. As they passed the van, Henry's face appeared at one of the back windows. Seeing that Turner had his hands tied, he opened the door and got out.

'Oh, thank God for that! You got him! Bravo!' He fell in beside Max. 'Who is he?' he said. 'I'm afraid when he pulled a gun and fired at me, I hid. Old habits and all that.'

'His name is Kyle Turner and he's leaving,' said Max. 'But not in his car – he's donating that to his kids.'

Henry looked baffled; Turner turned to protest, then thought better of it.

When they reached the parked Mercedes, Max shouted, 'Keys!' and Turner rummaged around in his pockets. Throwing them on the ground, he looked expectantly at Ant.

Strap-key in hand, Ant hesitated. She had a flashback to

Grey's office and the moment she had picked it up for the first time. This was the tool that had meant freedom, and now she had to give it to her scummy father. She felt like throwing it *at* him, not *to* him. But she understood the logic, and before she could change her mind, she hurled it as far towards the road as she could. It spun through the air, landing thirty metres away in a puff of dirt.

'Fetch,' she said, but Kyle was already running towards it. He dipped, picked it up and kept going; he didn't look back.

'Bye then,' said Ant.

'We need to move on,' said Max as they headed back towards the container.

'But I thought—' began Mattie.

'Hopefully we've bought some time,' said Max, 'but in case we haven't . . .'

'Then I'm looking up Henry's numbers,' said Ant. 'Looking for those records. I'll be two minutes.' And she took off for the river.

By the time she got a decent signal, Ant was only a few metres from where the drone had interrupted her swim. This time she ignored the water. In the shade of a large tree, she stopped and checked her photos of Henry's calculations.

'CBS,' she said out loud, 'then two threes, an eight and a two.' She turned as Max appeared beside her, phone in hand.

'It'll be quicker with two,' he said. 'I'll read them out, you look them up.'

She nodded and waited, fingers hovering above the keys. *What were you trying to tell me, Brian? What was so secret you had to hide it in a code?* She saw again his agonized face, heard the tunnel door closing, pushed by his dying kick.

'OK. There are twenty-four combinations with the CBS prefix,' Max said. 'First up, CBS 8332.'

Ant hit the keys. 'It's a song called "Wages of Love".' She shrugged. 'Next.'

'Did you love Brian or something?' he asked.

'No. Next,' said Ant, impatient.

'2338.'

She typed; he waited, already looking at the next number.

'Nothing. There's nothing.'

'OK. 3832.'

'That's something called "It's Your Turn",' said Ant, shaking her head. 'Move on.'

'3283,' said Max.

'Nothing,' said Ant, frustrated.

Oblivious to everything except the numbers, they stood side by side, their faces lit by their phones. Four more combinations followed; each met with a swift 'Nothing'.

'8323,' said Max.

Ant's fingers typed, and then her body tensed. Max saw the shift in her stance. 'What is it?'

But she was reading. As fast as she could, she scrolled through the words on her screen.

'Ant, what is it? Let me see!'

She read from the screen, '*CBS 8323. Catalogue release number from 1980. "Bankrobber" by The Clash.*'

'I've never heard of it,' said Max, peering over her shoulder. 'You said your Brian was into his music. Did he ever mention The Clash?'

'Might have done,' said Ant, 'and he wasn't "mine".' She read on. 'The song is a story, Max. A crime story.' She looked up. 'About someone whose father was a bankrobber . . .'

Max read from her screen. 'Brian's dad was a bankrobber?' he said. 'How does that help us?'

'No . . .' said Ant slowly. 'Brian said *Grey* would go mad. This is about Grey, not Brian.'

Ant and Max got it at the same time, their eyes popping.

'Assessor Grey's father was a criminal!' gasped Max. 'Can that be right?'

'Let's assume it is,' said Ant. 'And let's also assume that he was never caught.'

'Which makes Grey—'

'A strutter!' exclaimed Ant. 'But he hates strutters. More than anyone else. So he must have gone to great lengths to cover up his past. He would never have got where he is now if this is true. This changes everything.'

'Why wouldn't Brian just tell you?' wondered Max. 'Why put it in a code?'

'Too scary,' said Ant. 'Too dangerous. If it's true, if the leading campaigner and enforcer of the heritage-crime laws is actually a heritage criminal himself, this must have been as clear as he felt he could be.'

Max stared at her. 'This is huge, Ant.'

She nodded. 'If we can prove it, yes. Otherwise it's useless.'

Three sounds in rapid succession brought them back to reality. A desperate shout from Henry. A car starting and accelerating hard. Then, coming towards them, heavy running footsteps.

Ant and Max spun round to face whatever was coming their way. There was no time to hide, barely time to brace themselves. But then Ant saw that it was Henry, saw the anguished look on his face, and knew with a gut-twisting certainty why he was running.

Mattie.

Henry took a deep breath. 'Your brother!' he gasped. 'He's been taken!'

Ant had known fear all her life, but never had she felt the numbing terror that now scorched into every part of her. A breathless, distraught Henry got as far as 'That man . . . he came back . . .' before Ant started sprinting towards the container.

Mattie si ale.
Mattie's gone.

She yelled his name over and over as she searched the woods, but there was no reply.

Mwen kite l'ale.
I let him go.

The container was empty, the van was empty, the woods were empty.

Papa ale ave't.
Papa's taken him.

And the car was gone. On the dirt track by the houses, a thin cloud of dust still hung in the air, marking its route.

Pitit la mouri.
He's dead.

Mwen mouri.
I'm dead.

Tout bagay fini.
It's all over.

Ant fell to her knees and howled. The rage, horror and grief of the last two days boiled over in a torrent of unstoppable emotion. She cried with such force that Max was unsure whether to approach her. He waited for the storm to calm, then knelt beside her.

'We'll find him, Ant . . .' His words were barely a whisper. 'We have to go now, but we will find him and get him back.'

She turned to him, her eyes raw. 'But *how* has he gone? How did that happen? He was with you! He was with

Henry! He was right here! I thought . . . I was only . . .' And the tears overwhelmed her again.

'He was in the van,' said Max, 'just getting some stuff. I thought . . . Henry was just there . . . and I assumed your dad had gone.' He pulled the car keys out of his pocket and threw them on the ground in disgust. 'Either these are fake or he has a spare.'

Henry shuffled towards them, then slumped down on the grass.

'What happened, Henry?' said Max.

He coughed and spat, then wiped his eyes with his sleeve. His hands were shaking. 'I was in my place, just putting some music on.' He paused, staring at the grass. 'Then I was walking around, calming down, you know? I heard a noise, like a bang, coming from your van. I should have called you then – I should have had my gun—' He broke off, swallowed, then slowly raised his eyes to Ant's. 'I went over . . . and saw that man climbing in. I called out to him and started to run, but I'm not as fast as I used to be. Before I was halfway there, they were gone. I could see he had a phone in one hand, but then he had . . . he had a knife in the other.'

Ant swallowed another cry, holding a hand to her mouth. Henry pressed on.

'He saw me and held it up . . . I froze . . . He was scary, Ant. Who is he?'

Max glanced at Ant. 'He's their father.'

Henry looked like he'd been struck. 'Your father? But then . . . he wouldn't . . .'

'No, no, he would,' said Ant. 'He absolutely would.'

'He must be a sick man.'

'You got that right,' she said. Then a thought: 'Why was Mattie in the van?'

Max and Henry shrugged.

'Did he have anything with him? When he was taken?'

Henry shook his head. 'Nope. Not as far as I could see.'

Ant hauled herself up and trudged wearily over to the van, Max following behind.

'We need to go, Ant – we need to disappear again.'

'I know.'

'We should get this to the Bug sites – we need to tell them about Grey. They're all we have now.'

'I know.'

Ant opened the driver's door and climbed in. 'Oh, I know what you were doing . . .' she muttered. She looked around, then dropped to her knees. Under the back seat, stuffed in amongst the springs, was Mattie's journal – a red HMP London exercise book. Head on the floor, she reached through the old crisp packets and tried to pull it free. It seemed fatter than normal, its cover catching on the wire. She got out her phone to light up the floor. Some of the book's pages were caught in the seat's suspension, and Ant picked them out one by one.

'You sure rammed this in hard, Mattie,' she said.

'What is it?' asked Max.

'He had a journal. It's stuck in the springs. Hidden in a hurry.'

Ant prised the wires apart and eased the book out. From inside fell a long brown case. Ant looked puzzled.

'What's that?' asked Max.

'It's the case the strap-key was in. He must have had it since . . .' She paused, thinking. 'I gave him the strap-key in the case to unlock the Pearsons before we escaped from the coach . . . But then he only gave the key back to me.'

'So was he hiding it?'

'Looks like it.' Ant stared at the journal and felt herself go weak again. Mattie's tiny handwriting filled the pages. She had never dared look at it before – prison was intrusive enough without people reading your diary – but now she flicked through to the last entry. Lines of small, neat script ran down one page; large, scrawled words down the other. She read them out loud:

'*Papa back. On phone. Someone's mad. Needs strap-key case. Hasn't seen me. Hiding.*'

She handed it to Max, who read it again.

'So your father was being shouted at because he had the strap-key but no case,' he said. 'And when you showed it to him, he said, "Does it come with anything?"'

She opened and closed the strap-key case. It was just a box – hinged like a glasses case, moulded to fit around the strap. She shoved it deep into the pocket where, until an hour ago, the key itself had been. No key. No Mattie. Ant was bereft. It felt like half of her had been ripped away. For about as long as she could remember they had been a team. They'd had to be. With no friends, no family, and parents who didn't or couldn't care, they had come to rely on each other completely. Five years younger than her maybe, but Mattie calmed her down, made her think, nagged at her impetuousness.

Everything she did, she did for both of them. When she was fighting, when she was stealing extra food, when she was charming the POs, she was doing it for both of them. When she wasn't with him, it usually meant trouble. Surviving life with their parents had been teamwork, surviving prison had been teamwork, and she gave herself no hope of surviving outside without him.

'I want to get him back, Max,' she said in a small voice. 'I need to get him back.'

'Agreed,' said Max. 'And we need to get away from here fast. Let's cut the van free before your dad comes back. Again.'

They instinctively glanced at the dirt road where they had seen Kyle Turner's car, but it was deserted. Henry headed off for his container. 'I've got some tools!'

Ant found Henry's knife on the ground where she had dropped it, and set about the roots. She hacked and sawed with such ferocity that by the time Henry got back, one wheel had already been released. His saw made short work of the rest, and within minutes the van was free. Max started the engine and carefully backed away from the tree.

'Henry, we have to go.' His voice was agitated now. 'You should disappear too,' he said through the window.

Ant was about to get in when Henry grasped her arm. 'I hope you find your brother. I . . .' He faltered. 'I'm sorry I couldn't stop it.' She nodded and climbed into the passenger seat. 'I put some supplies in the back,' he continued, 'in case you need them. And you should take this.' He handed her his cap and a battered old scarf. 'I hope . . .'

He was still talking as they pulled away. Max accelerated round the field, and by the time they hit the track they were already doing forty miles an hour. Ant pulled on the cap, tied the scarf around her neck and strapped herself in. She wouldn't complain if he was doing a hundred.

Max barely slowed as they joined the main road. 'Where am I going?' he said.

'Anywhere. Doesn't matter. As long as we aren't there,' she said.

Max took roads at random. He cursed and hit the steering wheel. 'Amos was right, after all,' he said.

'Excuse me?' said Ant. 'Right in what way?'

'There's just two of us left, Ant! What can we do with two? We need help. We've lost too many people—'

'Yes, we have, and whose fault is that?' said Ant, realizing she was crossing a line but ploughing on anyway. 'If you'd—'

'Are you blaming me for Mattie's kidnap? Seriously?' Max was aghast, his expression furious. 'Who ran off to get the signal? Was that you, Ant? Yes, it was. Did you ask him to join you? No, you didn't.' The louder he spoke, the faster he drove. 'And whose fault is it that we are here in the first place? Eh? How come my mum and dad were in prison, and HOW COME THEY'RE PROBABLY DEAD?' Max wiped his eyes with his sleeve. 'AND HOW COME YOU DON'T SEE THAT IT'S ALL YOUR FAULT!'

On a small country lane, the van was clocking sixty miles per hour and still accelerating.

Ant, her eyes closed, said nothing. She didn't trust herself. Her heart was breaking, but she didn't want Max to see that. He was right, of course – this was all her fault, and now she had lost her brother. If Max crashed the van, she hoped she died because she didn't want to feel like this for a moment longer. As the engine strained, she expected to hear the screeching and tearing of metal on metal. She braced herself.

I'm sorry, Mattie. Sorry, Dan. Sorry, Gina. Sorry, Daisy, sorry, Jimmy, sorry, Brian . . .

The van was slowing, its roar easing; Max's foot was off the accelerator, and she opened her eyes. He was gripping the wheel with clenched fists, jaw set and face flushed. They drove on in stony silence. Ant stared out of her window, seeing nothing.

After a few miles she heard Max sigh. 'This van is too big, too obvious,' he said. 'Wait . . .' He braked hard and pulled off the road. 'The Lithuanian plates are still on.'

They both leaped out, wrenched off the number plates, then froze as a police siren suddenly blasted through the air behind them. It was moving fast. Ant and Max threw themselves to the ground as the car sped past.

'That was close,' said Max.

'Was that for us?' Ant brushed gravel off her face.

'Who knows? But let's assume so.'

Imminent danger and fear of arrest had halted their battle, but they both knew it was unresolved. They were united in their need to rescue Mattie and the others – maybe even Dan and Gina – but beyond that there was nothing.

They had stopped in the driveway of what looked like an old garage. They headed towards a dilapidated main building with an empty forecourt, expecting to be challenged. A burned-out kiosk and a row of broken windows suggested safety, and Max ran back to the van to park it out of sight.

Then they sat on the rough tarmac, phones in their hands. Ant took a deep breath. 'OK. We log on. We tell them about Grey. Someone must know about his criminal past.'

'And if not, at least we can get the information out there,' said Max.

'You do the Bug sites, I'll check the news sites,' said Ant. They hit the keys, and while Max waited for the logon sequence to run, he peered over at Ant's screen. He was close enough to catch her phone when she dropped it.

'*Young strutter prisoner caught in Cornwall,*' he read out loud. '*Matthew Norton Turner, eleven, seized by police.* My God,' said Max, shocked and incredulous. 'But it wasn't the police! It was a gang operation, wasn't it?'

Ant felt numb. Mattie had been found by the police. The police would hand him over to Grey.

'His father was a bankrobber . . .' she said slowly. 'Grey's a crook. A gangster. They're all working for him. They're all the same.'

Max nodded. 'Of course . . .'

'So Amos was wrong,' she said. 'If we'd asked the Cloverwells to get involved, we'd all be inside. Yes?'

'Yes, Amos was wrong,' Max conceded. He was still reading, and held the phone up to Ant. 'There's one other thing you should see.'

The scrolling caption read: *Breaking: HMP Bodmin announce public re-strapping to take place tomorrow at midday.*

Ant stood up and threw a stone through one of the garage's windows.

'And now that includes Mattie,' she said. 'So. We have our deadline.'

67

Hunched in the corner of the twenty-four-hour fast-food restaurant, Ant and Max were trying to stay awake. They had used the cashpoint and had feasted on everything they could manage, their table littered with empty wrappers and cartons. If they did fall asleep, they wouldn't be the only ones; as long as you bought food, no one seemed to mind if you dozed off. Ant, with Henry's khaki army cap pulled low, counted four sleeping customers between her and the till. She checked her phone: 3.30 a.m. A woman dressed in the restaurant's uniform cleared their table, her necklace swinging as she swept the rubbish away. Ant and Max shrank back, but she took no interest in them and moved on to the next table.

Ant yawned. 'Keep me awake, Max. Throw ice at me or something,' she said. 'We mustn't miss the truck.'

Max noisily sucked the last of his milkshake through the straw. 'We don't know it's coming, Ant. Just because we saw it last time . . .'

'Correct,' said Ant. 'We don't. But it might. And if it does, we need to be on it.' She could tell he was unconvinced, but one of the Bug sites had reported that a TV truck had been spotted on its way to Bodmin, and this seemed the most likely refuelling stop.

'And then what?' he said. 'Once we're in, what happens next?'

'We find out what happened to Dan and Gina. And we tell Grey we know he's a crook. Threaten him. Get him to release everyone.'

'Really? On the basis of what? Even *you* can't think that's going to work—'

'Max, I'll go on my own if I have to. I *am* getting in there, and I *am* finding Grey. If you don't . . .'

'Ant,' said Max.

'. . . think we can do it, you just need to say . . .'

'Ant,' he said again, more firmly this time. 'Look.'

He was staring at the till. The woman who had cleared their table was cashing up, her attention divided between the till and the computer next to it.

'What am I looking at?' Ant asked.

'That thing around her neck.'

What she had thought was a necklace was now plugged into the computer. The waitress finished her work, hit a few final keys, then, as the machine shut down, pulled the necklace free. Ant and Max stared at each other.

'It's a memory stick,' he said quietly. 'That's what's in the strap-key case. It must be.'

Ant pulled it out of her pocket, opened it and took out the lining, as she had many times before. She shrugged. 'No it's not,' she said, holding it out.

He took the case and repeated Ant's inspection. 'It's got hinges,' said Max, running his finger down the spine of the case. 'Unusual.' He was frowning now. 'Don't see them much these days.' He tried to pull out the long pin which acted as the pivot for the two halves of the case, but it wouldn't budge. He squinted at the pin's head. 'Well, well . . .' he said.

Ant leaned forward, all tiredness disappearing in an instant. 'What?' she whispered.

With his fingernails doing the work, Max twisted the pin. It started to move.

'It's a screw!' he said. 'The thinnest screw ever!' Slowly he twisted the pin from the hinge and the two sides of the case fell apart.

Max held them up for Ant to see, smiling broadly. Embedded along the edge of the lid was a metal prong. She teased it out with her nails. It flashed in the headlights of a large truck that was just turning into the car park.

'A USB,' she whispered. 'And I've had it all along.'

Max stood up, brushing a cascade of food crumbs to the floor.

'Where are you going?' asked Ant, taking the pieces of case back.

'I'm going to smile nicely at that waitress,' he said. 'Then maybe we can use her computer.'

The Cable Broadcast and TV Services truck edged slowly towards the prison gates. Inside the cab, the two technicians were arguing. The driver, a large man with a CB&TV T-shirt stretched across his frame, was trying to calm his panicking colleague.

'It's OK. I'll explain that the missing passes are my fault. I'll say they're back at the office.'

It had just turned 5 a.m., but the woman's company T-shirt was already sweat-stained. This was only partly due to the early morning heat.

'This is HMP Bodmin,' she said. 'You don't get in without the right tags! You said they were here!'

'And they were,' he insisted, 'but I'll handle it. They *need* us – there's no other TV truck around. We'll be fine.'

The first steel barricade was set a few metres from the outer wall. Two prison officers approached as the vehicle came to a stop. The driver lowered the window.

'All right?' said one of the POs, peering inside. He nodded at the discarded burger containers. 'That's a healthy breakfast you've had there. Save me any?'

The CB&TV man forced a smile. 'Maybe next time,' he said.

'No worries,' said the PO. 'Glad you're here! They can't do much without you guys!'

'Well, there's a problem,' said the driver. He lowered

his voice to a conspiratorial whisper. 'I left our passes back at base. I know that's bad, but maybe there's some forms we can fill in? Can we get temporary passes? Like you said, with no cameras, there's no *Correction*.'

The PO looked as though his morning had just been ruined. He sighed deeply. 'Really?' The driver nodded sheepishly. 'OK, stay here.'

The man consulted with his colleague, and they both got on their radios.

'How can you lose security passes?' muttered the woman.

'You're not helping,' replied the driver.

While they waited, the PO carried out the usual vehicle checks: a chassis inspection followed by a cursory glance inside from the back doors. 'Your cameras had better be more switched on than you,' he said.

Twenty minutes later, and with a sizeable queue building behind the TV truck, temporary ID cards were handed through the window. The PO half smiled. 'You guys are fools. But fools that, today, we need. So this time we let you in. These only work outside, OK? You don't get into the prison with them.'

The driver nodded his thanks. 'Apologies again. We only need to be in the courtyard.'

'It's quite crowded already,' said the PO. 'You know where to park.'

The steel barricade lifted, and the truck trundled into the prison grounds. Two more barriers, and they arrived in the melee. The courtyard was teeming with workers, scaffolding and trucks. The noise of shouted commands, hammering metal and revved engines all flooded into the truck.

'Not sure I like the idea of a public re-strapping,' said the CB&TV woman, sounding unnerved.

'We do what we always do,' came the reply. 'We drive the truck, plug everything in and keep our mouths shut.' He opened his door. 'But first I need to get rid of some of that coffee . . .'

Ant and Max, painfully squeezed into a cupboard housing spare TV monitors, stared at each other. The silence suggested that the second technician had also gone for a toilet break, and Ant was exploding with impatience. Looking at Max, his face just a few centimetres away, she raised her eyebrows.

Ready to go?

Ant could feel Max's heart thumping like an echo of her own.

'Wait!' he whispered, listening intently. The cacophony outside made it hard to tell if anything was happening inside.

'She's gone,' insisted Ant.

Max nodded and pushed open the cupboard door. The truck was empty, its bank of screens dark. From their hiding place they pulled out a small cotton bag. Henry's 'supplies' hadn't been the food they were expecting. A selection of tools, bits of the drone and some tea bags were all bundled up with a leather belt.

'What do we take?' hissed Ant.

'Some tools might make us look busy,' said Max. 'Whatever we can carry; hide the rest.'

From their pockets they pulled out the stolen CB&TV security passes and slung them around their necks. They filled up with tools and then edged towards the open door. The truck had parked alongside a wall so the view was of mossy granite. Ant was about to jump out when Max hauled her back. He was passing her a small monitor from their cupboard.

'Take this,' he said. 'If we're both carrying them, we look important.'

'You look scared,' said Ant.

'I *am* scared.'

'What do I look like?'

Max, briefly taken aback, opened his mouth then closed it. He tried again. 'Mostly scary,' he said.

'Just "mostly"?'

'But you still look like the girl who is wanted by the police. Even with the hat and scarf.'

Ant pulled her cap down, then adjusted the scarf. 'I'll bear that in mind.' She took the monitor and stepped out. Following the noise of construction, she walked swiftly along the narrow corridor between the truck and the prison wall. She recognized where they were. Ahead was the prison courtyard where they had seen Daisy and Jimmy taken from the coaches.

At the corner she hesitated, Max swiftly at her side.

The courtyard was being turned into circus. Rows of plastic seating were being fitted together. It already resembled a small amphitheatre, with a podium in the middle and a viewing gallery at one end. Scores of workmen swarmed around, watched by prison officers stationed at regular intervals.

'It's like they're setting up a gallows,' said Max. 'For a public execution.'

'Well, let's see if we can spoil their horrible little party,' said Ant.

She ran her eyes over the CCTV cameras that ringed the courtyard, and hoisted the monitor onto her shoulder. Max copied her, using the screen as a shield, and they strode into the tumult.

The viewing platform seemed near completion: three-tiered, with seats and camera positions, it was the obvious place for the monitors. Ant took a few steps towards it, then suddenly wheeled away, heading for the first bank of seating. The framework was high enough to hide them from the security cameras.

'What's going on?' hissed Max.

'Denholm and McTavish,' said Ant, dropping her monitor. 'Those POs by the podium? They're from Spike! If Grey has brought staff with him from London, then we really are screwed.'

Max peered between the wooden slats. 'Well, they're coming this way,' he said.

'Did they see us?' Ant crouched down to see for herself.

'No, they look too casual.'

They shrank further into the shadows provided by the seats and watched through the gaps. The sweating POs slumped into two plastic-moulded seats – the wooden plank above bowed slightly. There was the sound of squishing water bottles.

'Could do with a beer,' said one voice.

'*That's Denholm*,' mouthed Ant.

'Not till this charade is over,' came the reply.

'*McTavish*.'

Max leaned in close to Ant. 'I think I'm just going to ask,' he whispered urgently. She grabbed his arm but he pulled away. 'They know you, not me.' And before she could protest he was gone.

Ant crouched down, holding her breath.

What are you doing, Max?

She caught glimpses of him between the wooden slats, moving at speed. He stopped right next to where Denholm and McTavish were sitting, and she heard the *clunk* as he rested the monitor on the metal handrail.

'Where would this go, gents?' said Max. 'I was just given it and told to find the director.'

Ant shifted till she could see Max's right leg. She imagined Denholm and McTavish sizing him up.

'No idea, mate, sorry.' *Denholm*.

'We're prison officers, not press officers.' *McTavish. Classic PO answers.*

'Fair enough,' said Max. Then, as if it was an afterthought, 'Quite a show later . . .'

Oh, I know what you're doing . . .

'Re-strapping,' said Denholm. 'Seen it once before. It's not nice. And there's quite a few to get through.'

'Serves them right and everything,' said McTavish,

'but no one likes this whole . . .' He was struggling for the word. 'This whole . . . *display.*'

'Really?' said Max. 'I thought everyone loved it.' There was the sound of more water being chugged.

'Yeah, and no one as much as our Dear Leader,' said Denholm. 'You seen the governor on television? He likes to make speeches when the cameras are on. Reckon he's writing one at the minute.'

Is he now?

'How many are getting done?' asked Max.

Ant picked up the forced casualness in his voice. *Here we go.*

'All the ones they caught,' replied McTavish. 'In age order.' Ant's heart rate kicked up a notch. 'Starting with the old guy, Blakely.'

'Right,' said Max, his leg bouncing with tension. 'Then the kids?'

'Yup.'

'Did their folks get out of that fire? I forget now . . .'

Ant wrapped her arms around herself.

'Some did,' said McTavish. The tone of his voice made Ant's stomach twist into knots. 'Sarah Raath got out. Mishal Noon got out.'

The silence that followed seemed to stretch for ever.

Denholm took another swig of water from the bottle. 'Ahmet Shah didn't.'

Oh, Amos.

'And the Nortons never made it. You know, the foster parents of those kids that were on the run?'

'Oh, right.' Max was barely audible. 'They had a boy of their own too, I think,' he said.

Ant felt hot tears on her cheeks and dug her fingernails into her palms.

'Shame. Terrible business,' said McTavish. 'They seemed like good people. Hey, you forgot your screen!'

They are really dead, and it really is *my fault.*

Seconds later Max reappeared under the seating and dropped to his knees, his face twisted with grief. Ant crawled closer, the gravel sticking to her palms, but he held up his hand.

'Max, I'm so sorry,' she whispered.

He shook with silent sobs, seemingly oblivious to her presence. She longed to comfort him, but he clearly wanted no help from the very person he blamed for his parents' deaths. They were kneeling no more than two metres apart, but it seemed to Ant as though a chasm had opened between them.

'Please don't blame me,' she breathed.

Above them, boots were moving. There was a sudden darkening, a shadow along the prison wall. They had company.

'And what have you two done today?' said Governor John Grey. 'Or do I know already?' He beamed. 'Max Norton? I knew we would meet sooner or later. And Abigail Norton Turner! How lovely to see you again.' He spread his arms. 'Well, welcome to Her Majesty's Prison Bodmin. I think you're going to be here for a long, long time.'

Improvise.

Ant flung a fistful of gravel in Grey's face. He howled in surprise and pain, and she followed up by slamming her head into his kidneys. As he crumpled, she hurled another volley of stones before POs with tasers took her down. Hit once in the hamstring and once in the neck, Ant felt all her muscles spasm with pain like she had never experienced before. Grunting, she collapsed. The agony lasted only a few seconds, but by the time it had subsided, rough hands had dragged her and Max into the prison building. She felt the strap-key case being pulled out of her pocket.

Ant vomited copiously; Max swiftly followed suit. When she opened her eyes, she realized they had an audience. Grey, holding a dressing to his bleeding face, stood in front of a squad of armed POs. He watched impassively as she retched and spat.

'Why don't you come closer?' she said in a harsh whisper. 'I could be sick on your shoes rather than wasting it on the floor.'

'Cuff them,' he ordered brusquely. Denholm and McTavish stepped forward and hauled Ant and Max to their feet, steel handcuffs snapping around their wrists.

'I want to see my brother!' said Ant.

'Sure you do.' Grey walked past them into a fiercely lit corridor. 'Follow me!'

Ant and Max were led past bemused staff, who moved aside as they realized who was striding towards them; a scrum of POs and press followed in their wake. Now reunited with their security passes, the two CB&TV crew fussed with cameras and headphones. Two flights of stairs and Grey swooped left, ignored a saluting PO who was holding the door open, and turned to face his new inmates.

'Unlock them,' he said to the POs, 'and wait at the door.'

As the cuffs came off, Ant caught Max's eye. He was spent. Exhausted, in pain and in mourning, she wasn't sure he could walk another step. Or say another word.

I'm on my own here.

Grey had gone over to the window where she had spied him on their drive around the prison. *A thousand years ago.* It was a sparsely decorated room, austere even. One desk with a small zipped bag on it, one chair. A computer screen. Whitewashed walls – no paintings, pictures or curtains. A modest green carpet.

Grey guessed what she was thinking. 'Each inmate is allowed seven possessions in their cell. I lead by example.' He turned to face them, still holding the cloth to his face, and Ant realized he was already wearing TV make-up. *The bag on the desk.*

'You'll need some blusher,' she said. 'Hides the blood.'

Grey pursed his lips, folded the dressing and put it in his pocket. He ignored her provocation.

'I have one more possession now. One that was stolen from me a while back.' From his jacket pocket he produced the strap-key case and opened it. 'Back in its box,' he said, stroking the key.

I know you're not watching, Max, but nicely reassembled anyway. He knows nothing.

Grey's voice was harder now. 'Do you know how much trouble you caused me? Do you know we had to change the strap design after you stole this? You cost the country millions of pounds – a debt you'll be paying off for the rest of your life! However long that may be . . .'

Ant got the threat. *So that's why the key didn't work on some straps . . .*

'So,' he said, TV voice back again, 'is there anything you want to tell me? Anything you've learned while you were an on-the-run?'

'Yes,' said Ant. 'I've learned that my friends are brave. And that as we were the first to escape from Spike, we are an inspiration to strutters everywhere. There will be many others.'

'Will there, Abigail? Will there really?' he said sarcastically. 'And that's it? Nothing else?'

Say nothing. He's fishing.

Ant shrugged. 'I don't know what you mean.' She focused on Grey, avoiding the strong temptation to glance at the strap-key case.

He nodded slowly. 'Oh, I just thought that after all this time you might have a list of grievances . . . against me, against the prison service . . .'

Say nothing.

'Would it make any difference?'

Grey smiled coldly. 'Maybe not.' He nodded to himself, as if he'd resolved an issue to his satisfaction. 'So.' He folded his arms. 'It took longer than I expected,' he said. 'But here you are. And what should I call you now? Abigail? Ant? The "goose girl"?' He raised a finger to his chin as though trying to work out an answer. 'Well, whatever. Same girl, same problem. And why the goose I wonder? It's a wild goose, I think . . . Am I right? A cross-breed maybe? Uncontrollable, untamed. How romantic, how *moving.* They make a lot of noise, I think . . . I am right, aren't I? And here's the thing . . .' He smiled with satisfaction. 'They bite when captured! We all need to keep our distance.'

Ant glared straight back and said nothing.

'And of course you have one more name! You are the *Not to Blame* girl too. I should thank you really. Because of you, I am now a governor. Because of you, the old ways are gone. John Grey is on the rise, Abigail. So thank you.'

She glanced again at Max, who was swaying slightly, eyes closed. Big tears rolled down his face. Grey noticed her concern and raised an eyebrow. 'Why so sad?'

Now she spoke. 'You killed his parents. Why do you think?'

'The *riot* killed his parents,' said Grey. 'And who caused the riot? Who provoked two whole prisons to attack a third? You did, Abigail. *You* killed his parents.'

Max was swaying now. 'Can he have a chair?' she said.

Grey smiled. 'Can he have a chair? *My* chair? Of course not. It's the governor's chair, and has been since 1897. He can sit on the floor if he can't stand.'

Ant took Max by the arm and eased him down. 'He says you can sit,' she whispered in his ear. Max allowed himself to be guided to the floor, where he sat with his head on his knees.

'I want to see Mattie,' she said. 'I want to see my brother.'

'Ah yes. The sorry tale of Matthew Norton Turner,' said Grey, preening.

Ant looked away, eyes narrowing. Something in Grey's tone, his words, his stance, seemed significant. Her head still throbbed from the taser but she forced herself to focus. And then she remembered.

Correction.

'That's what you said before Mattie's film.'

'I may well have done—' began Grey.

'All those lies . . .' interrupted Ant. 'Why did you do that? Why go to all that trouble?' And then, her eyes widening, she answered her own question. 'You *knew*, didn't you? You *knew* I would go crazy . . . knew you'd have to send me to SHU. Then MacMillan told me the plan . . .' She stood with her mouth open, everything suddenly clear. Terrifyingly, brutally clear. Her words were slow and quiet, almost hushed. 'It was *your* plan, wasn't it?' she said. 'You *let* me visit Holloway. *Let* me visit Pentonville. You *wanted* me to cause trouble!'

Grey's mouth twitched. He came closer, stopping just out of reach. 'All this time? It's really taken you all this time? There was only one person who was ever going to be able to cause enough trouble in both prisons, and that was you. All I had to do was . . . allow it to happen. I knew that MacMillan had got friendly with you. I had the plan planted, and he passed it on to you.'

'But I wasn't supposed to make it out of Pentonville, was I? Me getting back to Spike wasn't part of the plan, was it? I remember you saying I'd messed up.'

'I hadn't expected a full-on riot,' said Grey. 'That is true. A more minor incident would have been fine. Just enough to show up the whole useless system. Just enough to send shock waves through the prison service. To get rid of flabby thinkers like Gaunt and Burridge. But you complicated matters.'

'By surviving . . .'

'Yes, by surviving. But the outcome was satisfactory.

Holloway blew, Pentonville blew and Spike was invaded. You wouldn't have escaped that either, but the stupid governor opened the cell doors and evened up the sides.'

'Not *all* the doors,' said Ant quietly.

Grey shrugged. 'Couldn't be helped.'

Now Max cleared his throat, spitting blood onto the carpet. 'But it could. That's the whole point,' he said, his voice brittle but steady.

'If it was you that caused the riot, you could have stopped it, but you didn't. You could have saved my parents, but you chose not to. That makes you guilty. All this time I've blamed Ant for their deaths, but I was wrong. It was you.'

Grey waved his arms. 'You believe what you want,' he said. 'No one cares about you or your opinions. I'd even forgotten you were here. Take him away and lock him up with the others. Let's not concern ourselves with him any longer.'

The POs walked over and hauled Max to his feet.

Ant and Max exchanged a long, stricken look.

'I'm so sorry, Ant,' he whispered, then McTavish bundled him out of the office.

Ant stood, her head bowed. She shook with the effort of controlling her anger and her tears. 'I want to see my brother,' she repeated. 'Please can I see my brother?'

'Do you know, Abigail – in all the time we've known each other, that's the first time you have ever said "please".'

'Please can I see Mattie?' she said again.

'Once you've recorded a message for me,' said Grey, using his TV voice again. 'I want you to tell everyone in Bodmin that you are actually finally here. They've been worried about you, you see. Some indeed might have hoped you'd escaped capture. We just need to set the record straight. There are screens in the cells, so you can speak to all your old friends. And, of course, your brother. You need to apologize.'

Ant shook her head. 'I don't need to apologize to anyone.'

'Oh, but you do,' said Grey with obvious relish. 'The re-strapping, you see, is not going to be easy. You have experienced it before, but this is new. Improved. Ant-proof, if you like! There is an injection of anaesthetic, then titanium rivets go under the skin and latch onto the vertebrae. Perfect. Usually this procedure is performed by one of our medical team. But now everyone needs to know what happens if you break the rules. So today, to discourage the others and make sure there is no more nonsense, you and your Spike friends are going to re-strap *each other*.'

Ant felt faint, sensed her legs starting to buckle.

'Just a brief message,' said Grey. He inspected himself in a small mirror, then, satisfied, packed it away in the make-up bag. 'And you should know that if you try anything, say anything, do anything that I disapprove of . . . then, when it is time for you to re-strap your brother, the anaesthetic will have run out.'

70

The camera shot was in close-up. Her face was blank, her eyes dead, her voice flat. Only the throbbing vein by a goose tattoo on Ant's neck showed her true feelings. She read from a card.

'*My name is Abigail Norton Turner – some of you call me Ant. I was on the run after starting the riot at HMP London. This morning I was caught, having broken into HMP Bodmin. I will be part of the re-strapping today. I'm sorry for the trouble I've caused and understand the price we'll be paying.*' She paused, looked at the camera, then back at the card. She rubbed one of her tattoos as she read the final line. '*The sooner we can accept the justice of the new criminal code, the better life will be for us all.*' There was the briefest eyes-to-camera shot, then the recording finished.

*

Mattie was delivered to Ant's holding cell just before midday.

'You have one minute!' snapped the PO. 'Everyone's on their way. You speak so I can hear you at all times.'

Ant and Mattie embraced, sobbing. She held him tightly until he stopped shaking.

'You heard about Dan and Gina,' he whispered.

'Speak so I can hear you!' snapped the PO.

'Yes,' said Ant, speaking unnecessarily loudly, 'I did. Does everyone know here?'

Mattie nodded. 'If only your pass had worked!' he sobbed.

She pressed her hand over his mouth. 'Mattie, stop. We haven't time—'

He pulled away. 'And I'm so sorry I got caught, Abi! He just came out of nowhere! I couldn't shout out—'

This time she placed a single finger over his lips. 'I know, Mattie. I found your journal . . .'

He wiped his eyes and took a deep breath. 'Did you find Grey?' he said.

Ant frowned. 'He found me.'

There's so much I can't say.

'Where's Max?' he asked.

Ant sighed. 'They took him. I don't know where.' She watched his sad face take another blow. She glanced at the watching screw – another one she recognized from Spike. 'Listen, Mattie. You know we're re-strapping each other?'

His eyes filled with tears and he nodded, not trusting himself to speak.

'Mattie, we've survived everything else they've thrown at us. We'll survive this too. But we need to rehearse it.' She turned her back on her brother and raised her T-shirt. She ran a finger down to the base of her spine. 'That's the bottom vertebra. Right there. You feel it . . .' He placed his trembling right forefinger on it. 'Count up one – that's the strap vertebra. Don't use that one again please – go for the third or fourth.' She broke off and approached the PO. 'Do you have a pen please?' she said. 'We need to rehearse this re-strapping. I think I need to mark the spot for him if I can. It'll just take a second.'

The man shrugged and removed a marker from his breast pocket. 'That's about what you've got,' he said.

She took the pen, and whispered to Mattie.

'Hey, no whispering!' shouted the guard. 'I told you already! I need to hear everything – understood?'

'Sorry, Officer. Just trying to raise his spirits,' she explained.

'Well, I need to hear,' he said, checking his watch.

Mattie took the pen and Ant bent slightly. Over her shoulder she said, 'OK, let's do this. Mark me up. That's it, Mattie. The T four. Put a mark just to the side, an X or a circle. Or an arrow. Anything. Finished?'

'Almost,' he said. 'Just want to make sure.'

She felt the pen tip on her skin, then checked back with the PO. 'You ever seen a re-strapping?' she asked.

'Pen,' he said in reply, holding out his hand.

'Finished.' Mattie pulled Ant's T-shirt down. 'I put a circle and an arrow.' She took the pen, then handed it back to the PO. 'What's going to happen, Abi?' he whispered.

The PO's radio rattled. 'Stand by the door,' he ordered.

Ant and Mattie stood hand in hand. His grip was tight. 'It'll be the anaesthetic first,' she said. 'Small shot just where you put the mark. Then there'll be a new version of the strap-gun. Place the titanium where the needle went in and fire. I'll be fine – just don't hesitate.'

'I fainted last time . . .'

'I know, Mattie.'

'It's not going to be any better, is it?'

'No, I don't think so.'

They heard heavy footsteps in the corridor, and Mattie started to shake again. 'I don't think *I'll* be fine,' he said, his voice barely audible.

Ant hummed a tune, then softly sang the words:

'Manman ou pa la lalé nan maché,
Papa ou pa la l'alé larivyè
Si ou pa dodo krab la va mange'w.'

'And here comes the crab,' she muttered.

The door swung open to reveal a shuffling procession flanked by POs. Heads down, defeated, the strutters didn't even glance round. Ant and Mattie recognized their friends, but they seemed smaller. Beaten. Doomed.

'Join the line!' shouted the PO, and Ant and Mattie filed out. Daisy and Jimmy were allowed the briefest embraces before they were pushed away. Ahead of them, Amos was staring straight in front.

'Norton Turners in the last two places! Go!'

Blakely waved at Ant, as if he was in a supermarket queue. In front of him, the red-faced woman with blonde hair shuffled forward as though her shoes were full of lead.

Daisy twisted round, her face blotchy, her eyes red. She looked from Mattie to Ant. 'I'm so sorry about Dan and Gina,' she managed, before being hauled forwards.

'Thanks, Daisy. So glad your mum's OK!' she said. 'And you too, Jimmy.'

He turned and, eyes full of tears, acknowledged her briefly with a nod. 'I'm so sorry,' he mouthed. They shuffled forward a few steps. 'And sorry 'bout your dad, Amos,' called Ant. He said nothing; didn't even react.

'He's not talking much,' said Daisy.

'You know what's happening, right?' called Jimmy, finding his voice.

'Yeah.' Ant remembered what a mess his back was already. 'You OK?'

'Aim for the fourth vertebra if it's you,' he said in reply. 'And stay strong, Mattie!'

Behind her, Ant heard Mattie reply, but his voice didn't carry.

'The Durrows aren't here!' she called. 'Go, Lena!'

'Go, Tilly and Sam!' said Daisy. She twisted round again. 'Max?' she mouthed.

Ant shrugged her shoulders. 'No idea. He was taken . . .'

The line had shuffled to a halt in front of a set of double doors. A short woman with a ponytail looked along the row, then spoke into a radio. 'Guests have arrived.' She listened to the reply in her earpiece. 'Twenty seconds,' she said, arm out to prevent them walking on early.

'Like we care about missing our cue,' muttered Daisy.

Mattie tried to reach for Ant's hand, but a PO pushed him away. The red-faced woman was sick on herself and then on the PO next to her; Amos retched over his shoes.

'Just so you know,' called Ant, 'no tricks from me. Grey's a sadist. I'm not giving him any excuse to make it any worse.'

'Like how?' said Jimmy. 'Any worse than this?'

'Like refusing us anaesthetic . . . That kind of thing.' A shudder ran along the line. Mattie shot his sister a quizzical look but she shook her head.

Say nothing.

The ponytailed woman shouted, 'Matthew Norton Turner to the front. Abigail Norton Turner, stay where you are.'

Mattie clung to Ant, but two POs pulled him free. Ant wanted to scream, but there was no point.

'*Feros Tig ti fre!*' she called. 'Stay fierce, little brother!' She watched as he was led to the front.

'OK, you're on!' said the ponytailed woman, waving everyone forward. The POs pushed them towards the courtyard. As Ant passed the woman, she hissed, 'Shame on you,' in her empty ear. 'This isn't some game show, you know.'

The floor manager looked surprised. 'But you're the goose girl!' *Of course it is.*

Ant stepped into the courtyard.

71

They were at the opposite end to the viewing platform – now with a large video screen attached. The banked seating rose to the left and right, wrapping around the podium in the centre. Four drones hovered high above.

Ant knew that it would be hot, that the seats would be full; she didn't guess that it would be silent. Strutters from prisons all over the UK were crammed into the temporary stands to each side of her, but they made no noise. Everywhere she looked, faces were straining to see her, as if needing confirmation that she had indeed been captured. She made eye contact with many she recognized from Spike. Some nodded, others blew kisses. Most looked scared. *Bet you've been threatened*, she thought. Everywhere tense and twitchy POs watched the crowd, hands resting on their batons. *Bet you have too.*

The podium now had an autocue, a built-in mic and a long low wooden bench running along in front. At one end stood the strapping table with its padded top; there were two small boxes of medical supplies underneath it. In spite of the midday heat, Ant shivered. She heard Daisy give a little cry.

'Stay strong, Daisy,' she called. Then with a cupped hand over her mouth, 'It'll be over soon. We'll have our revenge.'

Daisy said nothing; her head was down, tangled, matted blonde hair falling over her face. A few metres in front of her, Amos tripped, causing the others to stop. He fell on his hands and knees, his chest heaving, and vomited hard. The nearest PO pulled him up so sharply that he stumbled into Blakely. It was only a small moment, but in a silent, small amphitheatre, the sounds of illness, fear and brutality brought the first shout from the watching strutters.

'Leave him alone!' someone called.

Ant spun round. She couldn't tell where the woman's voice had come from and no one was giving any clues, all faces staring resolutely ahead. She saw four POs run into a stand near the viewing platform, grab the first strutter they came to and haul her away.

'*Dixam pas!*' yelled another voice – from the opposite stand this time. Again, the only reaction came from the POs whose job it was to ensure an uneventful *Correction*. It wasn't starting well. '*Dixam pas!*' yelled someone else, male this time, and the POs launched themselves at the offender.

'*Bax! Bax!*' came the cry as more POs ran into the courtyard.

'This Spike talk is going to make him mad,' muttered Ant.

'Is it live yet?' asked Daisy as they reached the bench. 'Can people see this?'

'Think so, but if this carries on, Grey will have to pull it.'

'Can he do that?'

'Can and has.'

The newly arrived guards took up their positions – nearly every row now had a watching PO. The murmurs of anger and discontent died away. High above, the drones whined, one dipping away to a new position just outside the prison.

Daisy put an arm round Ant. 'He's going to keep you till last, isn't he?' she said. 'You're top of the bill.'

Ant nodded. 'Me and Mattie. He'll keep Mattie till the end. So I don't misbehave. But I want to go first, Daisy – I *need* to go first.'

'But you can't heckle, Ant. Please tell me you won't—'

'I know!' she snapped. 'I know, I know.' She held Daisy's hand. 'God, I'm scared . . .'

'What happened to Max?' said Daisy.

'They took him away. He'd just found out about his parents.'

'Poor, poor Max,' said Daisy. Then added, 'And you and Mattie too.'

'Have you seen your mum yet?' asked Ant. 'That was some good news.'

Daisy nodded but didn't smile. 'They've kept us separate. It's been like being in SHU.'

The screen flashed the word *Correction* in large yellow letters.

'Feels like someone is about to make a grand entrance,' said Daisy.

The viewing gallery in front of them had one central camera; the only other one Ant could see was directly behind them, on the podium.

She knew what Mattie would say: *Why are you checking camera positions?* Then she would say, *I'm not*, and he would say, *Yes you are.* And what she wanted to say to him was, *I might get a chance. Just one chance. But the price of me messing up is you getting re-strapped without anaesthetic. And I'm not sure it's worth the risk . . .*

The big screen switched to a shot of Governor John Grey, hands clasped in front of him as he walked. A ripple of sound came from the seats, a collective intake of breath mixed with hissing. To Ant it was the sound of fear, anger and hopelessness. She watched the screen as Grey mounted the podium. He'd always loved *Correction*, and was now relishing every moment. She watched the screen as Grey mounted the podium. He glanced at the bench in front of him, then around the stands, and finally at the podium camera. He removed a pledge card from his top pocket, placing it carefully on the lectern in front of him.

He was about to speak when there was a honking sound. Heads turned towards the far wall, where a solitary grey goose had just landed; it was flapping its way amongst the startled POs. There were a few nervous laughs in the stands as Grey waited, annoyed by the last-minute delay.

'Is that a goose?' whispered Daisy.

Ant nodded. 'A goose with good timing,' she said.

'That's some coincidence,' said Daisy. 'Doesn't look like a fighting goose, but maybe we have a friend somewhere after all.'

'Maybe . . .' wondered Ant.

A few POs tried to grab the goose, but it evaded capture, running and honking behind the stands, until it eventually took off and flew away.

Grey breathed deeply and tried again. 'Justice. Justice, ladies and gentlemen, is why we are here today. Justice is why you are watching this at home. When justice is attacked, the nation needs to respond. Not to take revenge – that is not our way – but to seek redress for crimes committed. And our redress' – he looked around the courtyard – 'is the re-strapping of these offenders.'

The central camera now switched to close-ups of the bench. Ant hissed, 'Look at the ground,' and suddenly all viewers could see of her and Daisy was the top of their heads.

Grey continued. 'Already convicted of heritage crimes, these criminals rioted, then escaped from HMP London. Many died in the course of this violence. This cannot stand. In accordance with our laws, each has received a statutory extra fifteen years to their sentence. In addition, it has been decided that as they brought this misfortune on themselves, they should carry out their own re-strapping.'

Clearly some in the crowd had not heard that this was to happen; gasps of shock and astonishment rolled around the courtyard.

'The message from Bodmin today is this: you cannot escape justice! In the end it will find you out and take you down!'

'Sounds as though he was expecting applause,' said Daisy.

'Misjudged his audience then,' said Ant. 'Maybe he heard it in his head.'

Grey motioned a PO towards the medical boxes. 'Commence the re-strapping!' he ordered.

Dread and fear swept along the bench. Ant felt every muscle tense. *How can I get selected without messing it up for Mattie?*

The PO opened the first box and removed what looked like a small crossbow. She could see a handle and trigger at one end, and the steel loading plate at the other.

'The new strap-gun,' she muttered.

72

A small whimper came from Daisy and she buried her face in Ant's shoulder. Ant watched the rest on the big screen. Putting the gun down on the table, the PO removed a black box from which he slid the first strap. It loaded in seconds. She heard the terrifying double click as its titanium needle slotted into position and was made ready. Then the collective shudder of six hundred terrified strutters.

'Prisoner Blakely,' said Grey. 'Take the strap-gun. Prisoner Raath to the table please.'

'No!' The shout came from Amos, who was on his feet. He turned to face Grey. 'I'll go first. I'd like to go first.'

'What is this?' called Grey, visibly furious, a wave of

surprise rolling in from the stands. 'The order is set. You cannot "volunteer" in my court, Amos Shah. Sit down!'

But Amos didn't sit down. 'I want to set an example,' he said, refusing to meet the eyes of anyone on the bench, his voice breaking. 'I . . . deserve it.'

'You do indeed deserve it,' said Grey, 'and that is why you will be re-strapped and back inside prison in a few moments. In the correct order!' Two POs pushed Amos back to the bench. 'Prisoner Blakely and prisoner Raath. Now.'

Ant felt Daisy's arms tighten around her neck.

I have nothing to say. I have no comfort to give.

'It'll all be over in seconds, Daisy,' was all she could manage.

Slowly Daisy unwound herself from Ant and was helped to her feet by Denholm. Ant glowered at the PO but he wasn't looking. Daisy stepped reluctantly towards the strapping table. From the stands came the sound of a woman crying. Ant recognized it as Daisy's mother Sarah. The effect was instantaneous. Daisy had recognized it too and she immediately stood up straight, wiped her face with her hands and walked purposefully to the table.

A voice from somewhere: 'We love you, Daisy Raath!' Then another: 'You're a hero, Daisy.' Ant was aware of the watching guards reacting, but her attention was on the hypodermic syringe in Blakely's shaking right hand. He looked as terrified as Daisy.

In the pin-drop silence Ant heard Daisy say, 'Make it a good one, please,' and then she leaned over the strapping table. She pulled up her shirt and lay perfectly still. Blakely stepped forward, his left hand poised above her vertebrae, seemingly unwilling to even touch her spine.

'The T four!' hissed Jimmy, who was now next to Ant. 'Fourth one up!'

Blakely counted the bumps on Daisy's back, found the T4 and placed his finger just to the left. Sweat poured off his face as he held the syringe millimetres from her skin. He wiped his eyes, muttered some words to himself and held his breath. Ant held hers. Six hundred in the stands held theirs. Just when everyone thought Blakely wouldn't be able to do it, he stabbed the needle into Daisy's back. Unsure how deep it should go, he pushed it in further. A few screamed; everyone shuddered. Blakely squeezed the anaesthetic home and pulled the needle out.

From the crowd: 'Keep strong, girl.' From the bench: 'Nearly there, Daisy!' Jimmy's voice.

Blakely now snatched up the strap-gun. He inspected it briefly, then moved it along Daisy's spine. With his left hand he held the gun's loading plate in place; his right finger curled around the trigger. The whole crowd heard him say, 'I'm so sorry, Daisy,' and he fired. The hiss of the compressed-air shot was followed by Daisy's scream. A short, gasping scream to begin, then a series of staccato, gasping cries.

The screen showed Daisy's back, new strap in place . . . but the angle was wrong – the plate sloped sideways and blood was running everywhere. Blakely flapped his hands and tried to adjust the position. Daisy screamed again.

A medic came and pulled him away; panicking and distraught, Blakely dropped the strap-gun, then stepped on it as POs tried to calm him down. Grey shrieked into his microphone.

The medic helped Daisy up but she collapsed in his arms. Those on the bench heard him call to Grey, 'She's done! She can't strap anyone now.'

A flash of annoyance showed on Grey's face before he remembered the cameras. 'Of course,' he said, and waved her away.

On the bench the full horror of what had been done was hitting home. Daisy's blood was still visible on the gravel and Ant was shaking with rage. Mattie was sitting very still, his eyes closed. *I should go to him.*

She got up, but a large PO pulled her down again. 'You're here, he's there,' he said. 'It's staying that way.' She slumped back next to Jimmy.

'The strap-gun is damaged,' he hissed from behind his hand. 'Look!'

On the podium, Grey was inspecting the trigger, which seemed to have lost its tension. He stepped up to the microphone. 'A new strap-gun will be needed. We will resume in five minutes.'

As the screens filled with ads, Ant looked around. The delay had supercharged the atmosphere. The brutality of Daisy's re-strapping had left everyone stunned, but now, with nothing to do but talk, the paralysis had worn off. Angry voices could be heard around the stands. In spite of the guards, people had their heads together, fingers pointing.

Behind Ant, Grey looked uncomfortable. His eyes roved around the courtyard, looking for trouble. He summoned a nearby PO and jabbed his finger in four different places.

'I see danger,' Ant heard him say. 'There. There. There, and there. Known troublemakers. Take them away – get them out of sight! Someone needs to get a grip.'

Jimmy edged closer to Ant. 'What are you thinking?' he said.

'A million things all at once,' she said.

'But mainly?'

She cupped a hand over her mouth again. 'Mainly that I can't afford to do anything because of what they'll do to Mattie. And that I can't afford to just sit here waiting to be shafted like Daisy.'

Fighting broke out in the stand near Ant. Now that the cameras were no longer live, four POs with batons were clubbing their way along a row. Grabbing their victim like a snatch squad, they then clubbed their way back again. In their wake they left sprawled and bleeding strutters. The crowd anger kicked up a notch.

Suddenly the ads had finished and the *Correction* logo was back. Ant and Jimmy spun round to face the podium in time to see a wooden box arrive, presumably holding the new strap-gun.

Grey had returned to the mic. 'Welcome back. Our

technical troubles have been sorted – apologies for the delay. The re-strapping continues. Prisoner Shah to the strap-gun, prisoner Noon to the table please.'

Amos was back on his feet. 'No! The other way round! I want—'

But Jimmy was already at the table, shirt removed. The dressing on his wound looked clean. *Not much room for Amos to aim at. Come on, Amos, make this easy on him.*

Amos took the hypodermic and, before anyone could react, crushed it beneath his shoe. He turned to face Grey.

Amos, what are you doing?

'I said this should have been me,' he said, and put the strap-gun to his head.

73

Ant and Jimmy reacted first. They launched themselves off the bench, Jimmy going for the rugby tackle, Ant going for the gun.

'Amos, no!' Ant jerked his arm up just as he pulled the trigger. There was an explosion of sound – the strap-gun firing, people screaming, gravel crunching. Ant landed on top of Amos's arm, the gun falling from his grasp. She picked it up – hot from the firing and, to her horror, sticky with blood. She spun round. Where Amos's ear had been there was now just a flap of skin; blood ran freely down his neck. 'Amos!' she yelled.

POs descended from everywhere, throwing her and Jimmy back onto the bench. She felt something under her stumbling feet – it was the half-fired strap. Picking it up, she reloaded it into the strap-gun and looked around for Grey. He was shouting instructions, but in that second his eyes swivelled and met Ant's. They flashed with fear, then darkened.

'Get the girl! Get the strap-gun!' he yelled, and she was immediately pinned to the ground. The strap and the strap-gun were wrenched out of her fingers, and then she was manhandled onto the podium. She was aware of Amos being carried away and a circle of POs around the bench, but in front of her Grey was smiling.

'*Correction* is overrunning,' he explained matter-of-factly. 'Unsurprising in the circumstances. But if, as I am told, we have time for just one more re-strapping, it is going to be yours. You will not escape again, Goose Girl! We go again! Prisoner Abigail Norton Turner to the table . . .' He paused briefly for effect. 'And prisoner Matthew Norton Turner to the strap-gun.'

Ant's face clearly exhibited all the horror Grey was hoping for. She was quickly led to the strapping table and pushed forward onto its still bloody surface. She heard the uproar and pandemonium behind her: Mattie shouting; cries from the crowd; then Grey making one final speech.

She gripped the side of the table and twisted her head round as far as she could. Mattie was being given the syringe, but he was staring straight at her. She nodded and mouthed, '*You know what to do.*' A PO appeared and held her head down, forcing her to look away.

Grey called for silence as Mattie approached the table. He held the needle in his left hand. There were shouts from the stands, but Ant's voice was louder.

'Mattie! Steady hands! Hold the syringe high!'

A small voice behind her. 'I'm here.'

'How much time on the clock?' Her voice was now only audible to her brother and the man holding her head.

'One minute. A bit less.'

Forced to look sideways, Ant noticed a sudden movement under the far stand. A green flashing light shone clearly in the space between two rows of seating. She swallowed, blinked, then looked again. It had moved to a different position but it was still there. A green light. A drone's green light. And if it was hiding, it wasn't a prison drone. Which meant . . .

Max.

My God, we have a chance.

Mattie's voice cut in. 'Abi! Less than a minute!'

'OK. Grab my T-shirt,' she said. 'When I say so, lift it up as far as it'll go. Then stand back. OK?'

'OK.'

Ant took a deep breath and closed her eyes. Heart hammering in her chest, she yelled, 'Now!'

She felt Mattie's hands tug hard. The fabric strained, then tore, out the job was done. She knew the TV shot would be a close-up of her exposed back.

Let them watch. Let them read.

En . . .

De . . .

Twa . . .

Kat . . .

'Is it clear?' she yelled at Mattie.

'Yes, it's clear,' he said.

'Can people see?'

'Yes, they can see.'

She stayed motionless. This was the moment. This was what she had wanted. Ant listened to the crowd. She knew they were reading. She could hear the words – muttered, then shouted. The PO holding her down was reading them too. He read slowly, as if unable to believe what he was seeing. He read it out again, every word sounding like the sweetest thing Ant had ever heard. She felt the pressure on her head relax. She twisted free. Glanced at the screen. She had a brief image of her lower back in freeze-frame – three lines of Mattie's small, precise handwriting:

John Grey
is son of gangster
James Lee Glancey

Then the screen went blank. Grey had pulled the plug.

'Was it on for long enough? Could you read it?' Ant shouted.

Mattie nodded and smiled.

Grey was at the microphone, deathly white and shaking. '*Correction* is over!' he shrieked, then jumped down from the podium. He ran over to Ant, snatching the strap-gun from Mattie. 'It might not be on TV, but *I* shall re-strap you now,' he hissed. 'Without the anaesthetic!' He lunged for her, but Mattie was ready. As the governor raised his hands, Mattie jabbed the anaesthetic needle into his leg. Instantly Grey pulled up, yelping. He tilted as the feeling drained from his leg.

'It's too late, Grey,' said Ant, smiling. 'It's over. You're the son of a crook. James Lee Glancey. Bankrobber, fraudster and thug. The whole world knows!'

The green light was moving again.

'I pulled the show, you idiot!' Grey said, trying to balance. 'I took us off air before anyone could read it!'

In the stands, strutter and PO alike watched and listened, his words amplified by his lapel-mic.

'It only had to be there a second,' said Ant. 'It'll be a screengrab all over the world.'

Grey hobbled towards her, strap-gun held at arm's length like a pistol. 'You're a criminal from a criminal family! A filthy strutter!' he said. 'No one will believe a word you say! Cuff her. Put her back on the table and let's finish this!'

Six POs moved towards her, batons and pepper spray at the ready. Ant noticed the green light had edged closer too, and now she could see its operator. The briefest of smiles.

'You're right, no one would believe me,' said Ant, ignoring the advancing guards. If we hadn't published all the details of your father's crimes. Everything you placed on the memory stick? The stuff you thought I hadn't seen? That's gone everywhere too. The crimes, the contacts, the bank accounts. The Liverpool heist, the Gravesend shooting, that security van in Plymouth.

The big houses you grew up in, the holidays . . . Everything. It really is over. You're a strutter, Grey. *You've just been found out.*'

'You can say anything you like, Goose Girl,' he spat, 'but we're not live any more. These words are going no further than this courtyard.' Then, to his guards, 'She is lying, of course. Put her on the table!'

It was Denholm who was nearest. He cuffed Ant to his wrist, but Ant held up her free hand and he didn't try to stop her. 'Wait! I have one more thing to say. Just hear this and make up your own minds.'

The other guards looked at Denholm, who nodded. She had permission to speak.

Ant addressed them directly. 'I know all these facts because of one of your comrades, Prison Officer Brian MacMillan. The first PO to die in the London riot. He risked his life telling me about Grey's father. MacMillan was used by Grey. Grey got me to go into Holloway and Pentonville, knowing it would cause trouble; he let the riot spread. MacMillan could have been saved, but Grey chose to let him bleed to death. John Grey is a monster. He is no friend of the prison service!'

'The man was an idiot,' spat Grey. 'He was chosen because he fraternized with your kind. My brave men here understand the bigger picture.'

'Your brave men?' said Ant. 'You told me in Spike that prison was full of "hopeless failures being looked after by hopeless failures" . . .'

Grey waved her words aside. 'They see the bigger

picture, understand the larger war. And in a war there are casualties. MacMillan was a casualty.'

Ant noticed unease on the faces of Denholm and his colleagues. Grey did not.

'The other guards who died?'

'Casualties.'

'And my foster parents?' said Ant.

'Casualties.'

'Amos's dad?'

'Oh, who cares?' said Grey. 'Just strap the girl.' Then, with sudden alarm, 'Who is that guard – the one with the green light?'

Ant didn't need to look. 'He might be dressed as a guard, but if you look carefully, you'll see it's Max Norton. The man whose dead parents you just described as "casualties". And that green light is a drone camera which has just broadcast everything you said. *Your* cameras may have been switched off, but *his* wasn't.'

John Grey, his face ashen, turned to face Max, who was beaming. In his palm lay the reclaimed drone camera, its green light still flashing brightly.

'Heard every word, Grey,' called Max. 'The Stamper has a great little microphone. That was some confession.'

The moment power left John Grey was visible to everyone. His shoulders dropped, his jaw sagged, his body seemingly deflating in front of them. By instinct he managed to straighten his tie and rearrange his hair but he was a man lost.

Ant ran to the lectern, picked up Grey's pledge card

and held it high. 'So! Freedom Question number one! What have you done today?' she shouted, to huge cheers from the stands. 'What!' she yelled, stepping towards him, her voice bouncing off the old prison walls.

'What!' replied the crowd.

'Have!' she cried, stepping closer.

'Have!' came the chorus.

'You! Done! Today!'

Each word was echoed back by a dangerously expectant crowd. The last word had taken her to within a few centimetres of Grey's puffy, drawn face.

Ant put her head as close to his as she dared, and quietly, as though in a private conversation, said, 'Wrong goose, by the way. This' – she tapped her neck – 'is a *fighting* goose.' Then, louder, 'So Freedom *Answer* number one,' she said. 'You lost. John Grey, son of a criminal, lost. *That's* what you did today.'

74

It was a dangerous moment. Ant sensed it; so did Denholm.

'This isn't a revolution!' he shouted to Ant, using his own cuffs to apprehend Grey.

'Sure feels like it,' she said as enormous cheers and wild stamping thundered in from the stands. Those in the front rows took this as their cue to charge forward, overpowering the guards. Everywhere fights broke out and batons started to fly.

'You better say something!' shouted Denholm, pointing at the podium microphone. 'Or it'll be London all over again.'

Suddenly Ant had Mattie at her side, closely followed by Max and Jimmy. They all grinned at each other, embraced briefly, then climbed onto the podium.

Ant grabbed the mic with both hands. 'Hey!' she said, recoiling briefly at the sound of her amplified voice. 'Friends! No rioting! No violence! We all lost people in London . . .' The charging strutters pulled up, the scuffles halted.

'Here's your moment,' said Max behind her. 'Do it! Make it good!'

She wiped her face with her T-shirt and smiled at him. 'Right,' she said, and took a deep breath. 'This here is Max Norton. In the riot he lost his parents – Gina and Dan. They were me and my brother's foster parents too . . . and better to us than our parents ever were. You all know people who died last week – and POs, I'm talking to you too. So let's get this clear. This man' – she pointed at the crumpled figure of Grey – 'is a crook. Not because of what his father did, but because of what *he's* done. *He* caused the riot; *he* is responsible for the deaths of our friends and families.'

A voice from the stands: 'Strap him!' Then many more. 'Strap him! Do it now!' Some of the strutters who had been advancing on the podium edged closer.

Denholm and another PO were holding onto the now-terrified Grey, part captors, part protectors. Ant sensed Mattie looking at her, but this time she didn't need his counsel.

'It's tempting!' she shouted. 'He has caused so much pain and misery for us . . . how sweet it would be see him strapped.'

'Do it then!' bellowed a voice. '*I'll* do it!' cried another, then more voices: 'Me too!'

But Ant had the mic and she used the amplification to talk over the shouters. 'Honestly, I'd love to. I'd love to make Grey feel a strap on his back; know what it feels like to wake up feeling violated and in pain. It would be sweet. But it would be wrong. Is Grey guilty of all the crimes committed by his father? No. No, he isn't to blame. He shouldn't become a strutter because *there shouldn't be any strutters*! He can go to prison for murder, corruption and torture, but not for what his father did, and not with a torture-strap on his back.' There was a scattering of applause, but Ant didn't miss a beat. 'But if he's not to blame, *I* am not to blame. My brother isn't to blame. My friends aren't to blame. None of us are to blame. None of *you* are to blame!'

The cheers and stamping started again.

'Give us a way out then,' prompted Jimmy.

She gave him a thumbs-up. 'So if we aren't to blame, we shouldn't be here. There doesn't need to be trouble because Mr Denholm here will be using the prison strap-keys to release you all. Every one of you.'

All heads whipped round to Denholm; he had clearly reached the same conclusion because he was barking some instructions into his radio. There were more ear-splitting cheers, but Ant held up her hands.

'But the law hasn't changed. Not yet. That's a longer battle. There are many more like Grey out there. So they'll come for you if you run, but you won't have that vile piece of poison sticking to your back if you do!' More stamping, more whooping. She was smiling broadly now.

'And in the place where your strap was, once you're healed up, get someone to write *Not to Blame* in beautiful, neat handwriting.' There was laughter at this, and Ant lifted Mattie's hand up, like a winning boxer.

Applause came next, and Ant saw Denholm's shoulders relax slightly.

'You agree to the de-strapping?' she called, incredulous.

'If that's what it takes to keep my staff safe, sure. Let the politicians sort it out. I'm leaving the service anyway. Most of us are. If people like that can be governors' – he stabbed his baton in the direction of departing, manacled Grey – 'we're all better off out.'

Two POs with boxes in their hands ran over. 'These are the strap-keys,' he said. 'We'll take it from here.'

Denholm glanced around, then came to stand next to Ant. 'Look, who knows what happens next, but if I were you, I'd get out. The police will be here eventually. And the drone ops say you have friends outside. That's where the goose came from.'

He turned to leave; then, suddenly awkward, his eyes on the ground, said, 'Oh, and thank you for the small kindness you showed me in Spike. I probably didn't deserve it. Now, if you'll excuse me . . .' He nodded a salute and headed towards the queue that was forming in front of the key-holders.

Jimmy came scorching past. 'Hey, Ant!' His eyes were shining. 'Ant, I'm staying. I'm staying with Daisy. She's in a bad way and . . . We've . . . I'd like to . . . be with her.'

Ant grabbed him and hugged him close. 'Get her

strong, Jimmy. Then get her out. And maybe Amos too, depending on how he is. We'll be together again soon.' She kissed him on the cheek.

Jimmy grinned. 'We were brilliant, weren't we?' he said and, before she could reply, ran towards the hospital wing.

Mattie tugged at Ant's arm. 'The POs say the gates will open when we get there. And we need to get there now.'

She grabbed his hand. 'Got it,' she said.

'And we should take Max too.'

'Why are you grinning?'

'No reason.'

'OK. I was thinking the same thing anyway.' She turned to where Max was talking to queuing strutters. 'Hey, Max Norton!' she called. 'You're wanted.'

The three of them ran for the gates. Across the courtyard, the strutters clapped, cheered, then parted to let them through. A small insignificant-looking blue door opened as they approached; it led through the walls of the old prison, past a raised steel barricade. Suddenly they found themselves on a tree-lined service road – facing a surprising welcoming party.

Ant saw Henry with what looked some old-timer friends. A few trees along three partially obscured figures showed themselves to be a radiant Lena Durrow with Sam and Tilly. Other figures she'd never seen before emerged from behind foliage, all clapping and waving. She recognized the father and daughter from the

Hampstead Heath coach rescue. There followed many tears and hurried, snatched conversations.

'That was my mate's goose!' called Henry. 'Nice touch, eh? Thought you might need some encouragement! These are my on-the-run friends.' He indicated his smiling, applauding colleagues. 'They wanted to see what you were up to! You done OK, kid.'

Lena was grinning. 'After you got us out of Spike, we couldn't be anywhere else,' she said. 'We heard what was happening and we all wanted to be here.' The children came and hugged Ant hard.

'Who are all these other people?' she asked, bewildered.

'Supporters,' said Lena. 'From local Bug sites. We've all been following you.'

They all wanted a hug, but eventually Max pulled her free. There was someone else to meet. A smiling woman in a fitted steel-grey dress stepped forward. 'Ant, this is Sara Hussain.' He smiled awkwardly. 'From Bristol Uni. She got me out. She knows about the Bug groups everywhere. Taught me about the dark web . . .' He ran out of words and the two women embraced.

'You are extraordinary, Ant,' said Sara, laughing. 'I've followed you and Max as much as I could and wondered if I'd ever get to meet you. So I am thrilled. You have done so much, but now you must go. We've arranged everything.' She pointed at a small car parked in a lay-by. 'The driver will take you to a small airstrip we can use.'

'Where are we going?' asked Max.

'You have to go to Germany,' said Sara. 'It's the only

country where you can operate. Your contacts there are waiting, Max.'

The sound of distant sirens sent Henry and his friends scurrying away; Lena, Sam and Tilly had already vanished into the woods. Behind Ant a steady stream of strutters were running for freedom.

'Go. Now,' said Sara. 'We'll talk on the safe sites.'

They ran towards the car; Ant, Mattie and Max all piled into the back.

As they drove towards the airstrip, Mattie took Ant's hand. 'Germany?' he said.

She looked at her brother, smoothed his hair and smiled. 'Germany,' she said. 'Remember all those German lessons Dan gave us? Maybe he guessed what might happen. Seems like time well spent after all.'

'Dad gave you German lessons in Spike?' said Max. 'More than I ever got.'

'Well, you'll have to let me do the talking then,' said Ant.

'Seems to work out like that anyway,' he said, and they all laughed.

In the silence that followed, Max shifted uncomfortably.

'Look. Thanks for mentioning Mum and Dad up there. And . . . I am *so* sorry that I even suggested you were responsible for their deaths.'

'Max, don't—' Ant began.

'No, listen, Ant. You and Mattie lost them too, and I basically accused you of killing them. Which was how it seemed to me then. But I was so wrong.'

Mattie scrambled over Ant and threw his arms around Max and started to cry. They held each other for a few seconds before Mattie whispered, 'I wish they could see us now.'

'Me too,' said Max, his voice breaking. 'I owe you both, big time.'

'Well, the trick with the drone was pretty neat.' Ant smiled. 'That'll do for starters.'

They drove on in silence. Eventually she asked, 'How did you do that? When you left Grey's office, I thought I might never see you again.'

Mattie pointed at the MCTAVISH name tag on Max's uniform. 'That's a clue,' he said.

Max laughed. 'McTavish got cocky,' he said. 'He got slack. Maybe he was thinking about *Correction* – who knows? We were alone for ten seconds just outside some office. I suddenly realized I could take him. Got in an elbow to his face. He was out cold – I pushed him into a cupboard and took his uniform. I realized I could go pretty much anywhere. So I went back to the TV truck, got that drone-cam working.'

'The drone without a microphone,' said Ant, grinning again. 'No one heard a thing.'

'Yup,' said Max, 'but that's just another thing Grey didn't know. But all I did was film. What you did was take on Grey. And win.'

'We haven't won though. Not yet. If they realize what we're doing—'

He put a finger against her lips. 'Agreed,' he said. 'But we beat Grey. *You* beat Grey.'

'What happened to Papa?' asked Mattie.

'Don't know, don't care,' said Ant.

'They were all in it together,' said Max. 'Grey. The Cloverwells. So he's probably back with his gang. With a few questions to answer.'

Mattie leaned close to Ant's ear. 'And we don't know about Mama. We don't know anything,' he said.

She turned to face him. 'Well, now we're out, maybe we can start looking?'

Mattie nodded enthusiastically. 'From Germany?' he said.

'From Germany,' she agreed, then laughed.

'What?'

'*Kampfgänse.*' She ran her fingers over her tattoos. 'The German fighting goose is going home.'

'I think they'll like you,' said Max. 'A lot.'

'Will we like your German friends?' asked Mattie.

Max smiled. 'Mostly,' he said.

'Which reminds me,' said Ant. 'You said I beat Grey. Well, you know how I did it?' She leaned towards him. 'By being "mostly scary". That's what you called me.'

Max laughed, embarrassed. 'I remember.'

'If I'm *mostly* scary, what's the rest of me?'

Max's cheeks flushed scarlet, but he said nothing.

Mattie whispered in his ear.

Max nodded, then turned to Ant. '*Sansasyonèl*,' he said

slowly, checking the pronunciation with Mattie. 'Does that sound OK?'

Ant beamed. 'So I'm mostly scary,' she said, 'but also "sensational"?'

'That's about it,' said Max.

From somewhere, Mattie had produced some paper and a pen and had started writing.

Ant and Max didn't notice.

ACKNOWLEDGEMENTS

I blame Michael Morpurgo.

In 2014, I contributed to his anthology of memories of the First World War, *Only Remembered*. I wrote about my great uncle Stanley Killingback, a lieutenant in the Royal Engineers, killed in action in France, 1916. I know very little about his life, but the image of my grandmother's Remembrance Day poppy tucked into the frame of her lost brother's portrait has always stayed with me. Honoured to be writing for one of our greatest authors, I fussed for quite a while to make sure that my few hundred words of text for the book weren't too embarrassing. I found a photo and a song to go with them before emailing everything to Michael. And that was that.

Except that it wasn't. That night I dreamed I was in a queue waiting for admission to prison. It had been discovered that my great uncle had been a deserter and as he hadn't paid for his crime, I had to do so in his place. It was the same for everyone in the queue with me – they were paying the price for someone else's misdemeanour. It was an image powerful enough to stick in my mind – and the idea of heritage crime was born.

My heartfelt thanks to the Right Honourable Charlie Falconer, Baron Falconer of Thoroton, and the Right Honourable Douglas Alexander for putting me on a sound legal footing, to Isabelle Dupuy and Sybille Wunderlich for the Haitian and German translations, and the extravagantly gifted team at Penguin Random House led by my editor Kelly Hurst. Oh, and Sam Copeland at RCW, always the most stylish of literary agents.

There are many organisations around the world who work for those who are *not to blame*. Check out Reprieve, Amnesty, the Prison Reform Trust and the Howard League for Penal Reform to find out more.